FAITHLESS

GRAHAM AUSTIN-KING

For Gillian

Alone, alone in a terrible place,
In utter dark without a face,
With only the dripping of the water on the stone,
And the sound of your tears,
And the taste of my own.
                    - Edna St. Vincent Millay

CHAPTER ONE

Robes hissed over marble. Soft cloth kissed the cold stone, whispering secrets punctuated by the faint slap of sandals, as the old acolyte led them on through the halls. Wynn looked around at the friezes, the torches burning in their sconces, anywhere but at the other man with him who shot him furtive glances as they followed the acolyte. The man who called himself his father. Betrayal and guilt were like old lovers, reaching for each other in the silence.

A trek through a maze of smaller hallways ended with a wait at a dark oaken door as their guide stepped inside leaving them in the hall. The thick wood of the door turned words into muffled whispers. And then the old man returned, waving them into the opulent study with a blank expression that looked carved into his face.

Wynn followed his father into the room, looking past the red-haired man to the priest waiting in his thick, dark robes. His face was deeply lined, and the hooked nose would have made him look severe were it not for the kindly eyes.

The rug was deep underfoot and the air was stale, with the smell of parchment and wax. The shelf-lined walls seemed to throw back the heat from the fireplace as he gaped around at the leather-bound books that ran from floor to ceiling. He ignored the two men as they spoke, dimly aware that the acolyte had left, and refusing to hear the clinking sound the coins made as they fell into his father's hand. Hearing it would make it real.

"Is he simple?" The priest's words cut through the fog just before his father's hand cuffed at his head.

"No, beggin' your pardon, your honour." Wynn flinched away from the hard eyes as his father glanced at him. "He's not simple, your holiness. Just lacking in manners."

The priest looked at Wynn, running his gaze over him until Wynn stepped back a pace. The man saw too much, looked too deeply. "And are you ready to enter the service of the Forgefather, lad?"

"No," Wynn told him, trying hard not to stare at the symbol of a hammer that had been branded into the priest's forehead. "I just want to go home."

"Little bastard!" Wynn's father hissed. Wynn flinched away from the furious hands that reached for him.

"It is no matter," the old priest said, raising a placating hand as he stood and made his way to the door. "Many who come here do not truly appreciate what it is they are being offered. I'll send for someone to take the lad in hand."

The wait was not long but Wynn squeezed every moment from it. He glared at this stranger who'd fathered him and who, even now, would not even meet his gaze. Within minutes another robed servant came for him.

The musty study was gone in moments and Wynn was escorted through marble halls with stylised statues and polished anvils too inlaid with gold and runes to serve any practical purpose. The grandeur receded as they passed into smaller, more functional corridors. They made their way down a long flight of stone steps before Wynn's escort spoke.

"It won't be as bad as you'll think it is in the next few months," he told him in a low voice.

"I'm sorry?" Wynn looked over at the man. His face was pale and heavily lined and his short beard was grey, but it was a face that had been aged by hard work rather than years.

"Just a bit of advice is all," his guide grunted. "Accept what's coming and it'll be easier for you in the end."

Wynn frowned at that. "What do you mean, 'what's coming?'" he asked, but the old servant just shook his head and waved him onward.

2

The stairs were tired and worn, giving way to a smaller set of corridors fashioned from plain stone that had none of the opulence of the upper temple. The hall stretched on, reaching out until the darkness swallowed it.

"How far do these passages go?" he muttered.

"We're far beyond the temple walls now," the servant told him without turning. "Closer to the mountain. This passage goes to the mines, though there may be others. The temple is vast. I doubt there's anyone who knows all her secrets."

Wynn paused, slowing his steps. "Mines? I thought I was to serve the temple?"

"There are many ways to serve," the servant replied. "It will become clear in time." He fell silent, ignoring Wynn's questions until the boy gave up and they approached the door. It was a heavy oak creation, reinforced with thick beams and iron bars. Two robed men watched their approach, and nodded a greeting to Wynn's guide before fumbling with keys and lifting the crossbar to let them through.

Another gate lay a short walk beyond them, its odd construction half-hidden in the low light. Wynn's guide reached for his arm as the door slammed shut behind them. He gave a bow of greeting to the shadowed figures manning the gate.

"To you I give this boy, into your charge," he said, the words oddly formulaic.

"May the Father take him and shape him," a leather-clad man replied with a polite bow. Wynn stared openly at the second figure and the bandage bound tight around his eyes. He suppressed a shudder as the man turned his head, appearing to look back at him despite the dark cloth. The man's gaze passed over him like a cold oil, clinging to his flesh.

"I'll be leaving you here," Wynn's guide said in a neutral voice. "One of these two will lead you down to Garl's man."

Wynn glanced at the men, dark leather, and robes that might have been woven from shadow. When he looked back, his guide had already

3

turned to leave. Wynn watched him walk away for a moment and as the man in leather took his arm he realised he'd never even asked his guide's name.

The locks clanked tight behind them, leaving the bandaged priest alone with just the door for company. The air beyond the gate felt damp and the darkness deeper, split by odd, bowl-shaped lamps that sent a pale green light to fight a pointless battle against the black. Wynn peered at the lamps as they passed, trying to see the source of the glow.

"Chemiks," the man in leather grunted, following his gaze. "There aren't many torches or lamps down here. They don't last long enough and down in the mines themselves any flame can bring on the Father's Wrath."

Wynn turned away from the lamp. "The what?"

"Later." The man gave him a long look, scratching at one stubbled cheek and then shook his head. "It's not my place. It'll all be explained in time."

"What's your name?" Wynn asked suddenly.

The man paused, frowning. "Liam," he grunted. "Now come on."

Wynn frowned after him and then hurried to keep up. The stone corridors led them down yet more stairs, steps worn low with the passage of feet, and caked in dust and chips of stone. The distant sounds of life made Wynn realise just how quiet it had been. The murmur of voices combined with their steady footsteps, the sound of metal on metal, and a thousand other noises that grew louder as the passage led them out onto a pathway overlooking a massive cavern.

Flat-roofed buildings were clustered tight over the floor of the cavern, and formed up into streets and squares. Large lamps sat on one corner of each building's roof casting the same chemik-light glow out over the streets. The buildings stretched farther than he could make out, eventually being claimed by darkness as the chemlamps failed to banish the gloom.

A huge fissure split the high ceiling, letting a thin band of sunlight illuminate a section of the settlement. Wynn gaped out at the city below and then hurried after his guide. It seemed a stupid thing to think of it as a city, but there was simply nothing else to call something that vast and sprawling.

It was the smell that struck him next. Whilst the temple had smelled like a combination of incense and scorched metal, and the tunnels and corridors leading to the cavern had been damp and musty, this place had the smell of life. Sweat, mixed with the smell of baking bread, and coal smoke, with a metallic undertone that he couldn't quite place.

"What is this?" he breathed as they passed the first of the buildings.

"This is Aspiration. This is where you begin your training."

Wynn followed Liam through streets and districts, passing collections of shacks that huddled in ragged circles around fire-pits where men cooked with large pots. These gave way to long, low, huts surrounded by storage shacks crammed with picks and crates which, in turn, gave way to elaborate, marble-fronted structures surrounded by high walls and fences.

"There are fifty or more mining crews down here," Liam told him. "I forget how many, exactly. Garl's man will decide which is yours."

Wynn turned to see Liam had stopped outside a wrought-iron gate and was muttering something to the guard stood within. The gate swung inward as the guard eyed Wynn, fingering the iron-bound club as if he were any kind of threat and not a lost fifteen-year-old boy.

A thick door gave way to an opulent hallway crafted from the same marble as the temple far above them. Wynn and his guide were passed through three sets of guards, and searched twice, before they were waved into a large study.

"And just who the fuck are you?" a voice growled out as Wynn blinked against the bright lamps.

"He's with me, Derint," Liam said as he followed Wynn through the door. "Another gift from Father Sorn."

"Another one?" The chair scraped back against the polished floorboards as the dark-haired man hauled himself to his feet and moved out from behind the desk. "Bit old for a priest's taste wouldn't you say?"

5

"I wouldn't say. I know enough not to comment."

"That's right, wouldn't want to stain the marble floors up there with a bit of truth now would we?" Derint hawked and spat, shaking his head. "Go on then, piss off."

Derint waited until the door had closed behind the man before looking back at Wynn. "And how much have they told you?"

"Nothing really." Wynn shrugged, wringing his fingers behind his back. "Just that I am to serve in the temple."

"Serve!" Derint snorted a laugh and then narrowed his eyes as he looked Wynn over. "Show me your hands, boy."

Wynn held them out, trying to keep them from shaking as Derint inspected them.

"You're no stranger to work at least," he grunted. "Farmer's boy?"

Wynn nodded.

"Drought hit you?"

"Not as bad as it hit some others," Wynn told him. And that was the heart of it, wasn't it? He clenched his fists without thinking.

Derint narrowed his eyes and grunted. "But your Da sent you anyway, didn't he? Sold you for a couple of coins."

Wynn shook his head at that. "It's just for a year..."

"He'll be back as soon as the harvest turns around?" Derint offered. "I've heard that one too. It's time you grew a little, son. I've got no time for snivelling rats down here. You'll know the truth and deal with it. You're here to work, plain and simple."

"I thought I was to serve in the temple," Wynn blurted.

The cuff caught him solidly on the side of his head and Wynn staggered, clutching at his ear.

Derint pointed one stubby finger at him. "That's the only warning I'll give you. Interrupt me again, boy, and you'll get what's coming to you." He sighed, shaking his head. "Listen this time and try to get it through that skull of yours. You're here to 'serve the temple," he mimicked, clasping his hands and looking up at the ceiling. "That's shit. You're an aspirant. There's nothing below you because you're as low as things get. In time, if you prove yourself, learn your lessons, and if luck dribbles out of your fucking arse, you might scratch your way up to novice and maybe onwards. For now, you belong to Garl. And for as long as you belong to Garl, you'll dig."

"Dig?" Wynn asked, knowing it for a stupid question.

Another sigh, followed by another disbelieving shake of the head. "What name were you given, boy?"

"Wynn."

"Wynn, this is the temple of the Forgefather," Derint told him. "You must have passed the forges and anvils in the temple. Where do you think all the iron and gold the priests are forging comes from? This is a mine, boy. The priests might claim you're searching for your faith or some such bollocks, but the truth is that you're supplying them with the gold and iron they pound away at. That's how you'll serve the temple."

He pointed at a plain wooden chair set in one corner of the office. "Sit your arse there and don't touch anything. I'll fetch someone to babysit you."

Wynn sat. In the space of three short hours, his life had been torn to pieces. He'd known about the Father's Gift of course. Everyone did. But being sent to serve in the temple for a year or two was one thing, being condemned to a life of sweating away in the darkness was something quite different.

Where was his father now? Probably way past Berentford. The road to the temple was a rough one and his journey would only get easier as he went on. Somehow Wynn doubted he'd be able to say the same. He sat and gnawed on his lip, staring unseeing at the hands in his lap until the door opened.

The man Derint returned with was lean in every sense of the word. His face was impassive, his eyes as grey as his hair. He looked as if there was not enough substance about him to form into a full man and so, stretched thin and gaunt, this was the end result. "Temple's latest aspirant," Derint told him, nodding at Wynn. "Take him and show him the basics, he can go onto Terrik's gang in the morning.

7

"This is Skerth," Derint said, turning back to Wynn. "He'll show you around. Terrik will find someone else to hold your hand until he judges you competent enough to wipe your own arse."

Wynn gave the man a small smile of greeting. Skerth, for his part, looked him up and down, shaking his head gently as he reached for the door.

***

"Keep close," Skerth told him as Wynn emerged from Derint's office. "I don't like babysitting, and I don't like saying stuff more than once. Pay attention, and keep up." He set off without looking back to see if Wynn was following, and led him at a pace out of the building. He took Wynn on a winding path through the town, along narrow streets that passed between the long buildings and warehouses, and eventually past the shacks as they made their way towards the farthest end of the cavern.

"You'll sleep in this one," the grey man told him eventually, pointing at a long building. "This is Terrik's crew. He's hard but life is hard down here. You might as well get used to it. Work well and you'll have no problems with him. His crew doesn't do as well as some, but it does better than others." He shrugged. "It's not a bad place to find your feet."

Wynn opened his mouth to ask about the priests again but thought better of it. Skerth went to a storage shack and rummaged around inside as Wynn looked around. It was a long way from the fields of home. Once you moved out of the light from the fissure the darkness pressed in, oppressive and smothering. The chemlamps glowing from the roofs of the huts didn't pierce far into the murk and the ceiling of the cavern was lost in the black.

"Put this on," Skerth told him, handing him an odd helmet as he emerged from the storage shack. "I'll give you a taste of it."

Wynn took the helmet curiously, turning it over in his hands and peering at the strange contraption on the front.

"Chemlamp," Skerth told him, tapping on the glass face of the light. He pointed at the cylinders on either side of the glass. "Red in this one, white in this one. They trickle down and combine here inside the lamp. Pull that switch out towards you to start it."

"What is it?" Wynn asked, peering at the sandy substance.

"Do I look like a chemiker?" Skerth asked. "Turn the damned thing on and get it on your head. Don't touch it," he added as an afterthought. "They get hot."

Wynn pulled the metal hook towards him and watched as the glass began to glow with a faint greenish light. "It's not very bright."

"It's bright enough, boy," Skerth told him. "It's as dark as a sinner's soul in there and that's not even the worst of it. Always check your lamp before heading in. There's enough chems in there to last two or three days but you don't want it failing on you. I don't imagine you'd ever find your way out without one. Now get it on."

The narrow streets opened up as they moved closer to the end of the cavern, giving way to broad avenues that were littered with chips of loose rock. The smell of smoke grew steadily stronger, an acrid stench that had Wynn coughing and covering his mouth.

"You get used to it," Skerth told him with a wry half-smile at his discomfort. "The smelt works is down that way. Outside of cooking it's the only real fire you'll see down here. Now, are you ready?"

"Ready?" Wynn repeated, cursing himself for the stupid question as Skerth nodded at the dark passage sloping down in front of them. Twin tracks ran along the floor of the tunnel, emerging from the darkness of the passage and extending out towards the smelt works.

Skerth sighed. "Let's go. Keep close." He stopped, looking down at Wynn's feet as though he were seeing them for the first time. "Are they really the only boots you've got?"

"I... uh."

"They won't last you two days down here, and your feet won't last three," Skerth told him. "See that Terrik sorts you out with some hard-boots first thing."

9

The passage sloped down gently and then levelled out for short stretches at regular intervals. "For the carts," Skerth told him, answering Wynn's question without him needing to voice it. "We pull them up by hand, the flat sections are where you'll catch your breath."

"Wouldn't it be easier to use ponies or something?" Wynn asked.

"Would it?" Skerth scratched his head. "Might be it would. But then you've got a hundred ponies or donkeys down here, shitting all over the place, needing their own food and water. That all needs hands to deal with, creates as much work as it saves probably. Besides," he fixed Wynn with a serious look, "animals won't go near the mines or any of the Carnath stones. They go crazy as soon as they get close. They tried with ponies and mules, all sorts, way before my time. Everything bolts or goes wild. I don't think anyone even thinks about it anymore."

Wynn took a chance on Skerth's temper, risking the question. "What are Carnath stones?"

"All of it really. They call this place the Mines of Carnath but some parts are a bit odd." He shrugged. "You'll see soon enough."

The passage continued on and the sounds of the smelt works and the cavern they'd left behind soon faded, swallowed by a darkness that pressed in on them. The chemlamps strung on the wall grew further apart and new noises drifted out of the black. These new sounds were woven from the hints of whispers. They were little more than the remnants of echoes, but they tugged at Wynn's ears as they gave voice to the gloom.

Skerth led him on, turning into side passages, and walking through a series of narrow tunnels until they reached a wide, rock-hewn staircase turning in a lazy spiral as it descended ever deeper.

Wynn looked from the stairs to Skerth and back again. The stone was set with an intricate pattern worked into the surface which threw back the light from his helmet. He knelt to trace his fingers over the stone. It felt too warm to his touch and faintly slick, though it held no trace of moisture. He stood with a faint grimace, wiping his fingers on his clothes. The stone put him in mind of flesh for some reason.

"What…" he began and gave up, not finding the words.

"Carnath stone," Skerth told him with a shrug. "These tunnels are rich in gold and iron, that's why the mines were started here." He started down the steps again, glancing back to be sure Wynn followed. "We weren't the first ones here though. Places like this are all through the tunnels and the mine itself. They're old, much older than the new temple and maybe even older than the one that stood before. Nobody knows who built them or why, or where they went once they had disappeared. You can pass through three miles of natural caves and tunnels and then suddenly reach stairs like these, or one of the bridges further down."

The stairs took them down through the darkness until Wynn's legs ached. No chemlamps were strung on the walls here and they travelled purely by the light of the small lamps on their helmets. It was a weak light that shook with each step and Wynn found himself reaching for the wall with one hand to steady himself. Skerth didn't slow and finally led them out to a plain tunnel and then to a broader passage set with cart tracks.

"We stay out of here as much as we can," he told Wynn, waving him back against a wall that curved away from the tracks. "This is a hauling shaft. The job's hard enough as it is without men in the way, but it'll do you good to see how it works." A faint grinding and clattering sound grew steadily louder as they waited, punctuated by grunts and curses as it approached.

Skerth pulled him to one side as the carts came into sight, loaded high with large chunks of rock shot through with quartz. Four men strained in the harnesses that were attached to the front of the train of eight carts. Wynn pressed back against the wall, giving extra room to the men as they moved closer, each step in time with the others. Two more men worked in their harnesses on either side of the train, with another four heaving at a broad beam attached to the rearmost cart.

"It's one thing to tell you," Skerth said. "It's another to see it. You'll be on a crew like that soon enough and know what it feels like. You don't want fools in your way when you're hauling. We don't ever walk the hauling shaft unless we really have to."

11

Wynn nodded, still watching the carts as they headed up the shaft.

"Come on," Skerth said, slapping Wynn's back hard enough to make him stagger. "Let's see those young arms get some work done." He set off back into the side passage, winding his way through the rocks.

"Most of the time we do pick work," Skerth told him, stopping beside a pitted rock face. "You look here." He pointed. "You can see the edges of the quartz." He tapped the milky stone in the scarred wall. "This would have had a vein of gold in it at some point. It's been picked clean and carted out. You see here?" He tapped at the rocks close to the low ceiling. "This reddish stuff is the beginnings of iron. They'd have had that out too if they could."

"Why didn't they?" Wynn asked, leaning closer to see where Skerth was pointing.

"Probably the roof," Skerth grunted. "Sometimes it's worth bracing a tunnel. We shore up the walls and roof with thick beams when we have to. You can only take so much out before you risk bringing the roof down on you. Most times it's not worth it. They'd have had a Listener in here to see."

What was a Listener? Wynn wondered about that for half a second until Skerth's words sunk in. "The roof?" Wynn said in a strained tone as he looked up.

"You better pull your head out of your arse, boy," Skerth said, prodding him in the chest. "There's been crews down here for ten lifetimes or more taking gold and iron out. Think how much stone that is coming down. How much these walls have been shaken. There are collapsed tunnels all over the mine. Most of the time a Listener gets to it first." He shrugged. "Sometimes they don't."

Wynn was quiet for a moment. "A Listener?"

"Forgefather's hairy balls! Do you ever stop with the damned questions?"

"Sorry I…" Wynn stopped as Skerth waved him to silence with a sigh.

"Don't worry at it, lad. I'd rather you were asking questions and learning than staying silent and stupid. I'll let Terrik explain that one

12

though." He reached for his flask and gave it an experimental slosh. "Let's get some water, all this talking has dried me out."

Wynn followed the lean man through the narrow tunnels and then out through the first of three broad galleries set with large chemlamps. The ever-present echoes of picks striking stone grew louder and more distinct as they went, turning from a distant whisper to something akin to birdsong.

"We'll take the ladders down," Skerth told him. "It'll be faster."

Wynn nodded, though he had no idea what the man was talking about.

The ladders proved to be exactly what they sounded like. Long stretches of wooden ladder, held in place by rusty brackets that had been driven into the rocks. Wynn peered down over the edge as Skerth adjusted his pack. The chemlamp was too weak to show the bottom of the shaft and the ladder extended down until the black swallowed it.

"I wouldn't," Skerth warned him.

Wynn gave him a confused look.

"Looking down there isn't going to make it any less of a drop," the older man said. "You don't want to know how far down it actually is, trust me. Just focus on the rungs under your hands and feet, I'll be right behind you."

"Behind me?" Wynn blurted. "You mean I'm going first?"

"I've done this a thousand times and then some," Skerth laughed. "I *know* I'm not going to fall. You think I'm going to go underneath you, as you piss yourself and tremble your way down the ladder? You're crazy."

"I..." Wynn shook his head.

"First rule down here, Wynn," Skerth told him with a serious look. "Keep yourself in one piece. Terrik will order you around, the others in your crew'll probably ride you for a bit too. You've got a brain in that skull. Learn to use it and you've got a better chance of keeping it on the inside of your head."

He walked Wynn to the edge. "Just go slow. There's no rush, not so long as your arms hold out, anyway." He grinned at Wynn's expression and looked pointedly at the ladder.

Wynn sighed in defeat. Heights had never bothered him but the way the ladder trailed off into darkness affected him more than he wanted to admit. The ladder extended well past the lip of the shaft, allowing Wynn to climb onto the rungs without having to lower himself over the edge. He clung to the smooth wood for a long moment while Skerth watched him with one raised eyebrow. The breath left him in a long, shuddering sigh, and he reached down with one questing foot.

For the first few seconds it wasn't too bad. He found the rungs easily and set himself a slow pace. Then he felt Skerth begin his own climb above him and his footsteps rocked the ladder, shaking it against the brackets set into the rock.

"It's shaking!" he called up in a panic.

"It does that," Skerth told him in a dry voice. "Speed up a bit, I'll slow down, a bit more distance between us won't hurt."

Wynn tried to move faster, focusing hard on the wall in front of him. Now that they had left the ledge behind them, the air felt colder, somehow wetter, and he fancied he could feel a cold breeze reaching out from the darkness behind him.

The climb seemed endless. Without looking down there was no judging how much farther there was to go, and looking up showed nothing but Skerth's figure far above him. Temptation fought with common sense and sent it scurrying. Wynn glanced down into the darkness.

The light from the chemlamp was blocked by his own legs and he cursed, leaning awkwardly to one side on the ladder to try and get a better view. The light shone down along the rock face making it look slick with moisture. Moss caked the stone in places and a white fungus sprouted here and there, bulging out of the cracks as if the stones themselves were leaking.

He traced the light further down the rocks, following the line of the ladder and then froze. The light from the lamp was weak but it still reached farther down than he would have thought. There seemed to be no end to the drop. The ladder extended down into the dark, into a blackness so total it seemed almost tangible. The fear took him so quickly it stole his breath and he froze in place, holding tight to the rungs of the ladder as his legs trembled hard enough to shake him.

"You made it further than most," the voice called down to him. "Don't worry at it, lad. Everyone freezes on their first time down here. You fill your smalls?"

"What? No!" Wynn glared up at the man's feet, outrage eclipsing his fear.

Skerth grunted. "Better'n most then," he admitted. "Keep going, it's only another four or five minutes."

Wynn glanced down and then looked up into the glow of Skerth's chemlamp, his face carrying the question.

"You can't trust your eyes right here, boy," Skerth told him. "Just keep going, you can't hang here all day. Aside from anything else, I'm going to need a piss before too long. You really want to be underneath me then?"

Wynn reached down with a foot, feeling for the rung he knew must be there. It seemed so much further than it ought to be and his mind was filled with visions of him somehow missing the next step and slipping off, his body tumbling over and over as it fell into the darkness that yawned beneath him. Rather than terrify him the idea was somehow comforting. Why not just end it all? Let go? It would be so easy to just let the black embrace him.

"Almost there, lad, just another inch." The words fought their way through the dark thoughts and then Wynn felt the wood of the rung under his foot. He closed his eyes as relief flooded him and he moved on. In minutes his foot touched rock and his eyes flew open as he looked around him in confusion. The bottom of the cavern spread out around him, loose rock chips littering the ground in the light of the large chemlamps on the wall. Where moments ago the cavern floor had been nowhere in sight, now he stood upon it. As he took in the sight, the sounds rushed in at him, echoes of conversation, the distant noise of picks striking stone. Wynn looked around himself in utter bewilderment. "What in the hells?"

15

CHAPTER TWO

"Up, you lazy fuckers! Move it!" Terrik's shout was met by a chorus of protests and muttered invitations for the speaker to explore various forms of self-abuse.

Wynn groaned and rolled over in the narrow cot, pushing himself up as his warm feet reached down for a frigid floor.

"Grint, you can babysit our little newborn today," Terrik called out again. "You can have clearing duty from the fire-mined section in the shaft you did last week."

"Piss on that!" The red-headed man surged to his feet. "I'm not losing tallymarks just so this piss-ant can learn how to toss rocks down a hole."

Terrik gave the shorter man a wearied look with his one good eye. "Just do it, Grint."

Grint shook his head, picking something out of his teeth. "Choose someone else."

Three quick steps between the bunks had Terrik in the shorter man's face, a hand buried in his shaggy hair, yanking his head back as a jagged blade too ugly to deserve a name was pressed to his throat. "Do you know how long it takes to clear a life's worth of blood from a bunkhouse, Grint?"

The strained squeak might have been words but they didn't carry to Wynn who watched openly while others averted their eyes.

"Too fucking long," Terrik answered for him, his voice a low growl. "Which is the only reason you're not flopping about on the floor right now. Do as you're told, you'll live longer. You can have an average tally for the day out of the crew purse."

The knife vanished with a smooth motion and Terrik planted the flat of his hand on Grint's chest, sending the man staggering backwards over legs and bunks amid a flurry of curses. Terrik glanced once at Wynn before looking to an older man in tattered grey robes sat beside the firebox. "A verse if you would, Father Lasris?"

The old man nodded, unconcerned by the near-murder, and closed his eyes, lost in thought. Finally, he spoke, "The Father spoke from the flame and revealed the truth to mankind. Our way lies lost to stone and darkness. Only by hammer and flame, by the grace of the Father, shall we find the true path."

Terrik grunted, casting an eye over the men climbing out of bunks and into clothes. "Get moving then," he told them over the low murmur of grumbling and hushed conversation, and turned for the door.

Wynn followed the others, pulling the rough work clothes on quickly and ramming his feet into his thick leather boots. He glanced over to where Grint had fallen but the man in the neighbouring bunk shook his head, warning him off.

"Just leave it alone, lad. He's a miserable shit at the best of times. Mornings were never his thing. Let him get something hot in his belly and you'll do fine."

He let himself be swept out of the bunkhouse by the others, falling in with them as they went through the morning routine of lining up in front of the massive cauldrons. The food was doled out by men large enough that none would question their portion. The porridge was thin, closer to a gruel than anything else, but it was hot and that was enough. Wynn took his bowl and found space at an end of one of the long trestle tables.

The air still felt strange on his freshly shaved scalp. "Lice," he'd been told. The process had been quick but not one he'd like to repeat. He spooned down his breakfast in silence looking around at the others with their shaggy hair. How long had it taken to grow back? Conversation was muted at the tables, with most of the miners hunched low over their bowls, focused on eating.

17

"Done yet, boy?"

Wynn turned to see Grint, a smile on his face that seemed at odds with the earlier argument.

"I… uh," he managed.

"Come on then." Grint waved him away from the table. "The sooner we get you pulling your own weight, the sooner we start pulling in full loads."

Wynn hurried to dump his bowl in the water with the others and rushed after Grint. For a shorter man he walked surprisingly fast.

"You need chems?" Grint asked as Wynn caught up with him.

"I don't think so." He peered at the vials on either side of the chem-lamp on his helmet.

"Nah, there's enough in there for today," Grint told him after a casual glance. "You'll want to get it filled tonight though. Got the marks for that, or you running a slate with Terrik?"

Wynn looked at him blankly.

"Nothing's free, boy," Grint told him through a scowl. "You came in what, day before yesterday and no one's told you shit yet?"

He sighed with a grimace as Wynn shook his head. "Grab an end of this and we'll go." He took hold of one of the wooden barrows lined up beside the entrance to the shaft and looked at Wynn, jerking his head at the handle on the other end of the barrow.

Wynn shivered as they made their way into the shaft, walking to one side of the tracks that led out towards the smelt works. Grint was clearly in no hurry, stepping to one side to let other groups pass them.

The air had the same chill to it but there was something more, a damp-ness that wormed its way through his clothes and leeched away at him.

"Your head cold?" Grint asked, nodding at Wynn's helmet. "You want to get some cloth and wrap it round your head before you get your helmet on. Stop your brain freezing until your hair starts growing back in."

Wynn nodded. "Thanks."

"Skerth gave you your first taste of the mines, right?" He looked back over one shoulder for Wynn's nod. "He didn't tell you the truth of all this then?" Grint said, over his shoulder, as he led them into a side tunnel.

"The truth?"

"This." Grint nodded at the walls of the mineshaft. "The mine, the temple – all of it."

"I… No, not really," Wynn admitted.

Grint paused long enough to turn and give Wynn a penetrating look. "Listen up then. You were probably told you were going to serve the temple. Family brought you in?"

"My father," Wynn said, just managing to keep his voice even.

"And now you're wondering if it's all been a lie," Grint said, nodding. "You're wondering if he didn't just sell you into slavery."

Wynn grunted, not trusting his voice. Finally, he managed, "The man in the fancy building, Derint, he called me an aspirant."

"It's not that complicated," Grint told him. "The priests need ore more than they need novices. We work down here long enough and we might just earn our way out. That's the lie anyway. The truth doesn't taste quite as nice."

"I don't understand," Wynn said.

"Don't waste time worrying over it," Grint said with his own shrug. "Us that are marked," he tapped a finger to the brand on his forehead. "We're split into the crews, Terrik's, Sedna's, Esther's, a bunch more besides. We all work to get as much ore out as we can. Every crew that makes tally for three months sends a man to be tested. If you pass you train as a novice, if you fail?" He shrugged. "Well then you're back down here."

"So this isn't forever then?"

Grint snorted at that, a harsh laugh tinged with cynicism. "If you want to believe that, lad. Me? I've been here too long."

"When do you get…"

"Marked?" Grint guessed. "First time you're sent to listen to old Father Lasris." He caught Wynn's expression. "It's not so bad. It's over quick and it heals fast. Don't worry too much about it."

19

He stopped beside a long section of wooden planks fixed to the wall of the tunnel. "Give me a hand with the door," Grint said as he set the barrow down.

"Door?" Wynn looked blankly.

Grint grabbed a handle set low on the wall and waved at another one closer to Wynn. "That, you daft sod!"

Wynn followed Grint's lead and heaved upward, not knowing quite what to expect. The section of wood moved sluggishly and then slid upward into a rack set into the stone above them. It moved in a smooth motion as chains clanked somewhere behind it. Grint stepped into the small wooden room that had been exposed, ducking to get through the low entrance.

"Come on." Grint waved him into the room.

"Where?" Wynn asked, looking for another way out of the room and making his way in anyway.

The room was little more than a wooden box with two chains running through the floor and extending up and out of the ceiling. Wynn froze as the room shook under them, and he gave Grint a frantic look.

"He took you down the ladders, didn't he?" Grint asked, sighing as he shook his head. "Think, boy! If we all went down those ladders they'd be in pieces within a week. Take hold of this." He shook the left-hand chain, waiting until Wynn gripped it with both hands and then pulled hard on a lever set next to the chains.

The room shook and Wynn looked at Grint in shock as the man took the chains from him and began pulling them downward, hand over hand.

"Lend a hand any time you like," Grint told him, grinning at Wynn's wide-eyed expression as the room descended into the shaft.

"Sorry." Wynn mimicked Grint's action, marvelling at the apparent lack of weight.

"Counterweight," Grint told him.

"What?"

20

"The lift, this box, it's on a counterweight." He looked at Wynn's blank expression. "You'll see at the bottom."

The descent was a blink compared to the ladders Skerth had taken him down, but Wynn's arms were still burning by the time Grint slowed the chain at the first of several loud clicks. Soon the lift came to rest with a gentle crunch of gravel.

"Counterweight." Grint pointed up the shaft as they climbed out of the lift. Wynn followed his pointing finger up through the criss-crossing cradle of wooden beams and into the darkness, but could see nothing.

"Wait," Grint told him.

Wynn watched, not really sure what he was looking for, until the lift began to move with a clank of chains, rising back up the wooden tower that surrounded it.

"Look," Grint told him, pointing again. As Wynn looked up into the black shaft, a darkness began to descend. Wynn pushed aside the memory of the darkness reaching for him on the ladders and focused on the sight as a stone block, easily the size of two large oxen and encased in a web of chains and ropes, sank slowly towards them.

"Counterweight," Grint told him simply and then waved him onward into the darkness. He led Wynn into a side tunnel and slowed, playing the light from his chemlamp over the walls.

"What are you—?"

"Shh." Grint flapped a hand at him. "I'm looking for something." He crouched, running his hands over the wall until he stood with a cry of triumph. "Here, look!"

Wynn stepped closer, crouching to shine his chemlamp into the small hole Grint pointed out. He shook his head with a shrug. "What am I seeing?"

"That's a tally-stash," Grint explained. "You'd probably find all of this out the hard way if I didn't tell you. Hashek was good enough to do it for me, so I'll do it for you. When your team takes a load of ore to the smelt works, they'll give you tallymarks for it." He reached into a pocket and pulled out a hexagonal coin, crudely fashioned from iron.

21

"It's normally split evenly between the team. Some just give everything they have spare to Terrik, he takes three in ten anyway, that's the price for being on the crew. Most keep it under their bunks, or pretend to."

"Why would they pretend?" Wynn asked.

Grint's laugh was a harsh bark. "Aren't you just the delicate little flower?" he said, ignoring Wynn's scowl. "Life's hard down here, boy. It's been a while since I saw anyone actually get caught for skimming a mark or five out of someone's purse but that don't mean they don't do it; they're just not getting caught."

"So people hide their marks in these holes?"

Grint nodded. "Most do. Not just marks either. I've been known to stash gold or copper from time to time if I find a good nugget. You never know when you're going to have a run of shit luck and I don't like getting lashed any more than the next man."

"Lashed?" Wynn blinked.

"What did you think would happen if you don't make tally? A stern talking to and no supper?"

"I hadn't thought about it," Wynn admitted.

"Time to start thinking then," Grint advised. "You got to pay for your chems, your food, and your place on the crew. That all comes out of the cut Terrik takes. What you do with the rest is up to you. Blow it on whores, drink, or joy-chems, whatever you like. Just don't miss tally. If you do miss your mark, Terrik'll loan you what you're short." Grint paused, raising his index finger. "Once, and once only, mind. After that you're on your own." He knelt to replace the rock in the wall and turned to go.

"Come on then, there's work needs doing."

Grint led him on through a network of small tunnels that ran between the main shafts, few, if any, had chemlamps and he soon grew tired of stumbling over rocks in the darkness.

"Where are we going?" he asked, aware of just how much frustration had come out with the words.

"We're clearing," Grint replied, as if that explained anything.

22

Wynn bit back a retort and rolled his shoulders in an effort to ease the ache. The barrow was not so heavy that the two of them couldn't manage it with ease but walking with it was a pain. He had to hunch slightly to stop his shins from bashing against it with each step, and the odd posture was already aching his back and shoulders.

"Clearing?" he asked.

"You'll see in a minute," Grint told him.

The tunnel opened up into a long gallery and Grint set the barrow down. "Catch your breath," he said reaching for his canteen to take a sip of water.

Wynn stretched, arching his back and massaging his shoulders.

"Try and bend your legs a bit more," Grint advised as he watched. "It'll stop your back burning so much."

Wynn nodded and then sniffed at the air. The smell of old smoke hung in the gallery and he looked at Grint in alarm. "Do you smell that?"

"The smoke?" Grint nodded. "It's nothing to worry about. The fire's long out and we set it on purpose, the smell just lingers down here is all."

Wynn blinked. "What? You set it yourself? Why?"

"Why did we set it? It'll make more sense if you see it," Grint told him, reaching for the handles to the barrow. Wynn groaned as he followed suit.

The walk turned out to be mercifully short and down a slight slope. The gallery narrowed and transformed into a tight tunnel that then bulged out on one side to form a large cave. Rubble littered the ground and the smell of scorched stone and smoke filled his nostrils.

"They call it 'firing'," Grint explained, waving at the wall. "Set a fire burning and heap more and more wood and coal on it, let it burn for three or four days and then toss water on the rocks and the rock face collapses."

"Collapses?" Wynn moved closer to peer at the rough stones.

"'Explodes' might come closer to it," Grint told him. "You don't want to be anywhere close when it does, anyway. It brings most of the face down and then we can get at the gold, copper, or whatever that was

23

in there." He shrugged. "It's faster than just chipping away at the rocks with a pick. Dangerous though. We don't do it that often. Plus, it leaves this mess," he said, waving at the rubble that littered the ground. "You follow a quartz vein with a pick and most of the rubble is small enough to go under your feet with no problem, or ends up in the cart to the smelt works. Most of what comes down when you're firing is just dead rock. It's no good to anyone and it needs clearing. That's our delightful job for the day, Wynn. We get to clear this lot."

Wynn looked around at the pile of tumbled rock in dismay. "We have to take all of this up?"

"Up?" Grint snorted. "No, thank the Father. We'll take it down. The Utterdark can have this lot, and may she fucking choke on it."

Loading the barrow was as simple as it sounded. Keeping it balanced and well-loaded proved to be a science and Grint cursed and muttered as he rearranged the rocks to his satisfaction. "Come on then," he grunted as he crouched for the handles. "On three." He counted and they lifted in unison, making it one smooth motion. "Remember," Grint said as Wynn managed the first step. "Keep your legs bent a bit, and don't lean forward to reach for the handles or your back'll be fucked in a week."

"How far do we have to go with this?" Wynn grunted as they staggered through the tunnels.

"Watch your feet," Grint told him, ignoring his question.

"My feet?"

"Don't step left when I do," Grint said. "Use the other foot, or we'll start swaying and tip out. I don't want to stack each bloody load more than once."

Wynn closed his mouth, concentrating on his steps. The chill of the air was a happy memory now and the sweat ran freely down his forehead and dripped from the end of his nose.

"Let's see if you feel it," Grint said, breaking the silence of the last few minutes. "I'm betting you will."

"Feel what?" gasped Wynn between breaths.

24

"Just stay back from the edge," Grint told him. "I'll dump the load this first time. You just watch."

Wynn followed on, bemused, as they made their way through a tunnel which seemed to get narrower with each step. The passage turned sharply to the right as the floor sank down, opening out into a large chamber dominated by a hole surrounded by a low wall. Wynn frowned at the reflections cast by their chemlamps and leaned in to examine the wall as Grint lowered the barrow to the floor. Unlike the rough stone throughout the mines, the stones that made up the walls of the chamber seemed polished and shone as if they were slick with moisture. He reached out one hand and was surprised to find the stone as rough as anywhere else in the tunnels, and not wet at all.

"That's just the edges of it," Grint told him.

"What?" Wynn turned to the man. "How do you mean?"

"The Utterdark. The bitch is playing with your mind already." Grint shook his head. "Remember what I said," he told Wynn, pointing a finger at him as he sank down to reach for the barrow again. "Stay back against the wall, even if it looks like I want help. I won't. Not this first time. Just keep away from the edge."

The edge. Wynn nodded but he was already looking past Grint to the low stone wall that bordered the ragged hole. The wall seemed to be constructed of loose stone, rubble that looked the same as the rocks he and Grint had hauled in the barrow. His gaze drifted above the wall, taking in the large chemlamps hung around the room that he had somehow not noticed before. The chamber was brighter than anywhere else in the mines, yet somehow the light didn't seem to pass into the gaping hole beyond the wall.

The darkness seemed to hang in the hole, lurking there as if it were somehow aware. Despite the wall, Wynn was tall enough to see some distance down into the depths without leaving the safety of the edge of the cave. He peered into the gloom, not really sure what it was he was looking for as Grint struggled and spat curses at the barrow he was trying to manoeuvre closer to the hole.

25

The first of the stones crashed against the side of the hole as Grint dumped them out, bouncing far out into the shaft and tumbling down into the darkness. Wynn blinked and stared intently. The darkness seemed to move, to flex somehow, and then the stones were gone, devoured.

"Soft," Wynn whispered, his eyes not leaving the hole. The darkness called to him. It wasn't the black of a cold night, it was the comfort of a warm bed on an early morning. All he had to do was reach out and embrace it. All he had to do was accept it. All he had to do was…

His head cracked back against the wall and Wynn slumped down to the ground, blinking tight against the jarring impact.

"Wynn?" A rough hand shook him and he opened his eyes against the pain.

"Shit!" Grint shook his head in obvious relief as he looked closely at him. "You alright, son?"

"What happened?" Wynn asked, pushing himself up into a sitting position.

"You came this close to throwing yourself in is what happened," Grint told him, holding up thumb and forefinger. "All I could think to do was shove you back."

"My head," Wynn groaned, reaching through the stubble on his scalp with probing fingers and wincing at what they found.

Grint winced. "Sorry about that."

"What happened?" Wynn repeated himself.

Grint sighed and sank down next to him. "Skerth took you down the ladders for a reason. Though I think he's a bloody fool for doing it that way. There's something down in these mines. They call it the Utter-dark. It's like…" he looked up at the cave's roof and scratched at his neck. "It's like a piece of the night come to life. You probably felt it calling to you on when you climbed down the ladder. You felt it just now too."

"What is it?" Wynn asked, glancing over at the hole. He looked away with a shudder.

"Fucked if I know." Grint shrugged. "Some of the folks down here say there's no such thing, most of them if I'm honest. Admitting you've

26

seen it, or felt it, is just going to get you mocked. But you'll never find anyone come in here alone, not unless they're a damned fool anyhow. Why do you think the priests keep taking folks in? Aspiration's not so big we can take in each year for nothing. There's accidents now and then, and every few months someone will pass their testing and be taken up to the temple. More often than not though, it's because someone walked off into the dark."

"What happens to them?" Wynn asked, the pain in his head forgotten.

"No one knows," Grint said. "They don't come back. It's one of the reasons we work in teams." He shifted around so that he was crouched in front of Wynn. "Let me get a look at you," Grint said, peering intently at Wynn's eyes. He grunted. "You've a thick skull if nothing else. We're going to need to get you a better helmet though," he said, handing it back to Wynn. "It's no bloody use if it falls off anytime you turn your head." He pushed himself to his feet and held out a hand. "Come on, that rubble's not going to shift itself."

"But…" Wynn looked past him.

Grint followed his gaze and shook his head. "You'll be alright for now. Just be mindful of it. I kind of think it's a two-way thing. She don't come to you unless you go looking for her. You ignore her and she'll leave you be, mostly."

"She?"

Grint laughed with a shrug. "I don't know. For some reason it's always been a she to me. A cold, heartless bitch that wants to suck your soul dry."

***

Wynn had to stagger back to the huts in their small corner of Aspiration. He thought he'd known work on the farm, his father had driven him hard enough, but it was nothing to the bone-deep weariness he felt now. Somehow working in the darkness of the mines added another element to it, an intensity. The effort of having to turn his head

27

and shine the chemlamp every time he wanted to take a step, having to feel his way along with his feet when carrying the barrow and trying to keep pace with Grint, all combined with the sheer effort of carrying load after load of rocks, had left him drained and his eyes felt gritty with dust and fatigue.

Terrik's compound was loud. Its proximity to the smelt works meant that he heard metal crashing incessantly, and the jumbled echoes that spilled out into the cavern merged with the loud voices of those in and around the huts. The noise assaulted him from all directions as he trudged after Grint, first stowing the barrow, and then following him to refill the chem chambers in his helmet.

Grint gave him a calculating look as he popped the vials out of the clips that held them and placed them in a rack inside the hut. "I'll show you how to do this another time, you're pretty much done in. Come on, let's see what rats they drowned in the pots today."

Wynn sank down onto the bench, guided by Grint's hands on his shoulders. "Sit there," the shaggy haired man told him. "I'll fetch you whatever's hot."

"Boy? Hey, boy!"

Wynn raised his head blearily as an elbow nudged him.

"Grint ain't buggered all the sense out of you just yet then," the speaker snorted, shovelling another spoonful of something brown and wet into his face.

"I... what?" Wynn shook his head.

"Leave him be, Tresk," another man called out.

Tresk squeezed a dark scowl into a glance and threw them both at the man. Turning back to Wynn he asked, "You have fun picking up your little pebbles, boy?"

Wynn opened his mouth to speak but Tresk was already pushing on. "Clearing rubble while the rest of us did the real work? You think you can replace Canker like that?"

"I just did what Grint said," Wynn managed with a frown. What did the man want with him?

28

"We all got to put our sweat in," Tresk spat across the table. "We don't make the tally because of your scrawny arse and…" he fell silent as a hand reached down to set a bowl in front of Wynn.

"… and what, Tresk?" Grint asked in a low voice. "What are you going to do, knock him about? You going to do for him, Tresk? Find a loose face and set him to picking at it until the rocks take him? That's going to help with the tally, isn't it?" He swung a leg over the bench and settled in on the other side of Wynn before looking up again. "He worked a full day, harder than some others I've paired with. Leave him be, he's had a rough start of it." He paused, and lowered his voice. "The dark tried for him."

Tresk's eyes widened as he met Wynn's gaze and he looked around with a furtive glance. "Already?" he asked in a hushed tone.

Grint nodded. "At the black pit. First time I've felt it there in months."

"A touch this soon…" Tresk shook his head.

"Well now, my lads," Terrik boomed, making his way over to the table. "How did we do?"

"Fine," Grint answered quickly, giving Wynn a warning nudge with his knee. "He'll do just fine once we get him trained up."

Terrik frowned, reaching under the cloth tied across his missing eye to scratch with one finger as he looked at Wynn. "Not like we have a choice, is it? Tally's in two weeks. I'll leave it to you to get him moving."

Grint's expression twisted as Terrik held his gaze but he nodded with a grunt.

"Set him to working with some of the others. Get him on a pick team tomorrow," Terrik told him. "He can work with Killen and a couple of the others, show him how to follow a quartz line."

"You're going to get him on gold?" Tresk blurted, dropping his spoon and spraying stew onto the table. "He'll lose half of it to chips and shit strikes. We need a good crew in for gold."

Terrik turned his head slowly and looked at the man in silence before he spoke. "This is my crew, Tresk, earned by tally and more. You want out on your own? That can be arranged. You want to find your own ore? Haul it alone? Buy your own smelt-chits?"

29

Tresk shook his head, looking down at the table. "I didn't mean it like that, boss. I just…"

"I'll do the thinking, Tresk," Terrik spat. "You just hit the fucking rocks where I tell you." He looked around the table. "We lost a good man with Canker. We've got two weeks left to make tally, and less chance than I want to admit of making it. I'm going to want all of us to be on gold from now on."

Grint shared a looked with Tresk. "All of us? We only know two good veins and they're so small you could set the boy here to them with a rusty nail an' he'd empty 'em out."

"I know that, Grint," Terrik said, his low voice lifting. "That's why we're going to chance a Listening."

CHAPTER THREE

"Not that one." Killen took the pick from his hands and tossed it back into the heap. The woman was not the sort of person you would expect to find in a mine. Short and raw-boned she barely reached Wynn's shoulders. Her face was hard, and what beauty it held was tempered by her hollow cheeks and jaded eyes. "Look at the handle when you take a tool. If you're going to have this thing in your hands for the next twelve hours or so, you'd better make damned sure it's a good one." She reached down and selected a pick which looked much the same to Wynn.

"Try that one," Killen advised, scratching at her scalp through her close-cropped hair. She didn't look to be much older than him in years, but her eyes told a different story. Her eyes had lived.

Wynn hefted the pick, turning it over in his hands.

"Make sure the haft is smooth and that the head doesn't move about," Killen told him, watching until Wynn seemed satisfied. "This is Sott and Restik," she said, nodding at the other two men in the group. "Let's get moving."

They set off in silence, passing other groups as they headed into the mine. Wynn hurried to keep pace and reached to flick the tab on his chemlamp as soon as they passed into the darker passages. "How far is it to the first gold vein?" he asked, breaking the silence.

The air rushed out of him as his back slammed into the wall. Wynn gasped and fought to breathe past the arm jammed against his throat.

"Just keep your yap shut, boy," Sott rasped.

Wynn swallowed hard and nodded into the man's stubbled face as his feet struggled to reach the ground and take the pressure off his throat.

"Let him down, Sott," Killen said, squeezing the man's shoulder. "He wasn't to know. We don't talk on the job, Wynn," Killen told him as Sott lowered him down and stepped back, eyeing him with an unspoken promise of more. "We let other gangs know we're out here for gold and we're going to have problems with the carts."

Wynn frowned. "You mean…"

"Walk and talk," Killen said, nodding down the tunnel before setting off again. "What I mean is that we all have a tally to make, every crew does. This close to the end of the month, every team is scrambling to get what they need. Us more than most. It wouldn't be the first time a crew has come back to Aspiration with cracked heads and no gold. We keep it quiet for a reason."

"What, you mean you actually fight over it?" Wynn demanded, incredulous.

"We do what we have to do," she told him with a shrug. "You will too. Here, shine your chemlamp on my back."

Wynn watched as the slender woman turned and lifted the back of her shirt. The skin was pale from lack of sunlight but the silvery scars were clear in the lamp's light.

"Lashes," Killen told him as she turned around. "One for every mark we are below our tally."

Wynn sucked the breath in between his teeth. The mine was dangerous enough without the prospect of being whipped. "You mean, the priests…" he said, aghast.

Sott snorted at that. "You think they're going to get their hands dirty? No, boy, it's our glorious Sefin, Garl, and his lot that do that. You'll think different about your friend Skerth when he's watching you being tied to the post."

"Even a woman?"

"You'd best drop that right now, Wynn. That's surface talk. It's a different world down here," Killen told him. Her tone was light enough but her dark eyes made it clear she'd fought this point more than once and was tired of it. "Down here I'm just another crew member and I swing a pick as well as anyone else."

32

Wynn fell silent, following the others as Killen led them to the lifts and they sank deeper into the earth. The cold of the mines ate at him as they walked, and the small sack he'd stuffed with hard bread banged against his leg with every other step. The smaller tunnels had no chem-lamps and the wan light shed by their helmets did little to push back the blackness. His thoughts circled the memory of the Utterdark, fascinated by it but afraid to move too close. The pure seduction of the thing's touch on his mind had been unnerving. The lure of the deep had been a raging torrent, stripping away his thoughts and fears until it bore him away and dragged him down.

He shuddered, touched by a chill that had nothing to do with the temperature, and tried to turn his thoughts away from the Utterdark and focus on placing his feet as they walked.

"You ever see gold?" The question caught him off-guard and Wynn's head shot round to see Restik walking beside him, wincing against the sudden light from Wynn's chemlamp. He looked away quickly. "Sorry," he muttered. "No, not really. I mean, I know it's supposed to be a bit like brass…" he cut off as the shorter man shook his head.

"Not like that," Restik said, keeping his voice low. "In the rocks, I mean. You know what you're looking for?"

Wynn shook his head. "No," he admitted.

"Fuck's sake," Restik muttered to himself, fingering his scraggly beard. "You know what quartz is though, right?"

"Sort of a shiny kind of rock?" Wynn ventured with a wince.

"That's something at least," Restik grunted. "Killen'll show you when we get to the vein. Just take your time. Keep your strikes clean and try not to spoil too much."

The trek took the better part of an hour by Wynn's reckoning, though the dark made it harder to judge for some reason. They stopped twice on the route, once to retrieve a barrow from a storage cave and again to pick up a large chemlamp. Both times had Wynn hugging himself and rubbing his arms against the cold.

"Set it up," Killen told Sott, stopping in the passage abruptly.

Wynn played his chemlamp over the tunnel and realised it had widened out into a small cave on his left. Rock chips and debris littered the floor and he searched the rocks, tracing the light over the walls trying to pick out the gold, as Restik and Sott cursed and struggled over the chemlight on its three-legged stand.

"Wynn," Killen, waved him over. "You see this here?" she pointed to a streak of paler rock running down the wall.

"That's it?" Wynn blurted, stepping closer and peering with a frown.

"No, that's just a bit of quartz in the rock." Killen looked over to Sott. "Any time you feel ready, boys."

"Stupid. Bloody. Switch," Sott spat, punctuating the curse with blows against the lamp.

"Break it, and Terrik will nail your balls to a post," Killen warned with a sweet smile.

Sott glanced up and muttered something vile before turning back to the lamp and fitting the rod back into the slot on the side of the device, bearing down with a grunt. The big man let out a cry of triumph as the lamp gave a loud metallic report and began to glow softly. The light intensified until the chamber was lit as brightly as the streets of Aspiration.

"This here is what we're looking for," Killen explained running her fingers over the rock. "Gold and quartz seem to hang together. It's worth chipping this out and seeing what comes from it, especially when you're just learning. Now, over here," she waved Wynn over towards the others. "This is what we're really looking for."

The vein of gold ran down through the stone, looking for all the world as if someone had somehow poured it like paint over the rock's surface. Wynn looked in wonder at the gold, reaching out to touch it. It somehow didn't seem real.

Killen gave him a moment before she spoke again. "For now get over there and cut down that quartz, see if you can find a trace behind it."

Wynn nodded and set to work as the others began chipping and hacking away at the rocks. He eyed the quartz and gave an experimental

34

tap with the pick. The rock was more yielding than he'd thought it would be. He struck again, and then again.

By the time they stopped to rest, Wynn's arms were leaden and his face sore from the spray of rock chips. He ate in silence, mind numb as he chewed mechanically on the rough bread from his pack. It tasted of rock. Everything tasted of rock. The dust didn't hang in the air for long. It was too damp for that. But it seemed like it had coated his tongue. He forced himself to swallow and sipped from the waterskin to help it down.

His gaze drifted along his grime-coated clothes to his hands, made grey with the dust that had etched out every line and crease. He turned them over, flexing both slowly as he wondered at the wizened claws they had become, made ancient in the passage of a few short hours. Was this the new life he had been offered? A youth stolen, the theft missed by a mind too fogged with exhaustion to care about the loss.

Wynn looked over to the pile of quartz-heavy rock he had spent the morning hacking out of the walls. It didn't look like much. The others sat to one side, speaking softly beside the barrow already piled high with their gold-rich stone. He studied them in turn. Aside from Killen, not a one of them were under thirty, and Restik could be twice that. How long had they been down here?

He watched Killen. It was hard to put an age to her. Older than him certainly, but far younger than the others. How was it that she had come to lead this team?

He opened his mouth to speak but the crunch of rocks from the tunnel stopped the words before he drew breath. The others were scurrying to their feet before he could call out. A flurry of curses flew as shadows surged down the tunnel towards them.

"Grab your pick!" Killen shouted to him and then charged after the other two already rushing to meet the shadowy figures. Wynn watched as they clashed, picks reversed in their hands and the hafts crashing down in search of flesh and bone.

35

Two men were already down by the time he realised he hadn't taken a step. Wynn glanced down at the pick in his trembling hands as fear edged his feet backwards until his back pressed against the wall.

"Wynn, get in here!" Sott growled, ducking beneath a wild swing and jabbing the butt of his pick into a half-seen face, mashing the lips and cracking teeth. A cry of pain rose out of the wet crunch of the impact.

Restik fell as Wynn looked on, dropped by a pick handle that followed a well-aimed fist. The blow rocked his head back and his body sank like a dropped sack. The shadowy figures seemed everywhere at once and he blinked through the tears that blurred his vision. He couldn't do it. He couldn't go out there, and be part of that. Anger burned through his fear as he raged at himself and he smashed his fists down onto his thighs in an orgy of self-hate.

"Blade!" a voice called out above the fray and within the length of a gasped breath everything stopped.

Killen backed towards the light of the chemlamp with one hand buried in her captive's long, dark hair as she pressed a jagged length of iron to his throat.

"Back away," she told the men in front of them who eyed her warily.

"Do as the bitch says," her captive hissed out between clenched teeth. "You'll fucking burn for this, you know," he told Killen. "A few lumps on heads is one thing, blades is too far. Keepers will do for you."

"I'll worry about the Keepers, you worry about this," Killen snarled, pressing the knife closer. She looked through the press of men. "Sott, you alive?"

"I'll live," the older man said with a grimace, probing at the side of his face with one hand.

"Get Restik back over by the wall," Killen told him. "Wynn, you help him."

Wynn darted forward to grab Restik's other hand and together they managed to drag him out of the way, propping him against the wall.

"Now, how about you tell your lads to fuck off out of here?" Killen said with a sweet smile. "Uh uh!" She warned as the man tried to pull away from her grip. "You stay until I'm good and ready to let you go."

"You think I'm stupid?" the dark-haired man spat.

"No," Killen smiled. "I think you're the one with my knife at your throat."

"We could rush 'em," one of the attackers ventured.

"Only if you fancy splashing through his blood." Killen shrugged as her captive shook his head violently.

"No, you boys go," he said, his voice strained. "We're done here."

Killen watched them slink away, shadowy figures that revealed faces filled with pain and worry as the light of the chemlamp found them. The man in her grip cursed, watching his crew vanish. She waited until the sound of their passage faded. Wynn felt the pounding in his chest beginning to subside by the time Killen sent the captive on his way with a shove and a kick that missed.

"You're dead, bitch!" he snarled as he glanced at Killen. "You'll be praying for Garl to lash your back bare when we're done with you."

Killen snorted. "Piss off, will you?"

"Fat load of use you were," Sott spat at Wynn in the silence that fell. "Stood pissing yourself in the corner while Restik's getting his face pounded on."

"Never mind that now," Killen muttered. "Have a look at Restik, see if he's in one piece." She turned to Wynn and beckoned him closer, reaching for his shoulder, and leaning in as she spoke. "You've never been in a fight, Wynn? No fist fights with other lads?"

Wynn shook his head, looking everywhere but at Killen's face.

"Well you're going to have to toughen up," Killen sighed. "It doesn't happen all the time, more often when it's close to tally, but if you back out of a fight like that again you'll be walking along with my boot sticking out of your arse."

Restik let out a heartfelt groan behind them. Killen turned and crouched down beside him, speaking in a low voice.

"Best we clear out I think," she announced. "That was Vashek's crew if I'm any judge, and they're an evil bunch of sheep shaggers. They'll be back soon as they scrounge up enough men."

They moved soon after Restik hauled himself to his feet. Despite his injuries he reached for one end of the barrow and the four of them made their way through the tunnels to the carts waiting for them on the main shaft. Killen made Wynn wait with Restik while the others made two more trips, loading the ore-rich stone into the waiting carts and gathering up the supplies. The older man stood in silence, throwing black looks at Wynn but otherwise ignoring him until Killen and Sott returned.

The harnesses were worn, and dug in painfully to Wynn's shoulders as they set off, but he moved without protest as they strained to get the carts moving, hauling the load up the tracks of the main shaft Skerth had shown him on his first trip into the mines.

"Nobody bothers the carts," Killen called back to him. "The side tunnels have always been fair game but once a load is on the tracks then it's off limits."

Wynn failed to hold in the sigh. "So we're in the clear then?"

"No," Sott growled out between panted breaths. "We are not 'in the clear.' Because of you we left half our take down there. Because of you, we had to clear out. Vashek's lot know we couldn't hold it. We're already way below tally because Canker went for his little walk in the dark. Our only chance was the Listening and now we might not have the gold to stump up for that."

"I don't understand," Wynn said, glad for relative darkness for once. At least it hid his face, his shame.

"That's because you don't know shit!" Sott snapped. "Just do as you're damned well told from now on. If Killen says piss there, then you piss right fucking there. If she says smack that man's face in with a pick, then you fucking well do it. I'll tell you this for free, boy. If we end up getting the lash from this, you'll get it twice."

"Alright, Sott," Killen said. "Calm it down. What's done is done."

38

The older man glowered but said nothing and leaned further into the harness.

"What's a Listening?" Wynn asked after a few minutes. "I've heard it said a few times now but no one ever says what it is."

"The Listeners are a weird bunch," Killen told him. "They act as their own village, keep to themselves and never step foot down in the tunnels unless they're paid for a Listening."

"They don't mine?"

"Let me finish." Killen hushed him. "They claim the Listening is a gift from the Forgefather. Whatever it is, the Listeners can find gold, copper, whatever metal they're asked to. They search the tunnels and it's as if the rocks themselves are whispering to them, telling them their secrets. That's the way they tell it anyway. Either way, a Listening brings ore. Sometimes it's enough to keep the lash off your back. Sometimes it's enough that you won't need to worry about the tally for months."

"Why don't they just mine it for themselves?" Wynn asked.

"Most of them are too old or weak to swing a pick," Killen laughed. "Even if they weren't it wouldn't do them any good. They're all blind, every last one of them."

"Blind?"

"They put their eyes out when they first find the power," Killen said, suddenly quiet. "It's not a good business."

"They come in the night, I heard," Sott put in. "I heard it said that the Listeners can hear the power wake in those that have it. They come in the night and drag 'em out of their bunks and put their eyes out, right there in the street."

"You don't know shit, Sott," Restik muttered.

"I know what I heard," Sott shot back over his shoulder to where Restik worked with Killen at the rear of the carts. "I heard them come for a lad in my first crew. Dragged him screaming out into the street, they did. Pulled him out while the rest of us lay in our bunks and pretended we didn't hear a thing, hoping like hell they didn't come back for anyone else. I'll never forget the sound he made when they took his eyes." He spat onto the rocks. "I saw him again, must've been a year or two later. He looked just like the rest of them by then, eyes all bound up and wouldn't say two words if he could help it."

The incline soon stifled any conversation as the weight of the carts bore down on the harnesses. The aches of Wynn's muscles were nothing compared to this. They were a breath in the face of the hurricane. The pain that he felt through his shoulders eclipsed anything he had ever experienced.

Every breath was a battle and Wynn leaned into the harness to ease the strain, trying to match what he could see of Sott's stance. It didn't work. After five minutes the sweat was dripping from his face and down his back. He lived for the brief sections where the shaft levelled out. By the time they reached the final rise leading to Aspiration Wynn was beyond pain, sucking in breaths in brief, frantic, gasps.

Killen urged them onwards, only slowing at the entrance to the smelt works. "You two can drag this in, grab some of the smelters for help if need be. I want to get to Terrik before Vashik does, and I've no doubt he's going to want to speak to our little hero here."

Sott nodded, still breathing hard as he gave Wynn an evil grin.

Wynn flushed as the eyes turned to him and, for the moment, the pain in his shoulders was forgotten. He shrugged his way out of the harness and followed Killen, feeling Sott and Restik's eyes on him as they went.

"I'm sorry, Killen," Wynn muttered as they passed between two storage huts.

"For what?" Killen looked at him with genuine surprise. "For not getting involved in the fight? I've seen and heard a lot worse about first-timers. You didn't piss yourself, that's a plus. You carried your load on the carts. If we hadn't been on a gold run it would have never happened."

"But…" Wynn stopped,

"I'm not saying it was a good thing," Killen said, looking over at him. "Just that I wouldn't spend the rest of my life worrying about it. You'll hold your own next time, right?"

Wynn nodded, sensing that there wasn't really another option.

"That's not to say that Terrik isn't going to shit his britches," Killen told him with a smirk.

Wynn winced and opened his mouth to reply but Killen was already moving. He followed with a groan.

Killen glanced back at him as they reached the compound. "After you, sunshine," she told him, waving at the hut with a grin.

Terrik looked up at Wynn as Killen followed him through the door and leaned back in the chair.

"I was wondering when you'd show up," he observed, wiping his nose with the back of his hand. "Vashek's already been in, throwing a fit and making all sorts of promises he can't keep. A blade, Killen? You know better than that."

Killen winced. "Didn't really have much choice, Terrik. There were more men than we could handle any other way. I didn't actually use it anyway. I just threatened him a little bit."

"How much of a little bit?" Terrik asked, narrowing his one good eye.

"I held the knife to his throat and threatened to let his men splash around in his blood," Killen said with a shrug. "It was that or let them take the whole load."

Terrik grunted, glancing at Wynn who stood silent by the doorway. "What about him?" he asked Killen.

Killen grimaced. "He froze."

"In the fight?" Terrik guessed.

Killen nodded.

"Piss himself?"

"Nothing that bad," Killen said, shaking her head as Wynn's cheeks burned. "Just didn't get into it."

Terrik grunted, looking past Killen at Wynn with an expression which gave away nothing. "Did they explain the facts of life to you yet?" he asked in a flat voice. "You understand about the tally and what happens if we don't reach the mark?"

41

Wynn nodded and tried to find something on the wall behind Terrik to focus on.

"Nobody has to serve in a crew," Terrik said. "You understand that? We work in crews because it gives us all more of a chance of making the tally. You want out, you just say the word and you're gone. Do you want out, boy?"

Wynn shook his head in silence.

"That's it then," Terrik told him. "Next time, you back your crew up. Or you leave, if you still can."

"That's it?" Wynn asked before he could stop himself. He'd been preparing himself for some level of punishment. For lashes. For something.

"Everyone gets one mistake, boy," Terrik told him and he hauled himself to his feet and moved to wave a finger in Wynn's face. "Just the one, mind."

"I'm not going to be punished? Lashed?"

Terrik and Killen both laughed at that.

"No, lad," Terrik told him. "You get lashed and you're no use to anyone until you heal up. That's not to say I'll not punish you. You lost us who knows how much gold, and as good as handed it to Vashek. You can do blackwork until I say otherwise. And give a damned good accounting of yourself while you're at it."

Wynn nodded as relief washed through him. For the moment at least, he didn't care what blackwork was.

***

Blackwork, as it turned out, was mining out coal. The cavern that held Aspiration had several tunnels leading down into the mines but only one of these led down to the coal seams. Wynn had slept easily the night after meeting with Terrik, relieved that the punishment hadn't been harsher and he woke to Grint's kick, rested and ready.

The boy that was waiting for him outside of the bunkhouse was no one that Wynn recognised. His skin was heavy with coal-dust, ground thick into his pores, giving his skin a grey pallor in the light of the chem-lamps that made him look ill, or dead.

"You Wynn?" the creature asked as Wynn emerged from the hut. "Name's Darug," he said in response to Wynn's nod. "Get your helmet, day's wasting."

Wynn followed the boy through the streets of Aspiration in silence, heading away from the mines and smelt works. Darug informed him the coal works was on the other side of the cavern. What further attempts Wynn made at conversation had been met with grunts and one word responses until he gave up. He felt a sense of relief when the Blacker's tunnel came into sight.

The tunnel was nothing like the mine he'd almost become accustomed to. It sank down into the earth and soon opened into a large cave. Mounds of coal were piled high and a line of Blackers, most of them children, stood queueing for something at the far end of the chamber.

"Pull that behind you," Darug instructed him, pointing to a wooden barrow on runners that looked much like the sleds he'd used as a child. Wynn took up the worn rope and followed.

A low passage that showed obvious signs of having been widened sank down into the earth, narrowing with every passing foot until Wynn was forced to walk single-file behind his tight-lipped guide. They passed the first of many low shafts leading off in different directions and Wynn grimaced as he peered down into a tunnel that was little more than waist high.

"Why are they so low?" he asked.

"Coal don't hide like gold or copper," Darug told him. "Either it's there or it ain't. It ain't worth spending all day looking for it neither, there's enough down here that's easy takings. We just dig out what there is and go. No need to make the tunnels any bigger than they need to be."

The darkness deepened the further they went as the gaps between the chemlamps grew wider, and then the lights stopped altogether.

"It's helmet lamps only from here," Darug told him with a grin. "Not scared of the dark are you?"

Wynn met the boy's gaze with one as impassive as he could manage and wondered at Darug's age. Somehow this boy knew nothing of the darkness he had experienced.

Darug led Wynn through the darkness for another half hour before stopping him at a low tunnel. His back ached already from hunching down under the low roof and he was soaked to the knees from splashing through the puddles that seemed to be every other step.

"You can work this one," Darug said, pointing. "The seam's about a hundred feet or so down here. Hack it out until you fill your barrow then drag it out to the main chamber with the rest. You should be able to get five loads done at least. Make sure the tallymaster sees you dump your loads each time."

"You're leaving?" Wynn blurted.

Darug's lip curled in contempt. "I ain't here to hold your hand," he said in a voice that matched his face. "You'll see the support pillars that've been left. So long as you don't do nothing stupid like hack one out, you'll be fine." He reached into a pocket and pulled out a length of grimy cloth. "Here. Tie this round your mouth and breathe through it. If you don't you'll be coughing your guts out before you fill your first barrow."

Wynn took the cloth, murmuring his thanks but Darug was already leaving, moving easily along the tunnel. The glow of his chemlamp faded as he splashed his way down the tunnel, and then Wynn was alone with nothing but the darkness as a companion.

The first hour was the worst as Wynn made his way into the shaft and went in search of the seam. The coal itself was easy to find in the walls. What had been left behind shone as if wet in the light of his chemlamp. Here and there, pillars of the stuff had been left at the edges of the tunnel, supporting the roof.

The roof. It both fascinated and terrified him. Water dripped through tiny cracks that he reasoned must run up through towards the surface. Wynn glanced up at it often, grimacing as he made his way along the shaft, as if it might collapse at any moment.

44

Water trickled along the passage in a shallow stream that ran towards the end of the shaft. How, or where, it drained out, Wynn had no idea, but the prospect of the shaft filling with water did little to improve his mood.

He dragged the sled along until he reached a likely spot where he could crouch down, out of the wet, and began to hack away at the coal. It came easily, falling in cascades which threw dust up to his face and made his eyes water. Wynn coughed despite the cloth tied over his face and worked on.

By the time he had filled five barrows his arms and legs were trembling and his eyes felt raw with the dust that clung to them. He dragged himself out of the shaft and back towards the bunkhouse.

"Get that shit off you before you go in there," Terrik called out, stopping him on the step before he could go in. "There's a sluice over that way."

Wynn followed the vague directions to the sluice, which turned out to be a cistern of shockingly cold water that emptied itself over the idiot who was fool enough to pull the cord hanging underneath it. Shivering and miserable, Wynn dried himself as best he could, and made his way to his bunk.

After two days Wynn ached. After five days of it he was ready to go in search of the Utterdark itself, if it meant he wouldn't need to carry on with the blackwork. He crawled from his bunk like some vile cave creature, dragging himself out onto the steps of the low building before retrieving his clothes from where he'd left them over a rail. They were stiff from the coal-dust and grime, and Wynn grimaced as he pulled them on over his smalls.

"No, Terrik wants you in the mine today, Wynn." Killen stopped him as he pulled the rough cloth up his legs. "It's the Listening," she explained in response to his look. "We'll need every hand we can use. Crews sniff around a Listener like flies around shit. We'll have first grab at it for as long as we can work but the other crews will be in as soon as we leave it alone. We're going to need every hand we can call on. Get something hot inside you, it's going to be a bitch of a day."

45

Wynn looked down at his clothes and then back up at Killen with a raised eyebrow. She cracked a rare smile and chuckled. "Yeah, I reckon you're used to rough days just lately. You really ought to try and eat more, you know? You're as thin as a rake."

Breakfast went into Wynn, that was as much as he knew about it. Spoon went to mouth and food went to stomach but his eyes were occupied, busy looking for the Listener. He turned at Grint's touch and followed his pointing finger to the robed figure making his way into the square.

"How does he find his way along?" Wynn asked in a hushed voice. The Listener was shuffling along but still moving at a reasonable pace and working his way around both men and obstacles without any difficulties.

Grint looked away from the Listener. "Who knows? It's strange, I'll grant you, but trust me, that's the least of it."

"Maybe they're not blind then?" Wynn suggested.

"Wait," Grint told him.

The Listener seemed to be heading directly for them, passing close to the trestle table. The hooded robe was a mottled dark grey that reminded Wynn of smoke. He stared openly at the Listener, taking in the dark cloth tied over his eyes under the hood. It was only as the man passed him that the marks on his face registered with him. Twin rivulets of dried blood ran from under the bandage and over his cheeks.

Wynn stared after the figure in horror as the meaning came to him.

"Now you think you understand what I meant?" Grint asked, speaking in a low voice. He shook his head. "You're just touching the edges of it. The Listeners have their eyes put out. Ignore how they find their way around for a minute, they could never be acolytes or priests if they're blind. They could never man a forge. They're down here until the day they die. You know the other reason we call this place Aspiration?" he asked suddenly, waiting for Wynn to shake his head. "It's got nothing to do with the fact that we're all aspirants. It's not about aspiring, it's about aspirating. You know that word? That's what they call it when you choke to death on your own vomit."

46

Wynn's eyes widened as he looked at Grint, perhaps seeing him clearly for the first time. All at once he took in the lines on his face, the touches of grey in his hair. "How long have you been down here, Grint?" he breathed.

"Too long," Grint muttered with a shake of his head. "Long enough to learn a man can choke on hope."

The crew followed behind the Listener, abandoning food and caught in his wake as he made his way into the mine. Chemlamps flicked on as miners fiddled with helmets, but the Listener didn't carry a light, or seem hampered by the darkness.

"You want to get ahead of the crowd and see this?" Grint asked.

Wynn raised an eyebrow. "How?"

"Come on." Grint waved him on, pushing past the throng at the entrance to the mines and then led him into the first side tunnel.

The nagging suspicion was confirmed as they reached the ladder. Wynn chewed on his lip as Grint motioned him on.

"I'm not sure I can," he admitted, scratching at his thumb with the other hand. "It was bad enough the first time but…"

"This time you know what's coming?" Grint finished for him. He nodded. "Look, I know what you mean. I've felt the dark too. Not like you did at the pit, but enough that I don't dismiss it all as horse shit like some do. You don't often feel it in the same place, is all I can tell you. Chances are this'll be fine but," he paused and lowered his voice, "I heard what happened with you and the fight. If you're too scared…"

"I'm no damned coward!" Wynn spat out, clenching his fists and missing the grin that flashed over Grint's face as he pushed past him to the ladder. It was thirty feet before he started to calm down and another ten before he realised he'd been played.

The descent went smoothly. As Grint had said, there was no sign of the deeper darkness that had hung in the gloom the last time, and the difference was marked. What had been an endless climb down through the blackness before, was simple now. Hand to rung, foot to rung. And repeat.

Grint joined him in moments and led him on through the tunnels without a word. The small side tunnel rejoined the main shaft just as the Listener passed and Wynn and Grint were able to fall into step with the throng that followed.

The Listener seemed to be turning at random, leading them from the main shaft into the maze of small side tunnels that twisted and intersected as they wormed through the rock. He stopped next to an irregular bulge in the tunnel that had forced it out into a small cave. Without needing to be told Wynn knew this was the remnants of an old firing and he glanced over at Grint, noting his confused frown as the Listener held one hand up.

"Silence for the Listener!" Terrik bellowed from his spot beside the robed figure. In seconds the voices filling the tunnel died away, leaving nothing but the faint sound of water dripping in the distance.

The Listener stood, waiting until all the echoes had died away. He gave the smallest of nods and moved to the wall. Wynn watched as the blindfolded man pressed both hands to the bare rock, leaning in close and whispering something that carried, but which was somehow impossible to make out. He leaned in closer until his forehead pressed up against the cold stone and then fell silent, listening.

Wynn glanced at Grint but received only a finger pressed to Grint's lips by way of reply. The Listener stood frozen, wrapped in a silence that held him as tightly as the arms of any mother. His head snapped up as he sucked in a breath with a hiss and moved to his left, head cocked towards the wall as his fingers trailed along the surface. He slapped the stone once and turned to Terrik.

"Here," the Listener's voice was soft. "Here you will find both gold and iron in quantities." He glanced at the wall as if he could somehow see through the thick bandage that bound his eyes. "As agreed the balance of your payment must be received by the rise of dawn."

Wynn turned away as Grint muttered something.

"What?"

"Hmm?" Grint shook himself. "Nothing, it doesn't matter. It's just, I worked this firing. There's nothing left in those rocks, not a trace of anything."

48

"You think the Listener's wrong?" Wynn said.

Grint frowned at the wall. "What? No. No, they're never wrong."

"Maybe it's just deeper in," Wynn suggested.

"Maybe…" Grint trailed off, frowning again at the wall.

CHAPTER FOUR

"For pity's sake, Kharios. No!" The lead acolyte spat, leaving his position to march over to him. "No, no. Damn it all, no! We've been through this a dozen times already this morning. Why can't you get the sequence right?"

Kharios grimaced, allowing his arms to drop out of position only to have his wrists snatched up before he could speak.

"First position with the left, Guard of Flame," the man growled, shaking his arm as he held it in the correct position. "Second position with the right, Calling the Light."

"Yes, Hastrit," Kharios mumbled, looking down at the floor.

"Stop looking at your ash-damned toes, Kharios, and show me," Hastrit glowered. "And do not presume to use my name, Novice. You may have been given your true-name but that doesn't mean that much. You wouldn't be the first novice to be returned to the mines, you know?"

Kharios bit on the inside of his lip to still his tongue. He moved into the first position, fighting the urge to glance at how he had set his feet as he held his arm before him. He reached high with the other, fingers clasping at air as he brought the hand down again, level with his face.

"Adequate," Hastrit said with a faintly nauseated expression. "If just barely." He shook his head with a sigh and glanced at the other acolytes surrounding the forge. "Go on, Kharios. I'd rather muddle through without you than have to stop every other minute. Go and practice. And for the love of all the gods, do better!"

Kharios bowed in acceptance but the acolyte had already turned back to the others who regarded Kharios with expressions ranging from mild irritation to disgust. He should probably have felt shame but all Hastrit ever brought out of him was anger. He left, making his way through the empty halls of the lower temple. As he walked he imagined just how the skinny man's throat would feel under his hands. Would he scream as Kharios drove his thumbs into his flesh? Would he beg as his windpipe began to give way? The fantasy fuelled his anger until he could almost feel the hands scrabbling at his chest. His thin lips curled in a smile as he passed the hallway that might have led him towards Ossan's chambers.

He slowed, shifting unconsciously to a lighter step. Placing his feet with care and avoiding the creaks that lay in wait like old enemies, until he reached the thin stairs that led down to the more austere novice's cells.

Any priest in the temple could call a novice to serve, though many chose not to. Ossan was something of an oddity in that he almost always had novices in his cells. It was something that no longer seemed strange to Kharios, but then, he knew the reasons.

The cells surrounded a central room which served as communal kitchen and practice area. Kharios went to the prayer candle without actually thinking about what he was doing. He bent to check the wick, making sure there was no chance of it burning out, before lighting the wood stacked in the firebox with a taper.

He hunched down into a squat as he watched the flames gnaw at the dry kindling and take their first experimental taste of the larger, split logs. He should have been able to do that ritual. He'd known the pairing of the sequences for long enough that he ought to have been able to do them without even thinking about it.

Kharios stood, arching his back, and backed away from the stove. He glanced at the kettle and fought down the wave of nausea that came at the thought of tea. A memory rose, unbidden and carrying a scent with it until it seemed that it filled his nostrils. A suffocating combination of smothering heat, dust, and that ever-present stink of old tea. It had somehow always managed to penetrate the mental cocoon he'd worked to wrap around himself. Denial is often the first defence of the abused. Rest lie upon lie often enough and it looks like the truth, even to the liar.

51

He stepped back, unconsciously flowing into the first movement, and glanced down at his feet in surprise. From there the motions came easily and he moved through Guarding the Flame to Calling the Light with no real effort, passing through Clasping the Embers and a dozen more steps and motions before he drew to a halt, wondering at himself.

"So you can do it, alone. When there is no one here to notice or care," he muttered, and then froze. The sounds of the temple didn't penetrate down to the novice's cells. The crash of hammer on anvil, or the creak of the bellows couldn't make it past the first stairs and their own practice forge sat cold and silent in the corner. The silence, when it could be found, was something he relished. The voices and creaks of the floorboards above had shattered that.

Kharios moved quickly, crossing the room to enter his own small cell and pulling the curtain closed behind him. He perched on the edge of his small cot, trying to hold onto the silence as the voices drew nearer. The laughter and bluster grated at him and he squeezed his eyes tight, fingernails digging into his palms as he clung to the edges of the fleeing quiet.

"Kharios, we know you're mouldering away in there. Get out here!" The call was followed by quick steps and the curtain torn aside.

"What do you want, Mikel?" Kharios asked with a sigh, looking up at the tall novice.

"Ossan's called Arren to serve as his novice." Mikel grinned. "Come, celebrate with us!" He waved a bottle at Kharios and turned back to the others, missing the stricken look that passed over Kharios's face.

Kharios took two steps and grasped the younger man's wrist, spinning him around to face him. "Tell me you're joking?"

"No!" Mikel said, stepping back to sweep his arm in an expansive fashion towards the novice sat beside the firebox. "Ask him yourself. Let's just hope he doesn't fuck it up like you did, eh?" he laughed, slapping Kharios on the back.

Kharios shrugged the slap away with a scowl. "This is a joke isn't it, Arren?" The young aspirant's face answered the question before his lips could move. "You haven't accepted it though, have you? You can refuse, you know?"

"Why would anyone refuse?" Mikel interrupted. "It's an honour! He'll have to do some menial things, of course. Cleaning up, and the like. But think what he'll gain. Private instruction from Ossan. He'll likely cut years off his training. He could be an acolyte and working the temple forges in a year."

"Calm down, Mikel," Arren murmured. "It's not that big a thing."

"What?" Mikel looked at the novice as if he'd gone mad. "Of course it is! You'll be leaving all of us behind." He glanced at Kharios. "Well, most of us anyway."

Kharios frowned at the look. "What do you mean by that?"

"You know Ossan always calls novices in pairs, Kharios," Mikel told him with a bitter twist to his lips. "You'll be the first I've ever heard of being called twice though."

"He's called me?" Kharios sank down into a chair.

"Oh yes." Mikel gave a tight smile. "He suggested you might be able to show young Arren the way he likes things done, didn't he, Arren?"

Arren ignored him, and looked across to Kharios. "You will accept, won't you, Kharios?"

"Of course he will," Mikel said, all grins and smiles again.

"Mikel, will you just shut the fuck up!" Kharios snapped.

Mikel stepped back, hands held in front of him warding away Kharios's anger. "I really don't think…"

"No," Kharios told him, jabbing his finger at the younger man as he advanced. "You don't think. You don't know. You just bleat away like a damned sheep stuck in a bush. Too stupid to shut up for a second and think things through."

"What's that supposed to mean?" Mikel shot back, his own anger rising. "Just what the hell happened to you anyway?"

Kharios shook his head, closing his eyes against the room for a moment.

"Kharios?" Arren's voice was soft. "You will accept, won't you? You know how he works, what he expects. You know we only get one chance with something like this. I need to make the most of this and I'd progress faster if you came too."

Kharios stood, the room was suddenly too small, too crammed with expectation. He drew in a ragged breath, running his hands through his long black hair. The air somehow felt stale all of a sudden. Stifling, smothering him. He pushed his way past Mikel towards the stairs leading up into the temple.

"Kharios?" Arren called after him.

He fled.

***

The temple halls were quiet. Morning services would have finished hours ago and the great forge would stand empty now. There were closer shrines and chapels but the forge had always given him peace. Maybe it was just the quiet.

His feet knew the way even though his mind made no effort to steer them. The temple was vast and despite almost two years spent in the novice halls he only knew small portions of it. He could easily find his way to the bindery, the chandlery, and any number of prayer forges and chapels but the majority of the temple remained a mystery.

His thoughts churned, tumbling over each other as his eyes did little more than keep him from walking into the walls.

It was his nose that told him he was getting close. The smell of the coals and heated steel called to him just as well as the ring of hammers would have done. He rounded the last of the turns and made his way along the broad corridor to the large doors that awaited him.

Despite their huge size, the doors swung easily on well-oiled hinges. Panels of bronze, steel, copper and iron covered every inch of them and Kharios rested a hand on the cool surface for a moment before stepping through. The fires had burned out but the embers still glowed red and sullen beside the great forge. The anvil itself was easily large enough for a man to lay upon and would be high enough to reach to his shoulder. Kharios followed the marble pathway that rose above the rows of pews as it climbed to the forge. His gaze lifted to the wall behind the altar and the stylised image beaten into the great gold plate. It was indistinct, vague enough that any image could have been made out of it with a little imagination.

"Impressive still, isn't it?" The voice was enough to startle him but Kharios controlled himself enough to conceal his jump, and turned to face the old man who'd spoken.

"My apologies, Father," he said with a small bow. "I thought I was alone here."

The old priest dismissed his apologies with a lazy wave. "No matter, I should be apologising for startling you. You're one of Ossan's novices, aren't you?"

Kharios nodded. "Yes, Father?" He made the answer a question of his own.

The priest snorted a laugh. "I don't really hold with all that scraping. Call me Savas." He nodded again at the plate on the wall. "What do you see when you look at it?"

"I..." Kharios faltered. "I see the Forgefather," he finished.

Savas gave him a knowing smile. "I doubt that you do, Novice. Not in any real sense anyway. I always see clouds," he said before motioning to the left side of the image. "Though that part over there always looked like a roast chicken to me."

Kharios couldn't help but look and the laugh burst from him like a bird startled from the brush.

"Don't stop," the priest told him as Kharios clapped a hand over his mouth. "There is too little laughter in the temple, too little joy." The priest stepped past him and carried on towards the altar, turning to Kharios with one beckoning finger.

"Do you know what this is?"

Kharios followed his pointing finger. "It's the great forge, Father."

The old man shook his head, and tutted through his short beard. "Savas," he reminded him. "All of this," he said waving an encompassing arm, "is the great forge. Some even refer to the temple itself as the great forge. No, what I meant is this." He brought his gnarled hand down on the anvil hard enough to lend a metallic ring to the slapping noise.

Kharios frowned, not sure where this was going. "It's the anvil, Father."

The priest matched his frown and gave a minute shake of the head. "Not the anvil itself. Any fool can see it's an anvil. What is it made of?"

Kharios looked closer. He'd always assumed the anvil was iron and never really given it any thought. Now that he looked closer he wasn't so sure. There were streaks of green, red and even a copper colour running through the metal. Each were no wider than a hair and never lasted long before sinking back down below the surface of the metal. "I…" he shrugged and spread his hands in defeat.

The priest laughed in delight. "Don't worry about it. Nobody knows what the anvil is made from. If you look closely you can see layers, almost like threads of colour running through the structure of it. It's almost as if it were woven rather than forged, but those are secrets long lost to us now."

Kharios nodded, sensing silence might be the best course of action.

"So much of our knowledge has been lost over the centuries," Savas said in a low voice, still looking at the anvil. "So much of our faith has been twisted, or forgotten." He glanced at Kharios. "There was a time, so the tales say, when we could speak directly to the Forgefather. When his voice rang clearly in the strokes of the hammer on the forge."

"Father!" Kharios gasped and staggered back a step.

"Oh don't be ridiculous, boy," Savas said with a tut. "It's not really blasphemy unless I declare it as the truth. I'm just telling you what the tales say. I doubt you're going to rush off to Ossan or any of the high priests now are you?"

Kharios cast guilty looks about him before allowing a sheepish grin. "No, I suppose not."

"Well then." Savas shrugged. "Of course this would have been centuries ago. Long before the fall of the old temple and the rise of the new. Sometimes I wonder just how much has been lost…" He trailed off, falling silent.

Kharios shifted his feet, wondering how rude it would be to simply leave.

"And how is life under Ossan?" Savas asked, his narrowed eyes at odds with his casual tone. "I can't say I've spoken to one of his novices before."

"It's… fine," Kharios floundered.

Savas caught the pause and gave a small smile. "It won't be forever, my son. I don't have the fondest memories of my own time as a novice. Work hard. Help those around you if you can. You'll soon pass on to acolyte, and more ritual than any one man needs. To my mind it's always been how we treat those around us in these early years that shape us. Perhaps even more than the Father's hammer. I've seen too many rise and leave their bootprints on the faces of those that helped them up. I've always felt that we have a duty to help our brothers and sisters rise along with us."

"Yes, Father." Kharios gave a small bow.

"Well," Savas said as the conversation fell flat. "I dare say you have studies and duties you ought to be attending to." He patted the anvil absently. "Don't let me keep you."

Kharios knew a dismissal when he heard one and, giving another small bow, he turned and left. The old priest's words turned over in his head and he muttered curses as they found an ally with his conscience.

***

Kharios looked on as Arren knocked at the thick oaken door, itself a sign of rank. Acolytes and novices were never afforded the privilege or the level of privacy that a door would provide. Arren glanced back, eyes shining with an enthusiasm that had Kharios working to cover the grimace it brought to his face.

"Just remember," he began again. "Try to stay close to me as much as you can. Don't let him get you alone, Ossan is—" The heavy latch clicked and the door swung inward, cutting off the rest of his warning.

"Arren," Ossan exclaimed in a cheerful voice. "I wasn't sure you would accept." He peered past the younger novice into the passageway. "And Kharios too! It has been quite some time, my son."

Kharios gave a small bow, biting at the flesh on the inside of his lip. "Father," he managed in neutral tones.

"Come in. Come in." The short priest waved them through the doorway with a broad smile. "You've no idea how the halls suck the heat out of these chambers. Honestly, for a temple filled with fire and forges it's as cold as the grave in here at times."

He bustled them through a series of narrow corridors into a warm living chamber thick with the smell of old books and brandy. "Now then, would you like a drink before we get you both settled?" He moved to a side table and picked up a bottle. "An undertaking like this is cause for celebration on both sides, I'd say. You are here to learn, I to teach. But I rather tend to think that both parties in this arrangement should end up learning a few things."

"No, thank you, Father," Kharios said with a small curve of his lips that might have passed for a smile. He nudged at Arren, already dumb-struck by the opulence of the place, until he declined.

"You're sure?" Ossan paused in the refilling of his glass, cocking the bottle at them both. "Well then," he carried on in response to their nods. "Let's get you both settled then. Kharios, the cells haven't moved, though I've expanded a little. You remember the way, I trust?"

Kharios nodded, not meeting the priest's eyes. The words were innocent enough but he'd learned the hard way that nothing was ever truly innocent with this man.

"I'll have the servants prepare some food," Ossan said, still beaming. "We'll eat when you get back."

Kharios nodded. "Come on, Arren. I'll show you the way."

The chambers rambled, and Kharios led the way through dark winding corridors that reminded him of the mines, until they reached the flight of stairs that led down to the cells. They were simple enough, almost as spartan as the cells in the novices' quarters. Set side by side the cells were barely large enough for the beds and small desks they held, but both had thick mattresses and warmer blankets than either of them would be used to.

Kharios dropped his small bag of clothing beside the bed and sank down onto the plain wooden chair, surrendering to the memories for a moment.

"Kharios?" Arren was leaning around the doorway, his face mirroring the concern in his voice. "Are you alright?"

Kharios closed his eyes for the length of a long sigh, puffing out his cheeks. "I'm fine, Arren," he spoke into the darkness behind his eyelids. "I just needed a moment. Come on, let's get back to Ossan. He'll be waiting."

The priest beamed as they came back to his study, bustling them through to a dining room and a table that groaned under the weight of enough food for five men. Kharios sat in the offered chair and fell silent, backing away from the conversation as Ossan smiled at the flood of thanks and questions that flowed from Arren. The room was suffocating. The fire burning in the grate seemed to suck the air from the room even as the smell of food and wine smothered him. Kharios pulled at the collar of his robes and tried to remain calm. The heat and smells were the least of it; they were nothing compared to the memories playing over and over in his head.

Ossan, for his part, seemed oblivious. He'd cast a handful of sideways glances at Kharios as he picked over the meal, but nothing more than that. If he suffered any guilt for their past, he wasn't showing it.

"Now then," Ossan said, pushing his plate away and sprawling back in his chair with his wineglass. "What do you expect from all of this? From entering my service for this time?"

Arren glanced at Kharios, perhaps seeking guidance, but Kharios offered nothing. Let the boy forge his own steel, break his own path. Kharios might have been talked into coming with the lad, but at this moment he'd rather have been anywhere else.

"To learn, Father," Arren spluttered finally. "It is a great honour!"

59

"Oh, I know." Ossan smiled back. "It's no small thing to be chosen to serve, even if it is just by me. I'll try to help you as much as I can in the time we have. But what do you actually want?" The smile fell away as he leaned in towards Arren. "Forget the honour and the ritual for a moment. You have your chance here to seize something. What is it you want?"

"To move on, Father," Arren breathed. "To progress. I don't want to go back to the mines, not ever."

Ossan nodded. "I doubt many would, but then there aren't many in the mines who really understand their purpose whilst they are in them. The mines are there to test you, to temper you. I'll make no apologies for them. We need both the ore, and the revenue it brings us. But their real purpose is to turn pig iron to fine steel. That's what you are, Arren. Or at least what you might become, fine steel."

He sipped his drink and looked at the boy again, pursing his lips. "You want to take the trials, to be judged. That much is obvious. You wouldn't be the youngest I've known to make acolyte, Arren, but I doubt there could be much more than a year or two in it. Too young, some would say. Even after all these years there are some that still say ambition stands at odds with the teachings with the Lord of the Hammer."

"And what do you say, Father?" Arren's voice was a strained whisper, excitement pushing it to be something more.

Ossan smiled. "I say more fool them, boy. If the Forgefather didn't reward ambition he'd have a priesthood of slack-minded fools." He drained his glass and reached for the bottle with the other hand, refilling both their glasses as he glanced over to Kharios with a smile. "Still can't tempt you, Kharios?"

The taste of blood washed over his tongue as he shook his head, hiding behind the mask of his blank expression. Was the man deliberately goading him? Taunting him with these double meanings?

"Well then," Ossan said as he sat back, resting the base of the glass on the swell of his stomach. "It seems we might all be able to be of some use to each other, Arren. In time you may even be able to assist with some of my more delicate projects. For now eat, relax, and let us see what the coming days bring."

***

"You idiot child!" Kharios hissed as they turned the corner. He grabbed at the lad, pushing him back against the wall of the hallway. "I told you to keep away from him."

Arren twisted away from Kharios's clutch on his robes. "What are you talking about? We're in his service. How could I possibly keep away from him?"

"Just… Just keep your head down, alright?" Kharios sighed. "He's not what he seems. He's…"

"He's what?" Arren demanded.

The words wouldn't come. His throat felt tight, and his pulse pounded in his ears as forbidden images surfaced. He'd worked so hard to lock all of this away. "Just be careful with him, Arren," Kharios managed, hating himself for it. "He's not the man he pretends to be."

"You think I don't know that?" Arren spat back. "He's an old man, Kharios. He doesn't have half the influence he pretends to but he can get me to the trials. You've been dropping these half-warnings and whispered hints since you heard I'd been chosen. Ossan suggested it but I didn't have to ask you to come with me, now I wish I hadn't. You're bitter, or jealous, or something. That's fine, just don't ruin it for me."

"Bitter?" Kharios stepped back away from him. "Gods above and below, Arren. This is the last place I want to be. I came because you said you needed me, not for any other reason."

"Why, in the Forgefather's name, would I need you?" Arren shook his head, looking down at the floor. "I asked you because I wanted any help and advice you could give me to progress. I wanted your experience from when you dealt with Ossan. But all you do is flap and warn without ever really telling me anything. You know why I really asked you to come, Kharios?" He didn't wait for a response.

61

"Because I felt sorry for you. You've been a novice so long you've forgotten that it's even possible to advance. I brought you with me to give you your one last chance. If you can't see that, if you won't even try, then why don't you just go back to the mines and give someone else their turn?"

Kharios opened his mouth to respond but the boy was already pushing past him and rushing along the hallway. He stared after him, taking the first steps to follow only because there was nowhere else to go. Was Arren right? Was he just bitter?

The memories bubbled upwards, carrying guilt with them as they rose like foetid gasses. He gagged, forcing them down, but not before the image of the boy's face filled his mind. Even in death he'd carried the expression of pain. Blood had matted his hair and covered the right side of his face but the wreckage of his jaw and cheek were nothing to the look in his eyes. Death had brought no peace to his features.

"Brial," Kharios whispered the name as it drifted from thoughts he'd fought for too long to lock away. Perhaps remembering the name was enough, at least for now.

He glanced back towards Ossan's study, hands curling into fists and then falling loose to his sides. Nothing had changed. He was as powerless now as he had been then. He returned to his small cell, fell down onto the cot, and searched for sleep and oblivion.

Morning brought chores as he'd known it would. Kharios led Arren through the process of cleaning the private prayerforges; digging out the ashes and making way for the new fire. The boy was sullen, barely speaking to him unless he forced it.

"Lay the wood in a lattice, Arren," he reminded him again. "It'll draw air in from the grates underneath anyway but the fire will catch faster if you build gaps into it."

Arren gave him a look and shrugged, stepping back. "How do you mean?"

"Stack it like this." He showed him, placing the dried kindling in a lattice shape. "Now put some coal around the outside to hold it in place

62

and we'll get it lit. Ossan will want the forge ready in his workshop by the time he's eaten."

Kharios stood back again, letting the boy take the lead but staying close enough to step in if need be. Together they worked through the morning's tasks, lighting the larger forge in Ossan's workshop and letting the flames build before putting the layers of coal and coke on top, replacing the hammers and files in their places in the racks and refilling the barrels of water, salt-water, and oil.

"Ossan's a messy worker," Kharios muttered with a conspiratorial smile. "He'll dump a tool on the floor even if the rack's within reach."

Arren grinned back at him, teeth shining out of a face already black from coal-dust and Kharios couldn't help but laugh. "Look at the state of you, we'd better get cleaned up again before we eat."

Breakfast was lumpy porridge that was less than half-way to being cooked. The kitchen was small and cramped and the cook, a thin man who seemed to resent the very air they breathed, pushed them out as soon as the bowls began to look empty.

Ossan found them soon after, reaching to put arms about their shoulders. Kharios resisted the urge to throw him off. The man's touch was cold, like dead flesh had been draped over his skin.

"Now then, I trust you're well rested?" Ossan carried on before either had a chance to speak. "Kharios I assume you've taught Arren here how I like the forges prepared? You remembered that much I hope?"

Kharios began to stammer a response but Ossan was already turning, forcing Kharios to follow him in the narrow hallway, as he led them both to the workshop. He stood and watched as Ossan took the boy through the basics of smithing. It was the same script as the last time, Kharios noted. The old priest barely changed a word, pointing out and naming the various hammers, tongs and files as if a novice in the temple of the Forgefather would never have seen an anvil.

"Work the bellows, Kharios," Ossan instructed him, not taking his eyes from Arren. The young novice watched closely as Ossan took up a section of iron rod and heated it in the coals until it shone. "The legends

63

tell us there was a time when the Forgefather spoke to us directly from the flames," Ossan said as he began striking with the hammer, working the section of rod flat before laying it back in the fire as the glow began to fade. "That's probably the stuff of myth and nonsense but none can truly know for certain. You've heard the ancient tales of the Fall?" He glanced at Arren, catching Kharios's nod almost by accident. "There was a time when our temples could be found in every corner of the world. Now we are diminished, cast down because of wilful pride. What was our sin, Kharios?"

Kharios started, not expecting to be spoken to. "Ahh... Arrogance, Father."

"Arrogance." Ossan nodded and pulled the iron from the coals again, turning the tongs and folding the flattened area with deft blows. "We thought we knew the mind of the Forgefather," he said over the sound of the hammer. "We assumed he would support our seeking out the mysteries of truesteel and Listening. We were wrong, and as a result our Father withdrew from us, our faith dwindled, and this temple here above the mines of the Carnath, is all that remains."

"Our faith will sustain us, Father," Arren said, eliciting a fond smile from one direction and a look of disgust from the other.

"So it will, Arren," Ossan said, glancing over to Kharios. "Bellows, Kharios. Bellows."

Kharios pulled on the polished wooden handle, forcing air between the coals until the iron was closer to white than red. Ossan set it on the anvil and looked to Arren. "You're familiar with the Call of Iron?"

Arren cleared his throat. "The Call is only taught to acolytes, Father."

Ossan smiled through twitching lips. "But that's not really what I asked you, is it?"

Arren flushed. "I know the Call, Father."

Ossan stepped back, offering the forge to him. "Show me. Kharios, I already know that you know the counterpoint."

Kharios nodded as he began pumping the bellows again, working the chant around the rushing air.

64

Arren took up the hammer and began striking at the iron, blows landing in a syncopated rhythm that created an alien harmony within the roar of the bellows and the chant that flowed from his lips in a strong deep voice.

"That's good. Not bad at all," Ossan told Arren, stepping in closer to speak over the noise. "Don't focus so much on the rhythm that you don't listen, Arren. The Call is all about letting the Forgefather guide your strikes. Listen for the Father's voice, find his whispers in the sound of the blows. Don't let your own chant drown him out. The Forgefather can hear a murmur just as well as a roar." The old priest ran his hand along Arren's arm, brushing away a spark but it moved too slowly for Kharios to believe that was all it was. It lingered too long, and the wave of nausea and guilt rose high before it crashed down upon him.

"There is so much I can teach you, Arren," Ossan said, smiling. "If you'll let me."

The bellows faltered as Kharios's grip slipped and the sound from the forge was suddenly discordant and jarring. Ossan glared at the mistake and as Kharios met his gaze, the revulsion spilled out onto his face. It had lasted for only the briefest of moments, but Ossan had seen it. A challenge had been issued, tossed out into the silence of the moment, and as Ossan gave his cold smile of acceptance, Kharios wondered just what he had done.

"That was a foolish mistake, Kharios," Ossan whispered, scattering the stillness like carrion from a battlefield. "Do not do it again."

CHAPTER FIVE

"The path to acolyte is more than just memorising text and ritual," Ossan lectured, resting a hand on the great anvil. The temple was quiet, the next services not due for almost another hour. Kharios fought to look interested as his attention drifted, his gaze slipping off Ossan and playing over the gold plate depicting the Forgefather on the wall.

"The temple has expenses," Ossan droned on. "And our revenue is dependent on the goods that only we can provide. Temple-wrought iron and steel are the least of it. I don't doubt you've spent enough time in the smelt works to know the raw process of pulling iron from ore, but the ritual goes a good way further than simply heating rock and taking iron away from it."

Kharios and Arren nodded dutifully as the old priest looked up at them before continuing. "The Call of Iron is one of the first rituals any would-be acolyte learns, and perfecting it is the first step on the path to Adept. Calling the iron removes the impurities and flaws that any lay-smith, those that lack the guidance of the Forgefather, would miss. You can see how this would make temple-wrought iron desirable?"

Another look and another nod. Kharios fought down a yawn and wondered how long the old man was going to lecture on the obvious this time. He risked a glance at Arren as Ossan moved on to speak about copper and other metals, pointing in turn to the rings on his fingers that indicated mastery of the metals and their processes.

"If a novice is extremely attentive and talented, they might just leave my home wearing a ring of iron. It has been known before, though not in recent years. This is your first step on the path, and the journey is long. In time you may earn all eight rings of mastery," he said, raising his hands to let the light from the forge play over the rings on his fingers. For most, this takes the course of a life-time."

"Master?" Arren spoke in a tentative voice.

Kharios blinked at the title, frowning as he looked at the boy while Ossan smiled.

"Yes, Arren?"

"I'd heard tales, gossip really, that once there were ten rings?"

Ossan closed his eyes with a sigh. "You shouldn't listen to every tale you hear, my child."

Arren deflated, the enthusiasm fading from his eyes as Ossan watched him, a small smile playing over his lips.

"Ours is an ancient faith, Arren," the priest went on. "There are many aspects that have been forgotten. There are many wonders that were lost to us when the Great Temple fell and our lord turned his face away from us. There may have once been ten rings of mastery, who could say?" He reached inside his robes and pulled a dagger in an ornate sheath, laying it onto the anvil. "This, however, hails from the earliest understandings of the Forgefather. The pledging of ourselves to his service. Once, the oldest tales tell us, the Forgefather paid heed to those who pledged, and spoke his acceptance." He smiled at that, an old man sharing a foolish tale.

His smile faded, slipping off the stern expression that lurked beneath. "Stories aside, the oath is a sign of devotion to both the temple and our Father, and yours is long overdue, Kharios."

Kharios started, and met the old priest's eyes as he fought down a flush at having been caught daydreaming. "Mine, Father?"

Ossan nodded, no memory of the smile remaining on his face. "Your mark," he said, reaching to touch the brand on his own forehead, "is a symbol of the temple's pledge to you. To mould you and train you as an aspirant. To test you as soon as you are able. You have yet to bind yourself to us, to take your oath to the temple and to the Father. Pledge your life and soul to the Forgefather, Kharios. That you will serve him both in life, and then in death when he calls you to his hallowed halls.

"Think on it, Kharios. Thousands of blooded hands have pressed to this anvil as their oaths were made. Souls beyond counting, pledged to the Father and his church in both the old temple and the new.

"This is a simple thing but it is also among our most sacred rites. You have knowledge that none outside of our order possess. We guard our secrets jealously, Kharios. You will take the oath now, and be bound to our order, or you will return to the mines and serve us for as long as you draw breath."

The threat wasn't well hidden and Kharios felt an irrational surge of anger. He had nowhere else in the world that would have him, Ossan knew that. Giving him this choice was his petty way of sinking the hooks into him. Gritting his teeth, he nodded. "I wi…" he broke off, voice cracking, and he cleared his throat before trying again. "I will take the oath, Father."

Ossan grunted an acknowledgement. "Do you remember the oath, Kharios? You… left my service some time ago."

Kharios swallowed hard and cleared his throat. "Yes, I do."

"Are you ready then?" Ossan asked, pulling the black iron blade from its sheath. "It would benefit young Arren to see a pledging."

"What, now?" Kharios looked from the ancient blade to Ossan's eager face.

Ossan laughed at his expression. "I would say it's well past time, wouldn't you?" He reached for Kharios's shoulder, not noticing, or perhaps ignoring, the instinctual flinch as he pressed the hilt into Kharios's hand.

The urge to ram the blade into the old man's chest flashed through his mind and Kharios bit hard on his tongue. He looked down at his feet and drew a deep breath.

"Your god waits, Kharios," Ossan told him, a hint of impatience creeping into his voice.

Kharios blinked hard, mashing his eyelids together as if he might somehow improve the view when he opened them. He gripped the hilt and stepped up onto the stone block that held the anvil, drawing the black-iron blade across his palm.

68

"Thus I pledge myself, life and soul..." he faltered, the words abandoning him. The blade was sharp but the cut burned. It was not the stinging pain he had expected but something very different.

"To the service of the Forgefather," Ossan prompted him with a small smile.

"To the service of the Forgefather. May he take me and shape me, forging me under his hammer," Kharios continued. "May his light fill me and cleanse, that I might bring his message to others, until my fire fades and my days are ended." He brought his hand down hard upon the anvil slapping the bleeding palm against the hammer-scarred surface. He buckled against the pain, knees giving way as the cold iron seemed to claw at the wound. Bright lights flashed against the darkness behind his eyelids and a cold seemed to pull at him, as if the heat were being drawn from him and into the forge.

"Now you are pledged," he heard Ossan say. "Your soul is bound."

Kharios forced his eyes apart, rising from where he leant, half-slumped against the anvil. His eyes seemed to struggle to keep up with his head, his vision swimming half a pace behind. He made his way down the steps, on legs that swayed alarmingly underneath him, until Arren caught him.

"Good, Arren." Ossan's voice seemed to come from a great distance. "We are nothing without the support of our brothers. Let's get that hand bound up and then you can both show me what you have learned of iron."

***

Days passed into weeks, and then into months, until the passage of time was lost in amongst the endless tasks. Ossan piled work on them mercilessly. Long days at the forge were followed with hours spent poring over scrolls and thick, leatherbound books in Ossan's private library. Kharios threw himself into the work. The mysteries of the faith were intriguing, he was slowly relearning the knack of teasing the meaning from the scripture and, despite the aches and burns, there was something deeply satisfying about forgework.

Ossan had them working together for the first few months, encouraging Kharios to pass along the basics and what tips he might have remembered from his first time. Soon though he began assigning them to different tasks; chores that kept them apart for hours, and research projects that had them scurrying to different parts of the temple in search of obscure scrolls.

Once a week they would gather together over a meal as Ossan tested them with questions seemingly chosen at random as they devoured food more sumptuous than anything they were used to. Ossan's cook tended to provide simple meals that were easier to eat with a nose in a book.

Kharios picked at a bread roll as he waited. It wasn't unusual for either he or Arren to arrive before Ossan. He'd been waiting some time with the smell of the fresh-baked rolls assailing his nostrils, and eventually hunger had won out over manners.

He sipped at a goblet of the dark red wine as he waited. The dining chamber was warm from the fire and the wine slipped down too easily until he was forced to change seats, choosing a hard wooden chair in an effort to stay awake. The workload was wearing and he knew that it was starting to show.

Arren pushed through the doorway, flopping down into the closest chair and resting his arms on the table.

Kharios snorted a laugh. "That bad?"

"Worse," Arren managed, his moan muffled by his arms. "Ossan put me to memorising the fifty chants and then set me to forgework besides."

Kharios frowned slightly. "The chants already? I wouldn't have thought–"

Arren lifted his head long enough to throw a black look. "Thought what?"

"It just seems very soon," Kharios said with a shrug. "Calling iron is one thing. The rest…"

70

"Because you're oh so superior?" Arren said in scathing tones. "I couldn't possibly hope to match you?"

Kharios blinked, setting his wine down on the table. "You're not matching me, Arren. You're outstripping me. This is far beyond anything I did this early into my first time with Ossan. I hadn't touched the chants until I'd been here months." His voice grew softer as he spoke until the last words were a whisper.

Arren shrugged, tilting his head. "We have been here for months, Kharios. Or maybe I'm just better than you?"

Kharios smiled, letting that pass. "What forgework are you doing?"

"Copper inlaid steel," Arren sighed. "A sword. It's a nightmare," he admitted. His face relaxed as his guard dropped and Kharios stared openly.

"What?" Arren asked.

Kharios shook his head. The fatigue in the lad's face had aged him. He looked more dead than alive, not the young man Kharios knew he was. "You look like hell, Arren. When was the last time you slept?"

Arren grimaced. "It's these damned runes that Ossan wants in the blade."

"Runes?" Kharios blurted.

"Sigils? Glyphs? I've seen them mentioned with half a dozen different names in the scrolls."

"I know what they are, Arren," Kharios breathed. "I just can't believe you're working with them already. I'd never even seen them by this stage."

"I wish I hadn't," Arren confessed. "They're connected to the chants somehow and the surface ones are the least of it. Ossan wants sigils worked into the steel before it's shaped."

Kharios looked at him, frowning.

"Six sequences, put in with chants on every folding," Arren explained, smiling as Kharios finally understood and his mouth opened in horror.

"That would take months!" Kharios gasped.

Arren nodded with a sigh. "Ossan wants it done in three weeks."

71

"That's…" Kharios shook his head in disbelief. "That's just insane. It can't be done."

Arren sipped at the wine. "It's actually not all that hard," he said, unwrapping a finger from around his cup to point it at Kharios. "If you can get into a rhythm with it, anyway. The hard part is remembering which chant goes with which glyph series. It's a six series rotation and I keep mixing them up. I spend as much time preparing notes as I do in the forge, and I can't keep stopping to check them without having to reheat the steel each time. And…"

"Paper has no place in a forge," they chorused.

"How many foldings?" Kharios asked.

Arren's pained smile was answer enough. There was little point in folding iron or steel if you were only going to do it a handful of times. "I could help with the notes, if nothing else," Kharios offered.

"You'll do no such thing," Ossan announced in curt tones as he strode into the chamber. "Arren, if you find this task beyond your abilities, perhaps something more suited to your attention span would be better?"

The young man crumpled, paling visibly in a face already too long from sunlight. "Master, no. I—"

"I simply thought to help, Father," Kharios put in.

Ossan paused, chewing over that for a moment before he made his way around the table. "Yes, well," he said, somewhat mollified. "There are a number of techniques that can be applied for the runes and chants, Arren. If you were having problems you ought to have told me. Come to my chambers after the meal, we can discuss things and I'll go through them with you." His hand slipped off the back of Arren's chair squeezing his shoulder.

Kharios closed his eyes, saying nothing again, as he hated himself for the warnings he'd never given. Could cowardice be measured by silence?

**

Kharios lay in the narrow cot and tried to ignore the sobbing. It was a broken, distant noise, lurking on the very edges of his hearing as it drifted through the wall to his cell. The sound was barely audible beneath the louder grunts and panting that carried with them and Kharios was under no illusions as to what they meant.

It had been six months since Arren had been called to serve. In some ways it had been worth the daily slights and snubs that Ossan sent his way. He had learned so much. Rituals that he'd never heard of before; the mysteries of calling steel from iron, and taming copper, the histories of the church and hints of forgotten wonders. All of it paled next to the guilt. It gnawed at him, and on those nights when the sobbing came, it grew. Ossan sometimes called Arren to his chambers. More often though, he visited the boy's cell. Perhaps he took some sick pleasure from knowing Kharios had to hear.

He threw the thin blankets back and dressed in silence, fleeing the cell and the sound that filled the air as he raced through the halls towards the kitchens. A sullen red glow still peered from between the coals as he checked the stove.

"Father of flame, he who shapes us all, guide me in hand and heart," he muttered the prayer quickly, reaching to touch a taper to the coals and moving to light the lamps.

Water sloshed in the kettle as he shook it and he set it to boil, retrieving a clay cup and dried karas moss from the side. A light step turned his head and he stood as Ossan's cook paused in the doorway. "I didn't think anyone else was up."

The short man shrugged, glancing from kettle to cup. "You got enough water for two?"

"Should be." Kharios nodded and reached for another cup. "I'm sorry, I just realised I don't remember your name."

The cook snorted. "That's alright, son. Servants are like furniture, you don't name a chair do you? It's just there when you want to sit down." He sank into the wooden chair, resting his arms on the table. "The name's Fen."

73

Kharios studied the man through narrowed eyes. He hadn't recognised him but the cook was right, too often he ignored the various servants in the temple. "It's been a few years."

Fen nodded, wrinkled face giving nothing away as he absorbed that. "More than a few, I reckon. I'd almost forgotten you myself but the barrowman said he knew your name."

"Barrowman?"

Fen snorted again, as close to a laugh as he was capable apparently. "You think all this food grows inside the cupboards by itself? Jerf brings a barrow past by twice a week."

Hissing from the kettle called Kharios to his feet but Fen waved him down, pouring the water with a practised hand.

"I don't remember him." Kharios shrugged.

"No reason why you should do," Fen replied over his shoulder as he poured water through the dried moss and strainer. "I don't imagine you ever saw him. Your type don't tend to rise early enough."

"I've been up before six every day this week," Kharios protested, taking the clay mug and nodding his thanks.

"Six!" Fen laughed then, a step above the snorts but still through his nose. "Half the day's gone by then."

Kharios smiled but it faded too soon and he blew on the steaming cup of karas to cover it. Fen cast a look back down the hallway and grunted. "Guess you couldn't sleep huh?"

Kharios winced. "No. How do you stand it?"

Fen shook his head and buried his nose in his cup. "Not my business."

"Does it happen a lot?" The words stumbled out over his guilt.

Fen gave him a look. His expression was complicated, a jumbled mess of emotions but sympathy sang strongly from his eyes. "I... get paid enough to ignore the eccentricities of the priesthood. What men do together behind closed doors is their own business."

Kharios put the cup down. "Men, yes. Arren's hardly that though. He can't be much past thirteen."

The compassion faded from Fen's eyes replaced with something hard and ugly. "And he had no idea what he was getting himself into?"

The accusation was clear enough and Kharios sat back away from the table. "I tried to warn him."

"Then he knew." Fen slurped at his drink, smacking his lips. "You'll do him no good beating yourself up for it."

"I didn't try hard enough," Kharios confessed to his cup.

"Probably not." The chair scraped back as Fen rose. "Not much you can do now, short of dragging the boy out of there."

"Or sending him home," Kharios muttered.

"Novices got no homes," Fen snorted. "No bastard's going to stay here and take that if they got anyplace else to be. Me? I got an empty bed needs warming."

Kharios grunted into his cup, not meeting the man's eyes as he nodded a farewell.

***

Morning came too soon after the rest of a night that sleep hadn't liked the taste of. Kharios forced himself from his cot and dressed quickly, heading to the kitchen to spoon something into a mouth too addled with weariness to taste.

The morning chores had become second nature and his hands moved mechanically, going through the motions of clearing out the forge and laying kindling, coal and coke while Kharios's mind struggled to wake. He was touching flame to kindling before he saw Arren. The boy was silent as he dumped a load of coke into the bin beside the forge. He seldom spoke to Kharios at all now, often going days without saying a word to him.

"Arren!" Kharios abandoned his rush towards the boy as Arren flinched away from his touch, leaving him awkward and off-balance.

"What do you want?"

Kharios grimaced at the tone. It sailed past accusation and into the open seas of apathy. "I want to help you, if you'll let me."

75

The hope was brief, a hint of light in the boy's eyes that flickered and died as he turned away. "I don't need any help."

"Arren, wait," Kharios said, reaching for the boy's shoulder. Arren gasped under the touch, flinching down onto legs that couldn't hold him and he sagged to the ground.

"Holy blazes!" Kharios gasped, following the boy to the cold floor. "What's the matter with you?" Insistent fingers tugged at the soft robes, pulling fabric away from Arren's fumbled attempts at bandages.

"Did he do this?" Kharios breathed.

"I…" Arren faltered, eyes fixed on the floorboards as he spoke to the wood. "I tried to stop him. I tried to push him off…" His voice caught as he spoke, turning to something brittle and fractured.

His eyes were terrible, haunted pits. Kharios flinched away from his expression. "Come on," he said, as he tucked the robe back into place. "Let's get the bandage straight if nothing else."

"It's fine." Arren pulled away from him, clambering to his feet as he leaned on the wall.

Kharios took a breath, trying a softer tone. "It's obviously not."

"There's nothing you can do," Arren said, looking up to meet his eyes. "You've done too much already."

The tone drew his eyes back to the young man's face and Kharios saw the anger that waited. It pooled, threatening to brim over and pour out onto Arren's face. Despite all the warnings Kharios had tried to give him, Arren blamed him. He blamed him for everything.

"So go," Kharios managed through a throat grown thick with his own emotions.

"What?" Anger fractured, falling away from the confusion that lay beneath.

"Leave," Kharios persisted. "You still have some family somewhere, don't you?"

"A sister," Arren admitted. "But I can't just—"

"Why?" Kharios pressed. "Don't stop and think about it. Don't waste time weighing things up, just go. Go now before he can talk you round, or before he can send you back to the mines where you don't have a choice."

"I—"

"Go!" Kharios pushed.

"I can't. You know I can't."

The unspoken plea was loud enough for Kharios to hear and he let it drop. "What have you got left to do this morning?" he asked, looking anywhere but at the lad's face.

"Clearing the coke store out, and bringing in fresh wood and kindling," Arren said.

"So you need to go to the southern entrance for the kindling anyway?"

"I can't just go, Kharios." Arren shook his head, seeking comfort in the arms of denial. "I can't walk away now."

Kharios reached to grip him by the shoulders. "You could, you know," he told him, forcing the younger man to meet his gaze. "If you left right now, you'd be long gone before anyone thought to…"

It was lighter than a scuff but somehow it reached him through the noise of his own words. He tensed, body rigid as he turned his head in an agony of knowing. Frantic eyes found nothing despite their search, yet still they refused to accept it.

"What is it?" Arren hissed. "Did you hear something?"

"It's nothing," Kharios told him.

Arren glanced back at him from the empty corridor. "You don't believe that. Gods above and below, if that was Ossan…"

"It wasn't." Kharios shook his head. "Let me help you with the wood, it needs doing anyway and it will be easier with two pushing that cart."

Arren nodded dumbly but his gaze still reached past Kharios, sweeping the shadows of the corridor.

The kindling cart was unwieldy and best managed with two. Kharios hauled back against the handle, straining to manoeuvre the contraption out of the store and into the service corridor. The corridors ran the length of the temple, sitting on their own level that lay between

77

floors as they provided access to various priest's chambers without the need to cart coal, and messy supplies, through the temple's marble halls.

Arren pushed in silence, though conversation would be a challenge over the grinding rumble of the iron wheels. He turned often, looking over one shoulder as if he expected Ossan to be charging along the passages after them.

The rumble of distant carts spoke of other servants and novices and with each turn they took Kharios found himself breathing easier. If Ossan had heard them speaking he'd have stopped them already, wouldn't he? Fen had hinted at his own position before, it wasn't his problem. No, he told himself. The sound, if anything, must have been Fen.

The maze of hallways was broken up by well-balanced double doors that moved easily at the touch of the cart, swinging closed behind them. Twice they passed other carts, returning to their chambers with carts loaded high with kindling and logs. Arren remained silent until they passed through the heavy doors leading out to the storage cave in the side of the mountain.

Sunlight stabbed in from the open mouth of the cave and Kharios cursed, blinking against the light and moving into the shadow of the mound of split logs that filled one half of the cave.

Arren ignored him, filling his arms with logs and dropping them into the cart.

Kharios watched him with a frown. "There's probably never going to be a better time, Arren," he said, stopping him in a soft voice.

Arren's expression was haunted as he dropped the load into the cart. "I still don't know," he admitted.

"Ten hells, Arren!" Kharios snapped. "What's it going to take? Another lashing? Another three months of Ossan pulling you into his bed?"

Arren looked at him in horror. "You know about that?"

Kharios nodded, self-loathing clawing at him as it forced the words from his lips. "I can hear you at night, Arren. Our cells are side by side remember? Sometimes I hear you when you're crying in his chambers. You're not the first he's done this to. I tried to warn you. I'm so sorry, I should have tried harder."

"You knew this was going to happen? And you let me come anyway?" The accusation twisted Arren's face into something hard and ugly.

"Not for certain, Arren," Kharios said. "I did what I could for you."

"Oh yes, you were a fucking guiding light!" Arren spat on the cold stone. "You could have pulled me aside, spelt things out. How hard would that really have been, Kharios? And now you hand me this choice. Go back to that, or run – now, with no supplies, no real idea of where I'm going. Just me on the mountainside. That's your solution is it? Do you know what they do to novices who run?"

"I'm sorry, Arren." The words didn't sound enough. They weren't enough.

Arren shook his head, the accusation all the louder for its silence. He looked back once as he stepped out of the cave, wind already whipping at the thick novice's robe. His eyes said everything there was to say, but Kharios was thinking them already.

***

Heavy footsteps pulled him from the depths of sleep but the hands found him while he was still floundering in the shallows. His cry was cut short as a rag was shoved into his mouth and rough hands pulled a hood over his head before he even stopped blinking at the light.

Kharios struggled as he was propelled towards the doorway but the arms held him tight in a well-practised grip. He lurched in a deliberate stumble to one side and was rewarded with a crash and a muffled curse as someone hit the wall. The blow caught him on the back of the head before he had a chance to pull away.

"Don't be bloody stupid, Kharios," a voice told him. "You're not going anywhere without us. Walk nicely, like a good boy, and you'll have less lumps on your skull."

He was more dragged than directed and his stumbling steps were little more than an effort to keep him from falling. He lost track of the turns in moments, but the steps told him he was going down. A distant rumbling let him know they had passed through the service tunnels but beyond that he knew nothing.

Minutes stretched out in the darkness inside the hood until they lost all meaning. Kharios gave up on everything but concentrating on breathing. The hood was loose enough to breathe through but too tight to let the gag out of his mouth. Each breath took too long, the air forced through sackcloth and into frantic nostrils.

The hood was ripped away as he was forced back against a rough stone wall and Kharios blinked against the light as the figure drew closer.

"Where was he going to go, Kharios?"

He squinted against the light but the voice was too familiar to mistake, despite the rage that filled it. He pushed the gag out with his tongue, spitting it to one side.

"Who?" he asked Ossan.

The muscles in the old man's face flexed as his jaw clenched and he nodded to the man beside him. The fist slammed into Kharios's stomach, driving up and behind his ribs so that the air blasted out of him. His legs collapsed underneath him and he dropped to the cold stone as the hands released him, letting him fall.

"Arren," Ossan spat. "You encouraged him to try to run didn't you?"

Kharios shook his head as he gasped. His lungs screamed for air but he couldn't seem to make them work. He sucked in a desperate gasp, coughing it out again almost immediately.

"There's no point in denying it. I find it hard to believe you could be so stupid. I had you returned to the Novice's Halls after all that business years ago. Apparently you took nothing from that."

The rage had left Ossan's voice, replaced with something far colder. His skin felt like ice as he grasped Kharios's throat, hauling him up to his feet with a strength Kharios had never imagined. "You really are a stupid young man. You simply don't learn do you? Perhaps a return to the mines will provide more of an education. He nodded once at the men holding him and Kharios had just enough time to flinch before the wooden club crashed into his skull and he slipped into the darkness.

CHAPTER SIX

The voices were garbled, nonsense noises spoken as if through a mouthful of pebbles. Kharios tried to push the sound away, clinging to the last shreds of the sleep that had cocooned him, but it slipped through his grip like fine sand.

Agony found him, as he had known it would. Bitter aches that reached for him with a cruel glee. He curled up against the pain before he could think to stop. The movement brought fresh torment and the cry that slipped through his lips was close to bestial. It was the cry of a man reduced to the level of a wounded animal, too broken to know anything beyond the hurt.

He sensed movement near him but kept his eyes closed tight. The light would bring its own pain, and he had no intention of inviting it in.

Something brushed his swollen lips and he parted them as much as he was able, letting the crude spoon pour broth into his mouth. He swallowed before he registered the heat and his cough sprayed broth out as his jaw strained against the bandages wound tight around his face.

He had been right about the light burning his eyes, and he blinked and winced at it as if that might make a difference. Both the woman and the boy seemed familiar. She was small, with the first touches of grey in her dark hair. The sympathetic wince faded as she wiped the spattered broth from her own face. The boy's face was blank as he looked on, his eyes large in a face made dark with coal dust. Harsh braying laughter came from the other end of the small cabin, smothering her murmured apologies.

"I told you, Leesha. Leave him!"

She glared back at the speaker before reaching for the bowl again, a plea in her dark eyes as she spooned broth into his mouth. Kharios swallowed carefully, meeting her eyes and trying to put his own thanks into his gaze.

"I said, leave him."

Leesha closed her eyes for the length of her sigh. "It's my food, Bryant. I'll feed him if I want."

Footsteps thudded hard on the wooden floor. "It's *our* food, Leesha. Bought with the marks we earned together. Every mouthful you pour into this corpse is a waste. He's dead already, his body just hasn't got there yet. It's bad enough you picked up your pet here." He tried a half-hearted kick at the boy who dodged it with little effort. "You only just got this little shit to pay for himself, and now you drag this corpse out of the mine."

"He's not dead," Leesha snarled, setting the bowl down beside the empty one at her feet and ignoring the faint mewl of protest that escaped Kharios's lips. "He's getting better, you dumb bastard. He's putting weight back on, and he's staying awake for longer."

Bryant nodded, ignoring the insult as he scratched at his cheek through a beard turned black with coal dust. "Let's say he is. What's your plan here, woman? He gets stronger, he eats more, maybe he even gets that strap off his face when his jaw heals up. He's never going to make much though is he? Look at his hands. Fingers that twisted are never going to swing a pick."

Kharios raised his hand slowly, bringing it to his face. The splints were rough. The rags tied tight around scraps of wood made his swollen fingers look like jagged claws. He didn't remember his hands being struck. The clubs had done their work on his face and chest, and then his consciousness had fled, leaving his body to deal with reality alone.

He took an experimental deeper breath. The stabbing pain from his ribs told him all he needed to know.

"You don't know that, Bryant." Leesha was arguing. "He could help pull the sled if nothing else. It doesn't matter anyway," she carried on as Bryant snorted at that idea. "I couldn't just leave him there."

"Why not?" Bryant shrugged. "He's nothing to you. You should have just let him die." He looked at Kharios, making sure he met his eyes before he carried on. "I would have."

"Bastard," Leesha muttered as Bryant grinned at her.

"Bastard and proud of it, Leesha," he told her. "Family is for the weak. Blood means nothing, I learned that a while back. Maybe you should too."

"Don't you have somewhere to be?"

He shrugged. "Not until Lumphead gets back from pestering whores."

"Lumpet," she said, emphasising the difference. "Is burning through copper that should have been all of ours."

"We made tally well enough," Bryant said as he shrugged. "If I'd found that nugget I'd have kept it to myself too. You know," he said with a twisted smile, "if you want copper that bad you could always go to the Perfumed Row yourself. I'm sure they'd make room for one more."

Her expression said the words louder than her whisper. "Fuck you, Bryant."

"Anytime, Leesha," he said with a leer. "If you're going to give it away, why would I bother with the whores?"

He cackled a laugh as he ducked and made for the door, the empty bowl crashing against the wall behind him.

"Arsehole!" she called after him.

She waited, watching the doorway as his laughter faded, before kneeling before Kharios. "Do you want to try sitting up? It might make eating easier?"

He nodded carefully and between the two of them they managed to lever him up into a sitting position. She smiled that peculiar smile people seem to use with invalids and children and reached to spoon more broth into his mouth. The boy picked up the bowl she'd thrown in silence, nodding in acknowledgement as Leesha smiled at him.

"You're more alert today," she told Kharios. "The last few days you've barely been awake for more than a few minutes."

He nodded carefully, wary of inviting fresh pain.

84

"I don't even know your name," she said. "That's probably a good place to start."

He licked his lips. His tongue running over the swollen, unfamiliar landscape. He was missing as least a few teeth. "Arrri..." he managed, grimacing at the sound and giving up.

"Arri?" Leesha asked with an encouraging smile.

Kharios shook his head and reached to scratch out a letter in the dust on the floor. He stopped and looked up at her as she reached to touch his hand, stopping him gently.

"That won't help, I can't read," she confessed.

"Arryooos," he tried again.

Leesha shrugged helplessly. "Let's just call you 'Arri' for now," she suggested. "It's as good a name as any."

He nodded carefully. She was probably right. Getting words out of his mouth wasn't going to happen until some more of the swelling had gone down.

"Do you remember much?" she asked him.

He shook his head, shrugging.

"You know where you are, though? In the mines?" she asked, seeming relieved as he nodded again.

"We've not been able to speak before," she told him, sitting back on crossed legs. "Not even like this. You were too out of it with pain and fever. I think your jaw was infected or something. I couldn't tell if your fingers were broken or not so I splinted them anyway. My name is Leesha." She smiled in understanding as he nodded. "You got that already from when I was talking to Bryant, didn't you? This is Sylam," she nodded at the boy. "He doesn't speak. It looks like I need to talk for both of you for now. You've been here for a week. I found you in the mine, an old coal shaft that I didn't think anyone used anymore."

Kharios nodded. A Blacker's shaft. It would have been a good place to have him dumped. The real shock was that Ossan had left him alive. Novices didn't often vanish and the risk of what he knew getting out... He stopped himself, lips twisted into a painful smile before he could

85

stop them. Ossan didn't have to worry about word getting back to other priests. He was back in the mines. Back in Aspiration without a hope of ever getting out.

Leesha watched him, head cocked to one side in a silent question as the pained smile slipped from his face. She shook her head as she pushed herself back and then stood. "Who are you, Arri? What were you even doing in that part of the mine, and who did this to you?"

He drew a breath to speak and then spread his hands with a defeated sigh.

She smiled in sympathy. "You're a puzzle, Arri, if nothing else. I don't expect we'll find out much for a few more days yet. Do you think you can manage to feed yourself? There's more broth in the pot if you think you can do it, if not I'll feed you some when I get back."

He cocked his head, mimicking her pose to ask the question.

"Where am I going?" she said with an amused frown. "Well I can't just sit here all day, Arri. I have to get to work. I have a tally the same as everyone else.

"Don't touch your bandages," she warned him. "They won't be ready to come off for at least a week or two and we need to get you up and moving as soon as we can. Bryant was right about one thing; we don't have food to spare for idle hands. He already wants you gone. And Lumpet usually follows his lead."

He nodded and watched her as she moved around the cabin. Sylam followed close behind, like a puppy. She gave him a final smile before they stepped through the doorway, leaving him alone with his thoughts.

A week, and most of it spent unconscious. What had Ossan done to him? His questing hands reached for his face and he traced the bandages with his palms. They were wound tight around his face, binding his jaw in place as they ran from under his chin and over the top of his head.

Had the damage been done by fist or club? It didn't matter, he decided. What mattered was how long it might take him to heal. His gaze roamed around the small cabin. Two beds ran along the walls in addition to the one he was on. A small iron stove sat in one corner with coal piled in a crude bin to one side. A rickety table made up the rest of what must serve as the kitchen. It was basic but it was clean, and that said enough all by itself.

His fumbling hands retrieved the bowl Leesha had set by his feet and he set about trying to drink the broth. The spoon was crude, a hand-whittled piece of kindling, and the splints on his fingers made the task almost impossible. After the spoon fell for the second time he raised the bowl to his lips, cursing himself for a fool.

His swollen lips and the bandages around his face made the job harder than it should have been, and he poured as much broth over himself as he managed to get into his mouth. The pain seemed to lessen once he'd eaten though, or maybe he was just less light-headed. Instead, a dull ache reminded him not to try anything too stupid.

He sat back for a while, giving his stomach time to settle and adjust to having something inside it. He pushed himself forward, easing more weight onto his feet as he tested how his body might react. Aching hands pressed onto knees as he braced himself, careful to keep his fingers from touching. He'd have to do this quickly, he reasoned. A slow rise would never work, not in the state he was in. A lurch upwards had him staggering to one side as the dizziness hit. His leg buckled, and he fell hard, flopping sideways onto the bed. His head crashed down and the thin mattress slammed into his jaw, and for lack of a better plan, he screamed.

***

Boots thumped over the wooden floor and his eyes fluttered open in time to see the kick coming. Sleep fled, carried away in a rush of adrenaline as Kharios threw himself to one side. "Time to wake up sleepyhead," Bryant said with a grin.

"What do you want?" Kharios mumbled through thick lips. He almost smiled at that, the swelling was down and his words, though garbled, were clear enough to understand.

87

"It speaks!" Bryant raised his arms in mock celebration. "Time to get some work out of you, sunshine. Leesha might be happy to leave you here sucking your way through her soup but I'll be damned if I'm supporting you."

Footsteps thudded on the steps leading up to the doorway and Bryant turned, with a smile. "Look, Lumphead, Leesha's newest pet is awake and he's turned into a right chatty little bastard."

The newcomer grunted. Small and dressed in filthy coal-stained clothing, he had the look of an unwanted ferret and his dark eyes flitted about the cabin. "S'about time, I reckon."

"That's what I said." Bryant laughed again. "Time you were up and working, Arri. If you're awake you can cut coal."

"Kharios," Kharios corrected him.

"What?"

"Kharios, my name."

Bryant snorted and glanced at Lumpet long enough to share a grin. "Nah, I don't think so. Arri suits you better." Bryant stepped in and grabbed Kharios's arm before he really knew what was going on, and hauled him up onto unsteady feet.

His knees buckled almost immediately and Bryant ducked his head under Kharios's arm to keep him upright. "Father's boiling balls, he's a heavy bastard for just rags and bones," he gasped. "Get the other side Lumpet, we'll get some bloody work out of this sod if it kills him."

Bryant's behaviour suddenly made sense. The man reeked of drex; a potent drink made using lichen and various cave mushrooms which was just as likely to give you a case of the trots as it was to get you drunk. Kharios had always managed to stay away from it. The pubs of Aspiration were all carefully controlled. All food and supplies went to the Gilters first and what alcohol made it through to the pubs was highly sought after. Drex was brewed up, or distilled, in the poorest sections of Aspiration. Something in the process involved old vegetables, or something that stank. The finished spirit smelled as bad.

Leesha's cabin was built close to the coal works, about as low on the social ladder of Aspiration as was possible. Despite their drunken state, Lumpet and Bryant managed to move him along at a good pace, dragging him past the closest cabins where older men looked on with smiles or carefully blank faces.

He struggled for the half-a-heartbeat it took for him to realise that resisting was a bad idea. Better just to gut it out. He'd worked in these mines before, doing it again wouldn't be that hard, would it? If the pain in his face didn't stop him struggling, their fists surely would, and he was in no condition to argue. Other than the fact that he was in worse shape than a dropped egg, there were two of them, and neither man looked ready to let him go.

The Blacker shaft came into view and the edges of panic reached for him. "What about a helmet? A pick? I don't have any equipment!"

Bryant laughed. "What do you think this is? A Gilter gang? A helmet? Bang your head on the roof once or twice, you'll soon learn not to. As for a pick, you couldn't swing it right anyway. Not with those hands. There's enough leavings down there for you to fill a cart or two."

"What about light?" Kharios pressed.

"Here." Lumpet handed him a glass tube, half filled with chems and stoppered with a rough cork. Kharios took it and peered at it, confused.

Bryant took in his expression and barked a hard ugly laugh. "He's never even seen one. We've got a right posh one here."

"It's a glowtube, Arri," Lumpet told him. "Give it a gentle shake once it's good and dark. It should last you a few hours as long as you don't shake too hard."

"It *should*?" his voice was a strangled squeak.

"Get in there, precious." Bryant gave him a push towards the shaft. It was a light touch but he was unsteady enough on his feet for it to send him staggering forward, clutching the glass glowtube to his chest. He looked back once, and made his way into the shaft.

The first hundred yards weren't so bad. Chemlights were strung on the wall here and there and the passage itself was tall enough that he

89

didn't need to hunch. He kept to the edge and used a hand on the rock to support him as he made his way down into the cavern. The sounds of picks hacking away at the coal filled the cavern with echoes and Kharios almost didn't notice the Tallymaster sat at an opulent desk making notes in a large leather book. He paused long enough to look at Kharios, his gaze taking his measure as it ran the length of his body. Kharios flushed as the man looked back down at his work. He had been judged and weighed in one look. And he had been found wanting.

The sneer was probably well deserved, slight though it had been. What must he look like? Face bandaged up, no pick or helmet and only a glass glowtube to light his work. He was the very image of poverty. As low as anyone could get in Aspiration. Scrabbling around in the darkness to collect the coal that hadn't been worth the time for others to pick up.

"Chit."

Kharios turned sharply and winced at the pain that shot through his head. "What?"

"Take your chit," the Tallymaster told him, waving a wooden coin at him. His severe expression softened as Kharios stepped into the light of the chemlamp on his desk. "Take your chit. You don't want to be toiling in the darkness for nothing."

Kharios took the wooden coin and grasped it tight in his fist.

"I would try your luck in the south-western tunnels," the Tallymaster said in a low voice as he bent over his ledger. He glanced up, meeting Kharios's surprised look with unruffled calm. "They tend to attract larger crews and that always means more wastage."

The passageway sloped down, away from the carts and the Tallymaster surrounded by his mounds of coal. Kharios dragged the sled behind him, trailing his fingers along the wall with the other hand until the last of the chemlights faded. He shook the glowtube gently, hand held over the cork in case it came loose. The chems began to glow with a pitiful, wan, light that barely extended past his arm's reach.

His steps were slow, tentative things and one of his hands still reached for the wall. The glowtube did little to light his path and Kharios moved less by sight and more by hope and faith. Twice, other miners passed him, casting looks his way with their expressions lost in the glow of their chem-lamps. Each time Kharios had to wait until his eyes adjusted back to the near-blackness of the light of the glowtube. He took to avoiding them after that, shying away from the light as he ducked into side tunnels.

Loose coal crunched under his feet as he wandered. The passages all travelled downhill. Even in the darkness he could feel that much. Oddly enough, becoming lost was not among his worries. Instead he checked the glowtube frequently for any sign the light was fading.

Tunnel turned into passage, which turned into tunnel as Kharios wandered ever downward, the scrape of the sled grinding out a rasping melody as the echoes of picks provided a distant accompaniment. At last the crunch of the coal beneath his feet felt deep enough that there might be something he could work with. He knelt, scraping the fragments together between his cupped palms and shovelling them into the sled.

The first handfuls were slight and his splinted fingers caught and twisted against the fragments until he began to catch the trick of it. He worked in silence, each load into the sled marked a step towards getting out of the black.

The sensation of being watched grew gradually, as the cold seemed to seep from the rocks to suck the warmth from him. He stopped several times, pausing to peer into the darkness or to listen for the half-heard noises that tugged at his ears.

"Mine!" the whisper was the clearest yet and Kharios snatched up the glowtube, shaking it violently in an effort to coax extra light from it. The chemlight bloomed and he held it out before him, warding away the darkness as he twisted and spun, searching for the speaker.

"Who's there!" he called, his own voice thin and reedy.

The heat came all at once. Chems reacting at an ever increasing rate until the glass of the tube seared his hand. "Shit!" He dropped the tube, flapping his hand uselessly as the glass crashed and splintered at his feet.

"Shit, shit, shit!" Kharios moaned, dropping to his knees as the fine, sand-like, chems drifted down through the air, scattering over the coal chips at his feet. The light ebbed away slowly from the small pile of chems surrounding the shards of glass, and Kharios froze in place. Rooted, as if that would somehow help as the darkness fell.

He reached for the wall, thrusting out an arm he couldn't see through the darkness for a wall he hoped was still there. The blackness was total. Not the velvet night of above ground, when even the faintest of stars will provide some light. That darkness can even be a comfort. This was a darkness that held no warmth. It fell unopposed. And all unchallenged, it ruled.

His first steps through the black were terrified and blundering, as he walked with both hands pressed to the wall. For long moments he couldn't tell whether the passage rose or fell before him, and he froze in place as his heart hammered at his chest. Through his frantic breaths he slowly became aware of the sounds of the picks, reaching out to him through the silence. He was not alone, no matter how much the darkness tried to tell him he was.

The realisation was no comfort as the thought passed through hope and into paranoia. What was it that had made him drop the glowtube? Had he actually heard anything? Or had he just thought he had?

"Is there anyone there?" His breath formed the words, shaping them into something close to a whisper but so soft they would never reach anyone's ears.

"Mine!" the whisper came again, thin and plaintive. Yet even as he heard it, Kharios realised that there was no sound. The voice was in his mind, and the mine silent around him.

The thought brought another sound along with it, a note that hung in the darkness. He crouched slightly, turning his head and leaning closer to the wall until his forehead was pressed against it. His hands reached out, pressing flat to the coal on either side of his head as his eyes closed. The sound called him, pulling him down to his knees as his questing hands scrabbled over the rocks of the wall. A stone shifted under his palm and he ignored the pain of his splinted fingers as he picked away at it revealing a wider opening. He reached into the hole it left behind, working by feel until his hand closed over the lump. It was too hard to be coal and the song swelled as he pressed his hand to it, scraping it out of the hole even as the plaintive whisper called out from the darkness. "Nooo!"

An image filled his mind, coming and going between his blinks. He saw a face, low to the ground and picked out in blue light, its features twisted in anguish. Its hand reached out, making desperate snatches at the air in front of him as if it couldn't quite reach him. Kharios staggered back, the nugget clutched to his chest as he moved blindly, up the tunnel. Too late he remembered the sled he'd dragged down with him. "Fuck it!" he whispered, the sound too loud in the silence.

The image flashed once more. The man, or creature, or whatever it was, curled up tight as sobs shook its body and at once Kharios realised the man was dead. Fear unfurled lazily and embraced him. The pain fled his body, and in a panic, he ran.

***

"Arri!" Leesha pushed herself to her feet as he hobbled into view, staggering from wall to wall as he leaned on the sides of the cabins and huts passed. She ran to him, ducking her head under his arm and taking his weight as Bryant, and others he didn't recognise, looked on from the steps up to the cabin.

"Found your way back then?" Bryant called, picking at something in his teeth.

"Stupid bastards," Leesha snarled. "I told you he was in no condition to be working yet. You could have killed him!"

"Where's the glowtube?" Lumpet said, ignoring her and stepping past Bryant to thump down the steps.

The smile slipped off Bryant's face as he looked back to Kharios running his gaze over him and seeing the truth. "Where is it, Sponger?"

"It fell," Kharios admitted.

"It what?" Lumpet strode forward, stopping short of them as Leesha hissed a warning. "You broke it? You bloody idiot, those things cost! We only have three. Now what are we supposed to do?"

"Work in a team?" Kharios shrugged, stepping forward again as he made for the cabin.

Lumpet shook his head, outrage stealing his words as he sputtered.

"There's no point in working as a team on blackwork, Sponger," Bryant called over to them as they approached. "The tunnels are too small to work close to each other. We work together by sharing our gear. You owe, Arri. It's time to pay up."

The tallymark tumbled as it fell but the flash of copper worked into the surface of the dull iron was easy to see. Kharios ignored the cries of wonder, pushing past them as Leesha guided him into the cabin.

The bed was as hard as it had ever been but Kharios groaned in appreciation as he sank down onto it, leaning back against the wall.

"Where did you get the coppermark, Arri?" Leesha's voice was soft with hushed awe as if he'd just spun gold from straw.

"The same place all of the tallymarks come from," Kharios said with a tired smile. "And my name isn't Arri, it's Kharios. I can speak a little better now that the swelling is going down a bit."

She moved back away from him, pushing herself up from where she'd squatted in front of him. "I'm sorry. Kharios," she paused, trying the name. "I haven't really caught up yet. I went to work the shaft and when I came back you were gone. Now you're back, and you're speaking, and apparently dropping coppermarks like they're nothing."

He smiled at her apology. "It's probably me that should be apologising, Leesha. I'm just… I'm tired!" he admitted, sighing the word out and sagging down with the weight of the admission.

She nodded, chewing her lip as she thought. "I'll make something to eat." She glanced at the small kitchen and then out of the open door. "I expect Bryant and Lumpet will have gone for supplies. The others will probably have gone with them." She grimaced as she looked back at him. "I expect they'll visit a pub or two. Who knows what they'll bring back with them?"

Kharios leaned back against the rough wall, allowing his eyes to close as Leesha moved about the kitchen. The slosh of water and the faint grinding of her coaxing the coals in the stove back into life let him track her movements and he found himself slipping into a doze.

"So how did you get it?" Her question broke the silence and he jerked upward.

"What?" he said, blinking himself awake.

"The coppermark." She turned from the pot to face him. "Those two were too excited to think about it, but there's no way you could have picked up enough coal to get one."

He spread his hands in his lap, letting her see the marks.

"Forgefather!" she gasped, and dropped the stirring stick into the pot. She rushed over, pulling herself up short and kneeled down to get a closer look. "Gods above and below, Kharios. What did you find?"

"A gold nugget," he told her, closing his fists around the marks. "It must have been an old tallycache. I found it after the light smashed."

"If the light was gone then, how...?" she left the question hanging as she stared, wide-eyed, at his clenched fists.

"There was something down there, in the coal tunnels with me." He looked up at her as he spoke and his eyes were haunted. "It was something lost, or broken. Something left behind, like the echo of a person."

"A ghost?"

"No." He shook his head. "I thought it was at first, that's when I dropped the glowtube. But no, it wasn't like that. This was like a stain on the world. A memory of a person."

"And this thing led you to the gold?" She was trying to keep her voice neutral but he could hear the scoff in her tone. "You sound like those people who mutter about the Utterdark." She glanced at the pot on the stove, missing the black look he shot her.

"Just who are you, Kharios?" she asked, rising to stir whatever it was she had bubbling away in her pot. "You appear out of nowhere, beaten half to death. You've made no effort to get back to your crew but you don't act as if the mines are new to you."

"I'm nobody," he told her.

She gave him a curious look but stopped short of speaking, as a knock sounded on the doorframe.

"Travis!" Leesha smiled at the grizzled man leaning against the door. "Don't just stand there, come in."

The old man nodded his thanks, moving to one of the bunks and sitting with a sigh as he positioned his limp left arm into his lap. "Something smells good."

Leesha flashed him a smile as she stirred the pot. It was clearly flattery but just as clear that she appreciated the effort. "It's just a thick soup."

"You're the only one I know who can make it smell that good though." Travis smiled through his beard. The smile faded as he glanced at Kharios. "Reckon we need to talk, Leesha."

She nodded. "I'd expected you sooner."

He sucked on his lip as he looked at Kharios, his gaze taking everything in as Kharios tried hard not to stare at the stump of his wrist protruding from his shirt sleeve.

"He needed his rest, I expect," the old man said with a nod. "I'm Travis," he said, speaking to Kharios for the first time. "If this crew has a leader, I suppose I'm it."

Kharios nodded. "I'd thought maybe the leader was Bryant."

"He'd like to think he is," Travis snorted. "Most of the time he acts like he is too, so maybe I'm wrong. One day I reckon I will be."

"I don't—"

Travis stopped Kharios with one raised hand, cradling the stump of the other in his lap. "It don't matter that much, son. Fact is, we can't keep you. We just scrape by at it is, and you're one belly too many."

"Travis," Leesha began but fell silent at his dark look and raised finger.

"I can carry my weight," Kharios said.

Travis shook his head with a sigh. "It's not about that. I've been a Blacker most of my life," he told Kharios. "This damn place ruined the arm that you're working so hard not to notice. Thing is, we don't got no choice. We don't have the gear to bring in more coal, and we don't got the marks to buy it. We scrape by, same as every other Blacker crew out there. We share what gear we have. We share the food to a point, but it only goes so far. Too big a crew and things just don't work out."

Kharios thought hard, but he wasn't overrun with options. "Why do blackwork then?"

Travis raised a bushy eyebrow "Why not work in the mines you mean? With the gilters and all the other crews?"

Kharios nodded.

"No gear. No idea what we're doing," Travis told him, shaking his head. "Those mines are staked out. Crews have their claims and they'll put a pick through the head of anyone in the wrong place. Any new crew in there has to start blind. Without a Listener you could be chipping out worthless rock for months."

"What if you had the gear?" Kharios said, spreading his hands to reveal the pile of tallymarks.

Travis's eyes widened and he gnawed on a lip. He looked at Leesha for a second. "No." He shook his head again. "I told you, gear's not enough. Chemlamps, helmets and picks don't tell you where to work the rock. You don't get tallymarks for cold stone."

"What about the Listeners?" Leesha put in, excitement shining in her eyes. "Kharios has goldmarks, wouldn't that be enough?"

Travis scratched at one dirty cheek. "It might be. Might be it is, at that. Won't do no good though. Listeners won't work a crew without a priest."

"I'd never heard that," she admitted in a small voice.

Kharios watched the hope die in Leesha and closed his eyes against the sight as the sigh escaped him. "I am a priest," he said in a voice that would have been missed in a confessional. "I'm a novice of the Forgefather."

CHAPTER SEVEN

"Don't worry too much about clean strikes," Killen called over to him between the blows of her own pick.

Wynn glanced over at her and she winced, shading her face with a hand at the light from his chemlamp. "Sorry."

She nodded, brushing away the apology. "We don't have time to be perfect here. Just pick the damned stuff out."

Wynn shook his head to cover his embarrassment at lamp-blinding her and hacked away at the vein of quartz. It had taken the crew less than an hour to cut through the layer of rock that had concealed it and now it stood exposed, five thick veins that spilled down from floor to ceiling. Rock chips stung his face as he hacked at the rock, levering the larger pieces down to the floor as soon as he was able where they were pulled out to one side by the man acting as his shadow.

"Switch!" Terrik's voice boomed out and Wynn stepped back and to one side as his shadow stepped in, working faster than Wynn's numbed muscles were able to. He stepped out of the man's way, stealing a minute to catch his breath and take a mouthful of water from his flask.

"No time to dick about, Wynn," Terrik told him, his breath brushing the back of Wynn's neck. "Get clearing and loading."

Wynn jumped, pulling the scarf back over his nose. The man moved like a feather over glass, without a sound and leaving no trace. He flushed and moved into position, reaching out with his pick to hook the rocks towards him and loading them into the sled with a short-handled shovel. Already his muscles burned and the cloth tied over his mouth was wet from his laboured breath. The air was thick with dust, and light from the chemlamps cut through it in shafts that almost seemed solid. He was surrounded by a haze of grey that had blinded him every bit as much as the darkness it replaced.

"Carts are getting full." Killen's voice came out of the gloom to his left. "We're going to have to make a run soon, Terrik."

"You fill the carts; I'll do the thinking," the crew-leader growled back.

Killen took a breath, glancing at Wynn, and visibly bit back a harsher response.

"I am filling the carts, Terrik. I'm just telling you they're full. We'll be spilling gold all over the damn ground if we don't empty them soon."

The laughter of the miners was short-lived as Terrik's one eye glared out at anyone unfortunate enough to catch his gaze. "Fine!" he exploded. "Take Wynn in with you, he needs to see how this works anyway. And move your arse, we're ripe for the picking with half the damned crew gone."

Killen nodded her acceptance, though the gloom hid everything but the movement of her light. "Come on." She nudged Wynn with an elbow. He dragged the heavy sled behind him as they made their way out of the passage and back to the main shaft.

The carts were mired in rock chips and it took long minutes to get men into the harnesses and the loose chips out from under the wheels.

"Why's he in such a foul mood?" Wynn muttered as he leaned into his harness.

"Terrik?" Killen asked. She shrugged with a smile. "He's always in a bad mood. I think his good humour went with his eye. No, he just hates splitting the crew. There's always other crews out there that won't make tally. One might just be desperate enough to try something, even with the Listener's Peace."

"The Peace!" Tresk snorted from behind them. "The Peace ain't worth shit. Some crew wants to have a go, they will."

Wynn tried to look back at the man but the harness made it impossible. "The Peace?" He asked Killen.

"It's supposed to be part of the promise," she explained. "If you pay for a Listening, the Listeners encourage the other crews to leave you be while you work the finds."

"Encourage!" Tresk snorted a laugh. "One of those blind bastards comes at me and—"

"You'll shit your britches!"

Wynn couldn't place the speaker and Tresk's angry retort was lost in the laughter.

"Listeners or no, Terrik doesn't like being exposed like this," Killen told him. "If we leave the site completely, then other crews will move in. If we split the crew, we run the risk of someone trying something. We can hack ore out all day long but this stuff's no good to anyone until we get it to the smelt works. No matter what we do there's a risk."

"You really think something will happen?" Wynn asked, his words coming out in between his gasped breaths as the passage rose and the harness bore down on his shoulders.

"Can't ever tell," Killen said. "Keep your pick handy though. We're at least as good a target as Terrik is."

Wynn fell silent at that, and scanned the shadows as they hauled the train of carts through the pools of light shed by the chemlamps hanging from the walls. The half-heard conversation of the others fell to silence as the incline rose yet again. It had been hard to hear before, the conversation had been almost lost in the grinding of the wheels on the tracks. Wynn fought for air and found himself praying for each rest portion where the passage levelled out.

What relief Wynn felt at being out of the mines and onto a level surface faded at the acrid stench of the smelt works. It grew stronger as they approached until he coughed and his eyes teared. The carts ran easily on the level track leading towards the two large doors that marked the entrance. Both doors were open wide and two muscular men stood at either side of them holding wooden clubs. Both, crude and thuggish tools. Wynn squirmed under their gaze and they passed through the doors and into hell.

The passage curved and then opened out into a cavern, though the walls were too regular to be a natural formation like the cavern that held Aspiration. Huge machines pulled ore along on clanking tracks until it fell down into furnaces that were spread out across the cavern. Massive bellows wheezed and roared.

The heat hit Wynn like a physical blow. It had lurked, a sullen weight in the air as they approached, giving only a hint of what was to come until they had turned the corner into the cavern. Wynn gasped as his eyes teared again and the heat clawed at his throat. It was almost worse than the noise. The din was an assault on the ears; as if someone had taken all of the beasts and monsters of legend and trapped them inside a tin hut.

"Takes it out of you, don't it?" Tresk observed.

Wynn nodded, not trusting himself to speak just yet. He swallowed hard. "How do they stand it?" he asked, nodding at the large men working the closest of the bellows.

Tresk shrugged, glancing over at the robed Tallymaster speaking with Killen. "A man can get used to anything in time. Besides, they have their own compensations. You don't think a man gets that big eating the kind of slop we scrape by on do you?"

Wynn frowned at that until Tresk laughed openly at him. "All the food in Aspiration comes in through here, lad. Ore goes in, food comes out. And Garl runs the lot."

Wynn had no answer to that.

"Garl runs Aspiration as his own little kingdom," Tresk carried on. "Every Sefin has since the uprising and the pact with the temple. And it's not like we have a choice is it? We all have to dance to whatever tune he feels like playing."

"You want to watch that mouth, Tresk," Killen warned softly as she approached. "What whispers fall out can just as easily be rammed back in."

He gave her a tired smile. "You're welcome to try, Killen. As for Garl? I think I'm too little of a whisper for him to worry about."

101

"It's not Garl I'm worried about," Killen told him. "It will be Terrik's foot in your arse, not his."

"It'll be Terrik's foot in all our arses if we don't get back soon," Tresk warned.

***

The sound was just audible, on the very edges of Wynn's hearing. It was distorted and blurred by the thousand other echoes in the mines, almost lost between the distant sounds of pick striking stone, and dripping water. It hid beneath the memories of conversations that haunted the passages and caves, but it would not be ignored and it nagged at the ears until it hastened their steps.

The screaming became clear when they were still about five minutes away from the rest of the crew. The shafts of light streaming from their chemlamps swung wildly as they broke into a run. Wynn clutched at the pick handle as he ran, searching for his courage within the worn wood of the haft. The quartz they had hacked out of the wall had been rich with gold. The glints of the precious metal that clung to the milky stone had been obvious even to him. Killen and Tresk had made it clear that any number of crews might be desperate enough to try to take the site from them. Was that what this was?

The memory of his failure in the fight with Killen warred with the fear that tried to slow his legs. He was swept along by the others, stopping wasn't an option. The screaming grew louder, a single agonised cry rising over the voices and shouts of the others.

Wynn slowed as they approached the site. This was no fight. The site was a jumbled mess of fallen stone. Men fought to clear the rocks that filled half of the passage through air thick with dust.

"What the hell happened?" Killen called to the closest of the crew.

"What does it bloody look like? The tunnel collapsed," the miner replied, pointing up to the top of the pile of tumbled stone. "There was no warning. The rock face just fell between strikes and then the ceiling was coming down."

102

"Shut your yaps and get in here!" Terrik's cry was tinged with panic and he glared back at them as he heaved and clawed at the rocks.

Wynn moved without thinking. Quick steps brought him to Terrik's side at the sloped pile of stone but then he froze.

"Stick to the smaller ones on the edges," Terrik told him over the screams. "You pull the wrong one out and you'll just bring more down on us."

Wynn nodded, not really registering the words as he stared at the figures before them. Grint lay half-buried in the mess, grey and brown from dust and dirt. His face was smeared with blood and twisted in an agony he couldn't hope to contain.

A huge boulder jutted from the rubble, extending out over Grint's legs and hips. At least two bodies lay beside him. His screams stopped just long enough for him to drag in another breath, and then he began again in a mindless, agonised, raging. Pain was all the man had left to him.

"Wynn!" Terrik barked at him.

He knelt quickly, reaching with his bare hands for the stones. He moved mechanically, not letting himself think or feel as he tossed the smaller rocks to one side. Terrik and the others dragged the larger stones out of the pile. They focused on one small area, clearing a path to the larger rock. He forced himself to block out the screams, clenching his teeth as he worked on the rocks closest to Grint.

"Gods below, does he have to keep screaming like that? It's not like it's going to help."

Killen favoured the speaker with a look hard enough to make him stammer and turn away. She crouched down beside Grint, stroking his face while he roared again, and then stood and smoothly cracked the haft of her pick against the man's temple. The silence fell suddenly, revealing the sounds that had been lost in Grint's agony. Somewhere in the hush a man wept.

Wynn looked from Grint to Killen. "Is he...?"

She shook her head. "No, just out cold. Better to go like that than screaming."

Wynn shook his head in confusion. "I don't… What? Go where?"

She pointed. "Look at him, Wynn. Really, look at him."

The stone was larger than Wynn's chest. It lay across Grint's legs, pinning his body to the ground. Unconsciousness had relaxed his face but that just emphasised how twisted it had been before. Blood stained his cheek and flecked his lips and a dark stain pooled out from under the rocks that held him.

The crew worked in silence, pulling away the rocks that surrounded Grint and the others in a feverish effort that would have been madness at any other time.

Picks were wedged under the edge of the stone that pinned him but it still took four big men to move it. Grint's eyes fluttered and then opened wide as Terrik hauled him out. He gasped in a single breath, and then there was blood. His leg lay at an impossible angle, broken and twisted. Blood spurted through torn clothes where the shock of bone protruded.

Terrik swore and slapped his hands down over it, pressing down hard but blood welled up through his fingers and poured out beside his hands. "Help me!" he barked, his one eye wide and pleading.

Wynn looked on, helpless, as Tresk gently pulled at the one-eyed man's shoulder. "It's done, Terrik. He's gone."

"The hell he is!" Terrik snapped. "He's dead when I say he's dead!"

"Terrik," Killen's voice was soft. Cutting through where Tresk had failed.

Terrik stood. His limbs moved like a man twice his age as he let Tresk pull him away from the body. He looked back at the rockfall. Anger and grief passed over his features and he muttered something, then turned and stamped out of the passage.

The bodies were loaded onto the sleds like sleeping children. Wynn watched with the others as they were placed carefully as if any bump might wake them and carried away. And the silence grew.

Clearing the rocks was a grisly task. Blood had spread out over the ground with few chances to drain away and it had pooled and congealed.

Wynn slipped twice. Going down on one knee in a puddle of blood as the curses of others suffering the same fate echoed around him.

"The hells with this!" Killen growled, looking around at the others. "This site's as good as fucked now." She reached for Wynn's arm, pulling him up. "My day's done. I need a drink and we've a good man to send on his way." Her words were greeted with nods and grunts of approval as picks were tossed to one side.

News of the accident had spread. It was clear in the eyes of the miners they saw on the way out of the mines. Few spoke of it, and those that did try to offer brief words of consolation wilted in the face of Killen's glare.

There was a beauty in her pain, Wynn realised. Killen's face was usually marble; beautiful but expressionless, revealing little of her thoughts or feelings. Grint's death had forced emotions out, bringing a life to her features.

She turned as they left the entrance to the mine, following the tracks of the carts.

Wynn gave her a look. "I thought…"

"We need to see him off first," she told him. "Drinking can wait."

Wynn followed her without another word. She pulled off her helmet, letting it hang loosely as she walked, dragging feet that were too tired to leave the ground properly, but her expression never wavered.

The smelt works were silent. The doors thrown wide and the air still. Killen walked past the unguarded large doors and into the cavern. The machines stood as mute sentinels, watching with their tenders beside them. Wynn took a breath to speak, and then thought better of it at Killen's glance.

Miners stood in orderly rows around the belt that normally would be drawing rocks into the furnaces. Each face was grim. Each pair of eyes was downcast. Grint lay on the belt with the other miners who had died in the rockfall. The thought that Wynn had never even learned their names came and went, leaving no trace of its passing.

The already muted conversation fell silent as a figure pushed his way through the crowd. Wynn caught the movement and a flash of robes. Grey, the colour of wood smoke. A priest. He stood close to the bodies, muttering something that didn't carry.

The priest spoke up suddenly, his gaze rising to follow his voice. "Our brothers have been called to the flame," he began. His voice was flat. Empty. There was nothing of remorse or anything resembling grief in his tone. If anything, to Wynn, he just sounded tired as he droned on.

The words lost their meaning, and Wynn stopped listening, letting his gaze drift around the smelt works. The machines looked odd in their stillness and he frowned at the shadows against the farthest wall, until they moved. The Listeners stepped forward as one, picking their way from the farthest wall through the maze of machines and channels set into the floor. Not once did they stumble. Not once did they falter.

Wynn stared until their hooded heads rose, turning in his direction until it felt that their bandaged eyes must all be pointed at him.

"Let us remember him as we will," the priest intoned, his voice smothering Wynn's gasp. "And let his soul escape this shell to become one with the flame of the Father." He looked to the smelt worker at the entrance to the furnace, and gave a nod.

The belt moved sluggishly as the worker turned the huge wheel that powered the device, drawing the bodies into the open maw of the furnace. Wynn watched with the others until the first of the bodies were taken by the flames and then turned at Killen's touch.

"I think I've seen enough," she told him. "Are you ready?"

The crowd shifted to let them slip away. They weren't the first to leave. Wynn had seen figures drifting away from the back of the crowd since the priest first began speaking.

Killen did not speak until they were clear of the smelt works. Even with the majority of the machines and furnaces still and silent, the place still had an oppressive air. It had the feel of authority, of being judged and weighed, and it made Wynn's skin crawl.

Killen relaxed visibly as they stepped out into the main cavern.

"It's not just me then," Wynn said with a small smile.

Killen gave him a curious sideways look. "What isn't?"

"The smelt works," Wynn told her. "I don't like the feel of the place. You were wound as tight as a merchant's fist until we stepped out of there."

She shrugged.

"Where are we going?"

Her smile filled the place of an apology. "I keep forgetting you've not been here long. Aspiration is much more than the little portion you've seen so far. That's closer to being a mining camp than anything else. There are whole districts full of people that never step foot in the mines. The merchants who deal in chems and supplies, the pubs, the bars, gaming rooms…"

Wynn nodded and then paused, slowing his feet. "I don't have any money."

"I've marks enough for us both," she told him. "You can pay me back in drinks, or coin when Terrik cuts your share from the Listener take. Even with what's happened, we'll none of us be short."

She led him past Terrik's camp with its collection of huts and cabins, and into the city, cutting a path that led to the far side of the cavern. Her route took them away from mine, smelt works and coal works, and yet no closer to the Sefin's mansion and the home of the gilters.

There was no sign. No boundary marked the streets or buildings, but Wynn noted the change just as clearly. Between one street and the next the shops became more than just a source of supplies, selling chems or boots. Instead of tiny, functional shacks with surly eyed workers, they were suddenly broad fronted affairs. The shopkeepers often stood at their entrance, inviting those on the streets in to see their wares with expansive gestures and smiles.

Killen's mood shifted too, the black fog lifting from her eyes. She became animated, pointing out businesses as they passed. From pubs and eateries to shops that seemed to sell everything from clothing and boots, to complex chemikworks.

Killen stopped, moving to the side to avoid being hemmed in by a group of older children. They were dressed in rags stained dark with coal dust and they had spread out to weave through the press of people. "Go on, you little bastards!" Killen snarled out, pressing her hand tight against the pouch hanging from her belt.

She grinned at Wynn's curious look. "Thieving little Blacker shits will take the teeth from your mouth if you don't watch 'em. And the Keepers don't normally get involved." She moved to the edge of the street, watching the Blackers until they had passed on out of sight.

"Keepers?" Wynn asked.

"Like constables," Killen explained. "They work for Garl. Keep things running smoothly for him.

"We'll head to Lamplight's," Killen told him. She pulled him to one side to let a caravan of wagons pass, loaded high with sacks and barrels. "It's a good clean place, and Lamplight's always good for a laugh."

Wynn nodded with a shrug and let her hurry him along the street.

Lamplight's proved to be a large, rambling affair that looked as if it were formed of three or four buildings shoved roughly together. Unlike the majority of the buildings Wynn had seen in Aspiration which were built from stone, the pub was made largely of wood and the theme continued inside. Killen's boots clumped over the boards as she made her way through to the bar.

"Killen!" The man behind the bar welcomed her with a broad smile, hand closing around the coins he took from the men he'd been serving.

"Lamplight." She smiled back as they worked their way through the crowd. "I've brought you some fresh ears to abuse and a throat that's never been tainted with your demon drink."

Lamplight was a short man with wild hair that seemed to grow in improbable directions. He turned, thumping a crutch squeezed under one armpit on the wooden floor as he looked to Wynn with a broad, friendly smile. "Is that so? You're in for a treat then, my friend. I've the finest ales and spirits in Aspiration."

"Not that that's saying much," Killen muttered in a voice meant to carry.

Wynn smiled along with the chorus of laughs that erupted from the other patrons clustered around the bar.

"What can I get you then?"

Killen ran her eyes along the row of casks and well-polished bottles behind the bar. "Ale to start, I think. Do you have any Deeper's left?"

"Deeper's?" Lamplight raised a bushy eyebrow. "There is, but it's the last of it. I've been putting off broaching it. I can't let it go cheap, even for you."

"Even for me," she snorted. "Broach it, and we'll see how deep a dent we can make in it for you." She hefted her purse meaningfully and the man's eyes brightened.

"So what do you think of my place?" Lamplight asked Wynn as he set the drinks on the bar.

Wynn peered into the cup. The beer was dark, almost black, with a malty smell to it. He took an experimental sip and looked around at the pub. "It's lovely. I've not seen so many lamps since I got here. How is it you don't use chemlamps like everywhere else?"

"Chemlamps," Lamplight spat as Killen snorted into her cup and grabbed at his arm.

"Those bastard chemikers have this place by the balls, my young friend," Lamplight told him. "Between them and Garl, our glorious Sefin, they have this place sewn up. You see this?" he pointed up at the closest lamp. "This is as safe to use in the mines as any of those chemik powders!" He reached up with his crutch to hook the lamp down.

"You've done it now," Killen whispered to him with a smile that wasn't quite an apology. "I should have warned you before we came in."

"See this in here?" Lamplight poked a stubby finger at the flame of the lamp which seemed to be encased in a fine metal mesh. "Just this little piece of metal here is enough to keep anyone safe from the Father's Wrath. It's cheaper than chems, easy to make, and you won't find a single one of them in the mines. And do you know why?"

Wynn shook his head, interested despite the wry grins he was catching from Killen and the others at the bar.

"Because Garl gets a big sackful of marks from the chemikers every bloody month," Lamplight said, stabbing his finger down onto the bar. "That's why."

"His ears are starting to bleed, Lamplight," Killen warned him.

He gave her a black look and then broke out in a broad smile as he laughed. "Sorry, son. I've let my mouth run off on me again, and I've not even taken your name yet."

"Wynn," he supplied, taking a deep drink of the ale. It had a rich, nutty flavour that was far more complex than any ale he'd had before.

"Good to meet you, then." Lamplight's eyes flickered as he took in Wynn's forehead. "Not down here long then?"

Wynn shook his head and then peered at Lamplight's unmarked forehead with a frown. "How is it—?"

"Delicate little flower isn't he?"

Killen snorted again. "Leave him alone, Lamplight. He's still learning how things work. Not everyone down here works in the mines, Wynn. Or even for the temple for that matter. Lamplight was born down here. He's not alone. There are hundreds of families born and bred in Aspiration. This is the only home they know."

"The unmarked probably started with the whores," Lamplight explained as Wynn's frown grew. "That's one theory anyway. At some point some of the women decided that kind of life was better than working the mines. They swapped one shaft for another." He barked a harsh laugh as Wynn flushed and Killen shook her head.

"We still get a tally," Lamplight explained. "We just earn our marks in different ways."

"So you don't need to be down here?" Wynn asked. "Why don't you just leave? You could if you wanted to, couldn't you?"

"What? And leave all this?" Lamplight said, waving an expansive arm to another chorus of laughs. "I suppose I could but this is my home, Wynn. I've never known anywhere else. I don't know anything of the world above. Besides," he said, nodding down at his leg. "In case you hadn't noticed, I'm not exactly mobile."

Wynn's gaze followed the man's nod down to where the cloth was folded over and pinned in place. "What happened? Some mining accident?"

110

"To my foot?" Lamplight asked. "Nothing happened. I've never stepped foot in those mines." He snorted at his own joke and then caught Wynn's expression and laughed all the louder.

"Lamplight was born like that, Wynn," Killen told him in a soft voice. "Don't worry too much about it, he enjoys drawing attention to it. Making people uncomfortable must be good for business."

"Where else can you find ale this good and jokes this awkward?" Lamplight grinned.

Wynn took another drink to cover his embarrassment and looked around the pub as Killen and Lamplight chatted. The place was almost half full already. The miners were clear enough by their clothes but the others were obvious in the crowd. Their unmarked foreheads at odds with the near-slaves beside them.

Bitterness welled up, and his hands balled into fists. They might live in this odd underground city but at least they had the choice. He hadn't chosen this life; it had been forced on him. It wasn't even the life his father had thought it was. The lies of the temple were as blatant and unapologetic as they could be. That alone told him something. Either nobody ever left these mines to talk about it, or they were too scared to say a word.

"Why do you stand for it?" he blurted. "You're totally dependent on whatever food and supplies come out of the smelt works. If you left you could have a real business, have real control of your life."

Lamplight's smile faded as his eyes flickered to a corner of the room and back to Wynn. "You're not done educating your young friend here, Killen. Have a word with him. There's a Deeplighter in the corner and I don't want any trouble."

"A what?" Wynn looked back and forth between the two of them as Killen glanced into the corner.

"Which one is it?" she asked Lamplight.

He busied himself with a cloth and mug, not looking at her as he spoke. "White shirt, thick beard. He's been in here the last few days."

"What's a Deeplighter?" Wynn asked again, looking over at the man.

111

Killen took his chin and turned his head towards her with a warm smile. "Someone you don't want to be caught staring at." She took a drink and set her mug on the bar. "The Deeplighters work for Garl. They keep an eye on things, on the general mood of people, and those that are likely to cause trouble."

"So they'll let him know if people aren't happy?"

Lamplight snorted. "They'll make you disappear if you aren't happy. It all depends how loud you are about it. I remember, must be ten years back or more now." He shot a questioning look at Killen.

"Don't ask me," she laughed. "How old do you think I am?"

Lamplight didn't bother to respond to that, shaking his head with a sigh. "It was a bad business, one of the Blackers. He got it into his head that if he kicked up enough stink, if he got enough folks on side, then Arnsk would be forced to change things."

"Who's Arnsk?" Wynn whispered to Killen.

"Garl's predecessor," Killen told him, without taking her eyes from Lamplight. "Don't interrupt."

"He was wrong," Lamplight said, leaning low over the bar on his elbows. "The uprising he'd planned never happened. The five or ten that were planning it with him met their end in the same way, strung up and lashed to death. You ever seen someone get lashes, Wynn?" he asked, glancing over to the corner again. "It's not pretty. A nasty way to go too. They knew what they were doing, stopping often enough that the men didn't pass out too soon. So, no. I don't think of leaving. I don't think of complaining too much, either. I keep my head down and get on with the life I have. The tally's no different to the taxes I'd face above ground. As for supplies? I put my orders in through the Tally-masters, they get me what I need. I have no complaints, and if I did, they'd be bloody quiet ones."

Wynn nodded as Lamplight gave him a serious look. "I run a good place here. I don't need the Deeplighters bringing me trouble. You're welcome, so long as you can control your mouth. Otherwise find some-where else to drink."

"He's got it, Lamplight," Killen said, putting a protective arm around Wynn's shoulders. "He's new to all this, that's all."

Lamplight gave Wynn another long look and then gave Killen a curt nod before he left them, limping further along the bar.

"Well that went well," Killen breathed. "Are you always so good at first impressions?"

Wynn flushed, uncomfortably aware of the weight of her arm and the closeness of her body. Her smell filled his nostrils and he took a deep drink before he trusted himself to speak. "I'm sorry, I didn't mean to make things awkward."

"It's fine." Killen shrugged, letting her arm fall. "Let's finish these drinks and try somewhere else, there are enough places in Aspiration that we'll not be short."

Lamplight's gave way to half a dozen other bars and eateries. Wynn lost track of the names after the first three. The dark ale went down smoothly and he stopped noticing the bite of the drink as his cheeks slowly grew warm and numb.

CHAPTER EIGHT

The mines had no seasons. Nothing to mark the passing of the days save the small glimpse of sky at the very top of the cavern. The fissure was directly above Garl's mansion and just large enough to let some rainfall in. The smoke from the town drifted up and out of the hole, obscuring the view much of the time. Even when it was clear there was little to make out but a pale light.

Wynn squinted up at the fissure, made smaller by distance, and sighed. By his reckoning he'd been in the mines close to six months now, though it was impossible to be sure.

"Wynn," Terrik called as he stomped down the steps towards him. "Get your gear off. I want you up top today."

Wynn frowned at that. This was more than just unusual. A day spent in Aspiration, out of the mines, was a day's tally lost.

Terrik caught the look. "Father Lasris has asked for you."

Wynn blinked. "He *asked* for me?"

Terrik nodded. "It's not the first time, lad. I just couldn't spare you before now. He's been nagging me to send you for the last couple of months."

"What am I supposed to be doing?" Wynn asked, setting his pack down by his feet.

Terrik shrugged. "Whatever he says. Sometimes he wants nothing more than chores. Other times he'll lecture and question for hours. Who can tell with these religious types?"

Wynn thought about it for a minute. It would be a break from the tunnels if nothing else. "My tally?" he asked, giving voice to his worries.

"You'll get an average for every day you spend with him." He paused, wrestling with some thought before he spoke again. "I'd best warn you though, lad. You'll be marked this day."

"Marked?" Wynn said dumbly, his fingers reaching for the smooth skin of his forehead.

Terrik gave a grim nod. "It's not as bad as you think it will be. Lasris is waiting for you now. Might as well get something hot inside you before you head out."

Whatever it was that he ate, it was warm, he could remember that much. Everything else passed him by and the few attempts others made at conversation with him soon guttered and died as word of his calling spread. The looks though, those he took in. Looks of understanding, and of sympathy. At last, unable to bear the weight of the stares, he pushed himself to his feet and made his way out of the camp.

Lasris's cottage was set back from the rest of the camp, surrounded by a low wall of piled stones. The priest was a strange man who seemed to drift in and out of the camp at will, but he rarely spoke to anyone. There had been several times when Wynn had seen him in the long bunkhouse in the morning, having come in and slept in one of the cots during the night. Terrik seemed to take this in his stride. Noting the presence of the priest with nothing more than a grunt and asking him for a line of verse to send the crews into the mines with.

It had been almost a month since Wynn had seen him last. The priest had retreated to his hut over the last weeks and, were it not for the supplies that Terrik sent over to be left on the steps every few days, Wynn might have wondered if he still lived.

He paused at the low wall, resting a hand on the piled stone as he took in the cottage. Rough walls, bound together with a pale mortar, rose up to support a dark tiled roof. Smoke trailed up from the chimney and Wynn grimaced at the implication as knots grew in his stomach. He glanced back at the camp, expecting to find eyes on him, but it was already quiet. The crews had gone to the mine's entrance without him even noticing.

Why not just go then? The thought came to him unbidden and he toyed with it for a moment. There was no one to see what he did. Why not just leave? Excitement rose within him and died just as quickly. Where could he go, even if he could find a way out? Aspiration might be a home to the unmarked, but to him it was a cage. There was nothing waiting for him outside anymore. He was a slave, bought and sold. "All I'm missing is the brand," he muttered.

He glanced back at the cottage and jumped as he saw Lasris, stood in the doorway watching him. "In," the priest said in a flat voice, jerking a thumb at the house. He turned away, walking into the gloom inside the cottage before Wynn could respond. His sigh was long and hard as he took the first of his slow steps to follow the priest.

The interior of the small house was grim. Dark and spartan, the cottage was dominated by a large fireplace but beyond that, there was little besides a small cot in the corner. A long table took up much of the space, covered in papers, books and half-eaten meals.

"Sit," Lasris told him, waving at the closest of the two chairs in front of the fire.

Wynn sat, not taking his eyes from the old man in his dark robes who perched, bird-like, on the edge of the other chair. The priest peered at him, blinking too often as he looked out from under bushy grey eyebrows.

"Do you know your name, boy?"

Wynn blinked. The priest knew his name. He'd asked for him by name. "Wynn," he supplied, not bothering to keep the confusion from his face.

"Ah," the priest said sadly. "I had thought perhaps…" He shrugged. "No matter."

"What do you mean? I'm confused."

Lasris glanced back at him from where his gaze had wandered. "The Forgefather gives each of us our true name. I thought you might know yours already. It is not unheard of."

Wynn shook his head; this was going to be a waste of time. He worked to keep his expression neutral. "What am I doing here?"

116

A faint smile drifted across the old priest's features. "Spirited. That will serve you if you can learn to temper it."

Wynn grimaced as the old man went on. "You are here because I called for you. You were given to the temple's service. It is time we learned if you are simply rough stone, or if something more lurks within you."

"I don't understand," Wynn admitted.

"Look around you, boy. Where do you think this temple gathers its priests from? Have you seen priests of the Forgefather wandering the lands, holding sermon? No, because we worship here. Those who venerate the Father come here to us."

Wynn ground his teeth as the man's superior tone grated at him. "So why are you down here then?" he blurted, before he could think better of it. "Why aren't you up in the temple with the others?"

Lasris raised an eyebrow and regarded him in silence, letting the stillness draw out until Wynn fidgeted. "You regret that already, don't you?" he said, snorting a laugh. "I am here to atone for my mistakes. The temple tests us all. Some fail."

"What did you do?" Wynn asked.

Lasris sighed, sinking back into the chair. He seemed somehow smaller and older for it. "My sin is of no consequence. One day it may be that my flame will rejoin the fire. For now, I shall seek out what sparks and embers I can. Now, young Wynn who knows not his true name, tell me, what do you know of the Forgefather?"

"Not a great deal," Wynn said with a shrug that stood in for the apology. "He's the god of fire?"

"The Forgefather is the lord of creation," Lasris corrected him.

Wynn nodded, shifting in the chair in search of a more comfortable position. "So he made the world then?"

Lasris shook his head. "No. The Forgefather may well have formed this world but that was not my meaning. The Forgefather is the lord of fire and creation. His hand guides the very act of creating. It may be that our Father plays a role in every act of shaping but his spirit can be felt most strongly in the forge. Through the teachings of our Father we can

117

call iron to its purest form. We can spin steel wire as thin as spider's silk. Our temple was once the only source of truesteel in this world, sought after by princes and kings."

"So you're just a smith?"

The blow caught him on the side of the head and Wynn recoiled, blinking with the shock of it. Not at the force, it had been a light touch, but at the speed the old man had moved. He had uncoiled like a snake, whipping his hand out faster than Wynn could follow.

"I am a priest of the Forgefather," Lasris grated. "I am not *just* anything."

"Sorry," Wynn muttered, rubbing his head. "What do you want with me though?"

"That is why you are here," Lasris grunted, his eyes still hard and angry. "So we can see what shall be done with you." He shook his head and went to the fire, stirring up the coal with a poker until flames licked up again.

"Look into the fire," he said, jabbing towards the hearth with a coal blackened finger.

Wynn watched the flames lick at the coal, reaching out from the red embers beneath like clawing fingers.

"What do you see?" Lasris whispered, his breath hot on Wynn's ear.

Wynn flinched away and started to protest but the priest's hands grabbed his head, turning it back to the fire.

"What?" Wynn said, pulling against the hands.

"Look," Lasris repeated.

Wynn watched the flames, deciding to humour the old man. The small cottage was suddenly uncomfortably warm and the smell of stale sweat clung to the priest as he stood behind him.

"What am I looking for?"

"Just let the flames speak to you," Lasris muttered, sounding somehow further away.

Wynn shook his head and let out a sigh as he watched the fire. At least it was better than blackwork.

118

The blow caught him solid on the back on the skull and he crashed out of the chair, tumbling into the blackness as his body hit the floor.

***

The dull clack of metal and the gurgle of water drifted through the fog that held him. Wynn groaned as pain found him.

"Gods above and below, my head!" Wynn muttered as questing fingers reached for the throb at the back of his head. As if the recognition of one injury had woken the second, a searing pain coursed from his forehead and his fingers tentatively reached for this new injury, though he knew what he would find.

"Don't do that!" Lasris snapped, slapping his hand away. "It's clean now, you'll stop it healing so well. You'd be best to just leave it alone."

"You hit me!" Wynn accused him. Lasris only nodded.

"You hit me and then you branded me!"

"Did you want to be conscious for it?" Lasris asked with genuine curiosity. "I've tried it that way before. People never seem to want to stand still."

"What? No! I didn't want to be marked at all!"

Wynn stood, wheeling to face the old priest but the room tilted under him. His vision swam and he grabbed the back of the chair to steady himself.

"Careful, you're probably still a bit woozy," Lasris said.

"You knocked me out and then you branded me, like I'm some kind of cow," Wynn spat at the man. "Are you out of your mind?"

"It's entirely possible, I suppose," Lasris said, scratching at one cheek. "You're wrong about one thing though. You are some kind of cow. You belong to the temple whether you serve here, or in up the halls themselves."

He stepped back from where he'd been jabbing his finger at Wynn. "Now, how about a drink?"

"I… What? Okay," Wynn said. He sank back into the chair, collapsing down in on himself like a burning house.

119

"Here." Lasris handed him a tin mug.

Wynn sipped without looking, barely noticing the burn as he swallowed.

"Now then, let's get started," Lasris told him as he settled into the seat opposite. "Look at the flames."

Wynn stared at the man for the length of a long breath. "Is that supposed to be some kind of joke?"

Lasris shrugged. "I mean it this time," he said.

Wynn sipped the whiskey again and turned his head towards the fire, making sure he could still see the priest in his peripheral vision.

"Concentrate on the flames," Lasris said. The tone was the same gentle, guiding, voice the priest had used right before he'd clubbed him in the head and Wynn couldn't help glancing at him.

"Every flame is born with a purpose," Lasris told him. "Each has a touch of the Forgefather in it. It is said that if you could but train yourself to see and to hear, the Father would be everywhere."

Wynn watched the flames. Was there something in them? Memories surfaced, of watching the fire as a young child as he huddled close to his mother. The images were vague, dulled by the passage of time, little more than sensations and smells but he drew comfort from them.

"Good," Lasris murmured as a small smile played over Wynn's features. "That's a beginning."

Wynn shook himself. "I don't think so. I was distracted, I'm sorry."

Lasris shrugged, unconcerned. "What were you thinking of?"

"My mother," Wynn admitted.

"And you drew comfort from this?"

Wynn gave him a curious look. "Of course. She's my mother, why wouldn't I?"

Lasris nodded. "Indeed. But examine the feelings you had, are you certain there was nothing more? Something that perhaps you overlooked?"

"I don't know what you mean."

Lasris sighed. "Just try, Wynn. It's not that hard. Please, just humour me."

120

Wynn scowled and then winced as the expression pulled at the fresh burn on his forehead. "I'm sorry, maybe the hole you burnt into my face is distracting me?"

Lasris blinked, taken aback, before barking a laugh. "Maybe you're right." He stood and made his way to the door. "For now then, come with me."

Wynn followed him out and behind the cottage to where a rough forge waited.

"Seen one of these before?" Lasris asked, pointing at the anvil.

"Of course I have," Wynn snorted.

"Worked one?"

"No," Wynn admitted.

Lasris grunted. "At least you're honest. Work with me then, let's teach you how to light this bastard properly."

The next few hours were the purest misery as Lasris worked him almost to collapse. Clearing out the forge was the least of it, though the damp air of the cavern had managed to transform the ashes and dead coals into a thick, congealed paste. The priest had him build and rebuild the fire over and over until he had the kindling, coals and coke layered to his liking. By the time Lasris touched flame to kindling, Wynn would have bolted if he had either opportunity or the energy. Instead, Lasris set him to working the bellows.

"Now then," Lasris called over the noise of Wynn's pumping. "That looks about ready to me. Let's see what you can do."

"What I can do?" Wynn repeated, regretting the words as soon as he said them.

Lasris gave him a grin and handed him a hammer.

"Take those tongs there and pull the iron out of the fire. I want to see you working the hammer."

The heat was a physical thing and it pressed against Wynn as he reached for the tongs. His face felt as if the skin were drawing tight over the bones of his skull and, dimly, he wondered if he still had eyebrows.

"Gloves?" he asked Lasris as he looked around the forge.

121

"Use the tongs right and you won't need them," Lasris told him. "They'll only confuse your grip and ruin your strikes. This is an art, boy. Not just some clumsy pounding."

Wynn grimaced and took up the tongs, reaching for the end of the section of iron Lasris had set to heating in the coals.

"Now, let's see your hammer work," Lasris said.

Wynn tapped tentatively at the glowing section of iron and looked over at Lasris.

"It's not a bloody door, boy!" Lasris laughed. "You've a hammer in your hand. Don't tap at it, hit it."

Wynn struck hard at the iron, marvelling at how easily the metal flattened out under the strokes of the hammer.

"Good," Lasris said with a smile. "Now, try and merge your strokes. The hammer will rebound slightly as it hits, use that. It'll save your arm and it's something you'll need later anyway."

The priest fell silent, watching as Wynn hammered the iron. There was a rhythm to it and it was easy to fall into. He returned the iron to the coals as soon as the glow began to fade, pumping the bellows until the rod glowed like the sun before reaching it out onto the anvil again.

"Listen to the ring of the hammer, this is our church bell," Lasris lectured. "Try and hear beyond the sound, that is where we search for the voice of the Father."

The pounding of the hammer filled Wynn's ears until he couldn't tell when, or if, the sound ended. The pain of the brand was a nagging constant, flaring anew with each strike of the hammer, and every time he moved his head.

Lasris's voice seemed to drift away from him, becoming a half-heard drone in the background, until all he could hear was the hammer and the roar of the flames when he worked the bellows.

He stopped, clinging onto the edge of the anvil as the hammer fell from limp fingers. Somehow the ringing noise did not cease, it just went on and on echoing into what should be silence.

122

"Wynn?" Lasris's voice was distant, not able to draw his attention as he stared blankly into the flames. The edges of his vision were drawing in. He breathed in short, desperate, gasps as the light seemed fade from around him, narrowing until it felt like he was peering at the forge from the inside of a long tunnel.

Sweat was pouring from his face and he clung to the anvil as it grew darker still. The ringing transformed into a rushing roar as his own heartbeat pounded in his ears and he gulped desperately for air. In the centre of his vision, twin coals in the fire burned brightly. They watched him like two glowing red eyes. Finally, his knees buckled and he surrendered to the darkness.

***

Soft footsteps approached in response to his groan and a gentle hand pressed to his chest, holding him down as he sought to rise.

"Lay back, Wynn. Here, try to roll over and drink some of this." A cup was pressed into his fingers and a small hand guided it to his lips. He sipped, then gulped.

"Easy," the voice warned, but it was too late. He lurched upwards as his stomach heaved.

"Fuck, Wynn!" Killen leapt back as the mess spattered over the floor and her feet. "I told you, go slowly!"

"I'm sorry," he managed, wiping at his mouth with the back of one hand. He looked around at the empty bunkhouse. "What happened? How did I get here?"

"Lasris called for Terrik and a few of the others to bring you back," Killen told him, wiping at herself with a rag. "You passed out. Nearly fell into the forge, apparently."

Wynn closed his eyes tight against the memory and gasped as the pain flared again from his forehead.

"You'll get used to it," Killen told him, wincing in sympathy. "It's not so bad after the first couple of days, once it's had time to

123

get a good scab on it. Just try to leave it alone once it starts itching."

"He clubbed me," Wynn said.

Killen nodded. "He does that to everyone."

"You knew he was going to knock me out?" Wynn demanded, pushing himself up so he could sit back against the wall. "Why didn't you warn me?"

"You were always going to get marked, Wynn," she told him. "Knowing wouldn't have helped you."

"What?" Wynn demanded. "How can you say that?"

She crouched down beside the bed. "Think about it. If you'd known, and Lasris came at you with a branding iron, would you have just stayed still? No, of course not. He'd have had to get Terrik and some of the others to hold you down. It was always going to happen, telling you would just have made it worse."

Wynn pushed away from her, away from her touch. "Why did it have to happen at all?"

"Because that's the way life is down here, Wynn," she told him. A touch of anger or frustration crept into her voice, he couldn't tell which. She took a deep breath, closing her eyes for a moment. "It's probably time you grew up a little. There's no point in complaining about water because it's wet. There's no point complaining about the way things work down here, you won't change anything. You had to get marked because otherwise you can't earn tallymarks."

"What? But I've already earned marks," Wynn protested.

"Because you were going to be marked, and everyone who matters knew that."

He glared at her, hating her for her calmness. "What about Lamp-light and all the other unmarked?"

"Come on, Wynn. You should know this already. They don't get any marks from the Tallymasters," she told him, holding his gaze with her eyes. "Every mark they earn comes from crews like this one, from people like us."

Wynn gaped, his mouth shaping words that wouldn't come out. He gave up, closing his mouth with an audible clack.

124

"Are you done being sick on people?" she asked.

"It's not…" he stopped as the smile grew on her face. "I'm sorry," he said with a helpless shrug.

"Don't worry about it," Killen laughed. "Not too much anyway." She pushed herself up. "You should probably get something to eat. Lasris wants you as soon as you're ready."

"Again?"

She nodded. "Try to stay conscious this time," she told him, as she ducked out of the door. Her half smile bringing a small smile of his own to his lips.

He climbed out of the bed like an old man, taking care that his limbs were doing as they were told before he put too much weight on them. The floor was still damp under his feet from where Killen had cleaned up his mess. He hadn't even thanked her, he realised.

Breakfast was dry bread and water; he didn't trust his stomach much beyond that. It had already proven itself a traitor and he wasn't about to put fresh weapons into its hands. For all that, his head felt clearer as soon as he had eaten and by the time he was halfway finished he felt close to human again.

He made his way across the camp to the priest's small cottage, still chewing on the last of the hard crust. The priest must have been watching as he approached and the door swung open as soon as he drew close.

"You are well?" Lasris asked, looking him up and down, it was less a question and more of an observation.

Wynn nodded. "Well enough."

Lasris grunted, and moved to inspect the brand on Wynn's forehead. "Good. This is scabbing well. Leave it alone and it will soon heal."

Wynn's jaw clenched, trapping the words behind his teeth.

"Come then, let's see if you remember anything," Lasris said, waving Wynn around the cottage to the forge.

It had been freshly restocked, Wynn saw. Piles of coal and coke sat in their bins and the kindling was already piled high close to the forge. He glanced back at Lasris who nodded at the cold forge. "Set to then."

125

Wynn looked at the forge for a moment. Lighting it was no simple process, and Lasris had only shown him the steps the one time. This was obviously the priest's idea of a test. He got to work, slicing slivers of wood away from the kindling and piling them over the dried leaves and bark in the well of the forge, before reaching for the flint and steel. The wood was quick to catch and he set larger pieces and small chunks of coal into the flames, taking care not to knock the growing fire apart.

Lasris helped once, passing him a set of hand bellows so he could force the coal alight. By the time he had the coke loaded above the coal, and burning, he felt as if he'd been baked himself. The sweat was drying as fast as it could soak his clothes and the heat tugged at the brand on his face as he worked the bellows, forcing more heat from the fire.

He reached for the shovel again, loading coal, arranging it in a circle surrounding the burning coke, and close enough that the heat would cook the coal itself into coke. Finally, he shovelled raw coal, left out and exposed to the damp, in a horseshoe shape above the heart of the fire to focus the heat.

He stepped back then, watching the flames carefully as they flicked through the piled coal and coke, before looking to Lasris for confirmation. The priest nodded in approval and passed him a long iron rod.

Wynn gave the old man a questioning look.

"Never seen one of these?" Lasris asked. "It's a heating rod," he explained. "To test the power of your little fire here." He took the rod from Wynn, thrusting it into the fire and muttering to himself. Wynn stepped to one side to give the man room to work but he was doing little more than watching the flames, murmuring something to himself over and over.

Wynn found himself leaning closer to hear. It was a chant, not a mutter, and Lasris's brow was creased in concentration as he repeated it, adding a word onto the end of each cycle.

The priest fell silent and pulled the rod clear of the fire, holding the glowing tip out to show Wynn. "Well done, perfect forging heat. Now let's see what else you remember."

The hours passed swiftly as Wynn learned the rudiments of working iron, stopping only briefly to eat and drink. Lasris had him pounding the metal until almost flat and then folding it and pounding again, over and over as he corrected the angle of the hammer, Wynn's posture, and worried at the fire. He walked him through the use of the anvil, the racks of tongs, files, and hammers. The pain of his brand was constant, brought back to life each time he moved from the bellows into the heat of the forge.

Lasris lectured about the Forgefather almost the entire time and, despite the ring of the hammer, his voice was somehow impossible to drown out. It was an unceasing drone that only became animated when the man spoke about the art of smithing itself.

"Good," he told Wynn finally. "You come back in the morning and then the real work can begin."

"This wasn't work?" Wynn waved at the anvil with one hand while he mopped his face with a sleeve made rough with baked-on sweat.

Lasris gave him a rare smile. "This? Boy, this is just a beginning. You have no notion of what real work is."

Wynn flushed as Lasris caught his glance in the direction of the mines and raised an eyebrow. "You think the mines are hard work? Perhaps work enough for you?" the priest asked. He pushed on before Wynn could speak. "Know this, aspirant. This trial is the most important thing in your life. The friendships you form with your crew are nothing. You will leave these people behind, and they would leave you just as quickly. The only loyalty you owe is to yourself. The choice is always the same. Either learn in the temple, or die in the mines."

CHAPTER NINE

"What is that chant you do?" Wynn asked Lasris one morning as the man worked at the fire. He'd been working the forge for two weeks now, leaving the bunkhouse in the early morning and returning long after most of the miners were already snoring. The exhaustion had been crippling to begin with, a draining fog that seemed to fill his mind and slow his movements. Now he was almost accustomed to it.

Lasris glanced at him with a raised eyebrow, lips still moving.

"Is it some kind of chant to the Father? Something to bring the heat to the forge?"

Lasris drew the rod out and glanced at the tip. "Once, perhaps," he said. "Now it is little more than a way of marking time."

Wynn laughed at that. "That's it? I thought it was some kind of mystical chant, and all you've really been doing is counting?"

Lasris's usually dour face darkened and then split into a small smile as a snort escaped him. "What do you know of our faith, Wynn?" he said as he turned back to the forge. "I mean, really *know*?"

"Not much," Wynn admitted. "I'd barely heard of it before I was brought here. I mean, I've heard of the Forgefather, of course. I just hadn't heard much else about it."

Lasris grunted, taking a length of iron and pushing it into the coals. "In many ways we're a fallen faith, Wynn. We're a shadow of what we once were. There are people down here, down in these mines, who think of the priests and the temple as nothing more than slavery. In a way I suppose they're right."

Wynn blinked. It was one thing to think it. He'd said the same thing to Killen more than once, in nervous, hushed whispers. But it was another thing entirely to hear it from Lasris, a priest who lived in Aspiration.

"You're shocked to hear it from my lips," Lasris said, glancing up at him as one hand reached for a hammer in the tool rack. He shrugged. "You probably shouldn't be. The faith used to be something far more, and very different to what it is now. Our Father came into being as this world was created, He was an echo of the whisper that brought light to the darkness. I've heard a half a dozen different versions but that's the one that makes the most sense to me. The Forgefather was unintended, a glorious accident that brought power from the flames."

He fell silent, pounding away at the length of iron as Wynn watched. The strokes were deft and held only half the power Wynn had been using, saving the old man's arms, Wynn guessed. Lasris set the glowing rod onto the anvil and took a chisel, cutting through the soft metal with sure strokes. He shoved the one section back into the fire as the glow began to fade and took a drink from the skin set by his feet.

"Through the power of the Forgefather we created wonders this world hasn't seen the like of since. It's said we could spin wire thinner than a human hair, but with the strength of anchor chains. We offered up our own blood to the forges and the Father blessed them himself. His was the voice in the fire. Even those who didn't follow the faith could hear it."

"What happened?" Wynn asked, drawn into the story despite himself.

"The Fall happened," Lasris spat. "Somehow, all those centuries ago, we displeased the Father and he withdrew his grace. The fires fell silent and the faith withered until it is as you see it now, a sad and pathetic shadow of its former glory."

"And nobody knows what caused it?" Wynn asked in a soft voice.

"Oh we know what caused it," Lasris snapped, throwing down the hammer. "Pride caused it. Pride, and the creation of those blind abominations!"

Wynn turned, looking over one shoulder towards the distant cavern wall. "The Listeners?"

129

"The Listeners." Lasris nodded. "They claim that their power is a gift from the Father. I know it for what it really is. We all do, if we care to admit it. They have stolen the voice of the Father and in his silence he cursed them to rip out their own eyes."

He ripped the iron from the coals and slammed it down onto the anvil, working it flat and folding, until the red faded.

"Did you see how that was done?" he asked, without looking up. "How I managed it without pounding on it like you have been?"

Wynn nodded and then realised Lasris hadn't been looking. "I think so."

"Show me then."

Wynn returned the iron to the coals until it glowed the orange-white of candle flame. The hammer felt good in his hands as he worked the rod flat and folded the metal deftly, working it flat on the anvil again. He felt Lasris moving closer behind him and then the chanting began. His voice was deep and strong as he chanted in time with Wynn's hammer strokes. He shifted the rhythm and Wynn found himself following. The ring of hammer against iron forming a harmony with the chant. The priest somehow brought in a second chant behind the first, and at once the sound became song. The rhythm was so complex that Wynn gave up trying to follow it, or understand it. It was enough just to be surrounded by it. His ears caught hints of a third voice in the song, far softer than Lasris's voice, dancing between his notes as it added its own. It lifted him and tore at him, bringing joy and pain in equal measure, until it caught at his soul.

Lasris took the hammer from his hands almost tenderly as the tears ran unchecked down his face. "Now you see the edges," he said in a voice thick with regret. "That was the palest shadow of what was lost."

Wynn looked up to meet the old man's gaze but Lasris was already turning as the voice called from the front of the cottage. "Lasris! Where are you, priest?"

"Terrik," Lasris told him, though Wynn had already recognised the voice. "Wait here." He waved a hand at the forge. "Work the iron, get a feel for it. You need to improve your hammer work. I want to see you working faster than you have been."

Wynn watched him go, until the priest glared back at him. He flushed and reached to push the iron back into the coals. There isn't really any way to make a bellows quiet. The blast of air roars through the fire and ruins any chance of hearing anything.

He looked at Terrik as he pumped the bellows. The one-eyed man was speaking quietly to Lasris, their heads close together.

"… all well and good, Lasris," Terrik's voice broke through when Wynn stopped pumping. "But I need the boy earning his keep."

Lasris paused before replying, and Wynn took up the tongs, reaching for the iron in the coals as he felt their gaze on him.

Lasris's reply was lost in the scrape of the metal over the anvil.

"He shows some promise then?" Terrik asked.

This was ridiculous, Wynn decided. All three of them knew he was trying to listen. He shrugged as he set down hammer and tongs and turned to the pair, watching them openly.

"He does," Lasris acknowledged, turning his head to stare at Wynn as he spoke. "Though he is impertinent and apparently prone to listening in on other's conversations."

Terrik snorted as his lips twitched. "Promise or not," he said. "I can't have him here for weeks at a time and not paying his way."

Lasris grunted. Not taking his eyes from Wynn. "I need him at least twice a week. The rest of the time you can try and work him to death in your mines."

"They're hardly *my…*" Terrik stopped himself in mid-flow and let out a sigh that aged him five years as he shook his head. "Two days a week, but I want him back tonight." He glanced over at Wynn and nodded before he turned on one heel and was gone.

"Get to it, boy," Lasris snapped at him. "If I have to try and beat you into some kind of shape with only two days a week to do it in, then you'll damned well work."

131

***

The bunkhouse was quiet. Not everyone who worked on Terrik's crew lived in the bunkhouse anyway. Some saved their spare marks and had their own huts and cottages. Some, mostly the women, shared their homes with others. Despite that, the place was always at least two-thirds full and the rush of mornings was a cramped, sweaty affair. The place should be filled with noise. Men should be pushing and cursing their way through the press of people as they fought their way to the door.

Wynn shook his head, still half asleep as he swung his legs out of the bunk and shrugged himself into his clothes. The silence of the bunkhouse felt unnatural. He made his way outside, padding on quiet feet, and sat down at the top of the steps to pull his boots on.

It was just as quiet outside. The normal throng of miners making their way past Terrik's circle of huts was absent, and the cavern was muted and stilled. He paused, one boot half on and rested one hand on his helmet as he looked around.

The trestle tables, normally full of men and women eating, were empty. The cooking station was cold and still.

"What the hells?" Wynn wondered, getting to his feet.

"You picked a great day to come back to work."

Wynn started at the sudden noise in the near-silence, and turned to see Killen, a half smile on her face as she raised her eyebrows at him.

"Jumpy?"

"It's quiet." He shoved his foot fully into his boot and busied himself with the ties to cover his embarrassment.

"Yes, well. Like I said, you picked a good day to come back to work." Killen shrugged, motioning to the empty tables. "No one's working today. There's a reckoning."

"A what?"

Killen gave him a look that was somewhere between pity and contempt. "You've had this explained to you enough times, Wynn. Weren't you listening? You make your tally or you get flogged. That's the way it is here."

132

Wynn bit back something harsh and bitter. "Who?"

She shrugged. "Some chem-merchant I think. I'm not sure."

"A merchant," he blurted. The threat behind the tally was bad enough, but for someone to be flogged that wasn't even a miner. His mouth made nonsense noises, trying to find the words.

"What?" Killen frowned at him. "They make their marks the same as everyone else. Why shouldn't they have a tally too?"

"I…" Wynn struggled with it. He sighed, dropped his hands to his sides. "So why is nobody working?"

"Nobody works on a reckoning," she told him. "Everyone has to watch."

He dropped the boot as he stared at her.

"You think that's barbaric?" she offered, her features twisting into something hard and cold. "Cruel? That's life, Wynn. It's not really all that different to life above is it? What happens there if taxes aren't paid?"

Wynn closed his mouth on his protest. "You're right," he admitted. "It's no better where I'm from. There was a farm near to the one I grew up on…" He fell silent, staring into space as he shook his head.

She nodded. "Go on."

Wynn grimaced at the memory, regretting this already. "The Carsocks. Good people. I grew up with them really. I played with their twins in the fields when I was younger, and then worked with them on the ploughs when we grew a bit."

"What happened?" she asked.

He sighed. "The world? The weather? Everything, I suppose." He shook his head, looking down at his boots. "It was a war. Some place I've never heard of. I didn't even know it was happening until the tax-collectors came calling. We managed to scrape by the first year. It was hard but we had enough to get by, just. The second year though, that was when the drought struck. It just… It just didn't rain." He looked up to meet her gaze. "Do you know what that's like? It sounds like nothing but we had an hour of drizzle in a month when we should have had weeks of rain. The summer came early and baked what little water there was out of the soil. When we should have had plants already calf-high, we had bare, baked earth."

133

"Not what a farmer wants," Killen said, her voice soft.

Wynn snorted. "No, not really. We didn't quite starve the first year but by the time the following season came around we had precious little left to sow."

She looked at him blankly.

"Seeds," Wynn explained. "You're not from farming stock, I'd guess."

"No." Killen shook her head with a smile.

"We barely grew enough to survive on," Wynn explained. "But you need to keep back some for seed-stock for the next year."

"You didn't have enough?"

"We did," Wynn told her. "But the tax-collectors came again and the Carsocks just didn't have it. They argued first. Then they begged. I can still remember the day they left. The twins were putting a brave face on it but their mother was crying. It's their Da's face that stays with me. It was haunted. Like he'd failed, somehow. Not just his family but at life itself. He'd already given up."

"Is that how you ended up here?" she asked, breaking the silence. "Drought?"

He looked at her then and she recoiled from his expression. "Drought was half of it." He rammed his foot into the boot. "What time is this thing?"

"Not for hours," Killen told him. "That's why most people are still in bed."

Wynn grunted. "Why are you up then?"

She grimaced. "I can never sleep on reckoning days. I've been out of my mind drunk more than once." She gave a small shake of her head and looked at him. "The Keepers don't like that much. I wouldn't recommend it."

"So...?"

She shrugged. "We kill time I suppose. I could use something to eat. Terrik's slop-peddlers won't be working for an hour or more, and I think I need something that tastes like it hasn't been eaten once already."

Wynn laughed at that. "It's not great is it?"

Killen pulled a face. "Like sucking on a dead rat."

"I'll take your word for that," Wynn told her. "Where did you want to go?"

"Lamplight's has good food," she began, but hesitated.

Wynn frowned at her. "What?"

"Well, do you think you can behave yourself this time?"

He bristled at that. "I 'behaved' last time."

"Yes," she agreed. "Badly."

He glowered.

"No, look," she said, stopping him before he could speak. "You don't know Lamplight. You don't know how he works. He can be difficult at times, if he thinks he's being attacked or set-upon."

"I didn't—"

Killen fixed Wynn with a warning look as she lowered the finger from his lips. "You need to put yourself inside his head. He was born down here. He's had to fight his whole life. Can you imagine how hard it must be to function with just one foot in a place like this? He didn't even ever have the chance of being marked, and a lot of unmarked do choose that and ask. But the priests don't want someone like him. He's damaged goods. He's a reject. So he put up walls. He hides behind his humour, and behind making other people uncomfortable. Thing is, Wynn. He's cowering down behind them, hoping not to get crushed."

She shifted over to sit down beside him. "His lamps were supposed to be his thumb to the nose of the lot of them. To the temple, to Garl and his Keepers. They would have been his way of proving he was as good, or better, than anyone else. Instead the temple refused to even consider them. The revolt he mentioned came soon after, and he hasn't raised his head above the parapet since."

Wynn's eyes widened. "Then... You think he was involved in that?"

Killen sucked on her lip. "I don't know how involved he was but I'd say he probably has leanings in that direction at the very least. I expect Garl knows it too."

"So that's why the Deeplighter—"

135

"Was in there," Killen said with a nod. "Garl's sending a message. It happens every few months. If he didn't want Lamplight to know he was being watched, we'd probably never have known."

"So then, my asking questions…" he winced.

"No," Killen laughed with a shake of the head. "No, it probably didn't help matters much."

"Gods above and below," Wynn sighed. "And you want to eat there?"

"He has good food," Killen said with a shrug. "It's not that big a deal. At least, not now that you know about it. Besides, if you don't go back now you never will. It's like falling off a horse."

"Painful and humiliating?"

"No!" Killen said through a laugh. "You need to get back on, before you think about it too much."

"Been on many horses, have you?"

"I've never even touched one," she said, climbing to her feet and reaching for his hand. "But I've made a complete arse of myself more than once. Come on."

He let her pull him to his feet and, together, they made their way through the quiet streets. The air was damp and a thin rain misted down through the fissure in the cavern's roof, picked out by the shafts of light streaming through the droplets.

"How are you finding Lasris?" Killen asked suddenly after several minutes of silence.

"Hard work," Wynn told her, a wry smile twisting his lips.

"It's smithing," she laughed. "Not needlework."

"That's not what I meant," Wynn said. "He's hard work. He's fine when he's teaching forgework, but once he gets onto the stuff about the Forgefather it's like he's reading it from a book. He drones. It's enough to put you to sleep."

Killen shrugged, stepping around a man pulling a cart loaded high with goods. "It's not the most exciting topic, and, let's face it, it's his job. All he does is talk to aspirants about the faith. Maybe he's bored with it?"

Wynn grunted, unconvinced. "It's more than that." He shook his head with a sigh. "It's almost like he doesn't believe any of it."

Killen shrugged again as they rounded the corner and Lamplight's came into view. "Maybe he doesn't. Is unshakable faith a requirement for a priest?"

Wynn reached for the door. "It's probably pretty important, yes."

Lamplight's was still and he paused on the threshold for a moment, wondering if the place was even open.

"Come in, you're letting the smell out!" Lamplight called from behind the bar.

"The smell?" Wynn wondered.

"Well look who it is!" The man made his way out from behind the bar and came to meet them, his crutch thumping on the wooden floor. "And freshly marked too. Isn't that pretty," he said, leaning in to get a clearer view of Wynn's forehead.

Wynn flushed and looked away as Lamplight laughed and grinned at Killen.

"Yes the smell," Lamplight said. "I was looking forward to a nice quiet morning with everyone sleeping in. You start leaving that door open and the smell of my food will fill the place in minutes. You'll ruin my day."

"That good, huh?" Wynn smiled.

"You'll have to wait and see," Lamplight said with a wink. "Kris taught me a few things before the gods took him from me. Cooking was the least of them." His smile tightened as he spoke and pain and loss touched his eyes for the briefest of moments.

Wynn glanced back to Killen at that.

She snorted at him, rolling her eyes and shaking her head. "Table for two, Lamplight." She waved around at the empty chairs. "If you can fit us in?"

"Sit anywhere you like," Lamplight said with a scowl. "Keep that smart mouth closed and I might even bring some food for you to put into it."

137

She laughed and led the way to a table.

"Kris?" Wynn asked her in a low voice.

"He was Lamplight's partner," Killen said with a nod, matching his low tones. "It was a few years ago now."

"A man?" Wynn blinked.

"You *are* sheltered aren't you?"

Wynn shook his head. "I just…"

"I keep forgetting you're from farming stock. You've probably never even seen a city before Aspiration have you?"

Wynn shook his head, glancing over at the bar.

"Well then, yes, Lamplight loved a man. He loves men in general, I suppose. Don't get hung up on it. It's really not important. How much does it really matter what you have between your legs? Love is love."

"I suppose," Wynn managed, frowning. "I'd just never thought…"

"Now that I can believe."

"The Serapists say it's a sin, you know?"

Killen grimaced as if she'd tasted something foul. "The Serapists say eating lamb is a sin. Fish? Pig? Even cow. That's all fine. But lamb? Oh no, that's a sin." She leaned forward, resting her hands on the table. "You know what I think? I think the gods, if they care at all about anything we do, certainly don't care what we put where. They don't care if we eat fish, snake or fucking goat's balls. And they certainly don't care if you put that," she pointed. "Into there, rather than there. A hole is a hole, Wynn, and neither of them are especially sacred."

Wynn made a face. "That's blunt enough."

"I'm a miner, Wynn," Killen said as she shrugged. "I tell it as it is." She let the smile fall from her face, giving him a serious look. "Are you going to embarrass me here with this?"

"No! It just caught me off-guard is all." He tried a smile that was supposed to be reassuring. It sat uncomfortably on his face.

Killen looked at him in silence for a few moments before nodding and looking around for Lamplight. The man must have been watching their exchange, or at least waiting for the nod from Killen, before he made his way through the tables.

"What will it be then, my freshly-claimed sir?" he asked Wynn with a smile. "I have fresh eggs this morning. A mushroom omelette?"

"Where in the world did you get eggs?" Wynn asked.

"Chickens," Lamplight replied with a straight face that cracked after a moment to let the laughter through. "I have my own coop in the yard."

"I haven't even seen an egg since I got here," Wynn told him.

"Yes, well. I don't imagine they survive the journey down here too well," Lamplight said, wiping down the table with a wet cloth that was probably bringing as much dirt as it took with it.

"Two omelettes sounds great, Lamplight," Killen broke in. "Coffee too if you have it."

"Always, Killen," Lamplight told her. "I couldn't function without it." He worked his way back through the tables and through a doorway beside the bar.

"Does he really run this whole place on his own?" Wynn asked, looking around at the empty tables. "I mean, it's quiet now but…"

Killen glanced around at the tables. "He does it on his own when it's quiet but no, he has staff. He'll have others coming in later, I expect."

Lamplight proved to be as good as his word, bringing food and hot coffee in short order. Wynn first picked at the food and then devoured it in minutes.

"I told you it was good," Killen said around a mouthful.

"Forgefather! Why don't we come here every day?" Wynn asked as he pushed his plate away and reached for his coffee.

Killen grimaced. "Well, it's not what you might call cheap. You just ate the best part of a good day's tallymarks."

Wynn's face fell. "You're joking!"

"No, but if there was ever a day to do it, this is it."

Wynn felt for the marks he had in his pocket, squeezing the metal squares together. "You might have said something."

"You're not short are you?"

139

"No, but…"

"Live a little, Wynn," she said, sipping at her coffee. "Life's too short and hard down here."

He fell silent, pushing the remains of his food around his plate. A number of others had drifted in while they ate and the low buzz of conversation filled the room.

"What are you thinking about?" Killen asked.

Wynn shrugged. "Grint."

She nodded and winced as her eyes grew distant. "Bad business."

"It's not just Grint though, is it?" Wynn said, pitching his voice low. "Grint's death. Terrik's eye… How did he lose it anyway?"

"Rock chips," Killen told him, scraping the last of the egg from her plate.

Wynn grunted. "And now this flogging. This place is hell. We're sat here, spending an entire day's earnings on eggs, pretending that everything's fine."

Killen nodded. "It's what you make of it, Wynn. There's only one way out of here alive. You have a better chance than most right now."

"What, because of Lasris?" he said, picking up the near-empty cup again.

"Well, yes!" She reached across the table for his hand, pulling the cup down before it reached his mouth. "There is nobody else training for the test right now, Wynn. Not in our crew anyway. Not everyone gets chosen. You want out of here, that is the best way." She sat back, sipping at her coffee as she watched another small group make their way through the door. Lamplight moved to greet them.

"Does it really get me out though?" he asked, dropping his voice still further as he caught sight of Lamplight settling the newcomers at a table and then making his way over to them. "Or just into something else? There has to be another way."

Lamplight smiled broadly, looking at the table. "And how was it? I see clear plates, at least."

"Delicious," Wynn told him with a smile. "Easily the best meal I've had in weeks."

Lamplight's smile shifted and Wynn realised that the man was genuinely pleased.

"Where do you get the mushrooms?"

Lamplight laughed at that. "Do you know what you need to grow mushrooms, Wynn?"

Wynn shrugged and shook his head.

"Well, trust me, you only really need two things and we're not short of either down here." He reached to clear the plates onto another table. "I don't normally do this, but I'm going to have to move you along fairly soon. I need to close up in another hour or so if I'm going to be in time for Garl's lovely spectacle."

Wynn winced and glanced at Killen but if she caught his look she gave no sign. She stared into the bottom of her cup.

"You don't approve then?" Wynn asked.

Lamplight started to speak and then stopped, sucking in a breath through his teeth. He looked around quickly before pulling out a chair to sit with them. "No," he said in a low, angry voice. "I don't approve. I learned my lesson to keep quiet years ago but when Garl starts flogging women, it's hard to keep your mouth shut."

"A woman?" Wynn blurted loudly, drawing furious looks from both Lamplight and Killen. "A woman?" he repeated in softer tones.

Lamplight looked back and forth between them. "You two didn't know?"

Killen shook her head.

"Marielle," Lamplight told them. "She's been running a chemikers over by the Blackers for a few years now. Never did that well. She sells glow-tubes mostly but I heard she's been known to make stims too."

"Stims?" Wynn asked, looking blank.

Lamplight shared a look with Killen. "Chems for the body," she explained. "I've heard them called Joy-chems too. Some think they make life easier. They can make you so happy you don't care what's happening."

141

"Until you step off a ledge to play with the fairies," Lamplight said, folding his arms. "There are powders you sniff, philtres you drink. They're a bad business. Fill your head full of fluff."

"Not like good honest drink," Killen said with a grin at him.

Lamplight let the joke pass without a flicker. "A woman, Killen. Doesn't that bother you?"

"Why would it?" Killen shrugged. "There's nothing special about me just because I'm a woman. I work the same as everyone else. I have a tally the same as everyone else. Why should I get special treatment just because I have tits?"

Lamplight glanced at Wynn who shook his head.

"Fine, forget the fact Marielle's a woman," Lamplight said. "The lashing is wrong. She's not a marked, she has no chance of ever being tested. She's barely scraping by and probably got her own head full of fluff from the stims she makes. Is it any wonder she can't make tally? This place, they call it Aspiration, but there's no hope for the likes of her."

Killen looked around, scanning the few faces in the pub. "Deep-lighters, Lamplight," she hissed.

He waved a hand in a lazy dismissal. "There's none in here. They'll all be watching the crowd in the square."

The good humour slipped off Killen's face and she leaned on one arm as she stabbed a finger at Lamplight. "You keep talking like that and they'll be in here soon enough, and they'll be doing more than sitting in a corner and waiting for you notice them."

"Let them come," Lamplight spat, but Wynn saw fear in the man's eyes as they flicked around the room in furtive glances.

He cleared his throat. "What time do we have to be at this thing?"

Killen gave him an irritated look, seeing through the clumsy attempt at subtlety. "Mid-day, when the bell sounds. We'd probably best get moving."

"Killen, look," Lamplight said, laying a thick hand on her arm. "I didn't mean it. I don't have many people come in here that bring a real smile to my face. The fake one needs a rest now and then."

142

Her face softened a touch, the ice thawing in her eyes. "You can think and say what you like, Lamplight, but something like that will bring Deeplighters down on more than just you. This isn't much of a life but it's the only one I have."

"I'll watch my mouth," Lamplight promised, glancing around again at the other faces in the room. "Saying it more quietly doesn't make it better though."

"I thought you learned your lesson with Arnsk and the Blacker," Killen said.

"You would have thought so, wouldn't you?"

"Stay safe," she told him. "I don't know anyone else with chickens."

A small smile grew on the man's face as she led Wynn to the door.

***

Aspiration had come to life while they ate and the streets were filled as people made their way towards the Gilded Quarter. Wynn saw the difference almost immediately. Normally this quarter of Aspiration was filled with conversation and laughter; with life. That was gone now and it was visible in a dozen different ways. From the expressions on the faces, to the slow, penitent pace. This was not a people drawn to a spectacle, this was a people cowed and driven.

The river of close-packed bodies opened for them, swallowed them, and swept them along. They did not speak, and the silence chased away any words Wynn might have had. The quiet was oppressive, as Aspiration's people marched willingly to watch a bloodletting. He met Killen's eyes once during the journey but looked away quickly, not liking what he found there.

The Gilded Quarter was packed. The cold, perfect marble of the buildings stood in stark relief to the press of bodies, dressed in rags and filthy mining leathers, that shuffled through the streets. Wynn moved along with the others, the look of faint disgust had been on his face for so long that he felt a mild ache as his expression shifted.

The square was still, a silence that came from resting feet. The people of Aspiration stood in quiet rows, facing the steps leading to Garl's mansion, and the line of black-clad guards that stood at their base.

A solid wooden post rose out of the marble blocks to one side of the steps. If it had been anywhere else but the cavern, rain might have worked to wash away the blood. Here, the rain was seldom strong enough to form puddles, foiled by the plants that grew on the sides of the narrow fissure in the roof. Dark stains ran down the post and had spilled over the front of the marble block, the blood had sunk deep into the pores of the rock. Sometimes even a stone can scream.

The doors to the mansion swung open as bells called out the noon hour. Black-clad guards marched a slight figure to the post. She seemed frail, surrounded by the guards, but her situation made her look all the smaller, as if she had shrunk down inside herself.

Wynn glanced at Killen but the woman's brown eyes were fixed on the spectacle. Her face was a plain mask that told no tales. Marielle made no sound as the guards bound her to the whipping post, arms held high above her head.

Movement caught at Wynn's eyes and he watched as a figure emerged from the mansion. He was dressed in finery that Wynn would never have expected to find in Aspiration, rich velvets and polished leathers that seemed at odds with his grizzled face.

"Garl," Killen whispered to him.

The Sefin made his way down the steps to the post and stood, looking out over the crowd as a large guard shook out the whip.

"Aspiration is here for one reason, and one reason only," Garl began, his gravelly voice rolling out over the crowd. "To provide the temple of the Forgefather with the raw materials it needs, both with novices, and ore. All who live in Aspiration, marked or unmarked, must meet their tally, and all know the punishment for failure. This woman was warned twice over her production and sale of stims. She was warned twice and still she failed to meet her tally. Our rules are simple, but they must apply to all—"

144

"Where's your tally then, Garl?" a voice cried out from the back of the crowd. Wynn turned in shock, following the wave of turning heads. A dark haired man in coal-stained rags stood at the middle of a widening circle as people shuffled away from him.

"Oh, Curk. You stupid, stupid, bastard," Killen breathed.

The guards surged off the steps, charging into a wall of people that recoiled, making way for them as they rushed toward the man who was now struggling to fight his way through the crowd and away from the guards. Raised voices didn't cover the sound of several heavy blows that landed before the guards even reached the heckler and he could be seen struggling against the hands that held him.

"Get off me you bloody Deeplighter bastard!" Curk shouted.

Curk's protest turned frantic as the first of the guards reached him, feet lashing out as he was pulled to the ground.

"Gods, what do we do?" Wynn hissed at Killen.

"Do?" she replied, her lips barely moving. "We do nothing. And we keep quiet."

The crowd parted noiselessly to let the guards through with their struggling captive. He screamed, kicking wildly as he was dragged up to the post and bound in place, facing Marielle.

"One is here for not meeting the tally," Garl called out. "This one will face the same punishment for sowing dissension. While you live in Aspiration you answer to me. Aspiration belongs to the Sefin under the Pact. I will brook no interference with that."

He looked out over the crowd, meeting gazes for a moment. A curt word and a nod, and then the first strokes of the whip fell. A whip doesn't pass through the air. It cuts a path through it, hissing with cold spite.

Marielle sucked a breath in through her teeth with the first touch, her back arching as much as her bonds would allow. The second lash had her crying out. From there on she screamed with each touch of the whip until there was nothing between her cries but ragged gasps for breath.

145

Her clothing, already close to being rags, parted as easily as the pale skin beneath. The guard struck with a clinical accuracy, lashing the same place until blood began to flow and then moving upwards an inch or two and beginning again.

"Bastard's climbing the ladder," Killen breathed.

"What?"

She looked at him, disgust clear in her eyes. "That whip is designed to cause pain, it's not a weapon. It won't draw blood unless you really try for it. Rast is cutting her on purpose. They call it the bloody ladder. It's a sick game. He's doing this for fun."

Wynn looked at those closest to them. They stood in silence, most faces impassive though a few winced at each stroke of the whip.

Marielle had fallen silent. She hung limp from her bonds as the blood coursed down her back.

"Enough!" Garl called out and the large guard glanced over at him with a frown, looking back to Marielle with obvious frustration. The red, angry slashes ran the length of Marielle's back, stopping just below her shoulders. The ladder was incomplete. He raised the whip once more.

"I said, enough!" Garl snapped. "Cut her down. It's time our little heckler paid his price."

Marielle fell into a boneless heap and Rast took up his position with a broad grin. The man who had called out had his face pressed to the whipping post but his fear shone out in the way he stood, knees sagging and legs visibly shaking.

Curk took the first lashes without a word, hissing as the lash drew its first blood. The guard grinned broadly as he began a new stroke.

"I'm going to cut a ladder in your back, boy," the guard snarled out between lashes. "Carve you up."

The movement wasn't much. Curk was bound too tightly by the wrists for him to slump down away from the lash. Instead he lifted himself up slightly, rising up on the ball of one foot and twisting as the lash fell. The red weal was barely bleeding but it ran through one of the existing cuts, ruining the ladder.

"Little bastard!" the guard hissed. He lowered the whip as he stared at Curk's back in dismay. Emotions played in a slow parade across his face, but the anger grew until it outshone the rest. The next blow was brutal, landing with as much force as the guard could muster. He gave Curk no time to rest, ignoring his screams as he rained down the strikes in a torrent. This was no measured punishment, this was rage.

It took the blood pooling at Curk's feet for Wynn to realise what was happening. Though the guard seemed filled with fury, his strokes were not without control. With the same skill required for the bloody ladder, Rast was laying each strike of the whip in almost exactly the same place, carving a deep furrow into Curk's back.

The whip cut deeper into Curk's flesh and his screams grew agonised, and then hoarse, before he fell silent, sagging down as far as the bonds would let him. Garl looked on, unmoved as the whip cut through bloody flesh. He gazed out over the crowd through narrowed eyes, settling on faces and then moving on. He stilled Rast with a word, letting the silence fall before he growled out at the faces watching him.

"Meet your tally."

CHAPTER TEN

Leesha spoke first. "You're a what?"

"A priest," Kharios repeated himself.

Travis pushed past Leesha, stooping to bring himself to Kharios's eye level. "What are you doing down here then?"

"It's a punishment," Kharios said flatly.

"I can tell that!" Travis laughed. "What the hell could you have done to get sent back to this hole again?"

"Does it matter?" Leesha put in. "Who gives a shit? If we get a Listening we can get out of bloody blackwork. We can get some real gear, maybe even build the crew up."

"Look at her, getting all ambitious!" Travis snorted, grinning at Kharios. The smile fell as quickly as it appeared. "We don't know how we even get a Listener? What do any of us know about them? They need a priest but who knows what else they might want? What if they'll only work for the marked? Except for Arri here, there's not a marked face in here."

Leesha shrugged into the silence. "We can try," she said. "It's the priests that care about the mark, not the Listeners. What's it to them?"

"You're right," Travis said, nodding. "Arri could go and talk to the Listeners. See what they say."

"Kharios," Kharios corrected, in a voice robbed of all its strength. "Why does it have to be me? Send Bryant or Lumpet."

Travis frowned, sharing a look with Leesha. "What's the problem?"

Kharios flinched under the weight of their gaze, sinking back against the wall of the cottage. Facing the Listeners. Alone. His hands curled into fists, clutching at the fabric of the blanket.

Leesha's soft voice fought through to him. "Would you like me to go with you, Kharios?"

His look said enough, and some it probably shouldn't have.

"Not now, though," Travis said. "You're in no state to go anywhere just yet. Get some rest. You can both go in the morning."

***

Aspiration was still waking as they made their way through the streets. Cold chimneys released the first thin wisps of coal smoke that caught in the dim, grey, light carried down from the fissure. Here and there, large chemglobes burned, pushing back the darkness.

"How did you come to be marked?" Leesha asked, breaking the silence as they walked.

Kharios gave her a look.

"Well, we have to talk about something," she said, raising her hands to ward away his expression. "Why not that? Did you ask for it? I've heard tell that some people do."

Kharios closed his eyes for a moment, shaking his head. "Not that," he muttered. "Pick something else."

She sighed and followed him through the streets. "Okay, something else then. What is it about the Listeners that bothers you so much?"

He stopped dead, looking at the older woman in genuine astonishment. The question was so outrageous he couldn't find the words for a moment. "Have you ever actually seen a Listener?" he managed finally.

She shrugged. "They don't really come near the blackworks. I've seen some from a distance over the years I suppose. Why?"

He shook his head, starting off again. "There are stories about them in the temple. They hate us as much as we hate them. They're an abomination. I can't believe the temple lets them stay here."

"Really?" Leesha shrugged away his statement. "I always thought they look rather sad. The ones I've seen did anyway. It can't be easy to survive down here, blind and alone."

149

"They're not blind," Kharios told her, his words flat and hard.

"They're not? Why bind their eyes up then?"

"Because their eyes are cut out," he replied, not looking at her. "They're not blind though."

She gave him a sideways look. "You're not making sense. You do know that, right?"

He spread his hands. "I know. It doesn't make it any less true though. You'll never see a Listener walk into someone, or trip over something. I don't know how they do it but somehow they see."

He fell silent, gnawing on his lower lip as much as the pain in his jaw would allow. Whatever was in the tea that Leesha kept feeding him dulled it to an ache but it he was never completely free of it. He toyed with it, like a child picking at a scabbed knee.

"You didn't answer my question," Leesha said.

"Are you hungry?" Kharios turned, cutting across her path as he headed towards a street vendor.

Leesha hurried after him, glaring at the side of his face as he looked over the bubbling pots.

"Any soup?" he asked the vendor and then glanced across at Leesha. "For the record, I am so sick of bloody soup."

She scowled at him in silence.

"Soup?" he asked again as the vendor looked back and forth between them.

"Not that's even close to being ready," the man apologised, looking curiously at the bandage that ran around Kharios's face.

"Broken jaw," Kharios explained, pointing to the bandage. "What have you got that's soft?"

The street vendor looked over his pots and shrugged. "I've got a thin stew," he suggested. "I suppose you could pick out the bigger pieces?"

"Good enough," Kharios told him. "You want anything?" he asked Leesha as the vendor ladled stew into a stale heel of bread.

She shook her head, still glaring at him as he handed a single iron-mark over.

"Fine," he sighed as they set off again. "You want to know what my problem with the Listeners is? They scare the shit out of me. And they should scare you too." He lifted the stew to his lips and blew on a steaming spoonful before sucking at the broth.

Kharios knew the way to the Listeners' enclave. Anyone who'd spent any length of time in Aspiration did. They were set apart from the rest of the city, close to the wall of the cavern.

Where most of the buildings in the city were clustered close together, sharing what light came down through the fissure, the Listeners huddled in the deep shadows of the cavern wall. He slowed as they passed through the last of the streets, coming to a stop at the edge of the city.

The streets of Aspiration had been formed by the buildings on either side of them, not by any real effort to build a road. Lichen and moss had been cleared by the passage of feet rather than any conscious effort. The emptiness that marked the boundary between Aspiration and the home of the Listeners was just that, empty.

Kharios looked out over the expanse. The damp, grey stone that made up much of the floor of the cavern was pitted, and broad strips of sandy mud, thick with chips of stone, cut through the field of grey. Footprints led the way to the distant camp, a narrow channel that anyone going to the Listeners must have followed.

"Is that it then?" Leesha asked. "Out there? Alone in the dark?"

Kharios nodded with a grunt. Not trusting himself to speak.

She looked back and forth between the camp and his face. "Why do they live like that do you think?"

"Nobody else will have them," he said, and forced himself to take the first step.

The air was damp and somehow colder now that they'd left the streets behind them. Though the walk was only a matter of minutes, it was long enough for both of them to feel it. Kharios clenched his teeth as tightly as his jaw would allow to stop them chattering. He told himself it was just the cold rather than anything else. The cavern bred peculiar breezes and drafts at the best of times. The first lies are often the ones we tell ourselves.

151

A low fence, roughly fashioned out of stakes and scraps of wood, bordered the home of the Listeners with a narrow entrance marked out by burning torches. A pair of dark figures stood at the entryway, bandaged faces tracking them as they approached.

"Hello?" Leesha called, as they approached. "We need to talk to someone about a Listening."

Her only reply was silence. The dark robed men stood, impassive.

Kharios shrugged in response to her confused look.

"Is there someone we can talk to?" she tried again.

"Let's just go in," Kharios suggested.

She glanced from him to the entryway with a worried frown.

"You cannot enter." The Listener's voice was flat, expressionless, as he stared at Leesha. "He must go alone. You are not welcome. You were not chosen. You have no place here."

Kharios blinked, this was unexpected. "I..."

"You go on," Leesha told him. "I can wait for you here."

He gave her a black look. "Thanks, ever so much."

Both bandaged faces turned to regard him. "What do you want here?"

"Ahhh..." words left him.

"Just tell them," Leesha said, prodding at him.

This was ridiculous. He sighed, scowling at her as he turned. "Like she said, we want to arrange a Listening."

Both Listeners nodded, it was a formal motion that was closer to a bow. "I will take you to one who will hear your petition. Follow me." One of the Listeners turned, leading the way into the camp.

Kharios looked back at Leesha as he followed. Her encouraging smile didn't help.

The home of the Listeners was unlike Aspiration in so many ways but they began with the silence. The cavern that held the city did some odd things to sound. Some noises, the sounds from the smelt works especially, seemed amplified so that they carried clear across the city. Others seemed to fracture into a thousand tiny echoes that carried the snatches of conversation, and other sounds of life, in an endless, half-

152

heard, murmur. Neither sound seemed to have carried to this place and the silence hung in the air like smoke.

The outermost row of huts was more of a screen than anything else, Kharios noted, blocking the view of the interior of the camp. None of the huts looked used, though it had been impossible to tell from the other side of the fence. Once he passed beyond them, following his silent guide, the shape of the enclave became apparent.

Orderly rows of buildings surrounded a larger central construction, visible above the rooftops. The streets took them in a broad spiral, bringing them closer to the centre of the camp. Kharios looked at the buildings as they passed. They were rude compared to even the Blackers' huts. It wasn't that they were poorly made, or unstable, just that no effort had been made to make them appealing. They were dark, low structures with small windows.

What Listeners he saw on the streets ignored him, passing him in silence. A door stood open in one of the huts and Kharios snatched a look as they passed. A low table was visible through the doorway. A chair had been pushed back away from the book and the burning candle that stood beside it.

He frowned at that before rushing to catch up with his guide. The question died on his lips as they rounded a corner and the square came into sight. A large forge stood beside the building at the centre of the square. The bellows were still and silent but the smell of burning coke still hung in the air. A circle of Listeners surrounded the forge, their sightless gazes fixed on the anvil as they stood motionless and silent.

Kharios shuddered. There was something about the scene that seemed so very wrong. A forge is born for fire, and an anvil yearns for the ring of steel on steel. Silence has no place in a forge.

The guide led him to the large building and stopped at the door. "Wait here." He didn't wait for an answer.

Kharios pressed himself close to the building, staring at the ground, at his shoes, at anything but the scene before him as the minutes passed. He glanced up as the door swung open again and all but ran inside as the Listener beckoned for him to follow.

153

An older man with a badly trimmed beard waited inside the door in a well-lit hallway. Unlike the others, with their ragged, dark bandages, his eyes were bound with a strip of clean, white linen. He smiled in welcome as Kharios entered. "Welcome," he said. "I am Narris."

Kharios faltered. "I… Kharios," he managed.

"Come." Narris waved him on, pausing to nod in response to the Listener's bow as he left.

Narris led him through narrow hallways to a small room and waved him into a chair, which was set in front of a low table covered in papers.

"Can I offer you something to eat? A drink?"

Kharios shook his head. Hospitality was not something he had expected. But then, no part of this seemed to be meeting his expectations, whatever they had been.

"Well then," Narris said as he settled himself into a chair. "What can we do for you, Kharios?"

"You know my name?" Kharios blinked.

"Narris's lips twitched. "We know many things. We listen."

"How…" Kharios stopped as the smile grew on Narris's face. "I just told you, didn't I?"

"Not two minutes ago," Narris said with a nod. "Relax, Kharios. We are not the monsters you think we are. I must confess though, having you here is something of an oddity in itself. It is rare for a novice to be returned to Aspiration and unheard of for one to seek us out."

"You're certainly not what I expected," Kharios admitted.

"And what did you think we were?" Narris asked, giving a chuckle as Kharios flushed. "You don't need to guard your tongue, I'm sure I've heard it all already. Traitors? Abominations? Is that the beginning of it?"

"That and more," Kharios admitted.

"I suspect you're being diplomatic," Narris said. "I'm sure you've been told how the Listeners are the cause of the Fall. That the Forgefather punished his followers for our pride in seeking out this power," Narris said. "Is that about right?"

Kharios winced but nodded.

"It's all nonsense of course," Narris said. "But then, I'm a lying abomination." He shrugged. "I would say that wouldn't I?"

Kharios looked at his hands, picking at his fingernails until he realised it probably made him look nervous. The man was nothing like he had expected. The realisation of what he had been insinuating was slow to come, but doubt is a seed that, once planted, needs neither light nor love to grow.

"What else would you say?" Kharios asked, eyes narrowing.

That shocked Narris, he saw. The Listener sat back in his seat as he looked at Kharios. "You *are* an interesting one," he said finally. "You would be willing to hear our story? To hear the truth of things?"

Kharios was silent for a moment, and his voice, when he spoke, came softly. "Someone once told me the truth is like a piece of paper." He reached out for one of the sheets on the table.

Narris raised an eyebrow, waiting for him to continue.

"A piece of paper is a simple thing," he said, holding the sheet up for Narris to see. "But even paper has two sides to it and the truth is never as simple as that. If you really want to understand something you need to do this." He closed his fist, crumpling the sheet. "Only then can you see that there are many sides, many faces, and all of them are part of the same truth."

Narris laughed, delighted. "Who told you that?"

Kharios grimaced before he replied. "My father," he admitted.

"Ah." Narris left it at that, taking the rest of that story from Kharios's tone.

"Well then, I would tell you that none really know the whole truth of the Fall," Narris said. "It was centuries ago; no one could truly know. What is preached in the marble halls above is a story painted as the truth. The church of the Forgefather was strong back then. Temples could be found in almost every town and city. Whole legions of priests and defenders worked with kingdoms across the nine lands, as they petitioned us for aid with this cause or that. The forges of our church produced wonders that have been unmatched ever since."

155

"And then?"

"And then came the Fall," Narris said. "Any priest of the temple would skim over the fine details, probably with some sermon on morality and the sins of men. What little we know of the truth is remarkably dull. There was no cataclysm, no day of judgement. No voice called down from the heavens condemning us all as sinners. There was only silence, but even a silence can be terrifying if it falls in the right place.

"Between one day and the next the voice of the Forgefather fell silent. Our priests could no longer hear him in the fires of their forges. Holy rituals ceased to have any meaning, defenders were unable to call on the powers they relied on in battle. In a single night our church ceased to have any meaning. It was as if the Forgefather had never been."

"What happened?" Kharios asked.

"Well now, that is the question isn't it?" Narris replied, standing and making his way to a cabinet against one wall. He produced two glasses. "Are you sure I can't tempt you with a glass of wine or something?"

"You have wine?" Kharios blurted, before he could stop himself.

Narris chuckled. "Our work is not without its rewards." He tilted a glass at Kharios. "No?"

Kharios shook his head.

"Those far above us would have you believe that the Fall happened in that single night, when we fell from grace, and when the Forgefather withdrew his blessing. That's true, but it isn't the whole of the truth. The best lies almost always have a touch of the truth to flavour them. The Fall was what happened in the months and years afterwards, as our church crumbled in upon itself. Some things we still retain. Temple smiths are still among the most skilled in the nine lands but the temple is as hollow as its religion. The priests are faithless, muttering prayers and performing rituals to a god who no longer hears them."

"And the Listeners? How do you fit into all of this?" Kharios asked as Narris made his way back to his seat. "You're not actually blind are you?"

Narris let a small curve grow on his lips, saying nothing as he took a sip. "I don't recall ever saying that I was."

Kharios gave him a look.

"All of our eyes are whole, Kharios," Narris said as he settled back into his seat. He reached to pull the linen from his face, revealing perfectly normal eyes. "We bind them so that we might listen better. Sight confuses the ears; it is a distraction that we do not need. It interferes with our work."

Kharios gaped, staring openly at the man's eyes until he caught himself. "With your work?" he said. "And what is that?"

"We listen," Narris told him, putting a peculiar emphasis on the word.

"I see," Kharios said, though he didn't at all. Better to just drop it, he decided, straightening in the chair.

"To business then," Narris said, clearly catching Kharios's shift in position. "What is it you want from us, Kharios?"

"A Listening, if one can be arranged."

Narris leaned forward, looking intently at him. "And what is it you seek?"

The question threw Kharios. Wasn't that obvious? "Gold, silver? Anything that will help get me out of here."

"That last statement has the touch of truth on it." Narris nodded. "You wish to leave Aspiration?"

Didn't everyone? Kharios bit back the obvious statement. "I don't belong down here. I have already served as an aspirant. I have gone through my training and passed my trials. I was already taken as a novice."

Narris nodded. "And yet you are returned to the mines, to Aspiration. You believe this to be some form of punishment?"

"Wouldn't anyone?"

Narris didn't answer that, scratching idly at the back of his hand. "Every coin has two faces, Kharios. I wonder if the priests that sent you back here see the other side of it. It could be that you are unfinished, half-forged. You have simply been returned to the fire."

Kharios bit back a sigh, glancing around the room. The mysticism was beginning to annoy him. "Can we arrange a Listening or not?"

157

"That was never in any doubt. We will find what you seek. If, of course, you can answer the question," Narris told him, sitting back in his chair.

Kharios reached for the marks in his pocket. "What question? I thought this was about marks?"

"No." Narris shook his head. "Many feel the need to donate but the payment for a Listening has always been the answer to the question."

"And just what is this question?" Kharios said finally.

"Why do we listen?" Narris asked, leaning forward again and watching Kharios's face.

"Why do you listen?" Kharios repeated. "That's it?"

Narris spread his hands with a smile, saying nothing.

The man's smug smile grated. "So this is like a riddle? A game?" Kharios demanded. "People's lives depend on Listenings, and you're playing games with us?"

The smile faded from Narris's face. "Those are the terms. Answer the question, if you can."

"And you're not going to give me any more than that? Why do you listen?"

Narris smiled as he shook his head, sitting back to watch.

"Can I ask questions?"

"You may ask, but I will not answer."

Kharios bit back the next few comments that sprang to mind.

"Why do you listen?" Kharios muttered to himself, ignoring the old man's smile. "That's not a question. You listen to hear, everyone does." He glanced up at Narris but the old man was giving nothing away. "The question must be deeper than that. It's not why you listen, it's the purpose behind it. It's what are you listening *for*? What is worth listening for?" He fell silent, aware he was babbling.

Why would they be listening? What is there to listen for? What is there to listen for here? Here, in the mines.

He repeated the thought out loud and stuck on the last word. "What would there be for you to listen for in the mines?"

158

"Oh Gods above…" he gasped. "You listen for that which was lost, don't you?"

Narris nodded with a sad smile.

"This is why you only deal with crews who have a novice or a priest, isn't it?" Kharios said. "Nobody else would know the answer would they?"

The old man simply looked at him, expectant.

"You listen for the voice of the Forgefather," Kharios said.

"We do," Narris confirmed. "And those faithless above, who have forgotten the truth of the Fall, curse us for it."

Kharios sank back in the chair. "And so with every priest or novice that is sent back here, and with every one that returns above, you place someone else in the temple who knows the truth."

"Just so," Narris said.

Kharios shook his head. "Why don't you tell people? Why stay down here?"

Narris sipped, at his wine, looking at Kharios over the top of the glass. "We stay because we have little choice. Those above maintain the voice of the Father is gone. That he is silent, has turned away from us. We know this to be false. The voice calls to us. We find echoes of it every time we perform a Listening. If we were somehow to leave, that would be lost. And we stay because we have no choice. Many newcomers to Aspiration believe themselves to be slaves. That is not true for us. We know ourselves to be captives."

"Why the pretence?" Kharios asked suddenly. "Why allow everyone to think that a Listening costs so much if you're willing to do it in exchange for the answer to your question?"

Narris sipped at his wine again. "We do not charge but it does help with donations if people already expect to pay a large price. That's one reason. The other is more practical. If it were widely known that we charge no true fee, we would have no time for our own work."

"That's true enough, I suppose," Kharios said with a sigh.

"What did you come expecting to pay?" Narris asked.

159

"I had no idea," Kharios admitted. "I brought everything I have." He reached into his pocket and pulled out the handful of goldmarks.

"A not insignificant sum," Narris said, looking at the marks. "So then, shall we discuss your donation?"

***

Kharios closed his eyes as he fumbled with the strap on his helmet. Ossan's thugs had done a good job with his fingers. They might not actually have broken them, but the bruising and swelling had been enough to convince Leesha that they were. Either way they were next to useless when it came to fine movements. Trying to fasten the buckle felt like he was wearing two pairs of gloves. He cursed as the strap slipped out again and jumped as he felt small fingers touch his own.

Sylam gave him a shy smile as he fastened the strap tight under his chin.

"Thank you," Kharios murmured with a smile of his own.

"You done preening yourself?" Bryant called over. The big man looked uncomfortable himself in his new gear and his free hand picked at the leather mining apron he wore.

Kharios ignored him, turning to Travis. "How many of you have been into the mines before?"

"Only me," Travis admitted. "And that was so long ago that it barely counts."

Kharios nodded, looking around at the others. "Once we get inside, stay close. We're in no rush." Their fear was clear on their faces. Leesha and Sylam wore it openly. Bryant's was poorly concealed behind his contempt as he sneered at him. Only Lumpet and Travis seemed unconcerned.

"Lead the way then, priest," Travis nodded. "Let's go and find your Listener."

There was something odd about stepping into the mines again. The entrance shaft looked different somehow, though he knew it couldn't be. He left the chemlamp on his helmet dark for the time being, the light

160

from the large lamps strung on the walls was enough and his feet already knew the way.

Sylam huddled close to Leesha as Kharios talked Lumpet and Travis through the mechanism for the lift. The boy gasped once as the brake was released. It was his approximation of a scream, Kharios realised.

"It's safe," Kharios told him. "Don't worry."

He took them onwards, ignoring the muttered oaths that grew louder from Bryant the farther they went.

"You sure you know where you're going?" Lumpet asked finally. "Some of these tunnels don't look like they've seen feet in years."

Kharios glanced back, careful to look at the man's chest so the beam of his chemlamp didn't dazzle. "Yes, trust me. I spent years down here before I went to the temple. We're going to an older section but I know the way."

"Don't look like it to me," Lumpet muttered to Bryant.

Kharios ignored him, leading the crew onwards through the darkness.

"We're here?" Travis asked, as he drew to a halt.

"No," Kharios said as the others caught up. "The meeting point is quite a distance away; I would guess it's underneath the temple itself rather than the mine shafts we use now. It's probably in one of the oldest parts of the mine."

"So why have we stopped?"

"We need to cross one of the bridges in a minute. It's a bit… different," Kharios told them.

"Different how?" Bryant asked. "A bridge is a bridge, right?"

"You'll understand when you see it," Kharios told him. "Stick to the centre and don't look down."

He moved off before the questions could begin, setting a faster pace that had much more to do with forcing himself to keep going. He'd been avoiding thinking about the spider bridge since they set off.

The tunnel opened out into wide chasm. Light shone down from large chemglobes on the walls at either end of the bridge, illuminating the chasm and the walls close to the tunnel they were standing in, but little more than that. The darkness hung close to the side of the span and guarded its secrets.

"That's your bridge?" Bryant demanded. "Fuck that."

Kharios watched as the others made similar objections. He couldn't blame them. The spider bridge was a narrow span formed of twisting strands of stone woven closely together into an elaborate web formation. Even aside from the small gaps between the ribbons of stone, the span was barely wide enough for two men to stand next to each other. No railings or ropes stood in place to help prevent a fall, and the drop called hungrily to anyone stupid enough to look.

"It's not that bad," Kharios told them. "Not as bad as it looks anyway. Fifteen steps and you're across it."

"Or falling off it," Lumpet muttered, loud enough for everyone to hear. "What good is it to us anyway? There's no way we'll be able to bring carts across it. How are we going to get the haul out?"

"We won't be coming back this way when we work the site," Kharios admitted. He'd been hoping to avoid this and the chorus of protests made his reasoning obvious.

"Look, if went by the regular route we'd have stood out like a priest in a whorehouse. Anyone with one good eye can see this crew doesn't belong in here. We'd have half a dozen people following us. We get the Listening done and we can stake a claim with the Tallymasters. That's how it works down here. This is the fastest way in and out. This is the best chance we have of getting as much of this haul as we can. As it is we'll lose more than half of it."

"What?" Leesha spoke up, turning away from Sylam in shock. "Why?"

Kharios sighed. They didn't have time for this. "Because this crew is too small to work the site constantly. A normal crew down here has at least fifteen people in it that they can call on for a Listening. You work the site constantly and you've got less chance of losing so much."

"I thought you said we can stake a claim with the Tallymasters?" Leesha demanded.

162

"We can. We will," Kharios explained, sighing again. "Just because that's the way it's supposed to work, doesn't mean that's the way it does. Staking the claim will make sure we get something out of this. Enough to make up what the Listening is costing and more. We won't get it all, but we won't get anything if we don't get moving."

"Fine," Lumpet said, gesturing at the bridge. "You first."

Kharios swallowed hard. "Really?"

Bryant brayed harsh laughter. "You're joking, right?"

"Well it's just, if I fall then you don't get anything from the Listening."

Bryant snorted laughter. "If *I* fall *I* won't get anything from the listening! You brought us down here, choirboy. You cross!"

Kharios looked over their faces helplessly.

"Oh for the love of..." Leesha burst out, pushing past him. She stopped at the edge of the narrow bridge, pausing for a moment as she gauged the width, and then stepped out onto the span.

"Well, hell. If she can do it..." Bryant growled, making his own way to the span.

Lumpet followed, and then Travis, before Kharios approached the bridge. The stone had a faint greenish cast to it and the faded runes were just visible beneath the moss or lichen, or whatever it was that grew along the edges of the bridge.

"Come on!" Bryant's voice split the stillness and Kharios glared across the chasm at his smiling face.

The first step would be the worst, he knew. "Just don't look down," he whispered to himself, and placed a foot onto the latticework of stone. He kept his eyes fixed on the tunnel opposite. His eyes met Leesha's gaze for the briefest moment. Her sympathy clawed at him, raking his shame out of its dark corner. He looked away, there wasn't time enough in this life or the next to confront all of that.

He could feel the yawning depths with each step he took. The black called to him, pressing on his mind as he fought to ignore its seductive whisper.

He scrubbed hard at the sweat on his forehead with one arm, and thoughts came to him unbidden; the notion of that scrubbing somehow throwing him off balance, and sending him tumbling into the abyss. Kharios froze, the terror brought a clarity with it. Whether he had called the presence in the darkness to him or not, it was here. The Utterdark lay beneath him, waiting for a misstep.

His legs trembled and his jaw ached like it hadn't in weeks as he clenched his teeth together. The darkness whispered to him, promising release in its warm embrace. All he had to do was take a single step. Just reach a foot out into the air beside the bridge, and let it fall.

"Arri?" the voice cut through to him. He blinked, suddenly aware that he'd turned to face the edge. "Kharios, come to me," Leesha called him again. "Just follow the sound of my voice."

He took one hesitant step, and then another. The muttering grew clearer as he approached, low and insistent as Bryant and Lumpet spoke to Travis with a quiet intensity.

They fell silent as Kharios stepped off the bridge. Bryant and the others looked at him with expressions that ranged from curiosity to suspicion. Only Sylam ignored him. He stared out into the chasm, eyes locked on the darkness beneath the bridge. Kharios ignored them all, pushing past to move onward, and away from the chasm.

CHAPTER ELEVEN

It took them another hour to reach the meeting place. The narrow tunnels twisted and turned through the rock, intersecting and forming the maze known as the Spider's Web. It was an area of the mines Kharios had never actually been to, though he knew the way. This section of the mines was too old and mined out for anyone to pay much attention to. The crew had finally fallen silent after making him suffer through a barrage of questions that he'd largely avoided, as well as Bryant's mocking that he'd completely ignored.

Leesha hissed a gasp and grabbed at Kharios's arm as they rounded a corner. The Listener stood in the centre of the dark tunnel. She nodded once in greeting as her form was revealed by the light of their chemlamps.

Had she really waited here, alone in the darkness for them? Kharios shook his head at the thought.

"You're here to meet us?" he asked, speaking to break the silence rather than for confirmation.

"As agreed." The Listener gave a slow nod. "Are you certain of what you seek?"

That was unexpected and Kharios frowned as he answered. "That was all agreed with Narris."

She gave another formal nod. "Follow then," she said, and walked into the gloom. She seemed to have no problem navigating the small tunnels, despite the fact that all the lights were behind her and her eyes were bound in dark cloth. Kharios wondered at that. He'd not mentioned Narris's admission that none of the Listeners were truly blind, but watching this woman make her way through the darkness, without halt or pause, was enough to make him wonder how she did it.

The streaks of dried blood were just visible on her cheeks and, as she turned, he fought back a smile. What was it? Paint? Ink? It didn't really matter.

She stopped as they entered a larger cave, holding a hand up for silence as she approached the wall. Kharios glanced at Travis, smiling at his awed expression. The Listener stood with arms spread wide, her fingertips pressed to the stone as she muttered something too low to catch.

Kharios watched on, bored, as the others stared in wonder. The Listener moved closer, until her ear almost rested on the stone. Her eyes were bound, but that couldn't hide the surprise on her face or the frown that followed. She pulled away, shaking her head before moving back to Listen again.

"Is there some—"

"Silence!" she snapped.

She pressed her face to the stone again, whispering, listening. Listening. When she pulled her face away again, the bandage seemed darker. "Beyond this covering of stone, you will find what you seek."

"Gold?" Bryant asked, eagerness lifting his usual surly tone. "Is it gold?"

The Listener turned her face towards him. "You will find what you seek," she repeated. "Your payment must be received by dawn tomorrow." She glanced back at the rocks through her bandages, her forehead creased in a tight frown, and then pushed her way past them to disappear into the gloom.

"Well then," Bryant said, smacking his hands together. "You're the expert here, Arri. Now what?"

Kharios ignored the mocking tone and examined the rock face, letting the light of his chemlamp play over the surface. The stone seemed different somehow, less regular. The walls of the mines were far from uniform but even so, this seemed to stand apart. He placed one hand on the stone as he moved in closer, then he realised the difference. The wall wasn't solid, not in the sense of it being a single piece of stone.

"This is a rockfall," he muttered, then repeated it in a louder voice. "It's been here a long time, long enough for this crud to build up in between the stones and mask it, but it's still a loose pile. If we mine this, it'll come down on all of us."

"So what?" Lumpet demanded. "That's it? That's what we've bought? What a brilliant plan this was, Leesha."

"Shut it, Bryant," she snapped back. "When was the last time you ever came up with anything? When was the last time you actually did anything that helped any of us?"

Travis moved closer to him as Leesha continued on her tirade. "What do you think?" he asked Kharios.

Kharios gnawed on his lip. His jaw barely hurt at all now, though he wasn't quite ready to try chewing anything of any substance yet. "We need to bring all the loose stone down at once. If we pick at it, it'll just bury anyone at the bottom. I think we need a firing."

Travis nodded. "I've heard the name, I don't know the ins and outs of it though. You know what you're doing?"

"It's not that complicated. We build a bloody great fire and let it heat up the rocks for two or three days, then we throw water on it and it will bring most of it down in one go."

"Three days?" Travis gave him a look. "That long?"

Kharios nodded. "You need the heat to penetrate deep enough into the rocks or you'll just get the surface."

"That makes sense I suppose."

Kharios gave the ceiling a look. "If the roof holds, it'll be fine," he said in a low mutter.

Travis blinked. "If the what, now?"

Kharios shrugged. "The Listener wouldn't have brought us here if she thought the roof might collapse."

"And you're willing to risk your life on that are you?"

"How is it any different to a day in the Blacker's holes?"

Travis chewed on that for a moment and then nodded with a grunt. "I don't know that I'd mention it to Bryant or Lumpet though."

167

Kharios grinned. "I really hadn't planned to."

"What do we need then?"

"Wood, or something else we can burn," Kharios told him. "And lots of it."

"That," Travis said, "I think we can do."

It took the better part of the day to drag enough wood and coal into the mine. Kharios left them to it while he went through the tedious task of formalising the claim with the Tallymaster. The smeltworks hadn't changed, though the faces might have. He'd stopped paying attention to the faces long ago.

The coal was piled high against the rocks by the time he got back to the site. Travis knew what he was doing and had left large piles away from the wall to be fed to the fires as they burned down.

"Thought you'd gotten lost," Lumpet called as Kharios emerged from the tunnels. "I was about to send the runt out to look for you."

"Don't…" began Leesha, with a look at Sylam, but lapsed into silence with a sigh.

Travis shot Lumpet a warning glance. "Are we about ready then, do you think?" he asked Kharios.

"It looks like it," Kharios said with a nod. "Just one last thing." He reached down and unhooked the lamp from his belt.

"What's that?" Leesha asked, coming closer.

"It's a wrathlamp," Kharios explained, kneeling as he set the lamp on the floor and fished out flint and steel. "You've never heard of the Father's Wrath?" Kharios asked curiously.

She glanced at the others but received nothing but blank looks. "Should I have?"

"Didn't you ever wonder why we use chems for light instead of candles or lamps?"

"The chems are right here in the rocks," she said with a shrug. "Candles or lamp oil would need to come down through the Tallymasters. Why pay them when the chemikers can make light for a fraction of the cost?"

168

Kharios opened and closed his mouth a few times. "I hadn't ever thought of it like that before," he admitted. "Anyway, the Father's Wrath is something in the air that burns. Any fire might set it off and when it goes it's enough to wipe out an entire crew."

"And your little lamp will stop that, will it?" Bryant asked, moving closer to watch.

"No, but it will tell us if there's a danger of it happening."

Bryant nodded and looked on with the others as he set flint to steel and saw to lighting the wick of the wrathlamp. The fire burned with a healthy orange flame that shone through the mesh inside the lamp. Kharios looked up at the others with a broad smile. "Nothing. It's safe to light the fire."

"And if there had been something?" Bryant asked, speaking slowly as he frowned at the lamp.

"It would have burned with a blue flame," Kharios explained.

"I'm not a chemiker or a novice," Bryant said. "I know I'm not the smartest person in Aspiration by a long shot."

"And then some," muttered Lumpet, loud enough for anyone to hear.

Bryant gave the man an obscene gesture as he carried on. "So if this Father's Wrath of yours is started by fire..."

"Yes?"

"Well, wouldn't your sparks have set it off when you lit the lamp?"

Kharios glanced down at the lamp and then gave him a look of horror. Behind them, Lumpet or maybe it was Travis, started to laugh.

***

"Kharios." A finger prodded him again, harder this time, insistent. "Hmm?"

"The fire. It's your turn."

He shook himself awake, rubbing at eyes that were gritty with coal dust. "Hells demons and all their petty saints," he groaned softly. "What time is it?"

169

Leesha shook her head. "No idea. I've lost all track down here."

Kharios looked around the cave. The other members of the crew lay clustered together against the far wall. The heat from the fire, even burnt down as it must be, was oppressive and his clothes felt stiff with baked-in sweat.

He forced himself up to his feet, reaching for the flask of water as he stood.

"Where does the all the smoke go?" Leesha wondered looking up at the roof.

Kharios looked at her and then back at the sullen coals. There was little smoke rising now but even so, the air was clearer and fresher than it had any right to be. "I don't knosw," he admitted. "I hadn't really even noticed it until now. Nobody knows how far these caves and tunnels go though. We call it a mine but it isn't really. It's a cave system we just happen to mine in. There are air currents down here. I've even felt a breeze once or twice. I suppose there must be other openings leading out to the surface."

"Something like the fissure in Aspiration?"

"Maybe." He shrugged.

Leesha reached out a hand for the flask and took a sip. "How much longer do you think we need to leave it burning?"

Kharios scratched at one cheek. "It's probably had enough now. The fire's been going for what, two and a half days? Must be something close to that anyway. We may as well leave it burning until everyone else is awake though."

"It's your turn to be look-out then," Leesha said, curling up against the wall. "I'm going to sleep."

Kharios nodded, though her eyes were already closed. A quick look at the coals told him everything he needed to know. There was no way the fire would last until morning, and it certainly wouldn't produce the heat they needed for much longer.

He shovelled coal onto the fire, working his way along the length of the wall and stirring the sullen coals into life until flames flickered up to claim the fuel. Finally, he sat back out of the worst of the heat to watch. The smoke rose steadily but he immediately saw that Leesha was right. It wasn't building up like it should have. Instead it seemed to be drifting up to a single corner of the cave where three surfaces met.

Kharios stooped to grab his helmet and flicked his chemlamp into life. The fire had provided most of the light they'd needed for the past few days and it had soon grown too hot to even consider wearing a helmet.

His lamp sent shafts of light through the smoke, playing over the rocks until he found the right spot. A large crack where the irregular stones met was drawing the smoke out. A good thing too, he realised. He hadn't even thought about the smoke. If not for the crack drawing it out, they could all have choked to death.

The thought brought its own worries along with it. What was he doing? Getting a Listening might mean a better life for Travis and his crew, but what did it mean for him? Was it really going to give him any real chance of getting back into the temple? Did he even want a return to the temple? No, he decided. What he really wanted was to get out.

"Baby steps," he whispered to himself. "Do this first, then we'll figure out what comes next."

He sat, chin resting on his knees as he hugged his legs close to him, watching the flames. Eventually he slept.

"Some bloody watch you are," Lumpet grumbled as Kharios's eyes fluttered open. "Three days of tending this fire and then you go to sleep on your watch?"

Kharios looked in panic at the flames but the coals were still burning fitfully. There would still be more than enough heat rising from them to keep the wall from cooling.

Kharios looked back to Lumpet who now wore a broad grin. "Bastard," he muttered.

Lumpet chuckled and held a hand out to help Kharios up. "So now what, choirboy? What do we do next?"

"Now," Kharios said as he looked around at the others. "We throw the water and be ready to run like hell."

171

It had taken hours of work to drag the water through the tunnels. Ten large buckets stood in the tunnel beyond the cave, covered with lids and shielded by the wall from the worst of the heat. They carried them into the cave as quickly as possible but even the small respite from the fire made the heat hit like a physical blow as they came back in.

"Remember," Kharios called out. "It all has to be done at once, or this won't work. Try to aim for the section just above the fire. We throw two buckets each and then we get clear."

Bryant shook his head, muttering something to himself. The others just looked beaten. The heat had taken it out of all of them. Three days of sleeping rough and tending the fire had taken its toll.

"Ready?" Kharios called out, and five hands lifted the heavy buckets. "Now!"

The water hit the rocks and coals both and great gouts of steam flew up. "Again!" called out Kharios. There wasn't time to gawk. The second load of water crashed into the rocks and a deep cracking noise tore through the cave. The sound was felt as much as it was heard. Some sounds bypass the ears and speak directly to the legs. Kharios was already moving by the time the others had turned to flee.

The crash of tumbling rocks began before they made it out of the cave. The noise pushed at them, carrying them along with the clouds of dust, smoke, and ash that followed them into the passage.

Travis was the first to move, pulling himself away from the wall they huddled against. He moved slowly, making his way out to the centre of the tunnel and peered into the cave. "Well, son," he said as he looked back at Kharios. "It looks like you broke it."

The weakened rocks had collapsed, sagging down and then flowing like water across the cave until half of the floor had been covered.

"Great gods above!" Bryant's voice came from behind them as he made his way into the cave.

Kharios picked his way through the rubble, eyes scanning the rock as he went. Mining is a matter of volume, tons of rock might yield only a thimbleful of gold. He knew this, but even so, most of the rocks he saw were plain and dark. No ribbons of quartz ran through them, no tell-tale signs showing where gold or silver might be lurking. Worry went to seed in a quiet corner of his mind and quietly put down roots.

The silence grew behind him as the others picked over the rocks until Lumpet spoke up. "I'm no expert, Arri, but this is pretty much all plain rock. There's not even much iron ore in this lot so far."

"Maybe it's deeper in," Travis told him.

"This is 'deeper in', Old man," Bryant bit off the words. "Where's the gold, priestling? You promised us a fortune. There's barely anything fucking here!"

Kharios didn't turn. He couldn't have met the man's eyes even if he wanted to. His lips parted and then closed again. What was there to say? This had been his idea, and he'd failed them all.

"What's that?" Leesha asked, pointing to the recess the firing had carved in the rocks.

Kharios followed her pointing finger, letting his chemlamp shine into the hole.

"It's a bloody hole, woman," Lumpet sneered. "What does it look like?"

Leesha's expression was more scathing than any words could hope to be. "Since when do holes have fashioned stone blocks, Lumpet?"

She was right. Kharios clambered over the rocks, climbing over the slope to look closer. The blocks were partially obscured by the fallen stone but the small corner of the stone was clear enough.

"Careful!" Travis called. "You'll bring the rest down on us."

"If that was going to happen it probably would have already," Leesha said from somewhere behind Kharios. He barely heard her, as he pulled himself up. This wasn't a rock face; this was a wall of fashioned stone.

"What is it, Kharios?" she called over to him.

He looked back over one shoulder. "Well it was a wall. It looks like someone walled off a passage and then piled rocks here to make it all look like an old firing."

"A passage? A passage to where?"

173

Kharios didn't answer, he was already pressing closer, clambering up the rock slope that led to the hole. The rocks were still warm from the fire, though the falling stone had buried the coals, and his hands were soon slick with a paste of rock dust and water. His grip slipped as he climbed and the jagged edges cut into his palms as he pulled himself forward.

The hole was small, formed by fallen blocks. It would barely be wide enough for him to worm his way through, but the beam of light from his chemlamp shone through into the open space beyond.

"What can you see?"

Kharios glanced back down the slope. He'd almost forgotten the others were there. "Not much, I can make out a cave or something on the other side though."

"What are you waiting for then, Arri?" Lumpet called back to him. "Get in there."

"Me?"

"You're the one up there, ain't ya?"

Kharios muttered to himself as he looked back at the hole. It was going to be tight. He forced himself into the small tunnel before he could think about it too much. The hole wasn't long, it was just tight, and he wormed his way through it, reaching blindly out with one hand in front of him. The chemlamp was next to useless for the moment, shining onto the ground a foot in front of him.

The floor dropped away from him as he worked his way through. Blocks had fallen from the wall on this side as well. With no other options open to him, he slithered down over the rough stone, hands and legs spread wide against the edges of the hole in an effort to control his slide.

He crashed to the ground in a graceless flop that would have drawn laughter if he'd had an audience. Kharios let himself lie on the ground for a moment, waiting for the various parts of his body to tell him their sob stories. Other than a searing pain from his back where the roof of the hole had done its best to flay him, he seemed to have come out of it unscathed. His jaw ached, but then his jaw almost always ached.

He pulled himself to his feet, turning his head as he let the chem-lamp pass over the walls. The tunnel was plain. The walls were smooth, obviously worked stone that formed a shaft extending beyond the reach of the chemlight.

What was this place? Kharios followed the light, trailing one hand on the wall as he went. The darkness was oppressive. It combined with the stillness of this place and pushed down at him, making him somehow smaller and diminished.

The tunnel turned abruptly, and opened out into a wide chamber filled with crates and chests. Statues lined the walls, defenders stood ready with hammer and shield in amongst the crates, heads bowed and eyes closed as if deep in thought. A set of steps led up to an altar complete with anvil and forge, but it was the walls themselves that stopped him.

The carvings were intricate. Foot wide squares that ran from floor to ceiling depicting glyphs and rituals. He drifted between the chests, not really even aware that he was walking as he made his way closer to the altar. The walls here were lined with low racks covered in tools and imple-ments of forging. He turned at a distant crash, reminded suddenly of the others and cast a last look around the room, drinking in the discovery.

"Kharios?"

"In here," he called back to Leesha. "Keep going, there's a corner."

Travis was the first to appear, stepping into the chamber with a low whistle. "What have we here then?"

"It's old, whatever it is," Kharios told him, nodding at Leesha's wave as she came in with the others.

"What's in the boxes?" Bryant asked, quiet for once.

Kharios shook his head. "I haven't looked yet."

Bryant went to the closest crate, prying at the lid with his pick. "Papers," he spat in disgust. "What use are bloody books and scrolls to us?"

Kharios hurried closer, taking the scroll case from Bryant's hand with exaggerated care. He turned it over in the light. "Great Father!" he breathed.

175

"So it's some scribbling," Bryant scoffed. "We came looking for gold, Arri. Where's the fucking gold?"

"You really are a stupid bastard, aren't you?" Kharios muttered, plunging on as Bryant sputtered. "This is ancient, possibly even from before the fall. This is worth more to the temple, and therefore to Garl and the Tallymasters, than all the gold you could mine in a month."

"So what is this lot then?" Travis asked. "Some sort of store? Why was it walled up like this? I mean, this wasn't just kept safe, Kharios. This was hidden."

"How do you mean?"

"Look at these boxes," the old man continued, waving a hand. "If this were a store they'd be stacked neat. They'd be put in some kind of order so you could find stuff." He shook his head. "No, this lot has been shoved in here quick and then walled up. What in the hells have we wandered into here?"

Kharios sucked at his lip for a moment. "I don't know. I know this much though, I don't care. If we do this right, this find is worth a fortune."

"For paper and a couple of old statues?" Bryant blurted.

"If we can get them out to Garl, yes."

"That raises an interesting question, Kharios," Leesha said, looking up from the open chest at her feet. "How do you plan on getting this lot through Aspiration? We'd be spotted and set on before we even got out of the mine."

"We don't," Kharios said after a moment. "We leave it right where it is. We can wall this back up and cover up the hole easy enough. We can pretend we're working on a firing gone bad while one of us goes to see Garl."

"So we sweat in here while you saunter off to the Gilded Quarter?" Bryant scoffed. "Nice!"

"Do you have a better idea?" Leesha snapped.

Bryant muttered into his beard as Lumpet snorted a laugh.

She shook her head and turned to Kharios. "Go then! What are you waiting for?"

176

***

He was the obvious choice. He knew that, but even as Kharios made his way out of the mine it already felt like he was deserting them.

"So what?" he muttered to himself. "What do you really owe any of them?"

Nothing. Everything. The answers screamed out of the quiet corners of his mind.

The scroll case felt cold against his skin where he'd stuffed it down inside his loose shirt. It was poor concealment but it wasn't as if he had many options.

He slowed his pace at a noise from up ahead. Blundering into another crew was not what he needed. A miner alone wasn't a common sight, and for good reason. Miners worked in crews, the job just couldn't get done properly alone. A lone miner was someone with something to hide. More often than not they would be heading to, or from, a tally-cache. A lone miner was easy prey. A lone miner was dead.

The echoes of their conversation drifted back to him as he stepped over the cart tracks and pressed close to the stone, reaching up to his helmet to flick the switch that would stem the flow of chems. The light began to fade almost immediately but it wouldn't go entirely dark for hours, he knew.

Sounds do strange things in the darkness and he held his breath as he tried to decide if the voices were growing louder or softer. Louder. Shit! He eased backwards, pressing close to the wall as the light grew in front of him. The stones parted, a tiny side tunnel he had passed without noticing it was even there. He sank back into it, crouching down into the darkness.

The voices grew louder, meaningless noise transforming into words and conversation. Kharios pressed the face of the chemlamp into the floor, smothering what light remained. A month ago he'd been found by miners in the blackworks after Ossan's men almost beat the life out of him. Now here he was hiding in the darkness from the very kind of

177

people who'd saved his life. Hiding in the darkness so he could fight for a chance to return to the temple, to the corruption and the light. All in an effort to leave both temple and mines behind him.

His lips twisted into a grimace and he shook his head at himself. What had he become?

He moved in fits and starts, rushing through the silence until the sounds of others had him darting into corners and tiny passages. His pace increased once he reached the main shaft. It was too busy to hide in, and generally considered safe territory. A lone miner would still look out of place, but here it would simply raise eyebrows rather than raise fists.

Kharios ran up the shaft, his breath coming in pained gasps through a throat already choked with dust. This had taken too long already. The firing would attract attention no matter what they did. The smell of the coal burning had been filtering through sections of the mine for days. There wouldn't be many crews who hadn't heard about the Listening paid for by a Blacker crew, but even those that hadn't heard would have noted the smell of coal smoke by now. He'd placed a claim with the Tallymasters but that wouldn't mean a thing to the most desperate crews.

The lift was crowded. At least one full crew was jammed into the space, with men pressed to the wooden walls until there was barely room for those working the chains to move. He pressed against the wall, the scroll case jutting into his armpit as he turned his face to the corner. The bandages running around his jaw would draw their own attention as it was.

He filed out of the lift with the others and broke from the pack, rushing through passages and up the central shaft. Twice he drew curses as he scrambled past a train of carts hauled by sweating crews. And then he was free. He burst out of the mines into the dim light of Aspiration and stumbled to a halt looking around in confusion.

A moment later he was laughing at himself. What had he expected? There was nobody following him, nobody chasing him. A miner on his own looked out of place and would draw attention in the depths of the mines but, out here, or in the upper levels of the mines it was nothing special. He glanced back at the shaft leading into the darkness and made his way into Aspiration.

Not for the first time the oddness of Aspiration struck him. The very worst homes were those of the Blackers, on the far side of the great cavern. Blackers Town was its own bubble of poverty. A boil on the backside of Aspiration. It somehow didn't follow the norms of the rest of the city.

All the wealth in this strange place flowed from the mines and the smelt works, yet the closer you were to them, the poorer the area. Kharios passed the huts that were cobbled together from scrap stone and wood, or whatever was left over that others didn't want. These shacks were held in one piece by luck and a prayer. He shook his head and moved on to the more affluent sections of the city.

The Keepers' presence increased almost immediately, as if there were a mark painted on the streets beyond which there was no point patrolling. He felt their eyes on him as he hurried through the streets, keeping to the edges pressed close to the buildings.

It got worse the closer he drew to the Gilded Quarter. It took him ten minutes to realise he still wore the miner's helmet and apron. Most of those who lived and worked in this sector had rarely seen the inside of the mine and certainly wouldn't step foot in it now.

Kharios shrugged off the stares and looks of affronted disgust and turned onto Gilden Lane. The Golden Manse was just visible at the end of the road and Kharios began to relax. The hardest part of all of this would be convincing Garl to let him speak to a priest but just getting here had been half the battle.

He took a deep breath and moved on, and then staggered to a halt as Keepers blocked his path.

"Where do you think you're going, scrubber?"

Kharios took in their dark, polished leathers, and the dark iron helmets that covered their faces, as well as the black polish wood of their sticks before he spoke.

"I want to seek an audience with the Sefin," he said, keeping his eyes downcast.

"Oh do you now?" the Keeper said, nudging his companion with a snort. "And just why would he waste his time with a scrubber like you?"

Kharios paused for a moment before he spoke. "That's not your real question," he said. "Your real question is; why should you bother escorting me to him?"

The Keeper's face was hidden behind the helmet but Kharios could practically feel him bristle as he pointed a warning finger at him. "You cheeky little shit!"

"And the answer is because it's going to be worth your while, and it's far easier than patrolling all day," Kharios said quickly.

The Keeper's finger lowered slightly. "You better have something worth hearing or the mines will feel like a bloody picnic to you."

The Keepers took up position either side of him and marched him through the crowded street to the golden manse. The square was busy, filled with the colourful market stalls that catered to the pampered elites that populated this district. Kharios didn't bother to hide the disgust on his face as he looked around at them. Maybe one in ten of these people were marked, most had never set foot in the temple. They earned their marks and paid their tally by pandering to Garl and catering to the gilters. They not only accepted this life; the mine, the tally and its whippings – they actively supported it. They perpetuated it.

He spared a glance at the whipping post as the Keepers led him up the steps and into the manse.

"Don't worry, scrubber," one Keeper told him. "There's a fair chance you'll get a better look at it later."

The manse was larger than it looked from the outside and Kharios soon realised that it must be connected to several other buildings. The Keepers led him through layers of security; past guards and checkpoints, through secretaries and administrators, until Kharios was led into a small side room.

180

A fat man in plain clothing sat behind a low desk. He looked up as they entered, setting the pen down carefully beside the large ledger.

"Yes?" The word drifted out on the back of an exasperated sigh.

"This one says he needs to speak to the Sefin, Argus," the Keeper said, shoving Kharios forward.

"Really?" A thousand petty inconveniences and interruptions flavoured Argus's sigh. "And just what, do you think, the Sefin might want to discuss with this young man?"

The Keeper shifted his weight, feet restless on the thick rug.

"Dear Father, please tell me you at least know what this is about?"

"He just insisted he needed to talk to the Sefin." The helmet hid his face but the Keeper's tone made his worry clear enough.

The administrator pushed the chair back and clambered down to the ground. It was a laborious process made to look more awkward by his dwarfed legs. "I do hope you have more between your ears than this one," he muttered as he waddled closer. "Just what is it you want," he paused, taking note of the brand on Kharios's forehead. "Aspirant?"

"I need to speak to someone from the temple," Kharios said. "A priest."

Argus waddled closer, his not inconsiderable bulk somehow magnified by his diminutive height. "You're not in the temple, aspirant. This is a mine. There aren't any priests with authority down here."

Kharios met the man's eyes. "I need to speak to a priest. I've found something they will want to see. I'm sure something can be arranged."

Argus raised an eyebrow. "So certain are you? And you want the Sefin to arrange this for you? He's hardly your errand boy, aspirant."

"They will want to see this," Kharios said and reached into his shirt for the scroll case. The dwarf moved with surprising speed, darting backwards with a look of panic while the Keepers cursed and fumbled for clubs that were tucked away in their belts. Kharios pulled out the scroll case and froze.

"Gods above and below, boy," Argus breathed. "You nearly got your head pounded in then, and I doubt your little tin hat would have saved it." He shook his head with an explosive sigh. "This is not the place to be reaching for hidden things. Let me get a look at that," he said, reaching out a hand.

Kharios snatched the scroll case out of reach, clutching it to himself for a moment. Argus gave him a wry look and glanced at each of the Keepers. The message was clear enough, if Argus wanted it badly enough he would have it taken.

Kharios uncoiled slowly, handing the scroll case over.

The dwarf turned it over slowly in his hands. "This is... Where did you get this?"

"In the mines, there's a sanctum or something like it."

"Where exactly?"

Kharios paused long enough for the administrator to look up at him before he smiled.

"Not as much a fool as I thought then," Argus grunted and nodded. "I think we can probably arrange for you to speak with the Sefin. It seems that perhaps you do have something to discuss after all."

He stepped past Kharios, making his way to the door without looking back. "Well, come on then!"

Garl, the Sefin of the mines of Carnath, lolled in a chair gnawing at a chicken leg as he read papers with his free hand. He glanced up as Argus escorted Kharios into the room and looked back to his papers. The dismissal was so total that Kharios was taken aback for a moment. In one glance the man had examined him and rejected him as anything worthy of his attention.

"Why have you brought this here, Argus?" he spoke without looking up from the paper.

"I believe he has something worthy of your attention, Sefin," Argus replied in carefully level tones.

"I have people for this kind of thing, Argus. Petty, little people with small minds for small details." He peered past the edge of the paper with a smile that was clearly more for himself than for Argus. "That's why I keep you around. They don't come any better qualified than you, do they?"

182

"No, sir. That much is certainly true," Argus replied, unruffled.

A flash of annoyance passed over Garl's face and he pulled himself up in his chair. "Fine," he said with a sigh. "What is it?"

"The aspirant discovered this in the mines." Argus moved close enough to hand the scroll case over before moving back to his position.

"Did he now?" Garl held the case, turning it over in his hands. He twisted the case open with casual abandon, pulling out the brittle scroll inside.

Kharios hissed the beginnings of a warning before he stopped himself. Garl glanced at him with a raised eyebrow before scanning the scroll.

"This is ancient, aspirant. Where did you find it?"

"In a sanctum of some kind in the mines, sir."

Garl mulled that over for a moment, eyes narrowing as he considered Kharios. "And just where is this sanctum of yours?"

"I'd rather discuss that with one of the priests, sir," Kharios said in a voice that was far more confident than he felt.

Garl exchanged a long look with Argus. "What makes you think you will have any part of that conversation, aspirant? If you refuse to give me the location, I can easily have it beaten out of you."

"I'm not a well man, sir," Kharios began. "You can see the bandages on my face that cover a half-healed jaw. I'm afraid any methods of persuasion you employ may very well kill me, and then the sanctum would remain lost."

Garl nodded, pursing his lips as he reached for the goblet that sat on a small table beside him. He sipped and held the cup to his chest as he spoke. "I'm not entirely sure you give my men enough credit there, but your point is well made. What's to stop me simply having you killed here and now? I could have the mines swept with my own men until we find your little sanctum. If we don't find it then the priests are none the wiser, are they?"

Kharios gave his own small smile. "But then, you would miss out on the rewards which the priests are bound to offer, wouldn't you? What

I have is worth far more than your mines, Sefin, and this is just a small piece of it."

Garl's eyes widened and he motioned Kharios to continue.

"You called me 'aspirant' but I'm afraid you're mistaken, sir. I've already taken and passed through the trials. I am a novice of the temple and, despite my recent fall, I know enough to say with some certainty that these scrolls and artefacts are from well before the time of the Fall. We both know how valuable these items will be to the temple."

Garl considered him in silence with dark eyes until Kharios shifted his weight, fidgeting under his hard gaze. The Sefin's eyes twitched at that and then Kharios understood. This was all a game to him. He lived and breathed power. Wealth was a secondary currency to him.

"And you wish to be the one to deliver this treasure trove to them?"

"Merely its discovery, sir. The mines and all their varied treasures are your domain."

Garl grunted. "You're hoping you can buy your way back into the temple with this." He raised a hand, stopping Kharios before he could speak. "Don't bother to deny it, it's so obvious it's laughable. And what would you have me do with the rest of your crew?"

Kharios blinked. "My crew?"

"You don't expect me to believe that you found this sanctum all by yourself, do you?"

"Well, no," Kharios conceded. "Why does anything need to be done with them?"

"This is a mine, novice. Even if we ignore the fact that this city itself has needs, the temple above us has certain expectations. I can't afford to have my people picking through the mines hoping they might find forgotten scrolls and buried treasure, when they are supposed to be mining iron and coal, can I?"

"Surely the tally sees to that?" Kharios suggested.

Garl set down the goblet with one hand as he pinched at the bridge of his nose with the other, wiping at tired eyes. "A people aren't so easily cowed... What is your name anyway, novice?"

184

"Kharios."

"A people aren't so easily controlled, Kharios. The tally serves as a basis for control but there are far more people in Aspiration than my Keepers could ever truly manage. I govern because these people accept the order that is in place. They accept that this is the way of things. Hope is an illusion, a distant ethereal dream. If you start making illusions into reality, showing them that hopes can be realised, then the whole order of things crumbles. This mine and this city crumbles. The temple itself, crumbles. You do understand what it is I'm saying, don't you?"

Kharios was quiet for a time, hoping he'd misunderstood. He owed a debt to Leesha and Travis, to all of them. How much of a debt though? How many more chances would he have? Wouldn't they do the same thing? He raised his head, hating himself as he met Garl's eyes and nodded.

The Sefin nodded at him and looked to Argus. "Make arrangements for the novice Kharios to speak to an acolyte with the news of our discovery. Take this one with you and then we will discuss the other matter."

"You're a brutal and ruthless man, Sefin," Kharios said, the loathing was clear in his voice though he wasn't sure it was just Garl he loathed.

Garl nodded, unruffled. "I am. History is full of brutal and ruthless men. They usually call them 'victors.'"

Kharios closed his eyes for the length of his sigh. With one nod he'd just damned Leesha and the rest of her crew, all for a chance to get back to the temple. All for the chance to take the first step out of this place.

CHAPTER TWELVE

The journey out of Aspiration was almost surreal. Kharios followed along behind Skerth, surrounded by Keepers as they climbed the winding passage that led to the heavy doorway blocking the passage out of Aspiration. The Listeners tracked their approach, watching through bound eyes. They opened the locks without comment, reaching for keys that hung from chains around their necks before sliding open the grate in the door.

The acolyte waiting on the other side took the scroll case, and held it almost reverently as he looked it over, before handing it back to Kharios with visible relief.

He looked at Skerth and nodded to acknowledge a task completed. "You may leave. I will see the novice to where he should be."

Skerth grunted and glanced at Kharios, clearly weighing things. "Not many leave the mines twice. Don't come back again."

The acolyte led him away, up through the passage that would take them into the temple. It felt good to be back, despite what it might have cost – and Kharios was working hard not to think about that. He was back in the temple and that was a first step. That had to be worth the cost, any cost.

They passed through the lower portions of the temple, through halls and galleries that were as familiar to him as a mother's touch. It took several minutes but slowly he became aware of the direction they were taking. Not up to the upper temple, the archpriests and the Great Forge, but rather through passages he had hoped never to see again.

Somehow, on some subconscious level, Kharios had known it would be him. He was passed from acolyte to acolyte, and past subdeacons who marvelled at the discovery, all of whom peppered Kharios with questions but, in the end, it was a priest he was destined to see – and somehow Kharios had known from the start who it would be.

He'd spent months learning about the history of the church, of the Fall and how the numbers of the faithful had plummeted as the temple was attacked time and again in an orgy of plunder, until it was eventually razed to the ground. The number of modern-day priests was a tiny handful compared to the heyday of the church, but they still numbered in the hundreds. Despite all of that, somehow Kharios had known who he would be taken to see.

Ossan received them in his library. Kharios balked against that same stifling combination of heat and the smell of dust, books, and old wine. Once it had been the scent of study, a soothing aroma that helped put him in the right frame of mind to read. Now it was just stuffy and almost suffocating.

Ossan sat behind his desk, looking up with cold indifference as Kharios was led in. He looked pointedly at the scroll case Kharios held and reached out a hand without a word.

Kharios stepped forward to hand him the artefact, stepping back out of the man's reach as if he might grab for him. Ossan took the scroll case between his hands, turning it over and over with his fingertips as he examined it. When he did finally speak, he did so without looking up. "You know, I must confess, I didn't expect to see you again." His voice was low, dry, and only mildly curious. "I've thought about you a lot in the time you've been gone. It was a regrettable series of events." He looked up then, the familiar lines of his face set into a mask of contrition. "I think we could agree that there was fault on both sides, don't you?"

Kharios said nothing. There were no words to describe what he felt for this man. The anger raged within him in a swirling welter of emotions. Rage touched bitterness, touched regret, but all were smothered and tainted with his shame. His lip twitched at the corner of his mouth as his fingernails bored into the flesh of the hands he held clenched behind his back.

Ossan, if he noticed anything at all, was unmoved. "I think perhaps we should just move on." He smiled then, the same fatherly, exuberant, smile that had greeted two young novices so long ago. "And this!" he raised the scroll case. "This is a thing of marvels. All these long years we have had men toiling in those mines and nothing like this has ever been seen before. We never even suspected that any of the great temple had survived. This rude replacement that we now worship in, was cobbled together from the stones that fell, you know?"

Kharios nodded in silence. It was a tale he'd heard too many times before.

"Is this the only artefact?"

"No," Kharios croaked, speaking for the first time through a throat too long silent. He swallowed and licked his lips. "No," he tried again. "There is a sanctum, a room full of crates, boxes. There's even a forge-altar."

Ossan's eyes widened for a moment and then narrowed in thought. "How is it that it remained undiscovered for so long?"

"It was concealed," Kharios told him. "Hidden, I suspect. The sanctum itself was walled off and then made to look like the natural stone of the mine."

"And you just chanced onto this?" Ossan laughed, delighted. "Either you are favoured beyond any priest, Kharios, or you have the luck of ten devils and all their petty saints!"

Kharios managed a thin smile.

"Oh, for the love of the Father, boy." Ossan hauled himself out of his seat, snatching at a cane. "Have a drink and relax!" He made his way across the study. Bottle kissed glass and Ossan held out a brandy.

Kharios took the glass and sipped as Ossan smiled, accepting the apology that Kharios hadn't offered.

"There are many ways a novice can distinguish themselves but this is the noblest," Ossan told him, raising his drink in salute. "Nobody has performed such a service to the temple in my lifetime. Our names will be remembered, Kharios. Have no doubt about that. Our names will be remembered always."

Kharios drank, swallowing the vile stuff down before he could choke on it. He spluttered anyway, at least it gave him an excuse not to meet the old man's eyes for a moment.

"Now then," Ossan said, setting his glass down on a side table. "To the business of it all. How many artefacts would you say there are? Work enough for two men to carry? Three?"

Kharios laughed then. The old man still hadn't the faintest clue what he was being given. "No, Father. You'd need closer to twenty men and even then they will need several trips."

"Twenty!" Ossan sank back down into his chair. "Gods above and below, Kharios. And all of it is from before the Fall?"

Kharios spread his hands. "I didn't really have time to look. Finding anything of worth in the mines isn't the issue, it's keeping it."

Ossan gave him a sympathetic look that set Kharios to carving holes through his palms again. "I know, Kharios. You aren't the first person to rise from the mines you know?"

Kharios staggered back a step. "Did you...?" he breathed.

Ossan burst out laughing. He exploded into the kind of laughter that bends you double and robs you of the power to do anything but gasp breaths as your eyes tear. "Gods no, my boy. Not me. That's not what I meant at all!"

"Of course." Kharios's voice was flat. For the briefest moment he'd allowed Ossan in. The shock of thinking the old man had once suffered in the mines had brought his barriers down, but now they slammed back into place with the finality of a cell door.

"Well then, for now you can resume your duties as my novice. The cell is already prepared for you. Tomorrow you and I will supervise the recovery of the artefacts and we shall begin."

"Begin?" Kharios repeated.

"Begin the task of going through this trove of treasures, Kharios. I don't think you truly comprehend the opportunity this gift has given us. Tomorrow, I expect you might feel differently."

189

***

Kharios let his arms spread out from his body as he walked, brushing his fingertips over the chests and crates that filled Ossan's large storage room.

"Just tremendous!" Ossan said for the second time as he carefully removed scroll cases from a chest. He glanced back at Kharios. "Pull the fluff from your mind, boy. We have a great deal to do and little time in which to do it."

Kharios raised an eyebrow which drew a tut from Ossan as he shook his head. "You don't think the Three are going to allow these treasures to remain here do you? We have probably less than three weeks to examine this horde before they claim it."

"But…"

Ossan stopped him with one raised finger. "Oh, they will still allow us access, I'm sure, but it will be under their terms. Under their over-sight. I'd rather not wade through half a hundred stuffy priests to read the scroll I held in my hands yesterday."

"What other choice is there?"

"What choice is there?" Ossan snorted as he unrolled the ancient parchment. "None, of course. The Three will do as they will, unless I can persuade them otherwise. All the more reason to use the time we have." He lowered the scroll to look at Kharios. "Now if you can find the time, I'd appreciate some help here!"

Kharios did his best to hide his glower. Just being near the man made him want to grab for his throat, squeezing until the flesh gave way under his fingers and his face turned purple. Ossan was a means to an end though, it helped if he kept telling himself that. Whilst he would cheerfully beat the sick old bastard to death with the scroll he was holding, this discovery gave him the best chance of escaping him.

"Bring this chest for now," Ossan told him, tapping at the raised lid. "I'll have more brought up as we need them."

Kharios grunted as he lifted, following the old man out through the door and up towards the library.

190

Ossan settled in behind his desk with the single scroll he'd taken with him, leaving Kharios standing beside the chest he'd carried.

"You can start by seeing what has been discovered here," Ossan told him over the top of the scroll. "See if you can categorise things a little."

Kharios blinked.

"What did you expect, Kharios?" Ossan snapped. "You've managed to crawl out of the hole I put you into. Well done, I'm very impressed. Has it occurred to you though, that now that your hoard has been recovered you're of little use to me? I can have you returned to the mines just as easily as I let you out. Make yourself useful."

Kharios reached for a handful of scrolls and sat at a small side table. Reading in silence. The tension still hung in the air and several times he glanced up from the texts to find Ossan's gaze on him. The next day was no better.

Categorising the writings was not as simple as he had imagined. The temple script had changed only slightly in the centuries the scrolls had been in their cave, but the syntax and word usage made every other sentence into a riddle. At first he had hoped that the chests were grouping the books and scrolls by subject or by the authors themselves. Before long it had become clear that they had been thrown together with no apparent thought given to order.

The scrolls were the worst. The best of them were brittle and faded but many crumbled to pieces as soon as they were opened. Ossan's cries of dismay were too often matched by his own until the old priest threw the tatters down in disgust and announced that Kharios would examine them from that moment on.

The books seemed to have preserved better. Whether it was something to do with the fact the pages lay flat, pressed together under the weight of other books, or if was down to the humidity levels of the cave, he had no idea. Whatever the reason, Ossan seemed to be having better luck with them and Kharios cast black looks at the priest as he read.

"Sacrifice," the old man muttered.

"Father?"

Ossan looked up and nodded at the book he held. "Just more of the same," he told Kharios. "Cryptic hints. 'The Father's voice is found through sacrifice.'" He shook his head. "It's all like this. Nothing solid. Nothing I can use or be fully understood."

By the third day they had moved into Ossan's study and by the end of the week a full third of the room was covered by chests and crates of books. Kharios sat perched on a stool as he hunched over his small side table.

"This is ridiculous," he muttered to himself, pushing back from the table.

"Did you say something?" Ossan asked without looking up.

Kharios opened his mouth, thought better of it, then pushed on anyway. "I said that this is ridiculous. There's simply too much material here for the time we have."

Ossan sat back, fixing him with a cold gaze. "Do you have a more effective solution, novice?"

"I... It's just, I would have thought maybe some acolytes might be able to assist."

"Have you performed any of the rituals since I allowed for your return from the mines, novice?" Ossan pressed on as Kharios opened his mouth to speak, smothering the younger man's words with his own. "Have you worked the forge? Called iron? Have you restocked the supplies of coal or kindling? Have you, in fact, done any of the many duties you know must be attended to by novices or acolytes each and every day that passes?"

Kharios shook his head, mute.

"And do you suppose, that just maybe, there might be a reason for that, novice? That perhaps yours is the only mind, yours are the only hands that I can spare to dedicate to this task? That perhaps a level of discretion is required so that this research might continue?"

Kharios looked up, fighting down the flush that stained the portion of his cheeks visible beyond the bandages that still bound his jaw. "Discretion? I thought the Three were allowing this?"

"The Three are permitting me the honour of sifting through the detritus for gems worthy of their attention. I will decide what is worthy of sharing. That is my decision. Mine alone. I am permitting you the honour of assisting me. Unless there is somewhere else you would rather be, novice? Somewhere darker, perhaps?"

Kharios's eyes widened and he shook his head wordlessly before he bent his head back to the scrolls.

"A study nook, is what I meant, Kharios," Ossan said after a moment. "I've always found it best to study without distractions."

He didn't trust himself to look up. The priest's threat still hung heavy in the air no matter how he had tried to diffuse it. Ossan's veiled threat had just reminded him of the mines and of the people he'd left behind. He'd abandoned them to whatever fate Garl had decided upon, all as a means to further his own ends. How was he any better than Ossan? His voice was barely above a whisper as he spoke. "Perhaps you are right, Father."

They worked alone after that, Ossan in his study and Kharios in his novice cell. The already small room became uncomfortably cramped as the books and scrolls slowly took over. At first he tried to keep them confined to the crates, stacked first in one corner, and then outside of his curtained doorway as the pile grew. Soon, however, it had become clear that he needed to reference things he'd already read, and the pile of books on the small table grew until it spread and now covered half of the bed. Kharios was cocooned in a chrysalis of his own making, formed of notes and ancient parchment.

The search was maddening. The language was confusing and too often led him in circles as one meaning was eclipsed by another until he lost track of where it had taken him. As if that wasn't enough the text seemed to break off, frequently in the middle of a paragraph, continuing with a new line of discussion that had no relevance to what he had just read.

Despite all of the frustration, the reading was addictive. The texts assumed the reader knew rituals and church doctrine that he had never heard of, and the hints and snatches of knowledge were enough to keep

193

him tantalised. There was… something hidden behind all of the words he'd read. Mentions of the Father's voice calling from the flames or from the ring of hammer on steel were present in almost everything he read but there was something more. It was almost as if there was something just out of his grasp. A concept that danced around the edges of his understanding, delighting in his clumsy snatches at it.

Kharios sighed, setting the book down on his blankets and marking his place with a scrap of paper. He arched his back, knuckling at his aching muscles as he let out a deep, rasping, sigh and stumbled to his feet.

He lurched to one side before he was really fully upright, catching himself with one flailing hand on a wall as his foot flopped uselessly underneath him. Snorted laughter turned to curses as the numbness faded and the tingling of pins and needles began.

"Shit! Shit! Shit!" He gasped as he hopped and lurched out of the cell and into the long hallway that led towards the kitchen.

The pain had gone long before he arrived, seemingly taking the ache from his back with it as it passed. The old servant looked up at him as he rounded the corner and entered the kitchen.

"I have to admit you are one person I didn't expect to see again," Fen said, though no surprise showed on his face. "You want some of this?" He tilted the clay mug at Kharios.

Kharios nodded with a smile. "Please."

The cook hauled himself out of his chair and went to the kettle. "What happened to your face?" he asked as he took down a cup from the shelf.

Kharios winced, unsure how to answer. "A parting gift, shall we say."

Fen grunted. "Should've learnt your lesson the first time around, I'd say." He poured hot karas through a thin fabric strainer and handed Kharios the cup. "I might have something here for you, actually."

"Oh?" Kharios pulled up a chair and blew on the steam rising from the cup as Fen rummaged through shelves, taking down pots and jars.

"Found this one on the floor, down in the stores," Fen said, turning. "Don't know why I kept them really. I never expected you to come back. Never expected you to be alive, to tell you the truth."

He held his hand out and dropped the rings onto the table. One gave the dull clack of iron but the other made the clear chime of copper.

Kharios reached out, taking the rings and turning them over in his hands. "This is mine," he said, sliding the ring of iron over one finger. "I never mastered copper though."

"That's not what the master said," Fen told him, leaning into the table and wrapping his hands around his mug. His voice lowered, though there was no one else to hear. "I took that one to him." He nodded at the iron ring on Kharios's hand. "Asked what I should do with it. He told me to get rid of it, and this one too. He had it all ready for you. Seemed genuinely sad about the way things worked out with you both."

"Yes, I'm sure he was all cut up about it," Kharios said, shaking his head. "He had his thugs take to me with a club, Fen. They broke my jaw. They damned near broke my hands too."

Fen shook his head. "Best not to rake over it, son."

Kharios sat back with raised eyebrows. "Just ignore it then? Pretend it never happened?"

Fen sighed hard. "For a bright lad you are one stupid little bastard, you know? You didn't learn a damn thing from this did you? Maybe you need a few more knocks with a club to get the message. Ossan owns you. The church owns you. Unless you find a way out from under him, you'd best just do what you're told. There are worse things than a few knocks on the head, boy."

Kharios gave the old man an incredulous look and his mouth closed slowly. He sat back and fell silent for a long moment before he spoke again. "Why do you stay?"

Fen shrugged. "It's easy work. It keeps me fed, dry, and warm. There's not much else in this world for an old man on his own."

"But to just sit back and watch all this? To just ignore everything Ossan…" He stopped himself as Fen met his eyes.

195

"There are worse things out there, Kharios. I do what I can, when I can. Some things you can't stop no matter what you do. Those Blacker boys didn't have much of a life anyway."

Kharios blinked. "Blackers? What Blackers?"

"Ah shit!" Fen scrubbed at his eyes with one sleeve. "You just forget I said anything. That'd be best. The master will let you know about it if he wants you to know. Time I was going anyway."

Kharios caught Fen's sleeve as the old man pulled himself to his feet. "What Blackers, Fen?"

"No." Fen shook his head, tugging his arm away from Kharios's grip. "I did too much just giving you those rings back. I'll not stick my own hand in the fire. I learned my lessons years back. It's time you did too."

***

It felt good to be back at the forge. Days of searching through books and scrolls had given him an almost permanent headache and Kharios had headed for the forge almost as soon as he woke. It hadn't been a conscious decision; it was just where his feet had taken him.

He went through the process of preparing the forge without thinking about it. His body moved slowly, his mind elsewhere while he set about clearing out the firepot, making sure the airflow from the bellows was clear and strong, and setting the kindling, coal, and coke in place.

A glint from the store beside the forge caught his eye and his questing hands tugged out a half-finished sheet of copper. It had been roughly fashioned, hammered out from an ingot but with irregular strokes that made it little more than scrap at this point. Kharios turned it over in his hands. He knew this work. He knew these hammer strokes as well as he knew his own.

Guilt rose and stole the strength from his voice, turning the whisper into a breath that barely formed the name, "Brial." His anger rose quickly, shouldering guilt aside as he cursed at himself. First Brial and now Arren.

196

He lit the forge, pumping the bellows hard and raking fresh coke over until it could stand to be left for a time. The copper ring on his finger called to him, glinting in the light of the forge. *Liar!Coward!*

Copper could be worked without much need for the forge and he set to work with cutters, shearing out rough shapes. He worked without really thinking, letting the copper tell him what it wanted to become. He took a thin iron rod, heating it until it glowed almost white, and then set it onto a thick section of wood. The iron charred and scorched its way into the wood until he had a functional channel. Pounding the cooled iron rod against the cut copper sections provided the curve he needed. He lay the copper on the glowing coals of the forge just long enough for the metal to glow before quenching it quickly in the water barrel, and moving on to the next rough-sheared shape.

What was Ossan's game? Ambition was the root of it but what was the end goal? What was it that Fen had hinted about the Blackers? Somehow Kharios doubted that this was all about restoring lost glories to the church. He snorted as he worked. Who was he to argue or criticise? His own goals had been built around getting out of the church since the day he'd arrived. Was there really anything he wouldn't do if it meant getting out? His goals might focus on getting away from Ossan to begin with, but he couldn't see a future for himself in the temple. Did he really see a life for himself devoted to the Forgefather?

He froze, suddenly aware of what he was doing as he held the shaped copper in the coals with the long tongs. The chant had stilled on his lips but he'd been Calling Iron. Had the glow of the copper been responding? For a moment it had looked... He shook his head at the thought and began the chant again, watching carefully and then he laughed at himself as he pulled the glowing metal out and quenched it. It was a meaningless ritual chant, a way of counting time, nothing more.

The copper was just faintly warm when he pulled it from the quench. The leaf was rough, needing texture and finishing, but the shape was there, calling to him. Over the hours he moved into a rhythm, churning out the leaves and shaping them, adding texture and dimension as he chanted. Calling Iron fit perfectly with annealing, just as Drawing the Flame worked well with working the copper into thin rods. He lost himself in the process, in the simplicity of its complexity, until the forge was too cold to work.

The days fell into a pattern. He would work the forge first thing in the morning until the coke died. From there the rest of the day was devoted to study. He had categorised what scrolls and books he had, and returned to Ossan for more several times over. Ossan, for his part, left him almost completely to his own devices. He had looked sick the few times Kharios had glimpsed him; grey and somehow wasted, and utterly uninterested in Kharios's progress or activities.

Kharios shifted at the small desk. It had taken over a week before he realised just how stupid he was being. Ossan had always called novices to serve in pairs and his cells were arranged accordingly. He'd crammed his own cell full of notes and books until he barely had space to sleep before he realised he could simply expand out into the empty cell beside his own.

He scratched at his hand as he read over the same paragraph for the third time. It just didn't make sense. It wasn't a matter of the language being complex or confusing. The sentence just ended, and the next one had no relation to the first. He sat back with a sigh, his gaze drifting over the page as he ran his fingertips over the ancient letters.

The books, in particular, were works of art. The calligraphy alone was something he could never hope to match, but the margins around the pages were filled with stylised pictograms and images ranging from glyphs, to flames, to landscapes.

He froze with a frown as the soft pad of one finger traced over something, a raised character on the page. His questing fingers found it again in moments. It was a small, circular image. One of maybe a hundred that ran around the edge of the page. He peered closer. It was only barely raised, a thin layer of wax perhaps, or something worked into the paper? Whatever it was he would never have found it without running his hand over the paper. He turned the page, eyes searching, but there was no mark on the other side. This hadn't simply been embossed. It had been made deliberately to be hidden.

Kharios gnawed at his lip, dimly noting that there was no pain from his jaw now. The symbol looked familiar. He stared at it, frowning as his left hand scratched at the thumb on his right.

"Form!" His own shout shocked him and he ducked down, flinching at the noise. The symbol was the glyph for Form. It was slightly different but still recognisable. He'd used it a hundred times when folding iron. He'd taught Arren the glyph himself, correcting what the boy had taken from Ossan's lessons. But why bury this glyph here? It was nothing special, one of a hundred different glyphs that might be used when working iron or steel. Why emboss it on the edge of this page with nothing to show it was significant?

He ran his hands over the page as a thought struck him. Sure enough, three other glyphs stood out. Gold, Tempering, and Will. He marked his place with a scrap of paper and flicked through the pages. Some had no raised glyphmarks at all, others had two or more. There was one section of the book that went on for thirty pages with nothing.

He flipped back to the marked page, reading quickly to where the sentence shifted. Marking his place with one finger he ran his other hand along the margin at the edge of the page, checking each glyph in turn. There wasn't another Form mark for seven pages but as he read the first word his grin grew in triumph. It carried on from where the glyph marked sentence had broken off. It made sense.

Setting the heavy book aside he reached for another, scanning for glyphmarks and then searched for the next glyphmark that matched. Kharios sank back in the chair, heart pounding. It worked. He had found the key to reading the books. He had found the reason for Ossan to keep him alive.

CHAPTER THIRTEEN

The looks started the second week of his training with Lasris. Envious glances turned to black looks as the crew set off to the mines each day and Wynn headed for Lasris's forge. Glances had become accompanied with muttering and he'd almost been glad when Terrik had clawed him back from Lasris and sent him to the mines with the others.

Five days in the mines had left him aching as a different set of muscles were abused. He'd been grateful for his bed each night.

He swore again as he stomped down the steps and made his way across to Lasris's hut. The first of his two days a week with Lasris, he'd been woken by the priest leaning over his cot and jabbing a finger into his side until he got out of bed. The priest's grey and sunken face was not something he wanted to wake up to again.

The forge sat cold and silent in the grey murk of pre-dawn. Wynn arched his back, stretching out the kinks as he watched the drizzle mist its way down through the fissure high above the Gilded Quarter.

Lasris had made it clear that he had no intention of leaving his own bed this early, and that he expected Wynn to take care of preparing the forge. Wynn rummaged around in the gloom until he located the flint and steel, and bright sparks split the darkness. He pulled gently on the bellows, chanting softly until the kindling caught. The mechanics of lighting the forge had become almost second nature to him now. He barely paid attention as he added wood, set coal to catch the flames, and forced air into the fire. His chant grew with the flames and he basked in the heat, letting the warmth soak into his flesh.

The iron rod had been left close to the anvil and he glanced at the cottage before thrusting it into the forge with a twisted smile. Let the miserable old bastard sleep through this.

Wynn pounded on the glowing white and yellow length of iron with all the glee of a child splashing in a puddle. Any joy that pure fades quickly and he soon settled down to the business of folding the iron, working the chant of Calling Iron that Lasris had been trying to teach him, to the rhythm of his hammer strokes. His voice softened as he returned the rod to the forge, finding himself almost crooning the chant of Waking the Flame to the iron as it rested in the coals before reaching it out with the tongs.

Through it all the windows to Lasris's hut remained dark, and a sullen disappointment clung to him.

"It's a lovely noise, Wynn, but are you going to do more than just bang two bits of metal together?"

He managed to hold onto the hammer as he jumped, though it came close to leaving his hand and flying over his shoulder. He set it down on the anvil and turned to Lasris. "I thought you told me never to approach a man working a forge unannounced?"

Lasris met his gaze and then looked pointedly at the dark windows of the cottage. "I think I also mentioned that you should come and tell me when the forge was prepared. Not sit out here banging on my anvil like it's a fucking drum!" His voice rose with the final words letting the heat of his anger shine through.

"I wasn—" Wynn had enough sense to cut the protest short. "Where were you?"

"And do I owe you a record of my movements now, aspirant?"

Wynn flushed, looking away as he spoke. "No, I—"

"If you must know I was in the Gilded Quarter," Lasris interrupted him. He looked past Wynn to the forge and the length of iron that had cooled to a dull black against the glow of the coals. "I was passing your name to the Tallymasters for your trials."

Wynn spun to look at the priest in shock. "So soon?"

201

Lasris chuckled at that. "It's not really all that soon, Wynn. You've a few months left before you have to face them. You're far beyond most are at this stage."

"I am?"

Lasris snorted. "Don't let it go to your head. You have your letters already, that's all. Most of the aspirants sent to me don't. It's sped things up for you."

"I..." It was all too much and the words left him for a moment. "Will you tell me about the trials?"

"I'd be a pretty piss-poor teacher if I didn't," Lasris said with a snort. "They test for smithing, ritual, and creed – the core of the faith. What that means..." he raised a warning finger, stopping Wynn as he began to interrupt. "Is that you must show you have an understanding of the central beliefs of the church. That you have grasped a ritual such as Waking the Flame, and that you can apply the two of these together to the practice of smithing. Your trial will combine all three. Those that pass are lifted to the Hall of Novices. Those that excel might attract the attention of a priest who calls them to service as their own novice."

"What happens to those that fail?" Wynn asked, his voice a small, broken thing.

Lasris gave him a long look. "They return here, to serve in the mines until they are chosen to test again."

There had been a catch in the old man's voice and Wynn's eyes narrowed as he spoke. "That's not all of it, is it? What aren't you telling me?"

Lasris sighed, looking tired as the breath left him. "I probably shouldn't be telling you this but I'm past all that. They say that an aspirant can be called more than once, Wynn, but it never happens. You only really get one chance at this."

Wynn took a deep breath as he absorbed that and then met the priest's gaze. "How do we begin?"

The old priest blinked, taken aback, before letting out a hard, barking, laugh. "Damn me, but you've got some ambition in you. Good lad. Let's have a look at what you've been banging away at and then we'll go from there, eh?"

The weeks that followed fell into a cycle of exhaustion and frustration. Wynn would work in the forge whilst Lasris lectured him on everything from hammer strokes and metal structures, to the duties and rituals of the church. The days were long, but all too soon he would be back in the mines, hacking out iron ore as he worked the five days Terrik had demanded.

Terrik had moved him away from anything that required any real attention after the second week. He'd left more gold-rich stone on the floor of the tunnels than he'd managed to load into the carts, and only Killen's suggestion to move him onto less valuable ore had saved him from the man's wrath.

There was something compelling about the old priest's teachings. It was more than just the smithing, though he took a genuine pleasure from that. There was something about the faith of the Forgefather that nagged at him. Behind the ritual and sermons lay... something. It was as if he had been handed a puzzle and was just now learning to take the first steps at solving it. He carried it with him, worrying at it like a child with a loose tooth as he worked the mines, as he ate, and as he slept.

He lay in his bunk, lips shaping the chant to Waking the Flame. His body was a mass of aches and bruises. Half-healed burns decorated the back of his hands like pock-marks. The pain was little more than an inconvenience when he was working, but it was here, in the darkness of night, when he felt it. Every flex of his hands was enough to make the pain spark anew. He lay in the gloom waiting for sleep to claim him, even as it mocked him from the shadows.

The bunkhouse was filled with the sound of snoring men. Terrik's wheeze sang high above the others. The pitch somehow rose mid-snore and then the rumble became a snorted whine, the product of a nose broken at some point.

A sound lurked just below the snores. A whisper that clung to the silences between the indrawn breaths, striving to wrap itself in the stillness like a concealing shroud. Wynn's soundless chant ceased as he stared at a fixed point in the darkness. He sat up, squinting as he searched for the source.

The blackness shifted as he stared through it, looming towards him suddenly as if somehow made solid, and he jerked back on his bunk as he scrambled away from it.

"Wynn!" The hiss was still lower than the snores.

"Killen?" He frowned at the half-seen shape in the dark. "What are you doing here?"

"There's something you have to see. Come on!" She grabbed at his arm, somehow able to see better than he could, and urged him up.

"Fine! I can't sleep anyway, but get out before you wake anyone else up."

He shrugged his way into clothes in the darkness, and picked a path through the bunks and out onto the step.

"What are you doing here, Killen?"

She turned at his step, smiling into the face of his question.

"There's something you have to see." Her grin was broad and her eyes shone in the dim light of the chemglobe mounted on the bunk-house roof.

"Now?"

She plucked at his sleeve as she started to walk. "Come on."

He rammed his other foot down into his boot and scrambled to catch up. "Come where?"

She grinned at him, eyes still bright with excitement. "Lamplight told me about it years ago but I've only seen it once. You're going to love it."

The streets were quiet. Almost empty aside from a handful of shadows heading to their homes. Twice Keepers stopped on their patrols to watch them pass with glittering eyes, but neither pair of leather-clad men made to stop them.

The cave system was close to Terrik's compound, though in an area Wynn had never even known existed. Killen stopped outside a large cave mouth, and reached into a bag for a handheld chemlamp. "Ready?" she asked with a grin.

"For what?" Wynn asked, apparently speaking to himself as she thumbed on the lamp and ignored him.

The tunnels were broad with a high roof that made them feel closer to a succession of caves, than passages. Wynn looked at the walls as they passed. They showed no sign of tool marks and pale fungus sprouted in thick clusters.

"Are you going to tell me where we're going?"

"The pools," she told him. "It's not far now."

Wynn threw his hands in the air with a sigh and tried to ignore the look she gave him or her smile as he failed.

The passages narrowed until they were almost as tight as the crawlspaces of the blackworks. Killen led them on without pause or hesitation, though Wynn had no idea how she kept track of the maze of turns they passed through. More than once he asked how she could be so sure they were going the right way. Her looks grew darker with each asking until he gave up.

The light grew slowly. An azure blue that played over the rock walls at the end of the tunnel. Wynn looked from the walls, and the light that flickered over them with an undulating pulse, to Killen's face.

"It's chems," she told him, leading him around the corner. His feet slowed before hers as the water came into view. The cave was half filled with a pool, fed by a small waterfall that gurgled as it spilled over the rocks.

Wynn stared, struck for words as he gaped at the sight. The water was lit with a fierce blue light. It wasn't that there was a light source below it that illuminated the pool, the water itself glowed.

"It only happens once every few years," Killen told him in a hushed voice. "It takes rainfall and floods in just the right places up above to wash the right chems down through the rocks, or something like that. It drives the chemikers wild. They've never been able to copy the mix and get this kind of light."

205

Wynn nodded, still staring at the water. "How long does it last?"

"Not long, but this is the least of it. Look." She reached out a cup, crouching to fill it with the glowing liquid. "Drink some."

Wynn leaned away from the offered cup. "Is it… I mean, are you sure it's safe?"

"Don't be such a big baby," she told him. "Watch." And she swallowed the water down.

The glow began as she dipped out another cup. The skin of her cheeks grew flushed, but it was her eyes that made him gasp. The glow slowly grew in the whites until her eyes were cyan lanterns shining out of her face.

"Drink!" She thrust the cup at him.

He sipped tentatively but it tasted the same as any water he'd ever had. With a shrug he drank. The sensation began on his tongue, a tingling that spread to his cheeks and into his eyes. He reached to rub at them but it ended as swiftly as it had begun.

Wynn blinked, looking around at the glowing lake and the walls of the cave but there seemed to be no other effect than the glow.

"Is this it?"

Killen laughed. "Isn't it enough?" She turned before he could answer, walking around the narrow ledge that bordered the pool. The cave extended farther than Wynn had thought, curving away from the edge of the pool and leading into a narrow passage that passed behind the waterfall. The wall blocked the light from pool and within two turns, eclipsed it completely. Wynn looked over at Killen and then stopped dead. He could see as clearly as he had on their journey here, but the chemlamp swinging in Killen's hand was dark.

He looked from her glowing eyes to the dark passage behind them

She stopped with him, following his gaze down to the lamp and smiling up at him with her glowing blue eyes. "Now you know why the chemikers are so upset that they can't reproduce this."

"Gods below!" Wynn breathed, looking around him, somehow able to see clearly in the darkness. "Why don't they bottle this stuff?"

206

"It doesn't keep," Killen said with a shrug. "Any longer than an hour or so from the pool, and it just fades away. Nobody knows why."

She led him on through the passages, neither spoke but the roar of water soon made that all but impossible anyway as she led him out into another cavern. The falls were immense. They were fully ten times the length of a man across as they surged down from above and then fell into the darkness below. Even with his chemik-enhanced sight Wynn couldn't see the bottom.

Killen tugged at his arm and pulled him down until her lips brushed his ear. "I need to talk to you. That's why we're here. I needed somewhere I knew the Deeplighters wouldn't be able to hear us. It's about Lamplight. I think he's going to do something stupid."

"Deeplighters?" Wynn's forehead creased in a frown and he glanced back over one shoulder, following Killen's gaze. "Why would there be any Deeplighters?"

"There's a Deeplighter on every crew, or so they say." She looked at him, wondering. "How could you not know that?"

He shook his head. "Even on Terrik's crew? Who?"

She shrugged. "I don't know. It changes from time to time."

"How do you know so much about them?"

She looked down, avoiding his gaze for a moment. "Anyone can be a Deeplighter, Wynn. All it takes is need."

He stepped back away from her. "You?"

"I met my tally." Her voice was level, giving nothing away but her eyes sang their own song loudly. "Friendship and loyalty is just fine, Wynn, but in the end we all do what we have to do."

He gnawed on his lip, thinking about that for a moment before he spoke. "What did you mean about Lamplight?"

"I went to see him a few days ago. You remember that chemiker," she asked him. "Marielle? The one who was flogged?"

He nodded. It wasn't something he was likely to forget.

"We got to talking about it. He couldn't let it go."

"Maybe he was just grousing about it?"

207

Killen shook her head, the light from her eyes playing over the rocks of the wall. "No. You remember his story about the Blacker and Arnsk?"

Wynn frowned at her. *Where was this going?* "Yes?"

"I don't think he was as removed from all that as he makes out."

"How do you mean?"

She glanced back down the tunnel and then sank down, sitting on a rock jutting out of the wall. "I think he was related to the Blacker. Lamplight doesn't talk much about his past. He didn't have much of a childhood and he does his best to forget it, but he made it pretty clear that he knew the man."

"Really?"

"Yes. He makes a good show of talking down anyone who speaks up against Garl or the way things are, but his sympathies definitely lie in that direction."

"Are you serious?"

She gave him a long steady look. "I'm completely serious. Look at their lives, Wynn. The unmarked have a pretty awful time of it. You said it yourself the first time you met Lamplight. He hides it well because he's scared of who might be listening but it's obvious the Deeplighters are in there for a reason."

She sighed at his blank look. "They're keeping an eye on him, Wynn. The ones he knows about are sending a message but there's probably at least one or two that he doesn't."

Wynn shook his head and pinched at the flesh between his eyes. "Why are you telling me all this?"

She gaped at him for a second. "Because I thought you'd care! Lamplight is my friend, Wynn. I thought he was yours too. If he's going to do something stupid like take on Garl, then we need to talk him out of it."

"Do you think he'd listen?"

"I think we owe it to him to try!"

He looked away for a moment, her expression sat midway between being horrified and disgusted. "What do you want me to do?" he asked

208

in a small voice that sounded weak even to himself. "You don't even know what he's planning. If he's even planning anything at all. I mean, he's upset. I understand that, but in a few days maybe…"

"Just come with me to see him, Wynn."

He really looked at her then. There was something wrong. She hid it from showing on her face but it was clear in the way she held herself, in the way she avoided his gaze.

"I don't know," he said, watching her response. "I don't know if I can take that risk."

"What's the risk?" she demanded, a touch of anger coming into her voice. "You're talking to him, nothing more."

"Just how far have you gone with this, Killen? How deep are you?"

She spoke as if he wasn't there. Confessing her sins to the darkness. "I met with them a few times, that's all."

"There's a 'them' now? Who are they?"

"Just Lamplight and a few of his friends. We talked about how to make Garl and the Tallymasters take notice."

"Notice of what?"

"Of how bad things are!" she snapped and then sighed as the anger drained out of her. "I think just getting their attention would be enough for Lamplight. Just showing Garl that the unmarked aren't as docile and placid as he and his gilters believe."

Wynn scratched at the back of one hand, thinking out loud. "I don't know that I would want to attract Garl's attention like that." He glanced at her, eyes widening in realisation. "But then that wasn't the plan was it? There was never any intention of taking Garl on directly. Just what are they doing, Killen?"

"There's a chemiker, a friend of Marielle's. He thinks he can do something with chems."

"Just what kind of something?" Wynn pressed.

"Something destructive."

"Like a fire?"

"No, more like the Father's Wrath."

Wynn blinked. *I know this girl. This woman. This isn't like her. How could she be so stupid?* "An explosion?"

She nodded, avoiding his eyes again.

"Hell's demons and all their petty saints! When? Where?" He reached for her as she turned away, pulling her to face him. "Where, Killen?"

"I don't know!" she shouted back at him and only then did he realise he'd been yelling into her face.

"I don't know when they're going to do it," she repeated, her voice just above a whisper. "I just need… I need your help, Wynn."

The thought rose from nowhere, crawling out of the darker places within himself. A memory of Lasris telling him he had just one chance at the trials, and of his warning. Live and learn in the temple, he'd told Wynn. Or die in the mines. If he did this, if he helped Killen, he was putting that one chance at risk.

"I can't." The admission slipped out past traitorous lips.

She did not speak. Her expression would be enough to stay with him and haunt him. It went beyond shock and pain to something so profound there were no need for words. Her eyes mirrored the betrayal.

Her lips framed a question but she shook her head in silence before she could voice it. She looked down, blinking and scrubbing at her eyes with one cuff before she met his eyes again, turned, and left him.

The whisper must have come from his own lips. "Coward."

***

His life became the forge. Lasris worked him until his arms trembled, and he chanted rituals and prayers in his sleep. The days in the mine were blurred, half-conscious stumblings. When he made his way back to the bunkhouse, he often had no idea what he'd produced that day, if anything.

Killen did not speak to him again. Her gaze swept over him but she saw nothing more than the rocks of the walls. In her world, Wynn no longer existed. After the first awkward days he saw little of her. By the

210

third week he'd almost forgotten the conversation, or at least he'd worked hard to convince himself that he had.

Terrik worked his way down through the men sat on the steps of the bunkhouse as Wynn approached. His frown was made somehow more pronounced by the thong holding his eye-patch in place. "I need to talk to you, Wynn." It wasn't a request.

Terrik glanced at the men behind them and then waved him over to a spot around the corner of the bunkhouse, out of sight of the other members of the crew. He rounded on him, leaning in close enough that Wynn felt his hot breath on his face as he spoke.

"What have you done to Killen?"

That threw him and Wynn's face creased to match Terrik's own as he stepped back a pace. "I... What? Nothing."

"Well something's bothering her. She's not producing and I can't carry you both."

"You're... carrying me?"

Terrik glanced behind him at the corner of the bunkhouse for a second before giving him a frank look. "Wynn, just lately you're about as much use as wheels on a fish. As long as you're doing your training with Lasris, that's fine. Provided he says you're still doing well, that is. The bonus for having you pass the trials would pay the tally for the whole crew for months."

Wynn blinked. "There's a bonus?" he said, realising it was a stupid question as he said it. Of course there would be a bonus.

Terrik's laugh told him just what the man thought of that statement. "I'd not keep you banging bits of metal together if there wasn't, sunshine. Anyway, Killen's usually a good worker but something's throwing her off. You're two aren't speaking, that much is obvious." He sighed, shaking his head and then fell silent for a moment. "Look," he said. "There's a reason the women sleep separately from the men. It's not much, but it helps keep this sort of thing to a minimum. If you two are fucking, well that's your own business – unless you do something stupid and get her with child. But if you've fucked her head up so much she can't work? Well that messes with all of us."

211

"I—"

The explosion was closer to the centre of Aspiration than they were, but the noise was still loud enough that Wynn felt the pressure wave on his face. His head whipped around as the fireball rose above the line of the rooftops. There was a moment of shocked silence, and a scrambling noise from the corner of the bunkhouse. Then the screams began.

"Gods, Killen!" Wynn blurted, and his feet took him before Terrik's words could find him. The streets seemed suddenly packed. Miners crowded into the pathways between the buildings as they gawked at the rising flames, blocking his path as he fought to make his way through. Then suddenly, he was through the press of people, and he ran. He moved like a breeze through tall grass, forcing aside the slender reeds and whistling between the larger.

The smell of the smoke was thick in the air as he drew closer. His breath burned at the back of his throat and the smoke left a metallic tang that clung to his mouth. A ring of miners and Unmarked surrounded the burning remnants of the building. Wynn pushed his way through until he had a clearer view and was brought up short by a Keeper's hand pressed to his chest. "Stay out of the way."

More Keepers were flooding out from other streets, forming into a ragged circle around the hut and forcing people back, even as they glanced over their shoulders at the flames.

"Chem-store," a man on his left grunted, nodding at the burning wreckage. "Some chemiker must have fouled things up pretty badly to make that mess."

Wynn nodded silently, looking back at the flames. They had a white tinge to them, spreading out from the centre. This hadn't been an accident. He scanned the crowd and sighed as he caught a familiar face. Even before he looked he had known the man would be there.

Lamplight stood a couple of rows back from the edge of the crowd, watching the flames with a strained expression as Wynn made his way through the crowd.

"Lamplight!" He jumped, turning his head as Wynn drew closer.

"Wynn," he breathed, seeming almost to sink down in relief. "Made me jump there."

Wynn brushed past that. "Was this…" he stopped suddenly and looked around at the crowd. "Have you seen Killen?" he began again.

"I suspect you already know the answer to those questions," Lamplight said. "I know she came to see you."

"Gods above, Lamplight," Wynn hissed. "What was this supposed to achieve?"

"It was supposed to open some eyes," Lamplight snapped. "And keep your ash-damned voice down."

A line was forming as men passed buckets forward towards the fire, flanked by Keepers keeping the gawking crowds out of the way. Wynn stepped forward. "Let me help," he told a Keeper, who let him through to the lines with a terse nod. He reached for a bucket and passed it on, looking back at Lamplight. "Get in here," he hissed.

The man joined him with a studiously blank face, bracing himself with his crutch as he stood. Water hissed as it hit the flames, sending gouts of steam skyward.

"Try not to breathe in too much of the smoke," the barman advised in a low voice. "Who knows what's in it."

"You should have thought of that before," Wynn spat back.

The fire raged, growing taller despite the water that was thrown onto it. The flames were now far more white than orange, and the heat intensified until it drove the bucket line back so that the water barely reached the building. A crash sounded beyond the fire and dust billowed out as the adjacent building was torn down to create a firebreak.

Keepers called them off soon after that. The water had done nothing to save the building and there was nothing to do but let it burn. The cavern roof was lost to the smoke that boiled up towards the fissure high above them. Wynn watched it climb and turned, looking for Lamplight. He was gone.

The windows of Lamplight's pub were dark and the door locked when Wynn arrived. He knocked, and then pounded on the door with

213

his fist as he pressed his face to the glass. The tables were dark and empty. He couldn't see as far as the bar. If the man was in there he wasn't answering.

Wynn wandered the streets aimlessly and chemlamps were being lit by the time he made it back to the bunkhouse. Tresk nodded a greeting from the steps, pulling the longpipe from his lips and pointing towards the cooking pot. Killen sat alone on one of the trestle tables. She glanced at him once and turned away. The message was clear enough.

The others had eaten already but the bottom of the large pot still held a portion of something brown and gelatinous for him. Wynn scraped it out, and sat at the empty table chewing food that didn't need chewing and trying hard not to taste it.

He sighed, slumping down to the table and rested his forehead on the back of his hands for a moment. He'd been running on shock for most of the evening but his body hadn't forgotten he'd already done a full day in the mines. Anger or fear will let you ignore the price of pain for a while but the debt remains, waiting to be paid.

"Killen," he called softly. "Can I talk to you?"

He looked up to meet her gaze and then glanced behind him at the bunkhouse steps. Tresk had gone inside.

"We've got to talk about this," he said.

She was still angry. Even if he hadn't looked at her face he could have seen it in the set of her shoulders, in the way her fists were bunched tight enough to turn the knuckles white. "I thought you didn't want to get involved?" she said.

"Gods, Killen! I never thought you'd go this far. You can't possibly think Garl is just going to ignore this? That he'll let it go?"

She pushed herself back and stood. "Fine. You're right! Is that what you needed to hear?"

"No! I..." he closed his eyes as he sighed. "What do we do now?"

"We?" She shook her head. "No, there is no 'we'. You made that more than clear. I'll talk to Lamplight. He's so caught up in this that he has no idea. Deeplighters are probably watching him right now."

214

"What can I do?" he asked, helplessly.

"Nothing, Wynn." She sighed, suddenly looking older and tired. "I'll deal with it. You just go back to banging metal and singing over your forge."

"But if he's being watched…?"

"I'm not a fucking idiot, Wynn!" she hissed at him. "I know enough to be discreet. Go to bed, you're drawing attention to us."

"Fine, just promise me you'll deal with this soon."

"I'll do it in the morning. I can slip away easily enough once the crew is on the way to the mines. Just…" her voice slipped into another sigh. "Just leave me alone, Wynn."

He looked at her for a moment as her eyes tightened again, and left her.

Sleep was slow to come. He lay in the narrow cot listening to the sounds of the others as he stared at the fading glow of the chemlight. When he did sleep it was fitful and he woke long before the others, feeling that he might have been better off not bothering at all.

CHAPTER FOURTEEN

His muscles were sluggish as he dressed, ate, and then joined the line of men and women heading to the mines. Lack of any real sleep had left his head feeling fuzzy and half-awake. Stretching, and fighting back a yawn, he scanned the line for Killen. He finally found her and received a glare in return for his trouble.

The entrance to the mine was always busy first thing in the morning. Crews stood, packed close together as they waited their turn to go in whilst still leaving room for the carts to move up and down the shaft. He didn't see Killen slip away. Between one shuffled step forward and the next, she was gone. The knowledge didn't bring the relief he'd expected it to, instead he felt even more anxious. What if Lamplight and his friends had even more attacks planned? The more he thought about it, the more it made sense. There was little point in one isolated attack, after all. Killen might have come to him for help but she'd been involved with the attack to some degree. If Lamplight had persuaded her once…

He moved before he could think better of it, slipping through the line of men beside him and working his way back out of the shaft. Men were passing in and out of the mine and one more leaving wouldn't matter. He shuffled along until he was clear and then shifted into a jog. A moment later the jog turned into a run.

He turned a few heads as he sprinted through the streets, but not enough to do more than raise an eyebrow, he reasoned. Lamplight's looked as dark and closed as it had the day before. Wynn tried the door, though he'd known it was locked before he shook the handles. He leaned in to peer through the glass but there was nothing to see.

"Shit!" He turned in place, what to do now? A movement caught his eye as he leaned back against the doors. A face in the window of a small building across the road. The eyes widened as he met the woman's gaze and she darted back out of sight.

Wynn shoved his worry away. He had too many other things to think about right now. Killen had said she would speak to Lamplight. It was possible the two of them were inside but somehow Wynn doubted it. She had said she would speak to him somewhere discreet. "Where?" he muttered. Aspiration was not a community. The crews worked together to make meeting individual tallies easier, but in the end it was everyone for themselves. There were few places where you could go and not be seen, and fewer still that you wouldn't be noticed going into or out of.

He couldn't afford to stand around. Aside from anything else, the crew would know he was missing by now, and if Terrik didn't know already then he would soon. He started walking back towards the mine, sloshing the water bottle at his hip experimentally.

He froze, looking down at the bottle in his hand, before spinning and running in the opposite direction. A man, pressed back into a doorway, was a blur as he passed him, but Wynn didn't slow.

The cave entrance was close enough to Terrik's compound that Wynn had to travel by a circuitous route in an attempt to not run into anyone that might have recognised him. He strapped his helmet on and flicked the chemlight into life. The first part of the way into the caves was simple enough. The tunnel branched in places, but he remembered that Killen had always taken the widest passage. After a time however, they grew narrower and his choices became less certain until he came to a stop. He'd been guessing at turns for a while now, if he was honest. A glance back at the ground behind him showed his tracks where he'd been dragging his feet in the gravel, revealing the damper stone beneath. At least the way back was clear.

He followed his own trail back. The fear of getting lost was there, lurking and waiting to pounce, but it was manageable for now. The stone walls were rough and covered in moisture. One wet wall sprouting with mushrooms looks much the same as another. He followed the path back, passing through two or three junctions until he stopped again, looking in despair at the tracks that crossed his path. He'd been walking in circles at some point, and he'd already crossed his own trail. He had neatly created his own maze and it might take him hours to find the way out. For now, at least, he was lost.

The notion of being lost in here ate at him and he pulled his helmet from his head to check the chems levels three times before he caught what he was doing. The worry drove his feet until he was all but running along the passages, following a trail that might only lead him back to where he had already been. His breath came faster until his throat burned and he reached out a hand to brace himself against the wall as he bent double, gasping for air.

"Calm down, Wynn," he muttered between ragged breaths. "This isn't going to help."

He took three deep breaths and stood, looking around. "Okay, think. There's a way out of this."

The answer did not come and he set off again, moving slower this time toward the distant sound of water. He walked for a good five minutes until he stopped, cursing himself for a fool. It wasn't just moisture dripping from the walls; it was the distant lapping sound of the pools. He hurried through the passages, pausing each time the passages branched off to listen.

The attack came from nowhere, grabbing him around the neck and body and pulling him back off-balance. A hand pressed hard against his mouth, jerking his head back as another pressed the blade of the knife to his throat.

"Nice try, Deeplighter, but I think you've lost this one." Lamplight's voice was dark and hard, with none of its usual warmth.

Wynn made frantic noises until the hand moved enough to let him speak.

"Lamplight," he gasped. "It's me, Wynn."

218

"Wynn?" The voice was filled with suspicion. "What are you doing here?"

"Oh, let him go," Killen's voice called. "It's not worth torturing him over. Honestly, Wynn. You couldn't have made much more noise if you'd brought a horn with you."

Wynn spun as the hand shoved him away. "You knew it was me?" he gasped, turning to face the two of them.

"You're hard to miss, lad," Lamplight said, pointing at the chem-lamp on Wynn's helmet. "And you talk to yourself."

Wynn flushed.

"What *are* you doing here, Wynn?" Killen spoke over Lamplight's sniggering.

Wynn shifted slightly, turning away from the barman. "I came to…"

"You were checking up on me." Killen spoke for him. Her lips turned white as she shook her head and sighed. "I told you I would handle this. You're lucky it was Lamplight and me that found you. Some of the others would have just slit your throat and dumped the body."

"Better that you don't know any more of it, lad," Lamplight put in. "Go on, get going now. What we've done here, we've done. We'll live with any consequences for that. You're not in this, don't get involved."

Wynn started to speak again but Killen grabbed at his arm above the elbow, pulling him around and marching him away. "Just go, Wynn. You're not helping here and you're only going to draw attention where it's not wanted. None of this is really your problem anyway."

She pushed him on for a few steps, and then watched as he walked away. She was probably right, what had he hoped to achieve? She knew Lamplight far better than he did. Why would Lamplight have ever listened to him over Killen? He walked on through the tunnels muttering to himself. This wasn't really about Lamplight. This was about Killen, and he'd done nothing to pull her out of it. If anything he'd pushed her further in.

What did this really have to do with him anyway? He shook his head. "This isn't your problem, Wynn," he muttered, echoing her. Maybe she was right.

The journey out of the caves was far quicker than his trip in. He moved quickly as he passed into the tunnels he was more sure of. He pulled off his helmet as he emerged from the caves, flicking the chemlamp off and running an eye over the vials to check the levels. It was busier around the cave entrance than it had been earlier. A small group of men paused their conversation long enough to glance at him as he emerged from the cave mouth and Wynn hunched down under the weight of their stares. He hurried out of sight, jogging between two buildings. Had they been watching him? Were they watching the caves? The thought slowed his steps for a moment until he shrugged it aside. If Aspiration, and recent events, had taught him anything, it was to look after himself. The crews were an illusion. A means to an end.

The sound of rushing footsteps had him moving to the side of the path before the Keepers even drew close. He pressed himself to the building as they rushed past. The group numbered at least thirty and he stared after them as they ran back the way he'd come. It took a moment for the fact they had all held chemlamps to register, and another minute for him to realise they'd been headed for the caves.

He took three or four running steps after them before he stopped himself. "And what exactly are you going to be able to do?" he chided himself. "It's an entire troop of Keepers. They'd smash you into a bloody stain on the ground." He stared along the street as the normal sounds of the city reasserted themselves. There was nothing he could do.

He glanced back in the direction of the caves once, and then turned away heading for the mines.

***

Terrik woke them all early the next morning. The man looked sick; grey-faced and old. Wynn wondered if he'd slept at all.

"Get something in your bellies, we're heading out in half an hour," he told them.

220

"Why're we going so damned early," Tresk demanded, glancing out the window at the half-light beyond.

"To bear witness, you dumb shit!" a voice growled from across the room.

"We're not going because Garl wants us to go," Terrik said. His voice was dead, it held no life or depth. "We're going for Killen."

Tresk winced at that, muttering an apology as he looked down at the floor.

Wynn ate quickly, a hunk of bread that held no flavour, and followed the others into Aspiration. The crew walked in silence, making their way through empty streets that took the sound of their passage and threw it back at them.

The city woke slowly as they made their way towards the Gilded Quarter. Few spoke and it was an odd awakening as Marked and Unmarked shambled out of doorways and joined the solemn river of people flowing through the streets. Shops and stalls remained closed. The eateries, usually so loud and boisterous, stared out at the street through darkened windows.

The hush that held the city did little to lift Wynn's mood. He had caused this. There was no way to twist that fact, or hide from it. Killen had come to him for help. She had trusted him. And he had chosen to do nothing. That was the naked truth, and it screamed at him from the depths of his guilt.

Terrik glanced at him often as they walked. The one-eyed crew leader had said nothing to him since he'd run off towards the explosion, but it was clear he had his suspicions. The realisation that he was alone came to him unbidden. With Grint gone, Killen was all he really had left to him. The crew wasn't like a family. They were not friends. Tresk might grouse and grumble at him, that was about as far as it went. There were others in the crew that he barely even knew the names of.

Gilden Square was almost silent. Few people had ventured out so early and those that had, stood a silent vigil, facing the line of Keepers that stood guard over the spectacle.

221

A wooden platform had been erected over the steps forming a stage raised high above the level of those watching from the square. Seven posts stood close to the edge of the platform. Even from this distance Wynn could pick out which of the bound figures was Killen.

Wynn moved closer, edging past the quiet groups until he approached the line of Keepers. The closest of them watched him as he drew closer, gloved hands flexing on their clubs. Wynn barely noticed, his eyes were fixed on the post above him and the woman bound there. Her eyes were dull and, for a moment, he wondered if the bruises on her face meant she might be concussed, until she looked down at him. Her gaze held a handful of meanings. There was anger there, but that was the least of it. Her eyes held a deep regret, not for what she had done, that he was sure about, but for the fact she'd failed and for the lives she would leave behind.

"Killen," he said, his voice was a sad breath. He swallowed hard, glancing down at the hands trembling against his legs and barely recognising them as his own.

She twisted her head and forced the gag out of her mouth.

"Wynn," she called down with a smile and then winced in sudden pain. "Looks like there's going to be a show or something. Good thing I've got such a good spot."

Wynn turned to the closest Keeper. "Can I?" he jerked his head at Killen, making his meaning obvious.

The man nodded with a grunt that sounded hollow under the helmet. "Keep it quick."

Wynn nodded his thanks and edged past the line of men. "Gods, Killen," he managed. "I'm so sorry."

She shook her head. "It would have happened sooner or later anyway, Wynn. I'm Marked but I'll never pass the trials. Lasris would sooner pull out his own eyeballs than let a woman touch his forge. There's no way out of Aspiration for me, for most women. Why do you think I did this? For Lamplight?" She jerked her head, motioning to the big man, bound to his own stake. "He's a good friend, a nice man, but

222

no. I did this for me. I did this because there was this one tiny chance that we might be able to change things."

"And I ruined it," Wynn said.

She fell silent and let him suffer under her gaze. "You did," she said finally. "You led them right to us. You stupid, stupid, man." Her voice cracked as she spoke, letting the anger seep through. "Why couldn't you just have come with me to talk to him? Why couldn't you have helped me when I asked you?"

Wynn opened his mouth to speak but she bulled on, talking over him.

"You've killed me, Wynn. You may as well be the one holding the knife."

"I..." he shook his head. There were no words.

"Make sure you pass your trials, Wynn," she told him. "There are eyes on you now. You've marked yourself in ways Lasris never could. I'd bet the trials are the only reason you're not up here next to me."

"Alright, that's enough," the closest Keeper said, reaching for Wynn's arm and pulling him away. He didn't resist and let the Keeper push him back into the crowd. Killen's stare followed him and the accusation carried along with it.

The square filled as the hours passed. Wynn stood some distance from Terrik and the rest of the crew. He'd rejoined them to begin with but the sheer weight of people cramming into the square had shifted him away. He was glad for it. The force of Killen's stare was unsettling. She'd followed him with her gaze as he made his way back into the crowd and had stared at him ever since. She said nothing, mouthed no words. She stood in silence with the gag hanging loose around her neck, eyes boring into him.

The stare faltered at the sound of feet on the wooden boards. Garl moved slowly, stalking up the steps and onto the wooden platform as Derint and his guards followed. The Sefin paused for a moment, eyes sweeping the crowd, and then made his way to the closest prisoner, leaving his guards behind.

He said nothing, glaring out at the assembled people of Aspiration. Wynn had seen whippings before but nothing matched the pure fury in the man's eyes. He seethed with a cold anger as he looked over the crowd.

Garl moved with a casual ease, pulling the knife out from a sheath on his back and sweeping it around in a wide arc that ran through the prisoner's throat. Blood gushed out as the prisoner's eyes first filled with panic and then emptied and grew dull.

Garl did not pause. He moved on to the next prisoner, and then to Lamplight. The man strained against his ropes, screaming against the gag as Garl drew closer. Garl paused for a moment, meeting Lamplight's gaze and then drove the blade into his throat.

Wynn closed his eyes for a moment as the tears pricked at him and threatened to flow. He bit at his cheek as he forced himself to look. He had caused this, the least he could do is watch.

Garl worked in silence, matching the quiet of the watching crowd. The only sounds were the staccato spatter of the blood, and the muffled cries and thumps of the panicked prisoners as they thrashed and screamed into their gags.

Killen looked directly ahead, eyes fixed on Wynn as he watched on in horror. Garl paused as he reached her, fingering the loose gag about her throat. He whispered something to her but she gave no sign of having heard or listened. Garl frowned for a moment and then looked at her again, following her gaze. His eyes seemed to find Wynn in the crowd, though he knew there was no way the Sefin could pick him out. He drew the knife across her throat slowly, watching Wynn's area of the crowd for a reaction.

Wynn sucked in a breath as he stiffened. Did Garl see him? He tasted blood in his mouth as Killen sagged down against the ropes that held her. He held himself firm, biting down at the inside of his cheek as Garl's eyes swept over him, and then he moved on to the remaining prisoners.

He didn't hear Garl's words as he addressed the crowd. His speech passed Wynn by and he held himself rigid until the crowd began to disperse. He managed three streets before he found a darkened corner. And there, alone in the darkness, he let himself feel.

***

224

Lasris was waiting for him when he emerged from the bunkhouse. It had been six weeks since Killen's death. The days spent in the mines passed in a fog as he worked himself to collapse. Anything to make him stop thinking. Thinking led to remembering. To pathways that would only take him to guilt, and questions he didn't want to answer.

Forge days were something different. Working with Lasris gave him something to focus on and he'd thrown himself into it. Not just the forgework, but the ritual, the lectures, all of it. Somewhere, buried in the heart of this dead religion, there was a spark. A reason for it all. And he needed to find it. It gave him purpose and drove him on.

The old priest stood at the bottom of the steps and nodded at him in greeting as the others made their way past.

"It is time for your trials."

"Just like that?" Wynn blurted. "No warning, no preparation time? How is that fair?"

Lasris snorted at that. "What would be the point in testing you when you were expecting it? It is sooner than I would have liked but this is where we are. As for preparation, that would be defeat the purpose. You are not studying to pass a test. You are undergoing trials to determine if you are of worth to the temple. The priesthood had no interest in testing what you remember after weeks of study. They wish to know what you can do today, under pressure."

"You could have given me some warning," Wynn muttered, earning an amused look.

"Go and prepare the forge while I talk to Terrik," Lasris grunted. "The others should be arriving soon."

Wynn hurried across to Lasris's hut. 'Others', Lasris had said. What others? He was running blind, not knowing what to expect or what to brace himself for. He focused on the task of preparing the forge. Lasris must have cleared it out after its last use. The bellows vent was clear and an experimental pump produced only the smallest amount of ash and dust.

He busied himself with kindling, tinder and coal, building the fire up until he could cover it in coke. By the time he had the fire up

225

to forging heat he had already worked up a sweat and had it baked dry on him.

"He's not work-shy at least," a voice observed. "It's a better beginning than your last aspirant, Lasris."

Wynn turned to see a tall, thin, man stood with Lasris. He smiled at Wynn's expression. "Is he prepared?" he asked Lasris.

"As much as was possible within the constraints, Tomas," Lasris replied with a slight grimace. "You're aware of the situation, I take it?"

Tomas nodded. "Not what I'd hoped for you. This is your tenth trial now, isn't it?"

"It is," Lasris agreed, though Wynn noticed the clench in his jaw as he replied.

If Tomas saw the gritted teeth he made no sign. "Shall we proceed then?"

"Just you?" Lasris asked, raising an eyebrow.

"So it would seem."

Lasris grunted. "Wynn this is Tomas; he is the subdeacon who will be assessing you. Follow his instructions and try not to embarrass me."

Tomas gave Lasris a wry look, and turned to Wynn. "You are content with your forge preparations, yes?"

"Yes, subdeacon."

"Very well, begin with Waking the Flame. Have you a heating rod?"

Wynn reached for the length of metal, catching the scathing look Lasris gave the subdeacon.

He thrust the rod into the coals and began the chant.

"I wish to see your control as you channel the Father's presence. Bring the flame to one third of the length of the rod and then, when I tell you, push it out, back to the quarter line."

This was the test? Wynn worked to keep his face straight as he began to pump the bellows in time to his chant. He turned sharply as he felt the subdeacon draw closer, reaching around him with a section of fabric. "What...?"

"It wouldn't be much of a test if you could see the rod now, would it?" Tomas chided him. "Any fool can heat iron and watch the glow move along the metal. The Father gives us more control than that. Demonstrate what you have learned, aspirant."

The fabric was thick and wound twice around his face before the subdeacon was satisfied. Wynn stood in place, thankful that he still had one hand on the long tongs that held the heating rod and the bellows handle in the other.

He froze for a second before remembering that the rod was already in the coals. How long had it been in there? Panic threatened, and he forced it down quickly, beginning the familiar chant again, picking up where he had left off.

Not being able to see gave the task a new dimension as he concentrated on the chant. The rush of the bellows slipped between the tones of the chant, forming a complex rhythm that changed subtly every time he began a new cycle.

He knew from Lasris that this was little more than a way of counting out the seconds that had passed. To that extent, the entire faith was just a sham to fool the gullible. Yet the priests took it so seriously. The city of Aspiration existed purely to supply the temple with novices. Could it be there was something more to all of this?

He ceased the chant, pulling the rod out of the coals and setting it onto the anvil, moving by feel and memory.

He felt Tomas step past him to inspect the rod and grunt. "Well done. Now draw the flame back to the quarter mark." The man's approval brought a flush of pride that was gone in an instant as the complexity of the next task took hold.

Wynn began another chant, pumping the bellows to a slower, different, rhythm as he thrust the rod back into the coals. This was the hardest part, he knew. The lesser airflow would result in reduced heat from the forge, allowing the portion of the iron rod that was further from the heart of the fire, to cool. Whether he passed or failed this task would depend on how far into the coals he'd thrust the rod and at that moment, he had no idea.

"Adequate," Tomas muttered as Wynn set the iron back onto the

227

anvil. "Remove your blindfold and let us see what Lasris has managed with you."

Tomas questioned him for the next hour or more, testing him on the tenets of the faith. Wynn grew more anxious the longer the questioning went on. The subdeacon would occasionally pause between questions, considering the response Wynn had given and the silence only made the worry worse. Tomas walked him through what little he knew of Calling Iron, and the Anvil's Heart, before having him recite the Canticle of Embers and the rituals he knew already.

The chanting felt more complex now that he was performing to an audience. He glanced at Lasris but the priest's face may as well have been carved from stone. The man's warning that he would only have one chance at the trials filled his thoughts and he stumbled over his words.

Sighing, Tomas raised a hand to stop him. "Enough."

"I could do it again," Wynn offered, wincing.

"I think what I have heard is more than sufficient," Tomas said, with a look to Lasris. "I have one final question for you. Take some care with your answer. Do not waste my time with flattery or what you think I might want to hear. I wish to know the unvarnished truth. Understood?" He waited for Wynn's nod and then raised a questioning finger. "Why is it you wish to serve the Forgefather?"

Wynn went as far as parting his lips before he stopped himself. This wasn't an idle question, the warning alone told him that. It was obviously one that had been asked many times before, and the subdeacon had probably heard hundreds of glib responses. Asking to go home or to leave Aspiration wasn't an option. What were they looking for? He sifted through Lasris's teachings, catching Tomas's impatient expression.

"The truth," Wynn said finally. "I want to know the truth."

Tomas frowned slightly as he considered that. "Tell me more."

"This faith is old," Wynn began. "These things Father Lasris has told me of the Forgefather, about the ancient priests and Defenders, they are the tales and myths collected together from half-remembered legends. I want to know the truth about the Forgefather, about the faith

228

and the Fall. I want to know what it was that happened to make our church fall. What happened to the powers given us by the Forgefather? The Great Anvil alone is proof enough of the truth of the legends. What really happened? Where is the Father and what can we do to atone for our sin?"

Tomas nodded to himself. He wore a slight frown as he considered what he'd heard, and Wynn couldn't tell whether he'd passed or failed. He didn't look at Lasris, he didn't dare.

"Interesting," Tomas said, breaking the silence. "I'm not sure what you've given me here, Lasris. This is either a worthy aspirant or a shocking failure and I find myself quite unable to tell. For now, I believe he warrants further study."

Wynn glanced at Tomas in time to see his eyes narrow in suspicion. "Congratulations, Lasris. Your charge has passed his trial. Your penance approaches its end."

Lasris bowed his head in acknowledgement and turned away. "Take him then, Tomas. And leave me."

"So be it," the subdeacon said with a nod. "Come, novice. Your time here is at an end."

CHAPTER FIFTEEN

Wynn glanced back at Aspiration once as they left, taking in the chemlamps and the smoke rising up towards the great fissure. The city had not been a home to him in any real sense. Any comfort he'd drawn from it, any sense of belonging, had been taken from him. One look was all it deserved.

Tomas did not speak as they walked, not beyond the terse instruction to keep up with him. Wynn felt the man's eyes on him several times as they made their way up to the gate that would lead into the temple. The Listeners watched them as they approached, only moving to bar their way at the last moment.

If the subdeacon was surprised he gave no sign, his face was as calm and stern as ever. He drew to a halt and placed a possessive hand on Wynn's chest. "This one I claim under the pact." His voice was grave as he met their blindfolded gaze.

"As you wish," the leftmost Listener replied. "He has been forged and tempered in the fires of Aspiration. He is yours." He paused for the briefest moment. "And will you now acknowledge our task and purpose?"

Tomas's face grew, if possible, graver still. "I will not," he told them flatly. "You and yours have been judged by the Most Holy. I do not acknowledge your task. I will not carry your petition. You are the damned. I stand upon the one true path."

The Listeners bowed their heads in acceptance, fumbling with keys, and moments later the door swung open.

The temple was cold. It was a chill born of stones that had never known the sun's touch. The air held a faint dampness that sucked the heat from him as they walked through the shadowed halls. Aspiration had sometimes held a chill in the mornings, but the constant heat of the smelt works fed into the cavern and meant the place was hardly ever truly cold for long.

Wynn hugged himself, trying to coax warmth from a miner's tunic that was designed for warmer places. Tomas glanced at him as they passed through hallways and staircases and Wynn caught the faint curve to his lips.

"I will leave you here," the subdeacon announced, stopping abruptly. Wynn looked around in confusion until he caught sight of the door behind the priest, almost lost in amongst the shadows of the hall.

"The Master of Novices will place you where he feels most suitable. Give him this." He held out a silver coin and Wynn stared at it stupidly until Tomas thrust it at him.

Wynn watched the priest make his way along the hall until the shadows took him.

He knocked at the door, thinking as he did, that this was probably the first time he had knocked at any door in the entire time he had been in Aspiration. How odd that manners depend on the environment.

The Master of Novices was bent low over his desk, scratching a pen on rolled parchment. He looked up briefly as Wynn entered, taking his measure in one glance and then bending back to the parchment, apparently dismissing him as not worthy of note.

"Chit," he snapped, before Wynn could think of what to say.

"I'm sorry?" Wynn said, even as he realised that was a stupid thing to say. He took half a step forward, fingering the silver piece the subdeacon had given him, and held it out.

The priest shook his head with a barely audible tut as he looked up again. "Not entirely without wits then?"

He turned the coin over in his fingers before setting it carefully on the desk. "Who prepared you for your trials?" he asked, reaching blindly for a cup that sat perilously close to the ink pot.

"I was taught by Father Lasris, master," Wynn told him.

The priest's mouth moved, chewing on Wynn's words as he sucked on the inside of his lips. "Interesting," he muttered. "I like to know just what it is that I have been sent. Passing the trials is one thing but that tells me only that you can be taught, not what your abilities truly are."

Wynn nodded in an agreement that was ignored. The priest was talking at him, he realised, not to him.

"Very well then," he said as he pushed himself up out of his seat. "Follow me."

The corridors passed in a cold stone maze as Wynn was led through long hallways and down several flights of stairs until they reached a large room.

"Brial," the priest called out as they entered, beckoning over one of the white-robed men who were filing out of another doorway. "Take this one under your charge," he instructed as the novice came closer. "I assume I can trust you with that much at least?"

Brial's young face coloured as he nodded. "Yes, master."

"Very well then." The priest nodded, acceptance and dismissal all in one motion, and turned to leave.

"Brial," the young man introduced himself.

"Wynn," he replied, shaking the offered hand.

"You're probably freezing," Brial said, nodding at Wynn's thin miner's tunic. "I know I was when I got here. These robes might not look like much but they're warmer than what you're wearing."

The room served as a common area. Novice's cells surrounded the central chamber, each with its own hard wooden bunk and a small shelf.

"You can bunk down in this one." Brial pointed into the closest cell. "There should be a robe under the blanket and some sandals under the bed. If you change quickly we can still make it to Embers."

He gave the word a peculiar emphasis and Wynn frowned. "Embers?"

"Get changed," Brial repeated. "I'll explain it all on the way."

The robes were softer than they looked and Wynn pulled them on, grateful for the warmth as he tied the rope cord around his waist.

"There are prayers eight times a day," Brial explained as he led the way back into the maze of narrow hallways. "We're supposed to attend as many as we can but at the very least we must attend the holy hours. That's what I was talking about earlier. There are five named hours: Kindling, Fannings, Forgings, Embers, and Ash. Unless you have some duty, you're expected to attend all of them. Usually you'll be assigned a duty during prayers, but for this time at least, you can just watch."

The passage gave way to stairs, wider hallways and yet more stairs until they approached the upper levels of the temple. Brial hurried him through the halls until they approached the large double doors that had been flung wide. Two priests stood at attention on either side, one giving Brial a stern look as they rushed through.

The chamber inside was cavernous and Wynn moved sluggishly as Brial herded him through to the side of the room and the end of a novice's pew. He gawked up at the domed ceiling high above them, and then past the rows of empty pews at the huge anvil, standing on an island of stone that was almost completely surround by flames.

The priest at the anvil was dressed in far grander robes than those of Wynn and the novices with him. His voice was deep and sonorous but yet, somehow it didn't reach clearly to Wynn.

He frowned, and glanced at Brial, but the novice ignored him. He was watching the priest intently and repeated phrases at key moments. It took a few minutes before he realised that the novices must have memorised the sermons and the responses.

The room was obviously designed to inspire awe but the sound did not carry equally to all of it. The shape of the room was such that it funnelled the priest's voice out to the empty pews and the absent congregation. Novices were clearly less of a consideration, and the priest's voice was so affected by echoes and distortions that it was almost completely garbled by the time it reached Wynn.

"Kneel down," Brial hissed from the corner of his mouth.

Wynn followed the others as they knelt in prayer, murmuring along though he had no idea what they were saying until the end. "From the darkness unto light. From the fire unto form," he intoned, following Brial's lead and standing again.

The service passed in a confusing rush. Wynn found himself kneeling several times for prayers he couldn't hear properly, and singing along with hymns he didn't know. They stood, waiting after the final benediction as the priests and acolytes filed out.

"It gets easier," Brial told him as he ushered him out of the pew. "You'll have the hang of things in a week or two. And there's always the chance you'll be chosen too."

"Chosen?" Wynn replied, following along as the novices filed out.

"Any new novice attracts attention," Brial explained in hushed tones as they walked. "Any novice can be chosen to serve a particular priest. They live in the priest's chambers, assisting with research and other tasks whilst they train. It's a great honour, and the fastest way out of any of the novice halls."

Wynn shrugged. "The halls don't seem so bad."

Brial snorted. "Ours aren't the only one, there are seven. Ours are okay I suppose, there are better and worse. You're fresh from the mines, they wouldn't seem rough to you. I suppose it's not the hardest life but they only give you five years." He nodded at Wynn's expression. "If you don't make acolyte within five years then you are returned to the mines."

"I've never heard of anyone returning," Wynn admitted.

Brial spread his hands. "It's just what I've heard."

Wynn nodded, thinking. Had he known anyone who'd been returned to the mines? He didn't think so but then, would they have admitted it anyway?

***

The novice halls had a routine all their own and Wynn was pulled into the drudge of daily chores. He soon found he could split the tasks into two camps: those that were purely practical, and those that were ceremonial. The practical revolved largely around the fetching and cleaning that was needed to maintain and stock the temple and its many forges. For Wynn it became the ceremonial that grated.

He cursed as he saw the mess the candles had made, catching himself halfway through the words and glancing around in a flurry of guilt. The mess had built up in a mound of spattered wax that had grown up from the stone floor beneath the sconce. Almost all of the candles in the temple were supposed to burn constantly, with no flame ever permitted to go out. The result was that novices and any spare servants were constantly replenishing candles and wax-trays, or working in the chandlery to produce more.

Wynn jabbed at the edge of the mound of wax with the hand-shovel, metal scraping over stone as he cursed the name of whoever had left the tray to overflow in a litany of grumbled insults.

"Well now, isn't that just a lovely mess?" The voice came from behind and Wynn jumped, knuckles scraping painfully against the floor as the shovel skipped over the stone.

Malek's face twisted in sympathy as Wynn sucked the blood from skinned knuckles. "I'm sorry, Wynn. I..." he spread his hands helplessly.

"It doesn't matter," Wynn managed.

The novice winced as he looked closer. "Oh gods, you're bleeding."

"It's fine, Malek," Wynn insisted. Malek had been one of the first novices to approach him. He was a slight young man and Wynn privately wondered how he'd ever managed to survive the mines. "What did you want?"

"I almost forgot myself there." Malek shook his head, smiling at himself. "The priests should be arriving soon. Kamber sent me to fetch you."

It made him sound like a stray dog. Wynn shook his head with a scowl and shrugged. "What are you talking about?"

Malek stepped back as Wynn clambered to his feet. "Didn't Brial explain about a priest's choosing?"

"He mentioned something," Wynn admitted. "That a priest can choose a novice to serve at any time. It didn't sound like something that happens too often."

"It's not. They sent word a half hour ago."

"Bloody ash-damned hells, Malek. You don't give a man much time, do you?"

Wynn set off for the novice halls before Malek's stammered apology could really get started. The other novice irritated him for some reason. There was something soft and pampered about him that grated.

The novices were still waiting as they arrived, formed up into two long lines.

"You took your sweet time, boy," Kamber snapped as he caught sight of them. The large novice must have fought his way out of the mines without ever knowing the threat of the lash. Making tally had probably been easy for him but passing his trials must have taken a hero's effort. The Father, if he truly was the lord of creation, must crave balance in all things. Kamber might have the strength of an ox but he seemed to have the intellect of one as well.

Wynn gave an apologetic shrug, grateful that the man's ire seemed to be directed at Malek as he made his way to the end of the closest line. If the mines had taught him anything, it was that it is never a good idea to stick your neck out. Especially when the headsman is already looking at somebody else.

The Master of Novices had a penetrating voice that carried along the hallways. Wynn shifted and pulled his robe straighter, noting he wasn't the only one to fidget, as they approached.

The priest was a shorter man whose height seemed to have made way for girth. He wasn't fat by any means, but solid, and his robe only served to emphasise this.

"I'm sure you will be able to find a novice able to assist you on this project, Father Ossan," the Master of Novices said as he ushered the priest into the chamber and over to the ranks of novices.

Ossan for his part, looked unimpressed as his gaze swept over the young men assembled in front of him. He moved down the line running his gaze over the novices with a faintly offended expression. Twice he stopped to speak to one of them before moving on with a barely perceptible shake of the head.

Wynn forced himself to stop watching the priest as he finished with the front row and moved back to his own line. It seemed he stopped more often, though the conversations were whispered and brief. And then he was in front of him. Wynn froze, swallowing as his mouth went dry, suddenly unsure what to do as the priest considered him with a faint smile.

"And this would be our seeker of truth, now would it?" he asked the master over one shoulder.

Wynn's expression must have spoken louder than the master's voice as Ossan laughed, a kindly smile spreading wrinkles around his eyes and cheeks.

"Yes, word of your trial has spread, novice. I'm not sure I've heard Tomas ramble on with quite such enthusiasm in some years. Tell me," he leaned closer. "Just what was it that prompted that particular answer?"

Wynn felt his lips part as his mind went blank. Creativity failed him and he fell back on the truth. "I needed something that would get the subdeacon's attention, Father. I thought that a truthful answer might be something he hadn't heard that often."

Ossan looked startled for a moment and then threw his head back with a violent bray of laughter. Wynn cast a nervous glance at the Master of Novices who was looking back and forth between the two of them, unsure how Wynn's answer would be received.

"I like you, boy," Ossan said, wiping at one eye. "Would you be willing to serve?"

Wynn started to answer but faltered as the priest's gaze ran over him. There was something about the look that gave him pause. He mentally shook himself, what other options were open to him?

"I would be honoured, Father."

"Excellent!" Ossan clapped him on the shoulder. "Now to see if we can find a suitable study-partner for you. I've always found that these things work best with a pair."

237

"Might I suggest—" the Master of Novices began.

"No, I don't think so, Eskan," Ossan cut him off. "We both know you're about to suggest your pet ape, Kamber. He would be perfect if I had furniture that needed moving, but I suspect he'd struggle on his way to the end of a sentence if I asked him to read something. What I need is an agile mind. Someone thirsty for knowledge. Someone eager to serve." He walked away from the Master of Novices as he spoke, eyes running over the young men in front of him.

"And what have we here?" he asked. The uncomfortable sensation was even worse when Ossan was looking at someone else, Wynn found. It was an oily look, somehow as lost and hopeless as it was predatory.

"And what is your name, lad?"

"Brial." The answer was just barely audible as the young man squirmed under the priest's gaze.

"No need to be so nervous, boy. We're all here for the same purpose. We all serve under the Father." He glanced back over one shoulder. "Isn't that right, Eskan?"

"Of course, Father."

Wynn considered the Master of Novices. Eskan was fidgety and uncomfortable, casting frequent looks at the doorway. Was something going on here that shouldn't be? The master was very clearly worried about someone else walking in on them. Wynn briefly wondered what hold Ossan had over Eskan. Just what had he got himself into?

Ossan spoke softly to Brial, one hand squeezing his shoulder. He nodded in response to something the novice said and then beamed a smile, looking back to Wynn. "Excellent then. Wynn, this fine young man will be your study partner.

CHAPTER SIXTEEN

Ossan's study stank. It was the smell of a man who had lost himself in his work and struggled to find either the way out, or the way forward. It was the smell of frustration, overlaid with the stale stench of sweat, wine, and old food.

Kharios tapped on the open door again, leaning in to peer through the gloom of the study.

"What?" Ossan barked out the word as he slammed a hand down onto the book. He twisted awkwardly in his chair to look at the door. "What do you want, Kharios?" he demanded, squinting against the brighter light of the hallway.

Kharios eased into the room, setting the copper work down on a small table by the doorway as he hugged the books close to him.

"I think I've found something," he said, moving into the room.

"I'm beginning to think there's nothing to be found," Ossan sighed. "These books are nonsense, Kharios. There's not a page among them that makes any sense."

"I know." Kharios made his way over to the desk, setting the books down on a clear corner. "And I think it's intentional."

That silenced him and Ossan sat back in his chair with a slight frown as Kharios made his way to the desk. "Why?"

"I don't know," Kharios admitted. "But then why hide the books away in the mines at all?"

"The Fall," Ossan muttered.

Kharios gave the priest a curious look. "I don't understand," he said eventually.

"Think about it, novice," Ossan said. "The Fall brought chaos to half the civilised world. The faith dwindled as the Father's voice was lost. Defenders and priests were unable to call upon the power they once had. Temples were sacked and razed to the ground as looters sought the wealth and riches that we could no longer protect. This very temple is built upon ruins. Is it so hard to believe that this collection of knowledge was walled away for safe keeping?"

Ossan laughed at Kharios's expression. The sound was bitter and harsh. "It's no use, of course. The books are gibberish. You know that as well as I."

"I think I may have found the key," Kharios said in a small voice.

Ossan sat back up with a lurch. "What do you mean?"

"It's probably easier if I show you, Father." He moved papers and scrolls aside to make space and opened the two books. "Look here at this paragraph. The language is odd but it's clear that it is discussing the ritual chant for Calling Iron." He looked to Ossan and the priest waved him on impatiently. "Then, here, the following paragraph is talking about something else. Almost all of the books are like this. They lurch from topic to topic between one paragraph and the next."

"I know all of this, Kharios," Ossan said, there was a warning in his tone and Kharios wasn't fool enough to ignore it.

"But look here," Kharios pointed at the glyph built into the paper of the page, unable to keep a smile from curving his lips.

Ossan shrugged, shaking his head at the illumination. "And? The books are riddled with them. It's just decorative."

"I thought so as well, Father, but look, this one is raised."

Ossan ran his fingertips over the page, grunting as he found the raised glyphmark. He tried another, finding it smooth and flat, and then another.

"Try here." Kharios turned a couple of pages and pointed again at a paragraph close to the bottom of the page.

"So whoever did the illuminations used too much paint, or lead, or whatever, in a couple of places. So what?"

Kharios shook his head, waving Ossan's objection aside. "It's not paint, Father. It's ink, and besides, I think this is built into the paper itself. Anyway, that's not my point." He flicked back to the previous page, pointing out the last words in the paragraph. "It carries on from here," he said, turning the pages again. "These books aren't supposed to make sense. They function in a code. These glyphmarks are the key to the cipher."

"But why...?" Ossan shook his head and leaned closer to the book. "Show me again." The glower had fallen away from his face and he pored over the book running his hand over the glyphmarks to find the next section. "And it continues on," he murmured, "marked by these glyphs."

Kharios felt his own lips curve, matching the priest's smile. He took a half step back as Ossan read, suddenly sickened at himself. Even now, after all this time, the opinion of the man mattered to him. He was like a beaten puppy, crawling back to lick the hand of the man who kicked him.

"Great Father of the Flames, Kharios," Ossan gasped. "Have you read this?"

"Yes," Kharios said, his voice flavoured with his own disgust.

Ossan beamed at him. "This is incredible. There are implications here I've never even considered. This ritual it references... Do you see what this means, boy?"

Kharios nodded, adrift in the ocean of Ossan's enthusiasm.

"Of course, it would be easier if the sections were all transcribed," Ossan mused.

"I could help with that, Father," Kharios put in. It hadn't escaped him that, having handed the key to the books over to Ossan, he was in danger of making himself unnecessary again. "I've already made a start on some of it."

Ossan looked at him for a moment. It was a speculative stare that lingered long enough to make Kharios nervous, and reminded him of things he'd rather keep forgotten. Some things are left buried. Others need a little help staying in the ground.

241

"Do that," he said. "I take it you've found something similar in some of the other texts?"

"Most of them, Father," Kharios said. "Probably more than two in three if I had to guess. What I can't understand is how anyone was able to write like this, jumping topics every paragraph."

"They probably didn't," Ossan said with a shrug. "This is almost certainly not the original copy. We don't have the luxury of having transcribers in this, our modern church. From what I've read of the old temple though, they often couldn't read. They would have simply copied the symbols set before them. The bindery would have done something similar with the glyphs and illuminations."

Ossan turned back to the book, running his hands over the pages to find the next section. "I want you to keep this discovery to yourself, Kharios."

Kharios blinked at the back of the man's head. Who did he have that he could tell? "Of course, Father." He took a deep breath, steadying himself. "Father?"

Ossan didn't lift his gaze from the book. "Hmm?"

"I have completed my test piece for copper."

Ossan turned to look at him, curiosity in place of his earlier frustrated expression. "And just when did you find the time do this?"

Kharios fought to keep the wince from his features. "I did the forgework to clear my head, master. When I needed a break from the books."

"And so whilst I've been working into the small hours, you've been tinkering in the forge?"

Kharios gaped for a moment and closed his mouth. There was nothing he could really say to that.

"Well let me see it then," Ossan said, breaking the silence.

Kharios moved quickly to the doorway, retrieving the piece he'd wrapped so carefully in soft linen.

Ossan took it without comment, turning the object over in his hands as he unwound the cloth. The tree was set into a block of polished basalt and the leaves took the lamplight and spread it over the stone in a soft golden glow. Ossan lifted it closer to his face, tracing the turns of the gnarled trunk with his eyes.

"This is very intricate work, novice." He looked up at Kharios. "Three sections I would guess, held with concealed pins?"

Kharios nodded but Ossan had already looked back to the tree. "The colour on the leaves is quite impressive. How did you achieve it?"

"The leaves had to be annealed several times as I made them. They were just too brittle otherwise. I found that by using Waking the Flame I was able to bring the colour to the tip of each leaf and have it spread out from there."

Ossan frowned as he considered that. "Waking the Flame is an iron ritual, novice. Why would you use it on copper?"

"I was once told that Waking the Flame is little more than a way of counting time," Kharios said, watching the old man's eyes for his reaction. "I needed a way to regulate how much heat was going into the copper and to make it uniform across all the leaves. The rhythm of Waking the Flame worked perfectly for it…" he trailed off with a grimace.

"And now you feel you have done something wrong," Ossan finished for him. "That you have somehow cheapened a holy rite by using it to mete out the seconds as you worked. Is that right?"

Kharios's expression spoke for him.

"My son," Ossan began. "Ours is not an easy path. With the knowledge of everything that was lost in the Fall, it is hard to maintain your faith. I know this. Many have questioned. There are many who have had doubts. Are we simply casting prayers into the darkness? Scripture tells us that the Father hears every prayer, even if he does not yet choose to answer."

He pulled himself out of the chair, heading for the drinks cabinet. A bottle clinked against the glass and Ossan spoke as he poured. "It is for mankind to earn our Father's forgiveness, so they say, not to question. But is it not our questioning that makes us human?"

Kharios took a breath. "Even you, Father?"

Ossan laughed into the glass. "Even me? Definitely me. This place," he waved a hand vaguely. "This building is a church but there is little or no faith here. I've spent my life devoted to a god who does not answer prayers or even give any sign he still exists. Do I doubt? Of course I do. But it's so much more than that. Look at these writings you've brought back into the light. If I can find a key, if I can find something to reaffirm the faith of those that are lost, then it would change everything. Anything might be possible. Imagine what we could transform this church into if we cut away the dead wood. The Three have been guiding this faith for so long that they've filled every square inch with dust and stale rhetoric. This discovery, Kharios, could change the world."

He sank back into his chair with a smile. "If, we can find something." He reached out for the copper tree again. "You have a good touch, Kharios. A keen mind as well. I see great things in your future. Perhaps it is best if we let the shadows of the past stay in the darkness. Wouldn't you agree?"

Was that a peace-offering? Kharios nodded with a carefully blank expression.

"Excellent!" Ossan beamed again and took another deep drink from the glass. "As for your copper trial? You've exhibited a mastery I might struggle to match myself. Give me your hand."

He reached for a small drawer as Kharios stepped forward. "A master of copper. Born of earth, forged in flame, the Father takes you and shapes you as he will." He placed the ring onto Kharios's middle finger, closing his hand over Kharios's fingers until he folded his hand into a fist.

"Congratulations," he said with a smile. "Now, I believe you were going to transcribe these sections for me?"

Kharios nodded, glancing up from the two rings on his right hand. "Of course, Father."

"The sooner, the better, I think," Ossan told him. "Oh, and Kharios?"

"Father?" Kharios stopped, halfway to the doorway.

"Don't begin your work with steel or bronze until I give you leave. Is that understood?"

Kharios nodded. The man was looking at him intently and for once Kharios had no idea what he meant by it. He nodded again and turned for the door.

244

The ring was beautiful, formed into the image of a braided rope that twisted around his finger. The symbolism was obvious, tying him to the church, but as Kharios made his way back to his cell he wondered just who he had bound himself to.

**

The days had become ruled by the scratch of pen on paper. Ossan snatched the handful of pages away from him every time Kharios delivered them and sent him back to work with an admonishment to work faster.

His fingers ached where he gripped the pen. It was a dull pain and he was growing used to its presence, almost drawing comfort from it. Pain meant progress and Ossan was a furnace that he had been struggling to keep burning.

He'd considered asking Ossan for help transcribing. He'd even come close once or twice but the priest seemed obsessed with keeping complete control of the texts. Bringing in another novice or acolyte to help would have meant an end to that.

Kharios sat back and gasped as the cramped muscles of his back protested. He glanced at the candle burning and shook his head as he noticed it was burnt down to a stub. He'd missed another meal.

He stood, arching his back as he waited for the ink to dry enough that he could take the papers to Ossan. Even now the writings were nagging at him. It was hard to follow the text as he transcribed it. He'd begun by reading and then copying but soon he found that he was just copying text from one page to another and somehow not actually reading it at all. Scattered fragments had stuck with him and he'd found himself stopping, mid-sentence as he puzzled over the meaning of what he'd just read.

"Day-dreaming again," he muttered to himself as he scooped up the sheaf of paper. A figure in the doorway lurched back as Kharios jumped, papers flying into the air.

"Great gods above and below, Kharios," the figure snapped. "Get a grip on yourself. You scared me half to death!"

Kharios shook himself, crouching to retrieve the papers. "I'm sorry, Fen. I didn't expect anyone to be there."

The servant shook his head. "The master sent me to fetch you," he said, lips twitching as he fought down a smile.

Kharios glanced at the candle again. "Now? It must be past Ash by now?"

"Long past," Fen grunted with a nod. "I wasn't best pleased about it myself but there you are. He wants you up in the Great Forge, apparently."

Kharios shook his head and frowned. The Forge would be silent at this time of the night. What could Ossan possibly want that couldn't wait until the morning?

"I wouldn't waste time puzzling it out personally, but that's your own look-out," Fen said. "Me? I'm for my bed. You've had your message, do with it what you will."

"Thank you," Kharios said to the retreating figure. If Fen heard him he gave no sign. He gathered the papers up and hurried out of the cell. Fen wasn't the fastest person on his feet and Ossan's patience had never been that good to begin with.

The temple was quiet as he made his way out of Ossan's rooms. It was never truly dark. The candles that lined the halls were never supposed to go out, and each had been replaced with a slow-burner that had just the barest hint of flame reaching up from the wick.

Kharios hurried up the stairs and along the halls until he reached the great double doors to the forge itself. He glanced around as he pushed one open. Something about this felt wrong.

Ossan stood beside the huge anvil, one hand resting on its surface as he watched Kharios rush between the pews to reach him. "You certainly took your time, novice."

It was easier to accept the rebuke than point out that Fen was hardly the fastest messenger. "What are we doing here, Father?"

Ossan grinned then. His smile forced its way out on the wings of an enthusiasm which obviously couldn't be contained. "A ritual," he beamed. "A ritual which, if I am right, may well bring the power of the Father back to us."

Had there been any mention of rituals in the writings he'd given Ossan? Most of it seemed to be old scripture. He frowned as he fought to remember the scraps of text that had stuck with him. "How?" he asked, finally.

"The writings you brought me were vague. There is an assumption of knowledge that we simply don't have. Despite that, there was enough there to give me an idea. I have developed a ritual, building on some of the rites mentioned in the texts and from those we have already. If I'm correct then this ritual should draw the attention of the Father to us. It's a crude analogy but we will be seeking the Father with a great shout into the darkness. We will seek the Father through the bond of our pledges and the blessings of Mastery. We will force a response from the Father who has turned his face from us."

It sounded like it should have made sense but to Kharios it seemed fanciful at best. The fact that they were doing this in the dead of night wasn't lost on him. Ossan obviously wanted to avoid any embarrassment if the ritual resulted in nothing. "How do we begin?"

"As with any ritual," Ossan told him. "With the forge."

The great forge was oversized in every respect. The anvil alone was large enough that a man could have stretched out on top of it and still had room to spare. Great pits sat to either side of the island of stone that held the anvil. Prepared properly they would be filled with mounds of burning coals fed by the huge bellows.

Kharios followed Ossan to the small door set below the raised altar that held the forge. A short tunnel led them through to the twin rooms that housed the firepits. Ossan leaned back against one wall, motioning for Kharios to get on with it whilst he consulted pages of notes.

Kharios sighed and set to starting the fires. Stores sat to either side of the pits held supplies of tinder, kindling, and coal and within a few short minutes Kharios had twin fires burning. Ossan stopped reading long enough to help him shovel coke over the fires, instructing him on how to operate the wooden wheel that would drive the massive bellows hidden below the chamber. The heat was tremendous and Kharios found himself thinking wistfully of Ossan's smaller forge.

At last Ossan seemed content and gave a satisfied nod at the fires. "Over here," he called. "This will take both of us." The crank was thick iron connected to a mass of cogs and gears. "Throw that lever over there by you," Ossan muttered and took hold of the crank. The handle was obviously designed for two and together they strained to turn the large wheel. A grating of stone on stone accompanied the clacking of the gears as the fire pits rose ponderously up toward the anvil above them.

"Great gods below," Ossan gasped as they clambered out of the small tunnel. "I've not done that since I was an acolyte. It doesn't get any easier with age."

Kharios smiled in agreement and froze as he caught Ossan's cold glance. He was forgetting his place, that look said. This was not a partnership. Any glory would be Ossan's. He was simply here to assist.

The twin fires were raging now as the mechanism below the forge worked to force air through the glowing coals. Ossan pulled a second lever, slowing the bellows and motioned for Kharios to follow him up to the anvil on its altar.

"Begin with Waking the Flame," Ossan instructed him. "My own ritual will weave around yours."

Kharios frowned for a second, unsure how this would work. "What shall I use for a focus, Father? What am I calling into?"

"The rings, boy," Ossan said, as if that should have been obvious. "I will be throwing rings of mastery into the flames and crushing others on the anvil."

"Rings?" Kharios winced as soon as he spoke but Ossan seemed oblivious to his dismayed gasp.

"Rings," the priest nodded, reaching into a small sack beside the anvil and pulling out a fistful. "These rings of mastery are more than a

248

simple symbol of progression. They were blessed by the Father himself, long before the Fall. By weaving the destruction of just these few rings into the ritual we shall tug at the bond between man and god. We shall force him to respond, to acknowledge us!"

Was Ossan insane? The rings were possibly the most sacred items in the temple after the Great Anvil itself. The consequences for this could be anything. Kharios sighed inwardly, it wasn't as if he was in a position to refuse. If this failed, and the Three punished Ossan, perhaps he might even be able to escape out from under him. The thought brought a smile to his lips and he began his chant. The acoustics of the hall were such that his voice was taken and amplified, echoes chasing each other around the chamber. He faltered, glancing at Ossan, but the man seemed unconcerned about the noise and began his own chant in a rich, deep, voice.

The chants wove around each other, Ossan calling out hoarse instructions without breaking the rhythm of his own ritual. Kharios passed through Waking the Flame, and Calling Iron, and on to rituals he'd barely a passing knowledge of.

Ossan, for his part, seemed unconcerned as Kharios stumbled through Touching Gold and the Song of Silver. A flurry of sparks shot up as Ossan tossed iron filings into the closest fire pit. The coals flashed green for a moment as Ossan threw something else into the flames.

The first hammer blow caught him by surprise and he looked across to see Ossan set another ring onto the anvil, his chant rising to a hoarse shout as he brought the hammer down.

Kharios was looking as the hammer fell and his chant faltered as he watched. The anvil seemed to ripple slightly, almost pulsing in the air. Ossan didn't pause, perhaps he hadn't noticed. He set another ring onto the anvil, bringing the hammer down again.

Gold followed silver, followed bronze. The hammer strikes seemed deafeningly loud and Kharios felt a headache building with a pressure on his temples.

Ossan pulled out another ring and Kharios fell into a stunned silence. The ring was a shining steel colour but with the blue tint of truesteel.

249

"Father, no!" he gasped.

The priest fixed him with a glare so full of fury that he staggered back a step. "Resume your chant!" Ossan snapped, setting the ring onto the anvil. Kharios began again. He'd cycled through all of the rituals twice already and began with the first that sprang to mind, the first chant he'd learned, Calling Iron.

The hammer smashed down onto the truesteel ring and then simply exploded. Kharios staggered back as a shard caught him high on the forehead, dropping him down to his knees, gasping in agony as he grabbed at his face.

A low keening was coming from the anvil and Kharios pushed himself up with one hand. He felt gingerly for the wound on his forehead and brought his hand back, slick with blood.

Ossan was dead. More than dead. He lay slumped down over the anvil with blood still flowing from the split wreckage of his head. The shards of the exploding hammer had torn his forehead apart and what remained was a bleeding mess. Smoke rose from the anvil in dark, oily wisps that spiralled around the altar of the Forgefather in some unfelt air current.

Kharios gagged at the bloody spectacle of Ossan's body. The keening seemed to be coming from the anvil itself, or perhaps it came from the smoke. Kharios shook his head and rubbed at his eyes. He was probably suffering from the blow to the head, seeing things. This couldn't be real.

"What in the hells?" he muttered, shaking his head again.

His panic rose as the keening increased in volume until Kharios couldn't deny it any longer. He wasn't imagining this. The wisps of black smoke that had been floating around the room were coalescing into eel-like creatures of roiling mist and smoke that tore around the room, trailing streams of their essence out behind them.

Kharios looked around in panic and then froze as Ossan twitched. His hand flailed like a landed fish but quickly grew steady and the priest pushed himself up off the anvil until he stood upright. His face was a bloody ruin. Jagged holes showed where the shards of the hammer had torn through his skull. He turned his head slowly, gazing about the room with eyes that were darker than the lowest pits of the mines, and then threw his arms wide with a roar.

The sound that erupted from Ossan's throat was something that no man could have matched and Kharios watched in horror as the first of the streams of smoke crashed into his chest. Ossan, or whatever he'd become, staggered backwards and then the smoke began to pour back out from his eyes and mouth in an inky stream until it reformed into the eel-shape once more.

The difference passing through Ossan's body had made to the creature was obvious, and Kharios scrambled back away from the sinuous form as the face finished emerging from the mist, and from the burning eyes that now gazed at him with a growing curiosity.

Kharios didn't stop to think, he ran. His feet listened to the fear that screamed at them to move faster. He hurled himself down the steps leading to the altar, ducking under the mindless trails of smoke that were still passing in lazy turns around the room.

Stupidity made him glance back as he reached the doorway. The wraith watched him from the altar, unconcerned at his flight as Ossan lumbered down the steps after him. Another of the wraith creatures flew into Ossan's chest, staggering him. And then another. Kharios fled.

Kharios's screams echoed through the hallways as he fled, paying no attention to where he was going. He was dimly aware of doors crashing open behind him and some brief screams, but beyond that all was a blind terror as he flew through hallways and passages. He was only vaguely aware of the stairs, or of the priests he passed who looked after him as if he'd gone mad.

He was curled into a tight ball when he came back to himself. He'd huddled down inside a hall cupboard, nestled tight beside a mop and bucket. One eye cracked open wide enough to tell him that he hadn't closed the door fully when he climbed in to hide. He shuddered at the realisation and reached out to claw it shut.

The memories came flooding back as he sat in the darkness. There had been shouts, and rushing feet, and then the screams had begun. The

251

screaming had stopped some time ago, and he huddled in the darkness of the cupboard staring at the dim light that filtered through the crack. Fear, like anger and joy, can only be sustained for so long and exhaustion seeped in to fill the void that remained as it ebbed away. For want of any real alternative, he slept.

***

Kharios jerked awake in the darkness, lashing out convulsively and crashing his shin into something unseen as he flailed at the gossamer touch on his neck. A cobweb. Fucking spiders. He shuddered at the thought of how many of the things might have been crawling around on him whilst he slept. He shifted, and tried to ignore the throbbing pain in his leg.

The cupboard smelled of old soap, dust, and damp mop. Kharios wrinkled his nose at the smell and tried to shift into a better position. He dozed for a while, there wasn't much else to do. The smell didn't improve once he'd used the bucket. He ought to be grateful that there had been one he supposed. When you have to go, you have to go, and hiding had always had him wishing for a chamber-pot.

The aches in his back seemed to increase no matter which way he moved but it was the growling in his stomach that finally forced him to face facts.

"So now what?" He shaped the words with his lips.

No answer was forthcoming, but then he hadn't really expected it to be. One thing was obvious, he couldn't stay where he was forever. Even if the thing that Ossan had become, or the wraiths, didn't find him, he had no food or water. He listened carefully for a moment but the cupboard was as silent as it had been since he'd woken.

Was it morning yet? It had been late when Ossan had begun the ritual. How long had he slept?

He reached for the door, pushing it just wide enough to let him peer through the crack. The hallway was dim. The one candle he could see was a guttering stump.

There was nothing to see through the crack by the hinge and he forced himself up and out of the cupboard, moving slowly and listening for any sound.

Which way to go, though? For a brief moment he thought about working his way down to Aspiration but then, why bother? The whole point of becoming a novice was to escape the mines. With Ossan dead was there really anything holding him here now? Could he simply escape in the confusion? How many of the priests in the temple might have survived? The screaming he'd heard had been clear enough. Was there really anyone in a position to stop him if he chose to run? The realisation was an odd thing and he stopped in the hallway with a frown as he puzzled at it. He was free. For the first time since arriving at this cursed place, there was nothing to stop him from leaving. He made it to the end of the corridor before he thought about the others in Aspiration.

"You only get one life, Kharios," he whispered to himself. He'd had to fight to cling to the one he had and hell if he was going to risk it for people who wouldn't care if he lived or died.

He shook his head. "First you look after you," he muttered.

The sound was so slight that it took him several padded steps to really notice it. A whisper of cloth over stone accompanied by a shuffling scrape. He stopped, head tilted to one side. Was it getting louder? Shit! Yes.

He'd just passed a small candle store and he rushed back to it, easing the door shut behind him. The small room was dark but the door was old and sagged down on the hinges, letting a finger's width crack of light in. Kharios peered through the crack and waited.

The shuffling grew louder and with it came a scraping, dragging sound. The dim light revealed only a shadowy figure at first, dragging something behind it with a stunted, limping gait. As it drew closer Kharios could see the blood that had soaked through the grey robes the figure was wearing, and he bit down in the inside of his lip as he held his breath.

The acolyte moved in a slow but constant rhythm. One leg was very clearly broken below the knee, white bone visible where it had jutted

253

through the blood-soaked robe. The foot dragged along the ground at an unnatural angle with every lurching step, but there was no cry of pain, no flinching. Surely there was no way this man could be alive.

The acolyte seemed to pause as he drew level with the door and Kharios edged away from the crack of light. He might have told himself that he moved away in case the thing caught a glimpse of him through the crack, but the truth was that if it was coming to get him, he didn't want to watch it coming.

He huddled at the farthest corner of the small room, pressed back against the shelves as he clasped his hands over his knees. If anything, this was worse than fleeing Ossan. That had been a blind panic. This time he knew exactly what was on the other side of the door.

The shuffling sound of the creature moving on almost brought out a sob of relief and he clamped a hand over his mouth, pinching his nose and holding his breath as the shuffling sound receded.

Kharios eased out of the candle store. The hallway was on one of the outer edges of the temple, close to the temple walls but with no way of escaping outside. He glanced at a window set high in one wall. The glass was etched and frosted so that the daylight shone through and painted a pattern in light and shadow on the wall opposite – a cleansing flame. His laugh was stifled and bitter.

His padding gait gave way to a nervous jog and he passed through three hallways without incident. The temple was built into the hillside and, though there were other exits, they were all on levels below this one. The only way out of the temple, without passing through clear to the other side of the building, was through the main entrance.

The whisper may as well have been a shout and Kharios jumped, spinning around to face the small wooden door and the face that peered through the gap. "Is it safe yet?" the man asked in a hoarse whisper. "Did you see any of those people?" He was an older priest, crouched down low as he peered through the doorway.

"I don't think it's going to get any safer than it is right now," Kharios whispered back, glancing over his shoulder.

254

The priest pushed the door open and took half a step into the hallway, looking both ways down the hall. "Who were they?"

Kharios blinked. "Didn't you see?"

The priest gave a sheepish smile that faded quickly as reality intruded. "I'm afraid I just ran. I woke up to screaming and went to find out what was going on. I suspect a lot of people did. I got as far as the last hallway behind you when I heard someone being killed. It was an awful sound. Screaming and pleading and then silence."

"So you hid?"

The priest drew himself up, taking in Kharios's white robes. "Yes, novice. I hid. I'd expect you would too. And I'd ask you to moderate your tone, thank you."

"I'm sorry, Father," Kharios said, adopting what he hoped was a suitably chastened expression.

"Yes, well." The priest brushed the apology aside despite the fact he'd gone looking for it. "What is your name, my son?"

"Kharios."

"Kharios," the priest repeated, frowning as he sucked on his lip. He shook his head as he glanced back at him. "Father Keirnan," he introduced himself. "Did you see who they were? Some manner of brigand I assume?"

"I…" Kharios faltered. Who would believe this?

"No matter," Keirnan said. "I think best if you come with me until we know what's what."

"I was headed for the entrance hall," Kharios said.

Keirnan raised an eyebrow at that. "Flee? It can't be as bad as all that, surely?"

The statement was so ridiculous that Kharios couldn't keep the laughter from his face. Hadn't the man just finished telling him how he'd hidden at the sound of screaming and murder? "I hoped to find the other survivors outside."

"A gathering point?" Keirnan mused. "I suppose that makes sense. Shall we get started then?"

255

CHAPTER SEVENTEEN

Kharios followed Father Keirnan along the hallway. The priest had led off with a confident stride that had faltered and died within three paces. By the time they reached the end of the hall he had dropped into a fearful creep. The temple was silent again aside from the sounds of their passage, and Kharios cast frequent glances at the windows they passed.

The sunlight seemed to make a mockery of the events of the night, and Kharios had caught himself wondering if, somehow, it hadn't all been some kind of nightmare.

Keirnan stopped at the thick door, pressing an ear to the wood. "I don't hear anything," he muttered, looking back at Kharios. "I expect they'd all be long gone by now anyway. Still, let's be careful."

Kharios shook his head at the man's back as he eased the door open. *Let's be careful? The hells with that. Let's get out of here!*

The Grand Hall formed the innermost portion of the entrance to the temple. It was a grandiose affair with broad, sweeping steps, rich carpets and staircases leading up to galleries. Kharios edged out behind Keirnan as they made their way through the side door and into the Hall. Blood stained the marble, sitting in thick, congealed pools above the steps and covering the walls in spattered droplets.

"Where are the bodies?" Keirnan hissed, taking in the scene. "It looks like a bloody abattoir in here."

"Outside?" Kharios offered. Anything to keep the old fool moving.

Keirnan grunted and led the way down the steps. Kharios's head whipped around at the moan, and he shied back from the corpse of a priest as it shambled towards them, staggering down the stairs. The dark robes were thick with half-dried blood and the jaw hung slack and twisted.

"Great Father!" Keirnan gasped. "What's happened to you, man?" He glanced back over his shoulder. "Kharios," he said. "For pity's sake, help me get him outside."

Kharios looked at him, incredulous. How could he not see it? "Father, get away from that thing! Quick!"

Keirnan gave him a scathing look. "That's hardly—" He cut off as fingers clasped his shoulder and then screamed as they pressed in, sinking deep into his flesh. The thing's head shot forward, mouth agape as teeth sought flesh. Keirnan's scream cut off in a gasped gurgle as his hands scrabbled uselessly at the creature's robe. He slumped down, blood spraying from the ruins of his throat as the creature followed him down to the floor, tearing at his flesh.

He hadn't even been aware he was screaming until the thing's eyes turned to him. Kharios backed away, feet feeling for the steps. A sound behind him and off to one side turned his head and he saw another of the dead priests making its way down the stairs to the gallery. Kharios ran.

Robes are not well-suited to running and Kharios tripped twice, nearly falling, as he raced to the door. He whimpered, fighting back hysteria as he threw the door open and charged back down the hallway. A low moan from behind him urged more speed from muscles that were unused to the abuse, but Kharios was beyond caring about what his legs felt.

He crashed through more doors and down three flights of steps before he slowed. The sounds of pursuit had faded to nothing, and his frantic glances behind him showed only dim-lit hallways, but then fear is rarely interested in the facts.

"I suppose that means the main entrance is out," Kharios muttered. Shit, shit, shit! He was running out of options. His stomach growled again and he ran a tongue over dry lips. Now wasn't the time, but at some point, and soon, he was going to need food and something to drink.

The first corpse lay torn and broken against one wall of the hallway. Kharios peered around the corner at it for long minutes before he edged into the hallway. A bloody streak ran down the wall above it, mute testimony to its slide into its current position.

He studied it. Yesterday the sight would have been enough to empty his stomach. Now, he was just relieved that this body seemed to have stayed dead. That was the problem, of course. One dead body looks much the same as another.

Slow steps carried him closer, though not so close that he couldn't turn and run. Kharios grimaced. The bodies of the priests hadn't seemed to be very aware or intelligent. Other than the creature Ossan had become, who'd stormed after him with all the speed of a scared cat, they seemed to shamble along, barely aware of their surroundings until they got close. Would they have the cunning to lay in wait like this?

Kharios bent and pulled off his sandal. It wasn't much but he certainly wasn't about to get close enough to poke it with his finger. The sandal hit the body with a wet slap, sending the head lolling to one side. Kharios relaxed, shoulders sinking with a sigh. "Congratulations," he told himself. "You just hit a dead body in the face with your shoe."

He glanced at the body as he retrieved the sandal. It wasn't a good idea but sometimes you simply can't help yourself. It was a woman, he realised with a start. There weren't many female priests in the temple, which was odd as Aspiration had no shortage of women. But then, the only gatekeepers were men.

Aspiration! He stopped short of slapping his own forehead. Why was he skulking about in the bowels of the temple when there was an entire city below him that could offer help and shelter?

He passed more bodies as he descended lower into the temple. Some lay alone in the hallways and corridors. Others were clustered together in doorways, the doors ripped from their hinges and showing the scars of clawing fingers.

The passage to the mines was still. Had the creatures even made it this far down? Kharios already regretted the decision to keep pushing

258

down. It might have made more sense to try to make it to one of the supply exits that lead to the great stores of timber and kindling. In the end it had been a matter of practicalities. He'd lived in the temple and the mines for so long that he really had very little knowledge of the surrounding lands. Were there local villages and towns? How far were they? He honestly couldn't remember. He needed supplies. Food, water. There would be people in Aspiration who might help him.

The lamps were burning low on the walls and a number had already guttered out. Novices were responsible for supporting the many servants that worked in the temple. The daily tasks of replacing candles and replenishing the many oil lamps had now been left undone. It would not take long for the temple to be claimed by darkness. The chemlit mines might take longer to fall.

The darkness was almost complete around the gates. Five of the six oil lamps surrounding the structure were dark and the gates themselves hung open and broken. Kharios had never really taken the time to look at them in detail. The timbers were each over a hand's span thick in the frame that held the circular portal. They were worked into a complex pattern surrounding the gate. A lattice which wove the timbers around each other until they formed a structure as wide as a man was tall. Small gaps gave a glimpse through to the other side but no man would ever have been able to fit through. They served no purpose other than to demonstrate the power the temple held. You could see through the gaps. Two people with long arms might be able to reach through from either side and just brush fingertips. To pass through, however, required the gates.

The gate hung open and untended. Dark pools lay on either side of the portal as Kharios passed through. He had no need to look closer to see what they were. The heavy chains that had held the gate closed were twisted and broken. The locks, shattered and useless.

Shadowed murk gave way to the pale green light of chemlamps as Kharios passed through the second gate. This one had been built of iron and stone, constructed in defiance of the temple. Kharios stood for a moment, looking back at the shattered gates with their twisted hinges. What was he walking into? What other choice did he have?

Aspiration was still. The sunlight shining down from the fissure was enough to tell him it was still day, but beyond that he had no idea. With his frantic flight down through the temple he'd lost track of time completely. The streets looked empty from where he stood, overlooking the city. Smoke still drifted up towards the fissure. Surely that meant something? He shook his head. It could as easily be early morning as it could be evening.

He picked his way down the path to the city, moving slowly to keep his steps quiet. A thick silence hung heavy in the air. There should have been the murmur of distant conversation, the calls of market traders – even the distant rumble of the smelt works. Instead the city was as quiet as the halls from which he'd just fled. He stopped often, catching himself frozen by indecision. Was this really his only option? The silence of the city was unnerving. Even if he hadn't seen the pools of blood and the broken gates, the quiet alone would have been enough to tell him something was wrong.

The first of the bodies lay close to the base of the sloping path from the gates. A miner, still in his apron and helmet. He lay on the ground surrounded by the blood that had geysered when his throat had been torn out. More lay not far beyond him.

Kharios paused, letting his eyes show him what he'd been trying so hard not to see. Aspiration was a battlefield and the battle seemed to already be over.

He picked his way through the carnage trying to fight the feeling that this had been a huge mistake. His head was beginning to throb and he licked at his lips with a tongue too dry for the job.

The first priest he saw gave him pause. The body lay in a crumpled heap, crushed and broken from a flurry of blows. A mining pick still lay not far from the body. The priest's robes were soaked in blood, and torn besides, but they were white and that fact was enough to give him hope. No novice had a need to step foot in Aspiration. Their place was above in the temple. For the body to be that of a novice meant that it had been one of those taken by the wraiths above, and that meant these restless dead could be killed. Kharios pushed on, moving faster as he sought out any signs of life.

The creature hurled itself out of a small passage between two buildings, and flew at him. Kharios lurched back away from it, scrambling backwards and losing his footing as he moved. It moved in silence. No roar of attack. No cry of hunger. If it hadn't been for the sound of its boots on the stone ground, he would never have heard it.

"Oh shit, oh shit!" The words tumbled from his lips as he scuttled back in a panicked crab-like motion.

It snatched at his back as he got his feet under him, claw-like fingers raking at his flesh as it grabbed hold. Kharios lashed out with one sandalled foot, slamming it into the thing's knee hard enough to let him tear free. And then he ran. He sprinted along the street babbling his terror to anything that might have been close enough to hear.

They didn't move as fast as a man, he realised as he glanced back over one shoulder. Its movement wasn't quite a mindless shamble, but it couldn't match his sprint. So long as he kept ahead of it... He broke off as a miner burst out of a building, blood covering half his face from the wreckage of one eye.

Kharios shifted back into a run, outpacing the thing easily. He glanced back once as he turned the corner, heading into one of the larger roads. The dead were still coming. He might be able to outrun them but what happened when he needed to rest?

He slowed as he approached the remains of a barricade that had blocked the street at one point. Doors, carts, and furniture had been ripped apart and tossed onto the heap in an attempt to slow the dead as they'd approached. Bodies littered both sides of the barricade, and black scorch marks showed where it had been on fire at least once.

One end had been torn apart, sections of wood tossed aside as the creatures had broken through. Kharios sucked in frantic breaths as he slipped through the gap. He moved in a pained jog, one hand pressed to

261

his side as he sucked in air. The two dead men that chased him had given up. Either that or somehow he'd lost them. He hadn't seen or heard anything in twenty minutes now but he forced himself to keep moving.

It was the way they were so silent that unnerved him the most, he decided. A man, or even a woman for that matter, would scream or yell as they attacked. Even an animal would growl. These things didn't make any sound at all, other than the slap of their feet on the stones, and the effort of constantly being on watch for them was as exhausting as the running.

He looked around at the bloodied bodies. Priests and acolytes lay in a mass of gore. The blood covered the ground around them, where it had flown from countless wounds. The miner's bodies looked almost peaceful in comparison, if a violent death can ever lead to a peaceful state.

It had clearly been a running battle. Bodies were spread out along the road from where they'd chased the miners down one by one until they made a stand. Kharios would travel for two or three minutes between each gory scene. A priest's body, hacked limb from limb, surrounded by the bodies of miners. There were never less than five miners or unmarked to each priest. The significance of the numbers wasn't lost on him, and he had no illusions about his own fighting abilities if it came to surviving an attack. He looked back over his shoulder frequently, checking for any signs of movement. Any survivors would call out or make some sound, the dead would just chase him down in silence.

A distant yell was the first noise he'd heard that he hadn't made himself. He slowed as he drew closer, if it was a fight then approaching from the wrong direction would definitely not be a good idea.

Keepers, clad in their dark leathers and armed with long poles and sledgehammers, stood on a barricade of wood and rubble that rose almost twenty feet.

"Damn me. Another one!" the cry went up and Kharios glanced around in a panic until he realised that they meant him.

"No, I'm alive!" he shouted, waving one arm as if that somehow made it more believable.

Startled looks were followed with curses. "Get around behind us then, you daft bastard!"

Strong hands grabbed him as he climbed, pulling him up and over the barricade that blocked the end of the street. "Best get back into the square, son," the Keeper grunted and turned back to the street.

Gilden Square had been transformed. Men and women crowded around smouldering fires and cast fearful glances at the various roads leading into it. Each had been blocked off by tall barricades with men standing guard. Bodies littered the main path into the square, mute testimony to the fighting.

Kharios picked his way through the crowd for a time, suddenly unsure what to do next. He scanned the faces as he walked, looking for someone familiar. A double row of Keepers blocked off the end of the square and the steps leading up to the golden manse. Garl might be trapped in Aspiration with the rest of these people, but he clearly still considered himself a cut above.

"Kharios?" The call was wondering, almost disbelieving. "Is that you?"

Leesha sat beside a small fire behind him, twisting around to look at him. "What are you doing here?"

He gaped at her, eyes wide like an idiot. She was alive! Had Garl changed his plans, or had he just not got round to having the crew killed yet? He shook his head and fought for the right words until she patted the ground beside her and moved up to give him room to sit.

"What are you doing here?" she repeated herself with smile.

"I ran," he said, with a helpless shrug. "When these things attacked."

"The risen?" she asked.

"Is that what they're calling them?"

She nodded, looking into the fire. "The risen are the ones that don't know they're dead. The soulwraiths are the things that come out of them." She spooned something out of the pot set at the edge of the fire and handed a small bowl to him.

He took it with a wry smile. "Still taking care of me?"

Her smile was tired and forced. "Somebody has to, it seems."

263

That was probably best left ignored, he decided. "What did you mean, soulwraiths?"

"I haven't seen any," she told him as he blew on the broth. "Bryant told me about them. When one of the risen goes down, if they manage to kill it, the soulwraith escapes. He said it was like a thick black smoke that boiled out of their eyes and mouth that turns into something like snakes." She shrugged.

"And then what happens to it?" Kharios managed around a mouthful of broth. It had tiny pieces of meat in it and he realised it was supposed to be a stew. "Where are Bryant and the others anyway?"

Leesha shook her head, answering the second question without words. "They go into the closest person, Kharios. Living or dead."

"You mean…?"

She nodded. "That's why there are so many dead miners already." She gave a grimace at his expression. "It doesn't happen every time. One in ten, maybe less. The soulwraiths came down from the temple surrounded by risen priests. We didn't stand a chance. You can't fight off the dead, and the wraiths seem unstoppable. It's like fighting smoke. They pass into a person and it seems like they force that person's soul out, leaving the body to the wraith." She met his eyes and grimaced. "Bryant told me that sometimes you can see it, like a wisp of pale smoke that drifts away on the breeze."

He knew he probably shouldn't ask the question, but he did anyway. "What happened to the crew?"

"What do you think, Kharios?" she snapped, looking down and then meeting his gaze again with an apology in her eyes. "We're Blackers, Kharios. Nobody gives a damn about us. You remember where the hut was?" It wasn't really a question but he nodded anyway. "How close to the wall it was? When the risen came we had no warning. I've heard that they went for the priests and the Listeners first. Passing through whole sections of the city without touching anyone. Then, once they were dead, they came for the rest of us.

"There were a few screams but you ignore those if it isn't your crew, don't you? By the time we went outside they were everywhere. There was so much blood, Kharios. And nothing seemed to even slow them down. I saw a priest, he wasn't much more than a boy." She looked up at him. "He'd had his throat ripped out but he just kept moving. Five of ours, Blackers you know? They went for him with sticks. Got him down on the ground and just kept beating at him. He pulled them all down, one by one. Then he, it, just got up and kept on coming."

"Bryant?" Kharios asked.

She shook her head. "No, that was later. Gods above and below, Kharios. Can you believe this has just been one day?"

"No." He tried a tired laugh and then thought better of it.

"Where did they come from?" she asked him then. "I mean, I know they must have come down from the temple, half of them are priests, but why? How?"

He paused before he spoke. How much should he admit to? What good would it do her to know he'd been a part of this? "I don't know," he said. "How long have you been here?" he asked, looking around at the square.

"Since about mid-morning," she replied with a shrug. "Most of these people got here around then. They threw the barricades up during the night. Have to keep Garl and his gilters safe, don't we? They didn't do much good anyway. The risen just climb over them. They crawled up the sides of the buildings, even came along the rooftops."

Kharios glanced at the barricades. "So what stopped them?"

His question was met with a curious look and a shrug. "How do you mean?"

"Well, if they were rushing in that fast?" He gave her a helpless look. "Half the city in one night? Where are they all now?"

Leesha pointed at the far end of the square where Keepers stood ready. "Didn't you see the bodies?"

"That's only a few of them though. You made it sound like there were hundreds."

She shook her head again and reached down for a water bottle, taking a sip. "Not hundreds, not then anyway, but I take your point. They're out there. They seemed to stop when the day came."

265

Kharios looked up at the great fissure high above them, and then at the buildings at the edge of the square where the line of sunlight ended and the shade began. "Daylight? Do you think it's something that simple?"

"What do I know, Kharios? I'm just a Blacker. I can't see the risen being stopped by a little pile of wood in the road though."

"How are you still a Blacker anyway? What about the Listening?"

Her glance was hard. "We got nothing, Kharios. You might have earned your way back up to your temple but we didn't get a thing. We had the equipment but no real clue what we were doing, and the other crews don't take kindly to Blackers on their patch. Lumpet got the worst of it. I think he lost a couple of teeth. After that we stuck to what we know. We still have to meet the tally, you know?"

He let it drop and spooned at the thin stew for a few minutes, listening to the muted sounds of life around him. If he worked at it he could almost block out the memory of the night before.

"So what about Garl?" he asked between mouthfuls. "Has he said anything about the risen?"

"The Sefin?" she snorted. "You think he's going to bother with us? He's holed up behind good solid stone. I doubt he's even still there."

"Where else would he go?" he asked but she turned away, refusing to answer.

The broth was thin but at least it was something. Eating seemed to have woken his stomach and he emptied the bowl, wiping it out with the hunk of bread she handed him.

"Will you stay with me?" she asked him then.

He froze with a piece of bread halfway to his mouth. "How do you mean?"

"When the end comes? Will you stay with me?"

"It's not going to be like that," he told her, and wondered if the lie was just for her.

Her sad smile told him how convincing he'd been. "The sun is already going down, Kharios. If you're right, then we have a few more hours at most."

266

"Why is everyone so calm then?" he asked, dropping his voice.

"Maybe they don't know?" Leesha suggested. "People don't see what's right there in front of them. Or maybe they realise there's nowhere else to run?" She pulled herself up. "Come with me for a minute. I want to show you something."

He let her pull him through the crowd, towards the edge of the square and the line of shade that waited beyond the barricade. "Climb up," she told him, pointing.

"What?"

"Climb up," she repeated. "You can't see it from here."

"You're serious?" He gave her a look.

"Just do it."

Kharios sighed and reached up into the tangle of wood for a handhold. The barricade was more sturdy than it looked and he made good progress.

"Hoi there! What are you doing?" Kharios glanced down to see Leesha speak to the Keeper that had come running.

"He's looking at what's coming. Maybe you should too."

It took a few minutes for him to see it. The shadows were already deeper than they had been. Sunlight barely touched buildings only fifty feet from the barricade. He followed the line of the buildings and then jerked his gaze back to the foot. It was a boy, Kharios saw. He had probably been one of the Blackers but now the soulwraiths had claimed him. He stood, motionless in the shade, staring back at Kharios.

The risen filled the shadows. A wall of silent, motionless bodies that owned the sunless places. Kharios sucked in a ragged breath and ran his gaze back over the length of the street. They stood in every available shadow, lurking in the lee of buildings as the sunlight slowly ebbed and the line of shade drifted ever closer to the barricade.

Leesha said nothing as Kharios climbed down again. His expression must have told her something as he turned to face her. She looked at him and nodded once. "So you see?"

"We have to do something," he muttered.

267

She gave a bitter snort. "What, exactly?"

He grimaced, looking around as if an answer would simply present itself. "I don't know," he admitted finally. "The risen will cut through here in minutes. These barricades won't hold them."

She nodded with a simple acceptance. "I know."

"So why isn't Garl…" he stopped, looking around at the closest Keepers and lowering his voice. "Why isn't he doing something?" Kharios demanded in a hoarse whisper.

"What would you have him do, Kharios?" Leesha asked. "Every man, woman and child in here is going to die. And there's not a damned thing anyone can do about it."

Kharios shook his head and started back to the fire they'd left. He ran a hand across his face, stubble rasping under his fingers. He needed a shave again. He was trapped. Escaping Ossan? The flight down through the temple? All of it had been a waste of time. He may as well have stayed huddled in the cupboard for all the good it had done him.

Anger flared from frustration and his hands curled into fists. Damned if he was going to die here.

"What did you say earlier about Garl," he asked suddenly, frowning at her as he tried to remember.

"What?" she sighed. She suddenly looked very small. Small and tired. "I don't know."

"No, really," he urged her. "You said something about him not even being here anymore. How would he have got out?"

She started walking back into the square, glancing back to see if he was following. "I've no idea," she told him as he drew level with her. "It was just a thought, Kharios. I wasn't especially serious about it."

"No, but you're right. I can't see him staying here to die if there was any alternative."

She drew to a halt, looking over at the first of the fires. "If there was an alternative, do you really think all these people would be sitting here?"

He grunted with a scowl. "Unless nobody else knows about it, or has thought of it. There are no choices here, Leesha. We'll all fight when they come but these things don't really die. You told me that yourself. We have to get out of here."

"How?" she demanded, temper fraying. "You came down through the temple. Is it any safer up there?" She glared at him until he shook his head. "Well then," she said, as if everything were somehow settled.

"We can't go up. What if we went down?" He looked faintly surprised at his own suggestion as Leesha gave him a puzzled look.

"Down?" she asked. "What, into the mines?"

"I suppose," he said, scratching at his hands again. The damned itching seemed to be getting worse.

"What good would that do?"

He looked up at the fissure, thinking quickly. He'd said it off the cuff without really considering it but...

"There's water down there," he began. He spoke slowly, working his way through it as he went. "Whole rivers. It all has to go somewhere doesn't it? I mean, we think of them as the mines but they aren't really. They're just caves that we mine ore from."

"What difference does that make?"

"The difference is; this isn't some pit we've dug down into the ground. These caves stretch for miles. Who's to say there isn't another way out?"

"So you want to go blundering off into the dark?" Her voice was harsh, even scathing. "That's your great solution, Kharios? We could get lost. We'd end up starving to death in the dark."

"And how is that worse than this?" he demanded in a strained hiss. "I'll tell you this for free, Leesha. I don't want to die, but if I have to it'll be by dying of hunger or thirst while I'm trying to find a way to live. Not by waiting here for the risen to come and rip my throat out."

She stepped back, pulling his hands away from her miner's shirt where he'd grabbed her. She didn't comment, her look was enough.

"I'm sorry," he mumbled, looking away from her.

"How would we even get to the mines? The risen are out there waiting, remember?"

269

"Most of them are here, waiting for the sun to go down," Kharios said with a shrug. "I only saw two or three on my way here."

"The mines are the other way, Kharios," Leesha reminded him.

"Yes," he nodded. "So we'd have to wait for the sun to go down."

She frowned, not understanding and giving him a look like he was some kind of idiot. "So we're here, the risen are coming, and then what?"

"Then we run for the mines, while they're busy," Kharios told her, unflinching.

Her lips parted as she sucked in a breath and looked at him in horror. "You want to use these people as a diversion? As bait? To be ripped to pieces by the risen while we run?"

"These people will do whatever they want to do," Kharios told her. "I'm not responsible for them and they sure as hell aren't looking out for me."

"No." She shook her head. "Don't try and brush this away. If you're going to do this. If we are going to do this, we need to do it with our eyes wide open. This plan won't work if we all rush for the mines. We'd all just get pulled down and slaughtered one by one. You need people to stay here and die, to slow down the risen while we run away. That's what you're suggesting. That we sacrifice everyone left in Aspiration so you can live."

"Do you have a better fucking idea, Leesha?" he hissed. "I'd love to hear one."

She looked at him for a long moment but this time he didn't look away. She would be as much a part of this as he was. If there was blame to be had then she would have her share. "No," she said finally. "No, I don't."

CHAPTER EIGHTEEN

There was little to do but watch as the sun edged closer to the side of the fissure. Leesha had gathered up what supplies she had. It didn't amount to much. Kharios looked down at the two small sacks lying between them as they stood. Some stale bread, scraps of meat and cheese, and other odds and ends. It would have to be enough. They'd drank the skin dry. Water is too heavy to run with in any quantity and the mines were not lacking in it anyway.

People were drifting in towards the barricades. Some few moved towards the centre of the square until anger at their fate overrode fear but most stood ready to fight.

"Bloody fools," Kharios whispered to himself. They stood no chance. Death waits for everyone but they seemed to be rushing towards it.

The truth came to him as he watched them at the barricades. They weren't rushing towards death, they had decided that if they were to die, they'd go down fighting. At least that was the lie they had told themselves. The truth was probably something worse. They had convinced themselves that, somehow, they would win through. Their hope was probably a small, frail thing, but it was all they had left to cling to. Was what he was doing any better? Wasn't his plan to flee into the mines in the hopes he could find a way out, just the same thing?

The sun passed out of sight beyond the side of the fissure and a line of shadow moved steadily towards the barricades. There was a shudder that passed through the crowd like a wave as the shade touched and then passed the barricade. The tension was unbearable and Kharios met

Leesha's gaze as she plucked at his arm. "What are they waiting for? Why haven't they come already?"

Kharios looked behind him for a moment before the answer came to him. "They're waiting for the sun. For all the light to have gone. They want us to have nowhere to run to when they come."

Her face was stricken and he looked around again at the people pressing closer to the centre of the square, the few haranguing what Keepers remained on the steps of the Golden Manse, and those waiting at the barricades for the flood to come. "The hell with this," he muttered. "I'll be fucked if I'm just going to sit and wait for them. Let's go now."

"Are you sure?" she asked.

He reached for the sack by his leg, throwing it over one shoulder and set off for the far end of the square.

The barricade was lower on this side. There had been less attacks from this direction, Leesha had explained, which made sense he supposed. The risen would have had to work their way around the square to get to here, and what would be the point? He clambered up until he stood on the barricade and stared into the empty street.

"Do you see anything?" Leesha asked as she pulled herself up.

He shook his head and took the chance to look back at the square. The sunlight was just a narrow band, playing over the stones nearest to the barricade he stood on. It wouldn't be long now. They shared a grim look and then climbed down over the barricade into the unprotected street.

The first few steps were guarded, hesitant, things. Kharios looked around like a nervous sparrow, eyes darting from one shadow to the next. Leesha hung back slightly, letting him take the lead for some reason. It wasn't as if he could do anything to defend either one of them if it came down to it.

A roar stopped both of them and they looked behind them with frantic glances though they both knew what it meant. Screams were not slow to follow and they broke into a sprint. Leesha looked back over her shoulder often as they ran. Kharios stared straight ahead. He had no need to look. The roar was one he'd heard before. The roar came from Ossan.

A full sprint isn't really something that can be sustained, even when driven by terror. The sacks pulled them off-balance when slung over their backs, and tangled their legs if they were held anywhere else. Before they turned the third corner they had dropped into a steady run. The mine was easily twenty minutes run from where they were and the screams and sounds of fighting were already beginning to fade.

Kharios had slowed to a staggering lurch by the time they drew closer. One leg was protesting violently and a stabbing pain ran along the inside of his thigh with every step.

"There!" he managed between snatched breaths, pointing at a storage hut. They were rarely locked and Kharios crashed through the thin wooden door, snatching up helmets and vials of chems.

"Take this." He thrust a helmet at Leesha, dropping chems into his sack and grabbing for more. A quick look back the way they had come told him nothing but it couldn't be long before they were followed. Shadows were shifting at the further reaches of his vision. He squinted trying to see into the darkness and then caught himself, movement meant only one thing.

The smelt works were closed off. A heavy iron-bound door was set in place that Kharios couldn't remember ever having been closed before. He jerked his head at it as they raced for the entrance to the mine. "If he's anywhere, he's in there."

"Garl?"

"For whatever good it will do him," Kharios managed. "The cargo-lift goes right into the base of the temple. If he's in there, then he's locked himself in with the risen."

Leesha's answering grin was vicious.

The large chemlamps still burned in the main shaft. The walls threw the sound of their running feet back at them and they slowed to a walk as they made their way in. It was too hard to control their pace running downhill, and the ground shifted underfoot. Kharios led the way and they travelled in silence as the light from the entrance ebbed away and they were left with only the pale green of the chemlamps on the walls.

273

The mines held fast to any sound, throwing back echoes that could last for hours in the right circumstance. The chemlamps began to spread out as they descended and Kharios clapped his helmet onto his head, flicking the switch that would let the chems dribble through. He reached out to stop Leesha as she made to do the same. "Let's just run the one for now. We don't know how long they're going to have to last."

She gave him an odd look, eyes narrowing before she nodded. She doesn't trust me, he realised. Not entirely anyway.

He licked his lips, thinking what to say, but stopped at the sound behind them. Rushing footsteps crunched over the loose splinters of stone that made up much of the floor of the mine. Twin beams of light wove madly into the gloom as the miners rushed towards them. Leesha made to call out but he grabbed at her arm in time to hear the miner's shout. "Run!"

"Shit!" He didn't need to be told twice and they both broke into a sprint. He nearly fell twice before the slope levelled off, and the loose stones flew out from under his feet. He could hear the voices of the others behind them, between the crunch of his footsteps. The words were lost, but the tone was clear enough. They were panicked.

The lifts were well-lit by large chem-lamps on the walls and he yanked the handle upwards on the closest one. The wooden slats slid upwards, clanking as they went. Leesha grabbed at him as he reached for the braking lever. "We can't just leave them. Wait for a second."

He drew a breath but her expression was clear enough. These two, they would try and save. That was their penance. They might have left Aspiration to its fate but these two, they would save.

Kharios stood ready as Leesha took half a step out of the lift. "Come on!" she shouted. "You can make it, we're ready."

The pair were visible now. A man and woman, sprinting over the loose stone. The man yelled as he fell, crashing to the floor. He was up just as quickly, waving his partner on as she slowed. The fall was enough to give Kharios a glimpse of what followed them. The risen was small, probably a boy or a young man. It ran in a lope, the arms flopping use-

274

lessly by its sides as it came at them. The mere fact it was running was enough. The others hadn't managed more than a shuffling jog.

"Get away, Jaris," the man growled as she slowed to help him, ducking under his arm. He'd done something to his leg when he fell and his hobbling limp was too slow to give him much of a chance.

"Damn you, Brast, I bloody well won't!"

"Come on!" Leesha screamed at them as the risen lurched out of the murk, but it was too late.

Jaris fell without a sound as the risen grabbed her and pulled her to the ground. Her scream tore free of her throat as the creature threw itself at her, teeth tearing into her.

"Jaris!" Brast grabbed at the risen but it ignored him utterly, its attention fixed on the woman in its clutches. His scrabbling hands freed a pick and the creature crashed to one side as the glancing blow caught it in the back. The risen spun like a kicked cat and rose to its feet, eyes bright as it flung itself at Brast.

The mining pick caught it in the side of the head, the pick flying from Brast's grasp as the creature fell to the stone. Its blood was almost black in the green light, spattering over Brast's face.

"I got the bastard!" he grinned as he cuffed the blood from his face. "Jaris, did you see that?" he said, turning. And then, "Jaris!"

Brast scrambled over the stone. "Jaris!" his cry was a breathless gasp but it still split the darkness as he pulled her to him. Her body flopped limp against him and Kharios felt the grimace grow on his face.

"Kharios, look!" Leesha pointed at the body of the risen and the growing shadow surrounding it as dark tendrils boiled from the eyes and lips.

"Soulwraith," he hissed as the mist coalesced into the oversized eel shape and the face formed. The glow of its eyes grew steadily; twin pinpricks of light that shone sullen like embers.

"Brast!" Leesha cried out but if the man heard her over his own cries the warning was ignored. The soulwraith drifted towards him, the loose tendrils of its form trailing over the ground. Brast glanced up at the last, seeing the soulwraith approach and no longer caring.

The soulwraith struck, launching itself into his chest like a striking snake and passed into his flesh. He screamed then, an agonised cry of pain and loss. And then there was silence. In the glow of the chemlamps the miner's limbs spasmed twice and then fell still as his head turned slowly to glare at the lift.

Kharios grabbed at Leesha, propelling her backwards into the lift as his other hand reached blindly for the brake.

**

The lift lurched as the brake released and Kharios hauled down on the chain that extended out through the small holes in the roof, running it hand over hand as he dragged the lift down the shaft. Leesha didn't move. Her gaze was fixed on the open side of the lift as it descended.

The risen had dragged itself up, arms and legs moving sluggishly as the soulwraith assumed control over the new flesh. It lurched forward in staggering, almost drunken steps towards the lift, gathering speed as it came.

"Help me!" Kharios grated, kicking at Leesha.

She turned in shock at the light blow and reached for the chain. The lift was not designed for speed. Even with extra hands on the chain it wasn't moving fast enough and their view of the passage narrowed slowly as the risen surged towards them with renewed speed.

One arm thrust through the gap, grasping blindly for a moment. Both Leesha and Kharios pressed themselves to the back wall, flinching back from the arm as it snatched at the air in front of their faces. Kharios edged to one side and gave the chain a tug, nudging the lift down another few inches. The wood of the lift's ceiling touched the creature's questing arm, and it withdrew.

Kharios hauled down hard on the chain, sending them down another few feet, and then hung limp on the chain as he sank down to his knees.

Leesha spoke first. A shuddering breath that barely gave voice to the words, "Gods, Kharios. That was too close."

276

He didn't look at her but instead took deep breaths as he wiped his hands down over his face. "Let's just keep going."

The lift moved smoothly with both of them at the chain and they stole looks at each other, Leesha cracked a relieved smile for a moment. It fled as she glanced up at the wooden boards of the roof and the small slot the two chains passed through.

He drew a breath to speak but his words were stopped by a high pitched scream as something crashed into the roof, rocking the lift on its chains. Kharios grabbed at her, pressing his hand over her mouth.

"This lift was built for ten men or more," he told her. "It's not some little storage shack, you understand me? It was built for strength. It won't be able to get in." His eyes sought hers and held them. "We have to keep going."

She nodded, swallowing hard and casting frequent looks at the roof as they worked at the chain. The risen clawed at the wooden boards above them, even reaching fingers through the small gap the chains passed through, but it couldn't reach them.

The lift rocked again and they shared a glanced before looking up at the roof.

"Come on," Leesha muttered, heaving at the chains again.

The lift worked on a counterweight and whilst it was easy enough to move it down the shaft, speeding up the process didn't seem to be possible.

Leesha glanced up often and Kharios could see the first signs of panic beginning to show in her eyes. His own were probably five steps closer to it. The light of the chemlamp danced crazily around the small enclosure and the lift shook on the chains as the risen pounded and tore at the roof.

Something gave way with a sharp retort. Kharios didn't look up. Knowing wouldn't help him and there is a comforting warmth in ignorance. There was nowhere to run if the risen broke through. They were essentially trapped. He concentrated on the chains, reaching up to his full length and using his body weight to haul the chain down.

Leesha worked in concert with him, making her own pull as he released at the bottom of his movement and stood to reach again. The sweat was running down his nose and the clank of the chain almost drowned out the sounds coming from the roof.

"Out!" Leesha told him as soon as the first crack of the passageway appeared. Kharios gave one last pull and wormed his way after her. The wooden door to the lift was little more than a series of boards held on their own chain and pulley system. Leesha pulled down on the handle, slamming the door shut after them and jamming a rock into the pulley. It wasn't much, but it might hold them for a few minutes.

"Come on!" Kharios called her, already twenty feet from the lift and backing away. "Leesha, let's go!"

She nodded absently, picking up her sack and backing away from the lift. The sounds of the risen had increased in tempo as if they were working themselves into a frenzy. Another board gave way with a crack and they fled.

Kharios led, taking them away from the larger passages as soon as he was able, and sending them on a winding path through a maze of older passageways. The caves here had never been mined. Some acted as a shortcut from one area of the mines to another. Others were simply winding passages that had never known the cut of iron, as old and mysterious as the caves themselves.

Kharios ran until his lungs heaved and his throat burned at the cold air. He felt Leesha close with him as he slowed, her hand pressing against his back to stop herself from falling. "What's the matter?"

"Nothing," he gasped. "I just need a minute."

"Let's just walk for a bit, we'll make less noise anyway."

The light from the chemlamp bobbed with his nod. "Do you think they can follow us?"

"I don't know," she admitted. "The one that got Brast seemed different somehow."

Kharios moved to one side of the passage as it widened, letting Leesha move up beside him. "I know what you mean. It was faster for one thing."

Leesha sucked on her lip and shook her head. "It's more than just that. It seemed stronger, maybe smarter too." She looked around her, as if registering where they were for the first time. "Where are we?"

"One of the older passages," Kharios told her. "I'm not sure exactly, I wasn't keeping very good track. I just ran."

She stopped, reaching for his wrist as she looked at him, horror parting her lips. "Gods above, Kharios! What if it turns us back towards them? What if we just blunder into them?"

"It won't," he pointed ahead of them. "Look at the floor. It's still sloping down. So long as we don't head uphill then we're moving away from the lift, more or less."

She raised her eyebrows in response to his shrug. "More or less?"

He spread his hands. "It's all I've got, Leesha."

They walked. The mines were quiet. The miles of tunnels were normally never silent. Echoes bred echoes and the sounds of mining crews at work carried for miles. Now, with the miners of Aspiration either dead or taken by the risen, the mines were still and the sound of their passage slowed their feet each time they drifted into a run. They didn't discuss it. The risen were back there somewhere, seeking them out. It would only take one of them to hear.

Leesha flicked on her own chemlamp after the first hour. Kharios gave her a curious look and then nodded. He didn't need her to explain. The darkness pressed down on them both. The silence only made it worse.

The narrow passages opened out into a wider shaft. Tool marks showed on the walls but it was a passage that hadn't seen work in years. The echoes came as a whisper at first, a muted sussuration that grew into the thumps and scrapes of rushing footsteps.

Leesha grabbed for his arm as he looked back, pulling him into a run. The silence shattered as they ran, crashing footsteps and gasped breaths robbing them of any ability to hear. The shaft split and Leesha pulled him into the smaller side-passage, stumbling over rocks and shale. She crashed into the curving wall as loose stones betrayed her and one hand skidded down over the wall.

"Shit!" She sucked in a breath, cradling her hand in her lap. Blood was already welling up from the scrapes and she pushed herself awkwardly to her feet using the back of her hand.

One leg buckled awkwardly beneath her and she sucked in a pained gasp as she sank back down again.

The sound of scraping feet turned his head and Kharios recoiled as the risen shambled into the passage. It had been a smelt worker, he saw that at once. Nobody else in the mines had that kind of size. Its eyes glittered in the light of their chemlamps and it surged forward, arms reaching for them as they skittered back away from it.

Kharios took the pick from Leesha, wondering at her as she thrust it at him. Just what use was this going to be? He thrust it out at the risen, jabbing at its chest and then ducking below its awkward grab for him. The head of the pick made contact and he shoved the thing back away from them, stepping back himself.

"Run, Leesha!"

"I can't, you daft bastard!"

Something about that didn't make sense to him but now was not the time to argue. The risen lurched forward again, with all the grace of a drunk staggering out of a tavern. Kharios sighed, risking a glance at Leesha. Was he was actually going to have to try to kill this thing? He side-stepped another clumsy grab and struck. The pick passed the risen's warding arm and smashed into the creature, crashing through its cheek and angling upward into the skull.

The handle tore from Kharios's grasp as the risen smashed into the wall, sagging down like a broken marionette.

"Shit!" Kharios breathed, stepping back away from the blood that pooled slowly from beneath the mangled creature. He glanced at Leesha and then back to the creature. "Shit, shit, shit!" It seemed to sum things up.

The first traces of smoke drifted from the body's eyes and mouth in faint tendrils. Kharios stooped and grabbed Leesha's wrists, hauling her to her feet. He ignored her as she cursed and swore at him and ducked under one of her arms, taking her weight. Kharios hurried her away from the body, pulling her in a motion that was more than half-way to being a lurching drag.

"Kharios, stop!" she managed from between clenched teeth.

"We can't," he grunted. "The soulwraith."

She put her hand on his cheek, pushing at his face until he was looking back at the body. "Look at it!"

He stopped. The wisps of smoke were trailing out along the corridor. Not coalescing into the eel-like form of a soulwraith but passing back along the tunnel as if called.

"Can you stand?" he asked, looking down at her ankle.

She tested her weight, wincing slightly. "I think I'll be fine. So long as you don't drag me along."

He smiled at that, at the absurdity of their situation. The smile slipped too easily into laughter, and then she was laughing with him. Together they made a brittle, splintered sound that danced on the edge of tears. A harmony that matched perfectly with how he felt. Too fragile. Too close to snapping, or breaking entirely. It ended quickly.

They carried the silence with them as they started moving again. The hysterical laughter had shown Kharios just how close to panic they both were, and moving on seemed to help. There was no other real choice but it felt important to be moving because they chose to, rather than because the risen were driving them on.

A shuffling noise grew in the echoes that chased them. For a time, it was hard to tell if it itself was just another echo but it became steadily louder and then Kharios was sure. The risen were back there, hunting them.

Leesha hobbled along as best she could, but even with her arm around his shoulders they probably wouldn't match the pace of a risen like the one that had taken Brast. Kharios urged her onward fighting down his guilt at the darker thoughts that were coming to him. *Leave her*, they whispered. *You can't outrun the risen like this.*

He ground his teeth. "No," he muttered under his breath. "This one you will not fail." He hobbled on, trying to ignore the distant shuffling and the sound of his own thoughts.

281

The sound of the rushing water came all at once, hidden by some trick of the echoes and winding passages.

"That's a river. The High Span do you think?" Leesha asked him.

"It must be," Kharios grunted.

The tunnel narrowed until they were forced to walk single file, and then turned sharply and the bridge was before them. Between one step and the next the rough floor transformed into the polished stone of the High Span and the roof vanished into the darkness of the chasm.

The span rose up into the gloom; a pale marble arc that bridged the chasm before them. It was wide enough for two men to stand abreast, but just barely. There were no sides or railings. Instead a shallow lip lined the edges of the span. A mocking thumb to the nose of anyone with a fear of heights. It would do nothing to stop anyone falling. Kharios grimaced as he stepped out onto the polished stone of the bridge, concentrating on the path before him as he tried to ignore the empty air that yawned beneath them.

Kharios spun at a hissed snarl from behind them and staggered back away from the risen that stood at the end of the bridge. Its eyes glittered in the glow of the chemlamp and glared out from the wreckage of a face that had been struck by blade and hammer. Kharios stepped backwards, pulling Leesha with him until he saw that the thing wasn't following.

It stood at the edge of the bridge, shifting back and forth as it hissed and snarled at the stones before it. Kharios frowned as he watched. A bare foot reached out, and recoiled just as quickly from the stone as an audible hiss accompanied the wisp of smoke.

Leesha glanced back at him over her shoulder, confusion clear in her face. "What the…?"

"It can't step onto the stone," Kharios said.

Leesha shook her head at his statement. "I can see that! Why though?"

"Who knows? Are you complaining?"

She ignored that and watched the creature as it snarled in frustration. "You realise that's the first time we've heard any of them really make a sound?"

Kharios blinked. "You're right. It's almost like there are different kinds of them."

"Like bees or ants," Leesha mused.

He tore his gaze away from the risen. "How's that?"

"Workers or drones, and then the queen, or something like it," she told him over her shoulder as she watched the creature. "Maybe the risen aren't that different. They have the slower, almost mindless ones we all saw in Aspiration. Then there's the faster, more intelligent kind that got Brast. Like this one. Maybe it has something to do with how much of themselves the soulwraith leaves in the body?" She shrugged. "Who knows?"

"How do you know so much about bees?"

"Really, Kharios? That's what's important right now?"

He shrugged. "Let's take it for what it's worth. If they get caught here we can lose them." He motioned towards the other side of the bridge with a tilt of the head.

It felt odd to turn his back on the risen and he found himself glancing back at it as they made their way across the span. It stood motionless, hands raised level with its chest as if resting on something unseen, watching them.

"Come on." Leesha pushed at him. "Let's get going."

He sighed and walked on. The bridge was high, rising up in an exaggerated arc that would make for a challenge as they passed down the other side. The darkness swallowed the risen behind them, and the rush of water far below them was enough to cover any noise it might still have been making.

"It's amazing," Leesha breathed as they reached the apex of the span. She played the light of her lamp over the walls of the chasm, tracing the beam up the stone until the end of the light was lost in the darkness, then back down again, past the bridge and into the depths.

"How far...?" she left the question hanging as she leaned closer to the edge, one hand on Kharios's arm.

"Gods, Leesha," Kharios muttered, pulling her back. "Don't do that."

"You don't like heights?" she asked, teasing with a smile as she leaned out again.

"I don't like falling," he corrected her. "Neither does anyone else."

"Miserable bugger," she told his back as he set off again. He stopped as she caught up, unmoving as she poked at him.

"Come on," she protested. "You wanted to go, let's go."

He shook his head with a small motion and pointed. "Leesha," he managed in a weak voice.

She sighed, frustration creeping into her voice. "What?"

He pointed again, shifting aside so she could see past him. The risen filled the narrow passage leading from the bridge. They were smaller somehow, crouched low over misshapen legs as they watched them.

"How..." She looked back at him as she clenched her fists. "How did they get ahead of us?"

"Look at their legs," he told her in a defeated voice.

"What?" Her faced creased as she looked back and forth. "What do you mean? I don't have the energy for this, Kharios. Just tell me!"

"They're broken," he told her. "Shattered."

"What happened to them? We took the lift down. They couldn't have worked out how to use one of the others surely? There's no other way into the mines except for the ladders and there's no way that's faster."

"They didn't climb, Leesha," he said quietly. "They jumped."

She sank down slowly dropping the sack as she put her face into her hands. "No, no, no." She drew out the words until they became a wail that echoed across the chasm.

There was nothing to say. Kharios clambered down onto the stones of the bridge, sipping from the skin as he sat cross-legged. Leesha looked at him, incredulous, and then reached for the water.

They sat in silence for a while, listening to the water rushing beneath them as they picked at their food.

"How did you hear about the High Span?" Kharios asked, breaking their silence.

She looked at him blankly for a moment and shook her head. "You went back to the temple, Kharios. We didn't go back to blackwork right away. We kept working the mine for a while, found our way." She shrugged. "Miners talk. Even if they didn't, everyone's heard of the High Span. Even Blackers." She twisted her lips at the last, putting a tone of derision into the word.

He winced and she gave a wave of her hand, brushing her own words away with a helpless sort of shrug. "What do you think it's made of?" she asked then, leaning in to look at the bridge.

He looked down himself. "I don't know. I've only ever seen it once before and this is the first time I've been onto it."

"Didn't fancy it the first time huh?"

He shook his head with a laugh. "I suppose I needed a good enough reason."

She smiled up at him and then peered closer at the stone. "It's all one piece. Did you notice that? No blocks or mortar or anything. And look at these lines." She pointed and he bent against one arm to look. The stone was pale with faint greenish cast, though that could be from the light of the chemlamp. It was smooth, almost to the point of being polished, with faint strands running through it. The colours were varied, greens and blues ran alongside reds and rust. None lasted for long, emerging from the depths of the stone and trailing along close to the surface before sinking back into it again. It seemed familiar somehow but now was not the time to puzzle it out.

"What are we going to do?" Leesha asked him, pushing herself around until her feet hung over the edge of the bridge.

"I don't know," Kharios admitted. "Wait?"

She grimaced and shook her head. "How much patience do the dead have, do you think? I don't think that's going to work."

"I don't see that we have much of a choice, Leesha."

She pursed her lips as she tilted her head, conceding the point. "What if the soulwraiths come? The risen can't step onto the bridge but the wraiths could just fly over it, couldn't they?"

She didn't want an answer; she was building up to something. "What are you suggesting?"

"There's only one other way off the bridge, Kharios."

"What, jump?" He looked from her to the darkness below them. "Are you cracked?"

"If it's that, starve slowly, or be taken by the risen…" she shrugged. "I don't think that makes me mad. The water could be deep enough…"

Kharios shifted away from her, looking from one end of the span to the other. The darkness was too deep to see the risen but somehow he knew they were still there. "I can't do it, Leesha. I can't just leap into the darkness hoping there's enough water underneath to save me."

"Can you swim?"

"Yes, but that's not the point."

She gave a funny sort of nod, tilting her head and closing her eyes as she acknowledged the point. "I understand," she said. She paused, putting her hands down on the stone by her sides, and taking a deep breath as if she was going to say something more. And then she was gone, pushing off in one smooth motion and throwing herself into the black.

Kharios threw himself forward, arms reaching for her though he knew it was useless. The light from her lamp lit her fall, trailing down into the darkness. It illuminated the rushing water, closer than he would have imagined, and then it was gone.

He stared after her, gazing into the black as he tried to process what had just happened. She'd… just jumped. Somehow the reality of it just didn't make sense to him. He looked to either end of the bridge, looking for something to make it less real. The risen, if they were still there, were wreathed in the darkness that his chemlamp didn't quite penetrate.

He pushed himself up and walked slowly towards each end until he could see them. The risen watched him, silent and unmoving. "Forgefather!" he swore. She was right, there was no other way off the bridge. He glanced at the risen. Would he be able to fight his way through? The smelt worker had been slow and clumsy…

He snorted a laugh at the thought. He was no fighter. They'd tear him apart in moments. Even if they didn't, it was more than likely a soulwraith would claim him.

"Hells below and all the fucking petty saints," he swore, clenching his fists at his sides. He paced back and forth over the spot Leesha had dropped from. It made sense to jump in the middle, he supposed. There was more chance that the water would be deeper. Less chance of hitting rocks. He drew in a deep breath and let it out in a long, shuddering sigh. He was over-thinking this. Already he could feel his legs and hands shaking.

"Just do it, Kharios," he told himself. "Just fucking do it you bastard!"

He made sure the sack was tied tight to his belt and fastened the strap on his helmet. It was stiff. Miners didn't often bother with the straps.

He closed his eyes. Maybe it would be easier with his eyes shut. It wasn't, and he opened them again with a curse, turning around in a tight circle.

"Fuck it!" he roared, and ran for the edge, launching himself into space. He pinwheeled his arms as he fell, working to keep himself upright. His throat constricted, wanting to swallow even as he wanted to scream. Other parts of him clenched, and then he was crashing into the dark water, sinking down into an icy cold that was all too eager to claim him.

CHAPTER NINETEEN

Ossan's rooms were opulent. Dark hallways panelled in rich woods, and lined with lush rugs and carpets, gave way to a large library and study. Wynn followed along behind Brial and Ossan as the priest showed them around his chambers. It was hard not to be in awe. Compared to Aspiration, the priest lived in luxury.

The tour was brief, showing them the kitchens, library, and forge before ending in their own modest cells.

"I'll leave you both to get settled in and get to know each other," Ossan told them with a broad smile as he draped his arms around both their shoulders. "Call in to the kitchens if you get hungry. I'll have the cook prepare something suitable for tonight, to welcome you into my home. I imagine you could both use a good meal anyway and I always feel it would be wrong not to celebrate these beginnings."

Wynn fought not to flinch away from Ossan as he squeezed the flesh of his shoulder, pasting a smile he didn't feel onto his face.

"Of course, Father," Brial was saying as the priest stepped away from them. Wynn smiled again, it was easier this time now that Ossan wasn't touching him, and he nodded his thanks. He watched the older priest make his way along the hallway, turning once to wave at them both.

"Forgefather!" Brial whispered as the priest turned a corner. "Wasn't that something?"

Wynn cocked his head with a frown. "How do you mean?"

"This!" Brial turned in a circle, arms spread. "Look at this place. And Ossan himself, one of the most influential priests in the temple. I've heard it said that he's marked for great things. Maybe even to take a place with the Three when the time comes."

Brial couldn't be many years younger than Wynn was himself but there was something about the way he carried himself that made him seem younger still. His face didn't carry the marks of Aspiration. He had the brand on his forehead, the same as any priest, but the place gave most others marks that had nothing to do with the temple or the faith. It could be found in the tightness around the eyes, or just in the way people spoke. Brial had none of them.

Wynn picked the right of the two cells and sat on the bunk, testing the mattress. It was far softer than anything in the novice halls, and a world away from anything in Aspiration. He glanced up to see Brial watching him from the doorway. "What crew were you with, Brial?" he asked.

"Crew?" the young man frowned for a moment and then laughed at himself, coming in to sit on the bunk beside him. "You mean in Aspiration?" He waited for Wynn's nod. "Serpentis Crown. You?"

Wynn sat back, trying not to let the shock show. "I was on Terrik's crew," he managed. "It didn't really have a name." It all made sense now. Brial had come from a Gilter crew.

"Ah," Brial nodded. "One of the Blacker crews then?" He probably wasn't even aware of the way his lip curled slightly.

"It's not a Blacker crew." Wynn softened his tone as he spoke, aware he was grating out the words.

Brial waved his words away and shrugged. "You know what I mean, one of the lesser crews."

"Not a Gilter, is what you mean."

Brial shifted on the bunk, putting more space between them. "I didn't mean any offence. It's just how they were referred to."

Wynn sighed, pinching at the bridge of his nose. "I'm sorry. It's just not been the easiest time. I was told I would be serving the temple and then I ended up in Aspiration. It's just…"

"Not what you expected?" Brial finished for him with a laugh. "What was it like? On your crew, I mean?"

289

"Hard," Wynn told him. "We had to fight to meet tally every time. I lost good friends." He flinched away as Brial reached to rest a hand on his shoulder, his eyes filled with compassion.

"What's it like on a Gilter crew?"

"Ha!" Brial snorted a laugh. "Do you know; I don't think I've ever heard that term before? I suppose it makes sense. Gilt, gold." He shrugged. "I don't have anything to compare it to. It was hard for me. We worked with a Listener most days but we had to move fast to make it worthwhile. There was a lot of pressure, you know?"

Wynn nodded. A dark suspicion was growing that perhaps they weren't so very different. There were all manner of guilty connotations that came along with it. Wynn ignored it.

"Everyone hates the Gilters, as you called us," Brial went on. "They think we get some kind of special treatment. The truth is that any crew could be a Gilter crew if they worked hard enough."

"It probably takes a bit more than just working a bit harder, Brial," Wynn said, his voice carefully level.

Brial shrugged. "Yes, of course they would need a bit of luck too. But just think. What would happen if a crew had the marks to pay for two or three Listenings in a row?"

"They'd be hauling gold all the time," Wynn replied, speaking slowly as he thought his way through it.

"Exactly," Brial said. "Gold gives the most marks. It's got to be the easiest life, right?"

"I suppose." Wynn frowned, not sure where Brial was going with this.

"That's all a Gilter crew is, you know?" He glanced at the doorway as he spoke. "But it's not all as perfect as you might think. Our tally is at least twice that of the lesser crews and the Blackers, and that's not even counting the Sefin's Purse."

"The what?" Wynn asked.

"The Sefin's Purse," the young man explained, breaking off mid-sentence to let loose a massive yawn. "We have to give a third of our take directly to Garl. Our tally has to be met above that."

Wynn frowned at that. The Gilters had always been a privileged elite to him. A pampered class of miners who barely had to work in order to meet their tally. The finest merchants and eateries of Aspiration catered almost exclusively to the Gilters. Unmarked or regular crew members would never be allowed past the door. Rumour had it that even if they did, they could never afford the prices anyway.

"I had no idea," Wynn admitted.

"No reason why you should," Brial told him with an easy smile. "It's probably still an easier life than one of the lesser crews. With a bit of luck Torik's crew will become a Gilter crew before long."

"Terrik," Wynn corrected him with a smile. The boy... No. He stopped himself. He wasn't a boy. It was hard to put an age on him but he was more young man than boy. He was hard to dislike. He was naive and had undoubtedly been pampered during his time in the mines, at least compared to Wynn's own experience, but Brial was treating the temple as a new beginning. Maybe he should be as well.

They talked until hunger drove them to the kitchens. A cook, leaning in close over an elaborate pie crust, directed them to bread and soup with grunted words and gestures, without once looking up. The soup was simple but the bread was fresh-baked and soft. Steam curled up as he tore it open and Wynn ate slowly, savouring each bite.

He glanced up as he felt the eyes on him. "What?"

Brial's lips twisted as he smothered the laugh. "It's only bread, Wynn."

And just like that, the divide was back. They might have both suffered in their own ways, life on the Gilter crew had certainly never been the easy road that he had always imagined it was, but Brial had never wanted for anything.

"You've been too pampered. This is the best bread I've had in years," Wynn retorted, pulling another chunk off the loaf.

"Ha," the cook snorted, looking back at them over one shoulder. "Well one of you will get fed again."

Wynn grinned as Brial shrugged off the remark and tried not to look worried.

"What do you want to do now?" Brial asked. "We've still got hours before Father Ossan will want us."

"There's plenty of work needs doing," the cook grunted as he pushed the completed pie to one side and began rolling out fresh pastry. "Ossan always seems to think it does itself. While you two young'uns are here you'll be expected to pitch in and do your bit."

Brial bristled at that, shrugging off Wynn's arm. "We're here to study, not to pick up your sl…" he glared at Wynn as he poked at him and snapped angrily. "What?"

Wynn ignored him, speaking over the shorter man's head. "We'll be glad to help."

His words were met with a grunt and a nod. "There's coal and wood needs bringing up from the service tunnels. Follow this hall outside to your left and take the last door. The steps will take you down to the tunnels. The fuel should be waiting for you at the bottom. Ossan's store is back in that hall, in the room opposite. Bring a sack of coal in here when you're done. I'll be needing it by then."

Brial followed him along the hall, sullen eyes boring into his back. It was probably too much to hope that he would stay silent for long. Wynn sighed as Brial started to speak.

"Nice going there. We had an afternoon to ourselves and now we're lugging coal and firewood for the bloody servants."

Wynn gave him a hard look. "Somebody has to do it."

Brial gave a pitying sigh. "You're not in Aspiration anymore, Wynn. You don't have to limit yourself."

Wynn frowned, glad that the dim light hid his features in the hall. Just what was that supposed to mean? The door to the service tunnels was easy enough to spot and he busied himself with the heavy locks and bolts, reaching the key down from the hook set beside the door.

"What do you mean, limit myself?" he asked finally, giving up on teasing the meaning from it.

"You are what you are, Wynn," Brial said, following him down the steps. "You're here for a reason. Not everyone in Aspiration will rise. Not everyone can become a Gilter, and not just anyone could pass the trials to become a novice. It's just the way of the world. Cream always rises to the top. Back in Aspiration you probably felt awkward when the priests came calling for you, or during lessons with your tutors. It's okay now. There are no more envious eyes. You can just be you."

"I am being me," Wynn muttered as he reached the bottom of the stairs and turned towards the sacks of coal set neatly beside the steps. He stooped and hefted a sack of coal up onto his shoulder before he stopped. "What do you mean, 'tutors'?"

Brial gave him a curious look. "Your tutors? The priests that saw you all weekly for lessons?"

"Father Lasris, you mean? The priest who trained me for the trials?"

"No." Brial shook his head. "Before that. Didn't you have tutors for metallurgy and chemiks? Training in smithing?"

Wynn stepped past the younger man with a shake of his head, taking the coal up the steps. Brial might not see it himself but it was clear he'd lived a life very different to the rest of Aspiration.

Loading the coal was not pleasant. Brial complained constantly, a litany that Wynn worked hard to reduce to an annoying drone in the background.

They were both two shades from black by the time the work was done. The sacks were well-made but coal dust will sift through almost anything in time. Brial glowered at him well after the point when they'd managed to scrub it off and Ossan had sent for them.

"Come. Sit," Ossan said, waving them into the large room with his wineglass.

The dining room was large and the table was covered in more dishes than five times their number would need. Wynn perched on the edge of the chair. It was stained and varnished to a deep, rich shine and probably weighed almost as much as he did. Even so he perched, uncomfortable in the opulence.

Brial, he saw, had no such problems, settling into the chair and accepting the offered wine with a casual smile. Ossan didn't stand on ceremony, reaching for the closest dishes and heaping his plate high.

The food was rich and perfectly cooked but Wynn found himself only picking at it as Ossan and Brial ate. The priest finally pushed his plate back with a satisfied sigh.

"It's not something I do every day but new novices are an excuse I can use," he said with a smile. "It does help to have an exceptionally talented cook on board, of course."

"It was excellent," Brial said, refilling his own glass again. The wine was a rich red and Wynn had barely sipped at it before he felt it having an effect. Brial drank it like it was no more potent than water.

"To business then," Ossan said, leaning back in his chair and cradling his glass on his paunch. "A novitiate like this is generally beneficial all round. I have some expectations of course, you will have some tasks to perform in addition to your own studies, but I hope I can teach you both a thing or two. In return, I'd like to think you can assist with my own research."

"Your research?" Brial asked.

Ossan nodded. "Yes, so much of our faith was lost in the Fall. Not just the contraction of the church, but the physical records. The great library in the old temple is said to have been twelve floors high."

The interest on Brial's face waned as Wynn looked on, becoming forced and strained. If Ossan noticed, he made no sign but he barely looked at them in any event. He was sat back in the chair, eyes half closed as he went on.

"How much knowledge was lost? We know that the secrets of truesteel, for example, perished in the flames. What else was taken from us? Our faith is a shadow of what it once was. The Father has turned his face from the church and it lies upon us," he looked at them in turn, "to regain his favour."

"A research project then?" Brial's face was carefully neutral but Ossan must have seen something as his bearded face split in a smile.

"It won't be as dull as all that, my young friend," he said. "Novices are always the same. Always focused on the forgework and the rings of mastery. I've no doubt you'll leave here with at least an iron ring on your finger, Brial. Perhaps copper too." He smiled at the relief on Brial's face.

"And you, Wynn. You've been very quiet so far. What do you hope for?" His smile was open, even fatherly, but something about the man felt wrong to Wynn. He sipped at his wine to give him a second to think. "I do enjoy forgework, father, but—"

"Ahh, yes." Ossan smiled, interrupting him. "The seeker of truth. I remember. Well, I hope to find more than enough to spark your interest." His face grew animated as he spoke. "The destruction of the great temple was a sudden event. The mob ransacked the upper halls and the fire raged for days. The great temple soared far higher than this, our new home of the faith. The fire ate away the ceiling beams, mortar grew brittle and cracked, and the temple collapsed in upon itself."

He reached for his glass and drained it, looking down at the table as he sucked on his lip. "Water probably did as much damage to the books and scrolls as the fire did. It took months to dig out enough of the rubble to start salvaging what they could. The great anvil, the remaining stores of truesteel, a tiny smattering of books – that is all we managed to scavenge from the carcass of the temple. The knowledge we have amassed since has been brought from across the world, salvaged from broken churches and Defender's Halls. More than a few books have been bought at great expense from various private collectors. And how close do you think, after all this time, we are to recovering the secrets of truesteel or the lost rituals of the faith?"

Wynn shook his head wordlessly.

"We're adrift, Wynn," Ossan confessed, looking tired suddenly. "We have recovered much of our lost forgecraft, even some of the chemiks that once went hand in hand with it, but the deeper knowledge? The ritual and true understanding? It's gone, perhaps forever. Truesteel was said to be an alloy of steel, ritual, and faith." He gave a wry smile. "I suspect it might be slightly more involved than that, but the secret is lost to us now.

In any event, priests have spent centuries poring over the books we have recovered. It's doubtful you or I could discover much more. What I wish to focus on is the Fall itself."

Wynn glanced at Brial, the younger man didn't hide boredom well. "There are writings about the Fall?" he asked Ossan.

"Oh, hundreds." Ossan waved a derisory hand. "All the lamentations and gnashing of teeth any man could wish for. The blame is cast about in so many directions it's hard to find a group free of it. No," he said with a small smile. "I see no point in looking at writings from after the Fall. What I want to examine are those documents we have from immediately before it. The library perished but there are countless journals and diaries that were found in various chambers. I wish to search for some hint of the cause of the Fall itself. Find the sin, boy, and perhaps we can go some way to seeking forgiveness. Find forgiveness and we might reclaim our power."

Ossan called an end to the night as the wine ran low. He looked over to Wynn as they rose from their seats. "Why don't you come back to my chamber, Wynn?" he said through lips made slack with wine. "I've something that might be of interest."

Wynn glanced to Brial who gave a non-committal shrug from the doorway.

"Come on, I won't keep you long," Ossan said, moving around to drape an arm around Wynn's shoulders, pulling him closer. "You go on to bed, Brial. We'll speak again in the morning."

Ossan's rooms were close to the novice cells, up a short flight of stairs. Ossan staggered on the steps, leaning heavily against the wall and snorting a laugh at his own clumsiness.

He led Wynn in through a dressing room and past a private library until they reached the bedroom where he sank down to sit on the end of the large bed.

"Tell me, Wynn. Do they still use the lash in Aspiration?"

Wynn, shifted his feet, looking around. The bed was opulent and dominated the room. A small lamp burned in one corner, barely lighting the desk it stood upon. Cabinets and shelves lined one wall but there were few books. What was he doing here?

"They do, Father. Sometimes."

Ossan grimaced, shaking his head. "None of that Father business in here. Call me Ossan." He eyed Wynn slowly. "Were you ever lashed, Wynn? Show me."

"No, Father I…"

But Ossan's hands were already on him, turning him and tugging at his robe.

"Such soft skin," the priest marvelled, running calloused hands over his back. Wynn pulled away but the man, for all his fondness for food and wine, was stronger than he looked.

"Come now, Wynn. This doesn't have to be unpleasant. You show me a little affection and I help you in return. Is that really so bad?"

The man's hands were everywhere and Wynn jerked away at the dry touch of his lips on his back. The wine had taken its toll on him too and he stumbled as Ossan swung him round in a circle pressing him onto the bed.

A strong hand grabbed the back of his neck, holding him in place and Wynn struggled, twisting his face out of the blankets in search of air.

"No, please!"

Robes rustled and Wynn lurched away in shock as Ossan's hands grabbed at his hips, pulling him backwards towards him. A bare leg pressed against him. Ossan was naked.

Ossan slurred out a curse as a hand fumbled behind Wynn. Something too soft and yielding pressed against him as the priest thrust forward.

"Too much fucking wine," Ossan snorted. "You'll need to use your mouth."

Wynn tore free and threw himself across the bed, clutching his robes to himself and looking at Ossan with wide eyes.

The priest had slumped down onto the bed, chin sunk down to his chest as he muttered to himself. He looked up, feeling Wynn's eyes on his.

"Go on then. Get out!" he snarled, pointing at the door. "But breathe a word of this and you'll be back in the halls, boy. Understand? You'll rot there for your full five years until you go back to the mines."

***

"That took longer than a few minutes."

Wynn jumped and looked up at Brial.

"Did he have anything?" the younger man asked.

Wynn frowned. "What?"

"He was going to show you something, wasn't he?" Brial reached for his shoulders. "Are you alright?"

Tell him and you're dead. Or sent back to the Halls. Wynn shook his head. "No, he just rambled for a bit. He's drunk."

"That's going to be some project you're setting yourself up for then," Brial snorted. "Dredging through the diaries of long-dead priests and your only help is a man who drinks too much to show you anything. At least you'll catch up on your sleep."

Wynn looked askance at him and shook his head. The same thought had occurred to him. As much as solving the mystery of the Fall, and the truth of the religion as a whole, appealed to him, he had to admit that Brial had a point. But if it kept him away from Ossan's touch it would be worth it.

He looked away from the boy, the warning fading from his lips. Ossan had been clear enough with his threat.

"You have to have a break from the forgework sometime," he muttered. His response sounded as weak to him as it did to Brial. The boy's scathing look made that more than clear.

"Forgework is the whole point of this place, Wynn. Surely you've worked that out by now?"

That response had come too quickly. Wynn gave him a curious look. "What does that mean?"

Brial winced. "Nothing. I suppose research has its place. It's a fine calling."

"Just not for you?" Wynn finished for him. Brial grimaced again and fell silent. The cells were on the lowest level of Ossan's chambers, set beside storerooms that they had most likely been converted from. Wynn

298

checked the woodstove and blew gently on the embers as he stirred the fire back to life. "Fetch some water would you? I'll make us a drink.

"What did you mean earlier?" Wynn asked as Brial set the heavy iron kettle on to boil. "About the calling?"

"Forget it," Brial muttered. "I shouldn't have said anything."

He looked guilty, Wynn realised. "Tell me. Please?"

The younger man met his gaze with a sigh. "How did you come to be here?"

The change of pace threw him for a second and Wynn stumbled over his words. "My… My father brought me. My family are farmers and the drought had almost ruined us. I came so that they could use the Father's Gift to start again, get some seed-grain…" he fell quiet, the reasons sounded weak even to him.

"Not something you would have chosen then," Brial said, sprinkling the karas moss into the cups and breaking it up with his fingers. "I asked to come."

Wynn turned to look at him. "You asked?"

"Not for the religion," Brial said. "All the mumbo jumbo. I came for the forgework, for the training." He looked up from the cups, meeting Wynn's gaze. "Do you know how highly sought after Masterworks are? That's what they call forgework from the temple that was made by someone with their rings of mastery. A Masterworked sword, or piece of armour, can go for literally thousands."

"But surely that money goes back to the church? I mean, Ossan lives in comfort but…"

Brial laughed. "I wouldn't be in the church, Wynn."

"You can just leave? Don't they try and stop you?"

The kettle hissed and Brial busied himself with the business of making the tea, straining the karas moss through an elegantly wrought strainer. "I don't imagine they'd be overjoyed about it. To be honest, I wasn't planning on announcing it. The priests here aren't prisoners though. They're free to travel and many do missionary work. That's how I first learned of the temple."

299

"So that's your plan then?" Wynn asked, taking the offered cup. "To become a priest, take their knowledge and then…"

Brial winced. "You make it sound like a betrayal."

"Isn't it?"

"How much loyalty do you owe them then? You keep insinuating what a hellish time you suffered in Aspiration. Why do you owe them anything?"

Wynn didn't have an answer to that. He sat and huffed on his tea until it grew cold enough to drink.

***

Ossan put them both to work the next morning. Breakfast was a rushed affair, huddled in a corner of the kitchen, as they tried to stay out of the way of the cook and the handful of day servants who came and went.

The foundry was at the very edge of Ossan's suite of rooms. It was a large chamber with one third dominated by a forge and furnace. The remainder of the room was given over to a bewildering array of machinery and benches. A chemworks sat, isolated in one corner. Its contorted array of glass tubing and flasks shone faintly as they reflected the light of the powerful lamps set in the ceiling.

"Now then," Ossan said as he strode into the room. "I am aware you will have done some work as a part of your novice trials. Hopefully I can build upon that and not waste time rehashing things you already know." The man seemed unaffected by the wine he'd had last night. Wynn frowned for the briefest moment. Was it possible he'd been so drunk he simply didn't remember? The priest met his gaze for a second, and he had his answer.

Ossan nodded his head to the forge. "You two get that going and we'll see what you know of iron. In time I'd like to move on to copper and the married pairings like bronze. For now, though, let's see what you've learned."

The forge was well-maintained and larger than the smaller prayer-forge that sat on display in Ossan's chambers. Clever channels had been cut into the stone surrounding the firepit, that allowed for greater control of the airflow from the bellows and the two of them had the fire burning and up to forge heat in short order.

Ossan put him to working the bellows, and before long the muscles in Wynn's arms and shoulders were burning. The priest stood closer to the fire than Brial but seemed unaffected by the heat as he chanted, squinting through the light of the fire at the iron as it melted down inside the crucible.

"Now," he told Brial without taking his eyes from the molten iron. "Fetch those tongs and reach this out for us." He stepped back to allow Brial access and continued speaking. "You can stop now, Wynn. Come and see this. Note how the iron has taken on the colour and aspect of the flame? The heat and the power of the Father has infused the metal and now, with care, we can shape it as we will. Step over there, Brial," he said, pointing. "Toward the casting. Take your time, we don't want any accidents today. Now then," he said, taking up a position behind the boy as Wynn looked on. "Pour very slowly into the mould and we shall see what we can do."

The molten iron had the consistency of a thick soup and Wynn watched, fascinated as it poured into the mould, filling higher until the sword shape shone.

"Now, Wynn," Ossan said, looking down at the sword as the glow faded from bright orange to a cherry red. "What can you tell me about Brial's blade here?"

"Ahh…" Wynn faltered.

"Well obviously, it won't be a sharp blade," Ossan answered for him. "It would need to be placed on the wheel for that. But is it a strong blade? Will the strength of the sacred chants have passed into it? Of course not. In fact, this weapon would be all but useless. This is cast iron. It has a low melting point, which is why we find it useful, but it will also be brittle. Any warrior unfortunate enough to go into battle with Brial's blade would soon find himself in dire straits. In order to improve upon the strength of this mighty weapon we would need to hold it at an almost molten temperature and keep it there for days, letting it cool slowly. We don't have time for that, and so instead, more often than not, we will shape our iron rather than cast it."

He went on, taking them through the rudiments of heating and shaping iron. Ossan proved to be an attentive and thoughtful teacher as both of them took turns heating and shaping a simple iron rod. He called a halt close to mid-day, insisting that they both needed to eat and to take plenty of water.

"Brial," Ossan called as they headed for the door. "I want you back here in an hour. Wynn, I have another task for you."

"Father?"

"I think it would be a good idea for you to familiarise yourself with the great library."

Lunch was as simple and rushed as breakfast had been. Wynn slurped down a bowl of soup, ignoring Brial who muttered choice comments about the food and what Ossan was probably eating. He barely heard him. The blond man had been fighting down a smug smile since they left the foundry. In truth, Wynn wasn't remotely upset about the prospect of not returning to forgework. The foundry was impressive, and Ossan seemed like he could be a good teacher, but being around him was just too awkward. The memories of the night before were too fresh. Wynn had hung back away from Ossan for as much of it as he could, and had been grateful to escape to lunch. The library though? The prospect had him coughing over the bread he was eating.

He nodded a farewell to Brial as the young man stood and made his way down the passage, standing and taking both their plates over to the large pump and sink against one wall.

"Just set them there," the cook grunted. "I'll see to them later. At least you brought yours over. Your friend has ideas he's above all that, I reckon."

Wynn glanced back at the doorway and shrugged. There wasn't much he could say to that.

302

"No playing with fire for you this afternoon then?" the cook asked, a smile cracking his dour face.

"Father Ossan wants me to go to the great library."

"Probably best to leave the fire here then."

Wynn grinned. "Good advice. Do you have any idea how I might find it? I've never been there."

"Just head out of the chamber's doors and follow the hall to your right." The cook pointed. "Head down the stairs and from there any priest you pass can direct you to the library."

It felt strange to pass beyond Ossan's chambers and it took him the length of three hallways to realise why. He was alone. To a certain extent, he was free to go where he pleased. It was an odd thought, and not one he was used to. He hadn't had this kind of freedom since he left Aspiration.

The temple was vast, capable of supporting and housing a priest-hood far larger than the one that sheltered behind its walls. Wynn reached the end of the directions without passing a soul. He knew where Ossan's rooms were in relation to the grand chamber and the great forge, but beyond that he was lost.

With no better ideas, he headed for the grand chamber, passing down a flight of stairs and through a series of small passages until he began to see signs of life.

"Excuse me," he stopped a servant in dull colours. "Could you direct me to the great library?"

The woman stepped back, seeming shocked that he'd spoken to her for a second until she took in his white robes. "Of course, novice."

Her directions were as simple as they could be but he still walked for another ten minutes until he reached the library.

The temple had come to life around him as he passed into more heavily used areas, and the hallways soon become cramped and busy. Novices wove around each other as they walked, rushing about on various errands. The priests, clad in their black or grey robes, walked inside islands of calm as novices and servants rushed to get out of their way.

Wynn was still marvelling at this when the red-robed acolyte crashed into his shoulder, sending him sprawling. "Get out of the way of your betters, novice," the man grated, glaring at him as he picked himself up. He paused long enough to give him a look of utter contempt before striding off, leaving Wynn staring after him.

The doors to the library stood open and acolytes moved in silence past novices, priests and an assortment of brown-clad men. Wynn hovered in the entryway for a minute or two before being forced to step inside to make way for those behind him. The entrance chamber was a functional room filled with writing desks and lined with bookshelves. A brown-robed man caught his eye and approached with a smile.

"Impressive isn't it?" he asked, following Wynn's gaze through the double doors to the main chamber.

"Very," Wynn agreed, in a low voice. "I wasn't quite sure what to expect."

"I always enjoy watching novices catch their first glimpse of it all," the man chuckled. "It's probably childish of me but there we are. My name is Andrei, I'm one of the librarians here. "Is there anything in particular I can help you find? Or were you just curious?"

Wynn glanced at the other brown-robed men and women dotted about the room, and nodded to himself. "I, uh, Father Ossan sent me to familiarise myself with the library."

"Ossan," Andrei grunted with a terse nod. "I see. Well I can certainly give you a tour if you'd like?"

"That would be very helpful," Wynn replied with a smile.

Andrei gave a conspiratorial grin. "Don't mention it, it keeps me from sorting books, and that alone is worth it."

He led the way into the main chamber. It was dimly lit with chemlamps, the first Wynn had seen since Aspiration.

"You'll have seen these before, of course," Andrei said with a nod towards the closest lamp. "They last better than lamps or candles and, of course, there is no risk of fire or wax spilling. The library has five levels which are split roughly by century. The lowest level holding the oldest texts and, our own century's writings living on the uppermost level."

304

"So many," Wynn breathed, leaning on the rail to look down to the lowest levels. The rectangular opening lay in the centre of the chamber, dropping down through the floors until it reached the bottom. Wynn gripped at the railing spasmodically as a wave of vertigo swept over him.

"You don't expect the teachings of an entire faith to fit into a single book, do you?" Andrei laughed, oblivious to Wynn's discomfort. "Was there anything in particular you wanted to see?"

Wynn looked away from the drop almost gratefully. "The writings that date as closely as possible to the Fall," he told him. "Diaries and journals that might have been salvaged from the great temple."

Andrei shot him an odd look before catching himself and shrugging. "I'm sure we can find something."

The staircases were crafted from intricately wrought iron that spiralled down from level to level, passing down down through the rectangular opening at the centre of each floor. They were surrounded by solid iron bars, heavily stylised and decorated, but clearly in place to stop people from falling over the edge. It didn't help and Wynn did his best to focus on the books and desks lining each floor as they passed.

Andrei glanced back at him, noting the silence. "You get used to it," he told him. Wynn didn't believe that for a moment.

The bottom floor of the library was dark. The light from the chemlamps above didn't penetrate that far down, and the shelves were wreathed in shadows. Andrei reached a lantern down from hooks set by the stairs and flicked the switch in its base, letting the chems run. "It doesn't get much use down here. We tend to keep it dark most of the time. It's better for the records anyway and it's not worth wasting the chems most of the time."

Wynn nodded, looking around them curiously.

"Ossor has you looking for these journals then I take it?" Andrei asked as he led Wynn through the maze of shelves, stopping now and then to flick a chemlamp into life.

Wynn frowned. "Father Ossan, yes."

Andrei chuckled. "Sorry, bit of an inside joke. Ossor, you know? The constellation?"

"The great bear?" Wynn offered. "I don't get it," he admitted.

"Always with the pawing," Andrei said. His grin faded in the glow of the chemlantern and he shot Wynn a nervous look. "I didn't mean anything by it. Forget I said anything, okay?"

"Of course." Wynn shrugged and thought of Brial again and the man he'd left him with.

"The journals and diaries are very fragile," Andrei said with a cough. He cleared his throat and waved at the shelves in front of them. "They are the oldest records we have here."

"I'll be careful with them," Wynn promised.

"Oh you can't touch them," Andrei said quickly. "Not the originals anyway, they're all locked away in the archives. They all have a copy made but even that is precious. Every time we need to make a replacement copy we risk the original degrading further. The copies are not to leave this floor of the library, is that understood?"

Wynn met the man's gaze and nodded seriously.

"The records are organised by author so far as was possible," Andrei continued. "'A' will begin here. Given that there are a fair number of fragments, you will find a large section under 'unknown' but that's the nature of the beast I'm afraid, and I doubt you're searching by author anyway."

He stepped to flick on a chemlamp sat in the centre of a cluster of desks. "You'll find some paper and ink in each desk. Will you be needing anything else?"

"I don't think so," Wynn said, his eyes already scouring the shelves hungrily.

"Well then I'll leave you to it," Andrei said with a smile. "Don't hesitate to come and find me, or another librarian if you need help. Oh, and in case it helps at all, there are a number of examinations of the diaries already written. Vestok is the best one I can think of off-hand. You should find his work in the last row on the left behind us."

CHAPTER TWENTY

Darkness is timeless. The lowest level of the library knew nothing of the sun, or the passing of the days, and Wynn lost himself in amongst the books. The murmured conversations of others in the library were high above him, on the upper floors, and rarely did a sound travel down to him. Wynn worked alone, cocooned in his silence, as he lost himself in the diaries from another age.

The books were compelling. Not so much in what they said, but rather in the things they intimated. Most of the diaries and journals were merely the idle thoughts of the long-dead priests. Some were little more than a dry list of daily activities. Others though, spoke of things Wynn barely understood. They described long-forgotten rituals, and of priests communing directly with the flame, with the Forgefather himself.

Hunger forced him from the library the first day and the silent, dark chamber told him just how late it must have grown. He ate a cold meal that had been left out for him in Ossan's kitchen and collapsed on his bunk.

The days blurred, merging into one another as he continued his reading, surprising himself by how much pleasure he took from the solitary search. He saw nothing of Ossan at all. Brial, when he did see him, seemed quiet and withdrawn.

Ossan left him to his research for two weeks before sending for him to continue his forgework. The noise of the forge seemed somehow magnified by all of the days he had spent in silence, and for the first hour he found himself wincing with every strike of the hammer.

Cast iron gave way to wrought and Wynn worked with Brial, taking turns on the bellows as they perfected marrying the chant of Calling Iron to the practice of folding it.

"Now then, haul that out over here and I'll show you something totally new," Ossan said, stepping back from the anvil to give Wynn room.

The iron was a deep sunset orange and the air above it shimmered with heat as the priest leaned in close. A succession of gentle taps rang out as Ossan worked with a smaller hammer on a smithing stylus, and then he stepped back with a satisfied smile.

"This is the glyphmark for strength," he said, pointing at the cooling metal. He handed them both a slate and chalk. "Mark it out quickly."

The design was simple enough and Wynn copied it as Ossan returned the iron to the forge and pumped on the bellows until the metal glowed brightly again.

"Now," the priest said, as he deftly folded the iron, smothering the glyph. "Wynn, let's see you inscribe the glyph."

The chisel was fine-tipped and slender. Wynn bent low over the glowing iron as he'd seen Ossan do but flinched back almost immediately. The heat shouldn't have surprised him, yet it felt as if his hand had been holding the glowing metal, searing his flesh as he held the smithing stylus in place.

"Move faster," Ossan told him. "Five quick strikes and you can be done. Iron cools quickly and the metal is waiting for you. The pain is punishment for your making it wait."

Wynn struck hammer to chisel and worked the glyphmark into the iron. It was harder than Ossan had made it seem. The iron was pliable against the tip of the smithing-stylus and the chisel penetrated further than he would have thought.

"Adequate," Ossan sniffed, as Wynn stepped back. "If just barely. This is an art, Wynn. The technique requires you to move swiftly or risk burning your hands, but that is no excuse for sloppy work. This is process is a ritual itself, etched out in metal instead of by motion and chant. If we were simply making a mark in the metal we could have used a punch."

He turned and reached for Brial's shoulder, urging him closer. "You see how the lines of the glyph are marred and unclear? This is because Wynn was hesitant. This is a glyph. It's a sigil given us by the Forgefather himself. It is a command to the iron that it will be strong. That against the blows of hammer, rust, or time itself, it *will not bend*. Strike sure, and fast, Brial. You do not entreat the iron, you order it."

Brial flicked a glance at Wynn that barely met his gaze and took up the hammer. The stylus sang out five times as the hammer struck and Brial stepped away.

"Excellent!" Ossan beamed, leaning in closer to peer at the mark. He reached for Brial's shoulder, squeezing through the thin tunic. His hand lingered, and even as it slipped off as Brial shifted away, Ossan's eyes lingered still.

Ossan glanced at Wynn. Meeting his eyes for the briefest moment but the message was clear. You will say nothing. You will do nothing. Wynn bit hard on the inside of his cheek as he fought to stay calm, tasting blood. It tasted of cowardice.

The first two months were an orgy of discovery. Wynn alternated, shifting between library and forge every three days, and each new discovery was as bright and exciting as a young child spotting a copper penny in the street. The rewards of the research came slowly like a flower opening in the spring sun. The forgework brought a deep satisfaction with each technique mastered that eclipsed the burns and blisters on his hands and arms.

Before too long however, the demands they placed upon Ossan's household became obvious. The servants never demanded help, but it was made obvious in the subtle way that only a servant can manage that, if the pair were not to assist them in their duties, then the household would suffer. Drudgery, apparently, beckoned.

It was small things to begin with; loading the stores from the deliveries in the service tunnels, clearing out the prayer forge, and stocking the foundry. In time, it grew to daily chores that, coupled with the days they spent on temple chores in the chandlery, or the endless mopping and sweeping, had them rising earlier still and sapped at their energy.

Wynn found it harder and harder to concentrate in the library. The silence, once such a blessing, began to claw at his focus. The diaries were often as dull as the journals of a farmer; every day the same. He caught himself drifting to begin with – passing over whole sections of the text without meaning to, in search of something to anchor him, anything of any interest. Twice, he caught himself nodding off, his head sinking down as sleep reached for him.

The forgework was much the same. Brial fared better but still Ossan chided him for ill-timed strokes that came close to ruining pieces of work. Wynn suffered with burns, raising blisters that would not heal as the hammer rubbed against them.

"Have more care, Wynn," Ossan snapped, pulling him back from the forge as he flapped his hand against the pain. "You need two hands to work the forge, don't waste one through carelessness."

Wynn sucked as his fingers, wincing against the pain. "I'm sorry, Father," he managed between sucks. "I'm not concentrating."

"You haven't been focused in weeks," Ossan muttered. "Perhaps I push you too hard. The problem, my son, is that there is an expectation."

Wynn paused, taking his hand from his lips. "An expectation?"

Ossan shrugged, tilting his head to one side in an almost-apology. "The priesthood isn't without its own pressures. When one takes on novices there is an expectation for us to show off their achievements. It's a foolish and petty thing. The progress of a novice belongs to the student, not the teacher, but it is there nonetheless."

He hadn't thought of that. The fact that Ossan was under any kind of scrutiny or pressure had never even occurred to him.

"You realise, of course, that you won't be able to progress until you master these glyphs?" Ossan said. He spoke in a low voice, his words caught halfway between admission and apology.

Wynn nodded. There wasn't much he could really say to that.

310

"I could, help you. If you were willing to put in some extra hours?" Ossan offered. There was something about the way he spoke that made Wynn glance at him. His eyes somehow matched his tone. They glinted with something that made his words sit somewhere between an offer to help and a desire for something more.

It bothered him, though he would have struggled to explain why. Ossan obviously remembered what had happened in his bedroom on that first night but he'd tried nothing since. Had he just been that drunk? Wynn paused before he spoke, thinking. He wanted to say no. The man had given him enough reasons to want to say no. But then, Ossan was right, he wouldn't progress without mastering these glyphs. Brial might not be spending the time in the library that he was, but even ignoring the extra time he got at the forge, he had progressed far beyond Wynn.

"That would be very kind of you, Father." The words slipped past his lips, betraying him. He would rather be anywhere but alone with Ossan, even though he knew he needed this.

Ossan's hand reached for his shoulder, his cold fingers squeezing, and caressing. Wynn fought back the urge to shudder, pausing long enough to make it seem that he wasn't throwing the priest's hand off as he stepped back and away.

"Tomorrow, then," Ossan said, smiling. "You're in no fit state this evening. Get some rest and attend to your studies in the morning. We can meet in the foundry after you have eaten and attended Embers."

After Embers, that would mean that the servants would already be in their own quarters and that Brial would be looking to his own bed. Wynn nodded, avoiding meeting the man's eyes as the worries grew. The priest's eager expression found him anyway.

The time spent in the library was a wasted effort. His notes were jumbled and nonsensical threads of meaning he'd been trying to weave together from scraps taken from half a dozen diaries and papers. He pushed his papers away in disgust before gathering them together again and making his way up the spiral stairs. Losing himself in the chores helped. There is something comforting in the mindlessness of a simple

311

task. For a time, Wynn was able to push his thoughts away, to bury the worries beneath the familiar routine of clearing out ash and coals. Laying out kindling, wood, and coal to wait for the flame's kiss.

Ossan was waiting for him as he entered the foundry. The priest stood over the anvil, pounding the cherry-red steel as he chanted. Many of the words were lost in the ring of the hammer but the song itself was rich and clear, reaching to the farthest corners of the darkened chamber. Ossan sang to the soul of steel, strengthening and warding.

Wynn stopped himself as he approached. The figure at the forge was nothing like the priest who taught him. There was nothing of the wheedling quality to him, of the small man that reached for his flesh with cold, insistent hands. This man was a master of his craft, striking with precision as errant sparks flew wild into the darkness. His voice was rich and strong and the steel, Wynn knew, would listen and obey.

"Father?" he spoke softly. Shouting in a forge, even to be heard over the ring of the hammer, is seldom a good idea.

Ossan stopped the blow in mid-stroke, squinting in the darkness that lay beyond the glow of the forge. "Wynn? Is it time already?"

Wynn smiled as he stepped into the light. "Past time, Father. Embers is long gone, and it must be close to Ash by now."

"You should have come sooner," Ossan told him, chiding gently, though there was no real force in the words. He reached for the steel with a pair of long tongs and tossed it idly aside.

"Set to then," Ossan said, beckoning him closer with a wave at the forge. "There's fresh rods of iron in the bin there. Let's see what you manage tonight." He stood back and watched, silent as Wynn set the iron into the fire and pumped at the bellows until the red glow took root and bloomed into the bright sunset colour of forge-hot iron.

"Now then," Ossan said, his breath hot on Wynn's neck. "Move fast and sure. Strike at the iron as if you would command it."

Wynn leaned over the anvil, shrinking away from the man as he reached for the tongs. Ossan might be old but he moved faster and more quietly than most would expect. The priest's breath felt like it

312

had left a sheen of moisture on his neck and he fought to keep from wiping it away.

For the first time in a long while the hammer felt like it belonged in his hands. The healing blisters were far enough along to not impede him, and he struck fast and sure as he pounded the iron flat.

"Remember," Ossan told him, his voice passing out of the darkness that lurked behind the bright light of the forge. "This is not a complex glyph. It is your fear of pain alone that slows your hand. You must strike quickly. If you hesitate, you will fail."

Wynn ran his tongue over his lips as he turned to take up the smaller hammer and smithing-stylus from the rack. His jaw ached from clenching his teeth. He glanced at Ossan once before bending over the iron. His face was blank, a mask that fit too well for Wynn to see beneath it.

The tip of the stylus sat well on the glowing iron. Wynn set his teeth, and struck. The trick was not to let the tip become embedded in the metal, or come to rest. Strike and move on. Cut and reset. He barely saw the glyph he was carving into the hot metal, moving as fast as he dared and as slow as the pain in his hands would allow.

"Outstanding!" Ossan enthused as Wynn straightened up. "You see? I told you you could do it." He clapped Wynn on the back, the hand sliding down his back like oil, clinging and then cupping.

Wynn shrugged away, twisting from the touch, but it was his expression that Ossan shrank from. The priest's stricken expression softened and then grew hard as he snatched the hammer and stylus from Wynn's hands.

Ossan's look was thunderous. "Am I so disgusting to you, boy?" he said in an angry hiss. "I simply clapped your back and you lurch away like it's a leper's embrace."

"I... No, Father." Wynn floundered.

Ossan shook his head, anger filling the place in his eyes that confusion and hurt had left behind. "Do you know why I chose you to serve, Wynn?" He didn't wait for Wynn to speak. "I chose you because of the answer you gave in your trials. There is a mystery at the heart of our faith that we ignore. We tiptoe around it like a sleeping dog and pretend it isn't there. But you, you spoke the truth. We must reach past the dogma and assumed truth. We must seek out the root of our faith if we are to reclaim it. This is why I set you to searching in the archives, why I trusted you with such an important task. And in return you lurch from my touch as if I were diseased and repellent." His lip curled as he said the last, spittle flying from his mouth.

"I'm sorry, Father," Wynn began.

"No!" Ossan roared, his anger running wild and unfettered. "No more from you. Out! Out! Get back to your cell, novice. Your lesson is ended."

Wynn glanced back once as he hurried towards the door. Ossan had turned back to the forge. His face was unreadable but the fist curled tight at his side spoke into the silence.

***

Wynn crept into the temple the next morning, slinking like a guilty cat. Brial's soft snores followed him as Wynn passed his cell, and made his way up the stone steps, padding on quiet feet. Warm lantern light spilled out of the kitchen and Wynn's face came close to a smile as he entered.

"Thought you might be up early," Fen muttered, not looking up from where he stood, stirring a pot. He spoke again before Wynn could answer. "There's some food on the side for you there." The cook jerked his head towards a long table set by one wall. "The bread's still warm I reckon. You can take a cup of tea with you if you like."

Wynn nodded his thanks, avoiding looking at him. He knew. Somehow, Fen knew what had happened last night. Or at least, he knew enough that Wynn would want to be gone before anyone else might come into the kitchen or be about in the halls.

Fen took a tin cup and warmed it in the fire for a few seconds before filling it with hot tea. He pushed at Wynn and nodded once. His expression might have meant any number of things but none were anything either of them wanted to put into words. Wynn mumbled his thanks and left.

It wasn't until he'd turned into the wider passage that he realised he was going the wrong way. The huge doors to the Great Forge were already open and Wynn wondered, idly, how often they were ever actually closed. The chamber was empty, though the fires beside the great anvil still burned. It must be just gone Kindling, he decided. Wynn made his way past empty pews and towards the anvil and the great gold plate on the far wall. He realised, with a start, that he still held the tin cup and sack of food in his hands and turned to set them down on a pew hurriedly before snorting a laugh at himself. "Somehow, I doubt you care if I have my breakfast with me, Father," he whispered at the stylised image beaten into the gold.

He dropped to one knee before the wall and bowed his head. Was this how prayer was supposed to work? Despite his time in the novice halls and his time with Ossan there were few times he'd actually prayed himself. The prayers were caught up in ritual and formula until the actual worship itself was almost lost.

He shifted, somehow looking at the great anvil instead of the gold plate made the communion more real. Should he speak aloud? Or were his thoughts enough? Wynn stood, suddenly feeling foolish. No, not foolish – he felt like a fraud. The entire faith of the Forgefather suddenly felt like a sham. Where, amongst all this recovered ritual and pomp, was the faith itself?

Slow steps took him to the anvil and a curious hand reached out to rest on the surface. It was faintly warm to the touch, quite unlike the cold metal it appeared to be. "I'm sorry," he whispered. An apology to Brial and the god both. It seemed appropriate, and somehow it said everything he needed to say.

The library was quiet. Wynn waved a greeting to the brown-robed librarian at the desk and made his way to the stairs as she raised a tired hand in response. His feet clanged and rasped on the steps, shattering a

315

silence that was too deep to be comfortable. Libraries are thought of as silent places but Wynn knew this was never truly the case. A library is filled with the soft crackle of turning pages, and the gentle hiss as they settle against each other into each new embrace. The sounds of the rasp of pen on paper, whispered conversation, and muffled footsteps. The library felt cold and empty. It was a tomb for the trees which had been felled and pulped to hold the writings of this foolish faith, and Wynn winced with every noise his feet made as they struck the iron steps.

He sought refuge in the diaries, losing himself in the mundane routine of the lives of the long-dead priests who had become his companions. This dark and silent place would be his sanctum. Here he would hide away and try to make sense of the mess his life had become.

The routine was easy to slip into. He had taken to rising early and returning late. Ossan had made it more than clear that he didn't want to lay eyes on him for a time, and that suited Wynn perfectly. Fen, the cook, let him know what chores needed doing and passed on any instructions from Ossan to attend holy hours and assist with rituals.

Days passed before he saw much of anyone, and the library became as much a home as his own small cell. The library closed, however, and Wynn's mind didn't cease its churning with the closing of those great wooden doors.

Wynn stood and arched his back from where he'd been sat on his bunk, reading over the notes of the last few days by the light of a chem lantern. His pile of papers was growing daily. Hints were giving way to firm mentions and the barest outlines of descriptions of rituals and beliefs.

"Wynn?"

He looked up as Brial tapped gently against the doorframe.

Wynn managed a weak smile. "Hello."

"I wasn't sure you were awake," Brial said, stepping into the entryway. "I haven't seen much of you these last few weeks."

Wynn motioned wordlessly to the pile of notes and papers.

"You're busy at least." Brial shrugged. "What are you searching for? I don't think you ever explained it to me."

"Ossan asked me to search the diaries recovered from the ruins of the Great Temple," Wynn said, reaching for a sheaf of papers. "He wanted me to look for anything that might point to the cause of the Fall."

Brial grimaced. "Sounds dull."

"At times," Wynn admitted. "But then there are parts that are fascinating. The way these people took their power for granted. Creating flame from nothing but faith, or singing iron into shape without even reaching for a hammer."

Brial's eyes widened. "They could really do that?"

Wynn shrugged one shoulder. "That's what the journals say."

"Do you ever wonder if the whole thing is just made up? I mean, how do we really know that there ever was a Fall?"

"I don't know that I'd let Father Ossan hear me asking questions like that," Wynn replied with a smile and a glance at the doorway.

Brial gave a nervous grin, running his hands through his hair.

"Burn yourself again?" Wynn nodded at the bandage on Brial's hand.

The younger man glanced at his hand, shrugging.

"Hell's demons and all their petty saints, is that a ring? Is that a ring of mastery?" Wynn bolted upright, pointing.

Brial looked at his finger, turning his hand over as he looked at it. He met Wynn's gaze with an embarrassed smile. "Ossan gave it to me a few days ago. I thought he might have called you to attend the ceremony but he said it was a private thing."

"Gods, Brial. I knew you were ahead of me, but this?"

Brial flushed and looked away, letting his hair fall down across one eye. He swept it away with his hand as he looked back at Wynn "You know the funny thing? The test isn't actually that hard. It's certainly not anything much more than you have done already."

"Really?" He'd never really thought of what the tests of mastery might entail. Hell, he'd never thought he'd ever be taking one. A ring of mastery was unattainable. It was a badge of honour restricted to true priests, not someone like him.

Brial was nodding with a grin. "Really. Calling Iron, Waking the Flame, glyphs, some simple folding and enriching, and a test piece, and that's it."

"As simple as that, huh?" Wynn said with a wry twist to his lips. "Did you get your true-name too?"

The younger man nodded again, his smile becoming sickly and forced. "I'm not supposed to talk about it. I pledged myself on the great anvil too."

What did that mean? Wynn frowned for a moment. "Still, passing your test, that's amazing."

"I told you, it's really not that hard!" Brial insisted.

"For you, maybe," Wynn snorted. "Sometimes I don't think you understand how much more tutoring and training you had as a Gilter. Lasris did what he could but…"

Brial paused, taking a breath. "I could show you, help you. If you wanted, of course."

Wynn hesitated. It was a tempting offer. He was falling further and further behind and, whilst the work in the library was fascinating, it wasn't anything that was going to help with his own progression in the forge. If he was to move on to acolyte and away from Ossan then he would need two or three rings at least.

"I don't know," he told Brial. "I'd love to but I don't know how Father Ossan would react."

"We could do it on your own time," Brial suggested. "How could he object then? All you're using is coal and that would be used anyway."

"Okay," Wynn agreed, forcing a smile. "When would you want to start?"

"I'm not doing anything tomorrow night. Unless your arms will be too tired from turning pages and scribbling notes?" Brial laughed at Wynn's expression and ducked out of the doorway as Wynn searched around for something to throw.

"You're an ass, Brial!" he called.

The response came a moment later, muffled by the stone wall between their cells. "That's no way to speak to your teacher."

***

Wynn stopped, peering past Brial into the base of the forge. "Why are you laying the kindling like that?" The young man was placing the dried sticks in an intricate pattern.

"Look at the shape of it," Brial told him, not looking up from where he worked.

Wynn looked back at the pattern of interwoven sticks and frowned, there was something about it. "It's a glyph?" he guessed.

Brial nodded and stepped back to give Wynn a better view. "It's the glyph for flame. Father Ossan hasn't ever used it, so far as I can tell, but he seemed to appreciate that I went to the effort. It's a bit like placing a written prayer in the fire."

Wynn smiled. There was something elegant about the symbolism of that. "So where did you learn it? Gilter tutors I suppose?"

"Yes," Brial said, ignoring Wynn's derisory tone. "I'll draw it out for you later." He moved to the side, making room for Wynn to take over. "Let's go through what I did on the test of mastery."

He was a good teacher, Wynn decided after the first few minutes. There was no mocking or superiority to him. If he saw something Wynn was doing wrong, he simply corrected it and moved on. He took Wynn through Waking the Flame and Calling Iron before they settled into more practical aspects of forgework. A portion of this, Wynn knew, was a result of the teaching he'd received as a Gilter in Aspiration. The larger portion, however, must have come from Ossan, and Wynn privately rankled at being excluded from these teachings.

"Wynn?" Brial asked, slotting the word in between the hammer blows.

Wynn grunted, concentrating on the glowing metal he held in the long tongs.

"Does Father Ossan ever..." Brial stumbled through the sentence, drawing out the last word. "Does he touch you?"

Wynn froze for a second and then resumed hammering. "How do you mean?" The words came on their own, as though his tongue had

319

shaped them without his thought. He pounded on the iron, sloppy strokes that made a mess of the work he'd done already.

"He puts his hands on me." The confession was soft, making him sound like a young boy. But then, Brial wasn't all that many years from being a young boy, was he?

"I'm not sure what you mean?" Wynn said, shrugging as he returned the iron to the forge and stepped around to work the bellows. He chanted softly as he pumped, giving Brial the chance to speak. It wouldn't matter. Brial didn't need to say a word. He already knew exactly where the old man was putting his hands. His anger grew. It was a frantic raging against the injustice of Ossan's perversions. A murderous urge to run to Ossan's room and mete out the punishment that he so deserved with fist and hammer. But then, where would that get him? The man was a priest of the temple. Wynn was just another nameless novice. Who would take his word over Ossan? And then Ossan would have him sent back to the novice halls, or the mines.

Brial was speaking again but Wynn couldn't hear him. He wouldn't let himself hear him. In the middle of the realisation that he could never stop Ossan, a small voice in his mind made traitorous mouthings. A dark whisper that grew louder as Wynn recognised it for the truth and then shuddered away from it. "It will be him, or you, you know?" it whispered. "Ossan won't stop. He holds all the power here. In the end, if he doesn't have Brial, he will have you."

The decision came easily. Perhaps every betrayal does. In the end, they all begin with a lie. The small ones we tell ourselves to make what we do bearable.

It's not your fault.

There is no real alternative.

Anyone would do the same thing in your place.

"I wouldn't worry about it," he said with a shrug. "It's probably nothing." The lie slipped too easily off his tongue. He pulled the iron out of the coals again. "Tell me about the mastery piece you did?"

"What?" Brial frowned at him for a moment. "Oh, it wasn't much. I did a lantern. Father Ossan helped with the glasswork but the forging was all mine."

"Just a lantern?" Wynn glanced around at him. "I mean, I can see how that's dealing with thin plates but it doesn't sound that…" he broke off as Brial laughed.

"Hard?" Brial answered for him. "It wasn't, not most of it anyway. The thing was riddled with glyphs though. Each plate was folded iron, and I worked in glyphs for strength, and wardings against heat and rust." He shrugged. "None of it all that difficult but it takes time."

"I don't know half of those," Wynn admitted.

Brial nodded. "We'd better get started then, hadn't we?"

Over the next few weeks Brial worked him mercilessly, taking him through the process of casting iron; heating great pools of the metal in the massive crucible that filled one corner of the foundry. He walked him through crafting moulds, the benefits and drawbacks of quenches and slow cools, and then moved him onto wrought iron. Through it all he was patient, correcting Wynn without rebuke when he misstepped.

He was changing, Wynn realised one night. The boy that had entered Ossan's chambers with him was all but gone. This new Brial was drawn and haggard. He looked like he was losing as much weight as he was missing sleep. Wynn himself was returning to his bunk each night with arms that trembled, and legs that would barely hold him. He was uncomfortably aware that Brial's cell was silent and empty.

CHAPTER TWENTY-ONE

Wynn lurched sideways as he woke, a sound that was partway between grunt and snarl escaping his lips as he flailed his arms towards whatever had woken him. He grimaced as he sat upright in the chair, peeling a page of notes from his face.

"I didn't mean to startle you," Andrei said, lips twitching as he took in the spectacle. "You really can't sleep down here, you know?" He paused then as Wynn nodded and peered more closely at him. "Ashes and damnation, Wynn. You look like hell!"

Wynn worked his jaw which felt like he'd slept with his face on a bag full of rocks. "I don't feel much better. What time is it anyway?"

"It must be on the way to Fannings by now," the librarian told him. "Is Ossan really working you that hard?"

Wynn pulled himself to his feet and twisted, trying to work the kinks out of his back and neck. "It's mostly my own fault. I'm doing this research and then trying to fit all my forge learning in at night. It's not much fun."

Andrei grimaced. "That doesn't sound like a good way to study."

"It isn't," Wynn admitted. "I'm not exactly in Ossan's favour. I'm picking up what I can from the other novice serving with me." He ran his hand through his hair and glanced at the toppled pile of his notes.

"Even so, Wynn. I can't have you sleeping down here." Andrei paused, frowning as he followed his gaze and reached for the book laying open amid the mess. "And this!" His eyes grew dark as the skin pinched at the corners of his mouth. "This is not the way we treat rare and valuable books."

Wynn backed away until the back of his legs hit the edge of the desk. The librarian was not a large man but the anger in his eyes shone bright enough to give him pause.

Andrei took a deep breath, puffing his cheeks out as he let it out again. "What are you even looking for down here? You know you're probably the first person to touch most of these books in years?"

"It's complicated," Wynn hedged. He stopped, looking around them. "What are you doing down here anyway? I've only ever seen a handful of people down here and never you. I thought you had people for this?"

"One of the assistants heard you snoring. They came to get me."

"Nice of them," Wynn grunted.

Andrei managed a small smile. "You should be thankful they came to me. If Yorris had found you..." He shook his head.

Wynn gave him a blank look. "Yorris?"

Andrei sighed. "If you hadn't spent the best part of two months lurking in this gloomy hole, you'd have met him already. Father Yorris, he's the head archivist, and an unholy terror when it comes to these collections. These books are like his children. If he'd found you sleeping with one of them..." He trailed off with a shudder.

Wynn glanced at the desk, aware of how guilty it made him look. "I'm sorry, Andrei. It wasn't intentional but I am sorry if I put you in an awkward position."

The librarian waved a hand with a sigh. "No harm was done, I suppose." He glanced from Wynn to the pile of notes again. "Are you getting anywhere? I have to admit to some curiosity."

"I think so." Wynn turned and began pulling his papers into a more orderly pile. "It's all a bit tenuous. I mean, I always knew it was going to be, I've been working on hints rather than anything solid. Does that make sense?"

"None at all," Andrei laughed. "It might help if I knew what you were talking about."

"Father Ossan wanted me to research the diaries and journals for any hint of what might have caused the Fall."

Andrei turned the journal over in his hands. "The cause? Surely the Forgefather himself would have been the cause?"

"I suppose that's true but what led to it?" Wynn frowned for a moment. "Did you say it was past Fannings?"

Andrei nodded, still looking at the book in his hands. "Well past, I'd say."

Wynn stared at him in shock for a moment, the words taking their time to register. "Fallen saints!" he swore. "I need to go. I'm supposed to meet with Ossan."

"I'll just put this away for you myself then, shall I?" Andrei muttered, hefting the book.

Wynn gave him a grateful smile as the sarcasm went over his head. "Thanks."

The stairs clanged as he ran, clutching the pile of notes to his chest. Andrei's curses were probably following him and he was likely attracting the disapproving looks of who knew how many priests and librarians at the noise he was making, but both paled in comparison with the threat of being late for his meeting with Ossan.

In a way the rush through the halls was probably a blessing. He'd arrived at the library that morning after a mostly sleepless night spent worrying about this meeting. He had worked so late with Brial in an effort to make him tired enough to sleep, but it hadn't worked. Instead he'd laid awake, staring at a ceiling that was too dark to see, until he'd given up and gone to the library.

He'd had half a dozen minor meetings with Ossan. Each time the priest had picked at Wynn's findings, pressing him to work harder and find something more than hints and vague inferences.

The chambers were silent as he made his way in through Ossan's halls to the study. He paused in the doorway, glancing at the burning prayer candle that stood close to Ossan's desk.

"You're late." The old man's voice was too calm.

"I'm sorry, Father, I—"

"The reasons really don't matter, novice." Ossan looked up from the page he'd been writing and sighed. "The fact is you're late. Time has been wasted." He shook his head as Wynn reached for words which wouldn't come.

"Do sit down, Wynn. Let's salvage what we can from the time we have left."

Wynn perched in the chair and sorted through the sheaf of notes in his lap.

"Now," Ossan said, leaning back his chair and sipping from a long-stemmed glass. "The last we spoke about your research, you had identified several promising journals and were going to focus on those."

"Yes, Father," Wynn said. "I had originally thought that the problem would be finding any records that had survived the Fall. I had no idea that there would be so many."

Ossan nodded with a slight smile that did little to thaw his expression.

"As it turned out there were hundreds, maybe thousands," Wynn explained. "But the problem was that many of these were simply diaries or journals."

Ossan frowned. "Isn't that what I had sent you to find?"

Wynn winced. "Can I ask, Father, do you keep a diary?"

"No," Ossan admitted, shaking his head. "It's never really appealed to me. I'll admit I don't understand the attraction."

"Well the problem is that not everyone writes out the same way that they speak. The best journals I discovered," Wynn said, leafing through his notes. "Were those where the diary's owner had written almost as if they were speaking to someone. It was almost as if they'd used their diary as a confessional. The worst of them were little more than lists. The words probably meant something to the person that had written them but nobody else."

"And compounding this is whether they ever mentioned anything that might lead to the Fall," Ossan put in.

Wynn nodded, setting a thick pile of notes down on the floor beside the chair. "The fact that the Fall hadn't yet happened when these were written, complicates things as well. The best I could do is to guess at the things that might be relevant. I've written extensive notes for you as well, Father."

Ossan's nose wrinkled as his gaze drifted to the thick pile of papers still in Wynn's lap. "Summarise them for me, Wynn, if you would for now."

"I... uh." Wynn turned the pages of his report until Ossan snapped his fingers, holding out a hand for the sheaf of papers.

"Come now," he chided in a softer tone as he sat back down with Wynn's notes. "Surely you have something for me?"

Wynn flushed. "Arrogance," he said.

Ossan sat back, blinking at him. "Excuse me?"

"The overwhelming impression I had of the priests from before the Fall," Wynn explained. "They were incredibly arrogant. They wrote of abilities that I can only barely explain. There are mentions of Defenders calling down the power of the Forgefather and holding off what sounds like entire armies of various dukes and kings. But yet there is very little mention of the Forgefather himself. It's almost as though they acted like he was a tool to be used, or a beast of burden to be hitched to a cart. There is very little of anything that a person might call worship."

"That's it?" Ossan demanded. "Arrogance?"

Wynn closed his eyes for as long a blink as he thought he could get away with and wished for patience. Ossan wasn't getting his point.

"You're suggesting the cause of the Fall was that the Forgefather wasn't getting enough attention? That the god of flame and creation turned his back on his church and all mankind like some manner of petulant child?" Ossan's voice was scathing.

"I'm not sure what I'm suggesting. I..." Wynn took a deep breath; that had come too close to him snapping the words out. He tried again. "What do any of us know of the nature of god? What do any of us truly know?"

"Careful, novice," Ossan growled. "You're walking close to some dangerous ground there." He paused and looked closer as him as Wynn sank into the chair. "You don't look yourself, my son. Are you getting enough sleep?"

"No, Father," Wynn laughed. "I can barely remember what sleep is! Between studies in the library and then..." He clamped his lips tight.

"Working in the forge with Brial?" Ossan offered and then burst out laughing as Wynn bolted upright. "Did you really think I didn't know? Those are my tools, Wynn. I know when another hand has been at them."

Wynn raised his head to meet the man's gaze. "I'd expected you to be…" He shrugged. "I don't know."

"You thought I'd be angry?" Ossan smiled. "If I'm completely honest, I was a little when I discovered it. But then Brial teaching you serves to teach him as well. He's consolidating what I've taught him." He sipped at the wine again, giving Wynn a serious look as he peered over the top of the glass. "How far have you come?"

"I'm sorry?"

"With your forgework. How far along are you?"

"Oh." Wynn shrugged and then smiled. "Brial seems to think I could take the test of mastery tomorrow. I'm not so sure."

"Tomorrow?" Ossan smiled again and Wynn tried not to squirm as the gaze travelled over his body. "I don't think you'd be ready tomorrow, not with the state you're in. The next week though?"

"You're not serious?" Wynn gasped.

Ossan grinned at that. "Who says so? If you can have your test piece done." He sighed leaning forward and resting his hands on the desk, as the smile fell from his face. "My son, I know there has been a certain amount of unpleasantness between us. I don't take to insubordination easily and perhaps my temper flares too swiftly. I'm not about to stifle talent, though, and you have that in spades." Ossan sat back as he changed tack. "Have you thought about your test piece? I'm sure Brial has spoken to you about it."

"I'm not sure," Wynn admitted. "I thought maybe something associated with fire. Perhaps a candlestick or…"

Ossan pursed his lips as he looked up to the ceiling. "Possibly, possibly. I can see how that might be suitable. Provided you employ enough techniques of course." He gave Wynn a serious look. "You understand that I cannot help with this? If you have questions, I am happy to answer them or give advice, but the work must be all your own."

Wynn nodded. The meeting had taken a turn he could never have expected. He took a deep breath before speaking again. "Should I stop the research for the time being then, Father? To focus on the test, I mean?"

Ossan glanced up at him from the notes he was thumbing through. "I would suggest that's probably the wisest course. You'll need your rest, if nothing else."

"And once the test is over?"

The old man's lips twitched as he considered him. "Are you enjoying it that much, Wynn?"

"Enjoying it?" Wynn snorted a laugh and then stifled it quickly. "No, it's not really enjoyment. It's more like some kind of compulsion. It's an itch I can't scratch. There's something there, something just out of reach. Does that make any sense?"

Ossan was giving him a peculiar look. "It makes perfect sense, Wynn. I've had that itch for forty years or more." He flicked through the pages of Wynn's work. "I think you may have touched the edges of something here. You haven't solved any mysteries, not by a long way, but you may have gone some way to finding the direction we ought to be looking."

***

The foundry stank. The smell of smoke and hot iron, which has its own peculiar odour, filled the place and mingled with the stench of stale sweat and baked leather.

"Wynn, drink!" Brial thrust the waterskin at him and glared. "You're being an idiot," the younger man said. It wasn't an accusation, or even said with anger, just a simple statement of fact.

Wynn raised an eyebrow, drinking deep draughts of water from the skin.

"You're not going to get this done any faster by working yourself to death," Brial told him.

Wynn lowered the skin. "Don't you think you're being a little overly dramatic?"

"Am I?" Brial looked him up and down. "You've been at this for over five hours. That skin's almost full, which means you've stopped to drink maybe twice?" He paused long enough for Wynn's face to betray him. "And you're working in here alone. What happens if you pass out?"

"I'm not going to—" Wynn burst out.

"Really?" Brial cut him off. "Just look around you for a minute, Wynn. "Do you see anywhere soft for your head to land? This is all stone floor. Hell, you could have hit the anvil. You could have hit hot iron!"

"But I didn't," Wynn snapped. "Stop mothering me, Brial. I just need to get this done."

Brial bit back something harsh and looked at the lump of iron resting on the anvil. "You could have just cast this, you know?"

"So you've said before." Wynn hung the skin back on its hook and took up the tongs, setting them around the rod where it extended out of the misshapen lump at its end. He grasped the end of the rod itself with one gloved hand and gripped the tongs with the other, setting the iron back into the fire.

"So why didn't you?"

Wynn sighed, moving around to pump the bellows. "You know why. Because cast iron is too brittle, plus it rusts more easily. Besides," he said, slotting the words in between the rush of the bellows and his own panted breaths. "How much skill am I showing by pouring iron into a mould?"

"Enough," Brial said with a shrug. "As for rust, it would never rust in here. It's too hot all the time for any moisture."

Wynn shook his head. "That's not true and you know it. It's as cold as a Listener's soul in here first thing in the morning. You can see your own breath some days, and you know damned well that the kindling gets damp."

Brial shrugged again, beyond caring. "Even so, it'd take years. What do you care?"

"I care." Wynn bit the words off and began the chant again. He ignored Brial for a few minutes, pumping the bellows as he Called Iron until it glowed.

Gods above, he was bored. The process was hard work, but hardly taxed the brain. Heat the iron, fold another section of the rod into the mass, inscribe the glyph.

"Holy hells, Wynn. You're doing glyphs on every fold?" The curse was little more than a whisper.

Wynn grunted, not looking up from where he worked with the smithing stylus. He turned the iron with a deft twist of the wrist and levered the rod upwards, forcing it back on itself until he could begin hammering again, working in another fold.

Brial watched for a few minutes. "At least let me work the bellows for you."

Wynn shook his head. "It has to be all my own work, remember?"

"Hell's saints, Wynn. You don't do things the easy way, do you? It's exhausting just watching you."

Wynn stopped hammering long enough to give the young man a tired smile. "Shouldn't you be at prayers or something?"

Brial glowered at him. "Just promise me you'll drink?" he said, turning to leave.

"Yes, Mother."

"And eat something!"

Wynn shook his head with a smile as the younger man left. He was right about one thing though; the work was exhausting.

The recombining of the iron rods into a shape he could work with took the better part of three days. If not for the intricate glyphs that had to be worked into each fold, he might have had it done in half the time. As it was, by the time he began the actual forging of the piece, he felt wrung out. Aches fought with minor burns for his attention but his sleep-deprived brain only had enough focus for the job at hand. Fen, Ossan's cook, brought him food and water, joining in with Brial's nagging when he found food left uneaten

330

It was Brial who found him on the morning of the last day. He'd slumped down over a workbench, his test-piece still sticking out of the water barrel he'd quenched it in.

He came to at a low litany of curses as Brial shook him awake. "Ashdamn it, Wynn. I can't believe you slept in here."

Wynn pushed himself upright, working his jaw and rubbing at his face where it had rested on the wooden bench. "It wasn't exactly planned."

Brial grimaced and gnawed at one knuckle as he looked around the workshop. "I should have come for you hours ago. You know Ossan's going to be looking for you soon. Are you going to be ready?"

Wynn nodded. "They're done. I must have been up until a few hours after Ash by the time I was finished. I suppose I fell asleep polishing."

Brial frowned and glanced at the water barrel.

"That's the other half of it," Wynn said, following his gaze. "The first part is this." He shifted and revealed the medallion laying under his arm."

"Can I?" Brial asked, reaching for it.

Wynn nodded.

Brial lifted the piece, letting it hang on the leather cord as he examined it. "The detail is fantastic," he marvelled. "The textured effect you got on the anvil, and the glyphs! Is this every iron glyph here?"

Wynn grinned, unable to stop himself. "Most of them. I put in all the major glyphs. I didn't have the room for all the minors or the faith glyphs."

"I don't know how you even got these in. Most of them are tiny. What did you even use?"

Wynn shrugged. "I had to make a new stylus."

"So, what's that in the quench then?"

"Every anvil needs a hammer."

Brial lifted the hammer from the water, hefting it and turning it over in the light. "Flashy bastard," he muttered. "Come on, let's get some food into you quickly. If your test is anything like mine you're going to need it."

Wynn picked at the food. The porridge was hot and creamy but he wasn't really interested even though he knew he'd need it. Brial nattered at him, chattering away about this and that until he realised Wynn wasn't really listening. On the pretext of chores he'd finally left Wynn alone, though they both knew it was to give him space before the testing.

It was less than an hour until Ossan found him, striding into the kitchen in his thick black robes and rubbing his hands together. "Today is the day then," he declared with a smile. "How do you feel?"

"Tired," Wynn admitted, eliciting a small frown from Ossan. "But ready, I think."

"Good, good." Ossan smiled again. "It's natural to be nervous. Shall we?"

Wynn walked in silence as the priest escorted him to the foundry. Ossan spoke enough for the two of them, filling the silence with easy conversation that he somehow managed to carry alone.

"I'm sure Brial has walked you through this," Ossan said as they entered the foundry. "I know you're as thick as thieves these days. I remember my first test of mastery," he said, lifting his hand to gaze over the rings on his fingers. "I was so nervous I barely remembered how to lift a hammer. So, I'm going to take it slowly with you. I'll prompt you when necessary but, by and large, I'll just be watching. Understood?"

Wynn swallowed at the lump that filled his throat. "Yes, Father."

"Begin with lighting the forge then."

That, at least, was simple enough. Wynn gathered fresh kindling from the store and inspected the vents leading to the bellows. He caught himself as he started stacking the small sticks, casting a look at Ossan as he hesitated.

"This is it, Wynn," he whispered to himself, and began again, laying the wood out as Brial had shown him, forming the glyph for flame.

Ossan took him through simple tasks to begin with. Calling the Flame through a rod of iron. Forging small items; a nail, a horseshoe. And then onto more complex work. He had Wynn fashion a cube of iron, working from a rough casting and then shaping with hammer and file. He asked him to forge a section of folded iron, with different glyphs worked into every fold. And then he took him through the glyphs of iron, quizzing him on the thirty major and fifteen minor glyphs, their usage and meaning before moving onto faith glyphs.

"Good enough," Ossan grunted, turning the cube of iron over in his hands idly. "Now then, talk me through your test piece."

Wynn reached inside his shirt and drew out the amulet. "I have produced this, Father."

Ossan reached for it with a frown. "Go on…"

"I forged it from fifteen layers of wrought iron, each layer inscribed with the glyphs of strength, faith and fire."

"Names," barked Ossan, glancing up.

"Lar, Mer and Kelv," Wynn replied, not missing a beat. He was quick enough to catch the small smile that flickered over Ossan's lips.

"The image of the anvil I worked into the surface using a combination of stylus and fine hammer work. The glyphs on the surface contain all major iron glyphs and—"

"I can see the glyphs, Wynn," Ossan stopped him in a low voice. "How did you manage to inscribe them so finely? These are a quarter of the size of normal glyphs, maybe a fifth."

"I had to create a new stylus, Father."

Ossan grunted, turning the amulet to catch the light. "And you consider this to be worthy of a ring of mastery, do you?"

Wynn winced. That wasn't the reaction he'd expected. "No, Father. This is only half of the test piece." He unwrapped the hammer slowly, setting the velvet cloth aside.

Ossan took the piece wordlessly running his fingertips over the head and the lines of glyphs inscribed in each non-striking surface. He lifted the hammer to the light and looked closely at the twisting, braided-rope effect, that Wynn had worked into the iron haft, and down to the flaming torch that formed the butt.

"Lord of Fire and Flame," Ossan breathed. "This is truly spectacular." He shook his head, meeting Wynn's anxious gaze. "You do realise I was joking with you? The amulet was more than enough to demonstrate your competences. This though," he hefted the hammer. "This is a thing of wonder." He shook his head, drawing himself up and looking giving Wynn a solemn look. "Come here."

The priest's hands were cold as he reached for Wynn's head. "Upon you, Wynn, I grant the ring of mastery over iron." He winked then and Wynn fought down a smile. "Hold out your hand."

The ring was dull iron but as Wynn looked closer he saw the rows of tiny figures etched into the surface.

"A lost art," Ossan told him as he took the ring and slid it onto Wynn's index finger. "We have so few true rings of mastery left to us now. Be careful with it."

"I will, Father." Wynn closed his fist tight around the ring on his finger. It didn't quite fit.

"Congratulations Wynn, your novitiate will soon be at an end I suspect."

Wynn blinked at that. To earn the ring was one thing, to progress beyond novice was something quite different. "I, I don't know what to say, Father."

The priest smiled and shook his head. "There is nothing to say, Wynn. You have earned it. We'll have to get to the great forge tomorrow so you can pledge yourself to the Father. For now, enjoy the ring. That, and the gift of your true name."

Ossan reached out again and grasped Wynn's head in a tight grip, leaning in to stare into his eyes for a long moment. He whispered something, and then cocked his head to one side as if listening. Finally the old priest smiled and stepped back. "Of course," he murmured. "It's obvious really."

Wynn gave him a look.

"Your true name is something only a handful of priests would be able to discern." Ossan explained. "I can hear it calling out of the very essence of you, echoing the will of the Father. In our tongue it would mean 'seeker' or 'one who searches'. It's rather fitting, don't you think?" He smiled then, taking in Wynn's impatience.

"Kharios," he said. "Your name is Kharios."

Wynn said the name to himself. It sounded strange coming from his own lips. But yet it resonated, striking a chord somewhere deep within him, as if on some level he should always have known it.

He frowned. There was so much about this faith that was ritualised nonsense. So much that was clearly the efforts of old men trying to give meaning to the mundane. Making a fuss about the fact that hot iron will glow, or that wrought iron is less brittle than cast. What did this mean? The true name was real, he could feel that much.

"…for a celebration I think," Ossan was saying.

Wynn started, realising that he'd been ignoring the priest as he spoke. "A celebration?" he repeated.

"Well it hardly seemed appropriate with just one of you having passed their test," Ossan said, nodding. "What if you'd failed yours? But now that you've passed as well, and in such spectacular style," he pointed at the hammer. "It would be wrong not to."

He slipped the amulet around Wynn's neck and took up the hammer, ushering him towards the door. "I'll confess I've had Fen working on a meal all day. I expect it will be some time yet but I'd say you've earned a drink or two, wouldn't you?"

Wynn mumbled something, twisting the iron ring around his finger, but Ossan wasn't really listening to him anyway. The whole situation was surreal. A ring of mastery! He shook his head. He'd had a vague notion that he might be faced with the test one day, but it had held an air of fancy about it, in much the same way as he'd thought of being a warrior as a young child. The ring would lead to others. Three rings and he would likely be an acolyte, beyond Ossan and free from his clutches. He would be free to discover the truth about the faith, if there was one. His new name had compounded his doubts and questions. It muddied things he'd thought were clear. He followed Ossan through the halls of his chambers, letting the priest's words wash over him as he led the way to the dining hall.

He'd had two glasses of wine by the time Brial joined them, and Ossan was well on the way through his fifth.

"Brial!" Ossan called out in welcome, spreading his arms and slopping wine over his hand. "Come. Join us. Kharios here has passed his test of mastery and so I thought it time we celebrated both of your achievements."

Brial grinned and helped himself to a glass of wine. "Kharios?"

"His true name," Ossan said with a smile at Wynn. "Not all true names are close and secret things to be held tight and cherished. Some call out as loud as thunder to those that know how to listen for such things. To lock them away is both a crime and a sin."

"To Kharios then!" Brial raised his glass in a toast.

The afternoon drifted into evening in a celebration that Ossan seemed determined to turn into an orgy of excess. Plates littered the table, filled with dishes that were barely touched as the evening wore on. Ossan insisted on playing the role of host, sending the servants away and filling their glasses himself – though he filled his own twice as quickly as anyone else's.

The man drank as much as he spoke, somehow fitting the glass to his lips in between stories. Wynn looked on, bemused. Ossan was like a different person. Amiable and entertaining as he regaled them both with legends of the time before the Fall, and temple gossip, seemingly in equal measure. The priest who had all but banished him to the library after the incident in the foundry was lost, buried beneath the patchwork cloak of Ossan's personality.

Wynn drained his glass and felt for his cheek, it was growing numb. Time to slow down, he cautioned himself. Brial, had no such plans by the looks of things, almost keeping pace with Ossan.

The priest looked over at Wynn's glass and fumbled for the bottle, toppling it over and sending the last of the wine spilling out over the table.

"Oh bugger," he swore under his breath, standing to mop up the mess. "No matter," he told them, waving Wynn back as he sought to help. "I'll fetch another."

Brial watched on with twitching lips as the priest made his way out of the room in a route which swayed and lurched until he caught hold of the doorframe.

"Be right back," Ossan grinned.

Wynn met the boy's gaze and laughed. "He's a drunk as a skunk, you realise?"

"I'm not far behind him," Brial admitted. "Still, at least it keeps his hands busy."

Wynn grimaced and turned his face away to hide it.

"Oh come on, Wynn," Brial burst out. "You know. We both know you know. Why do you bother hiding it?"

"How do you stand it?" Wynn asked, without thinking.

"It's a means to an end," Brial said. His tone was casual but his face said more. It wasn't quite a shudder, but it came close. "Anyway, like I said. As soon as I get my rings I'm gone. You should come too!" He grinned as if the thought had just occurred to him. "Think about it. Two temple trained smiths with rings of mastery? We'd have kings and princes lining up for our work."

Wynn froze, glancing at the doorway for a moment. "I don't know, Brial. It's not something I've really thought about."

Brial let that pass with a shrug, sipping his wine again. He nodded at Wynn's ring. "So, Kharios? How does it feel?"

"A bit odd," Wynn admitted. "I can't decide if I like it or not."

"At least you can use it," Brial muttered. "You know what Ossan said about my true name being kept secret?" he said, reaching to drain the last of the wine in his glass. "It's horse-shit. I wanted to keep it secret because it's embarrassing. It's an ash-damned joke. He named me 'Diast', Wynn," he said as he caught Wynn's look. "It means 'beloved.'"

"It's not that bad," Wynn replied.

Brial scoffed at that. "Are you mad? It's like he's claimed me for his pet. He disgusts me. The sooner I can get out of here the better. Think about what I said about running with me once we have our rings. Two temple trained smiths could make a fortune."

Ossan lurched through the doorway and stormed across the room in three quick steps.

"Bastard!" Ossan raged down at the boy. His face was mottled in anger, the red flush rising up through his neck and cheeks. "You damned thief! You would simply take this training and use it for peddling swords? You're worse than any whore, letting me think you care when all you wanted was gold."

"Care?" Brial spat, rising to his feet. "Is this how you show someone you care?" He pulled his shirt up revealing a mass of bruises across his ribs. "You're nothing but a disgusting old man. I'm fourteen years old, Ossan." He threw the words at him, spite and fury touching each one. "You're just a sick old bastard preying on boys who have no choice but to let you." He looked at Wynn with venom. "And you let him."

The blow threw Brial sideways as the back of Ossan's hand slammed into the side of his face and threw him off the chair. Ossan gave him no time to get up but piled on top of him, fists rising and falling as Brial twisted under him, screaming past Ossan's roars of anger until the priest's glancing blows became wet thuds.

Wynn stood rooted by shock for a moment, and then rushed in, grabbing at the priest's arm as Ossan snatched up the fallen wine bottle. He snarled at him, shoving hard. Ossan might be old but a lifetime of smithing had packed solid muscle onto his frame. Wynn flew backwards as the bottle tumbled through the air and shattered on the stone floor. The air rushed out of him as he crashed down and his head cracked back against the flagstones.

Dimly he watched Ossan reach blindly over the table and his fingers close around the ornate haft of the hammer Wynn had crafted. His head hurt with that peculiar ringing pain that comes from an impact to the skull, and his vision was still hazy as he saw Ossan raise the hammer. It fell with a wet crunch and Wynn screamed out as it rose up, dripping blood and gore like the muzzle of some half-starved beast pulled back from its kill, and then the hammer fell again.

Something within him fractured then. The world seemed at once very bright but also hazy as if he were watching through a bright-lit fog. He was dimly aware of Ossan rising to his feet, staring down at Brial in

338

silence. And then he was screaming for Fen, calling out that there had been an accident. Wynn stood and looked down at the wreckage of Brial's body, ignoring the priest as he spoke and the snatches of conversation that drifted past him like leaves on a breeze.

"...shouldn't be blamed for it. I think back to the novice halls would be best, at least for now, until his fate is decided. Have him escorted there. I doubt he'd cause trouble but..."

He didn't resist as strong hands took hold of his arms and walked him out of Ossan's chambers. In the space of five minutes his life had changed utterly. Everything he'd accomplished in these last months had been taken from him. Wynn walked in silence, not trusting himself to speak as he was led through the halls. He sank down on the hard bunk after he was pushed roughly into a cell and looked down at his hands. It was only then that he realised his fingers were bare. The ring of mastery was gone.

CHAPTER TWENTY-TWO

Kharios clung to rocks he couldn't see as the rush of water pulled at his legs. He was soaked, and cold, and that was pretty much the extent of his knowledge for the moment. The rocks must have been worn smooth by years of rushing water and his grip slipped and faltered as he tried to pull himself closer to them. The current tugged at him as his grip shifted, sweeping his legs around behind him in a half circle that ended with his knees and shins crashing into another rock. His curse was lost in the sound of the river as he reached out blindly for a better handhold.

It took several attempts before he managed to haul himself up and out of the water and onto the rocks, before toppling down the other side and landing on what felt like shingle.

"Leesha?" His voice sounded loud in the darkness, even over the rushing of the river. He tried again, shouting this time and listening for her voice. Nothing. Shit.

"Light," he muttered. Light was the first thing. The darkness was total. Not the dim gloom of night above ground, but an utter blackness where the eye doesn't even attempt to adjust. Questing hands told him the helmet was still in place on his head and the chemlamp seemed to be in one piece, though the chems were probably soaked and ruined.

He pulled off the helmet, fumbling with the straps that had held it on his head, and ran his fingertips over the lamp. A sharp twist had the chemtube out, and he felt the cold rush of watery sludge as it drained out over his hand. Water must have filled the chemtube. If it had soaked the chemchamber itself then he was fucked. Or at least stuck in the dark for a few hours.

Did he even still have the chems? The thought bubbled up out of nowhere and his hands flew to the sack tied to his waist. Panic made his hands clumsy and he had to force himself to slow down to even work open the neck of the sack. The food was all soaked but the glass tubes seemed intact. The chemtubes were designed to be installed in the dark, and the ridges and dots worked into the glass told him which ones were which. Getting the tubes installed with hands that shook from the cold would be another matter.

The mind works strangely in total darkness. Deprived of sensory input it works hard to fill in the blanks. The thought of dropping the chemtubes from numb hands was enough to slow him and he sucked at his fingers in an effort to coax some warmth back into them. An image of chems spilling out from the shattered tubes played over in his mind and Kharios bit down on his own fingers to give himself something else to focus on.

He swore again as he gripped the tube with two hands, moving as slowly as he dared in an effort to keep it from shaking. The helmet he held gripped between his knees. It took several attempts to find the slot in the side of the chemlamp, and another three to get the tubes locked into place. He slid the switch only a fraction of the way across, letting just the smallest flow of chems into the chamber to mix together and activate. The chemik reaction caused heat. If there truly was a Forgefather, and if he was watching, then the heat from the reaction would be enough to dry out the chemchamber.

The light was minute, less than the glow shed by fireflies on a summer's night, but in the utter darkness it was glorious and Kharios let out a whimper of relief as it grew.

He wrapped his arms around his legs and watched as the light grew, clenching his jaw against the shivering. "Got to do something to get warm," he told himself. He could see the clouds of his own breath in the light of the lamp. If he didn't dry out somehow, the cold would kill him just as easily as any of the risen would have.

He glanced behind him at the thought. The darkness was too deep to see anything more than the hint of the movement of the river. The risen

341

would be out there somewhere. They couldn't stand on the bridge but would that have stopped them throwing themselves into the river after him? Fear has its limits and Kharios was simply too tired to care right now.

The lamp was already faintly warm to the touch, a good sign he decided and eased the switch over some more, increasing the flow. The light grew brighter and Kharios put the helmet back on for a moment to examine his surroundings. He lay on a dark shingle beach, pressed close to the sheer face of the rock wall and surrounded by a high wall of stones and boulders that held back the river. Bone-white sticks of driftwood lay bundled in amongst the rocks, evidence of some past flood.

With little else to do he emptied out the sack, spreading the contents out in the hopes they would dry a little. The bread had a hard crust, and hadn't been cut. There was a chance that it might be okay. The dried meat was soaked but that wouldn't matter. Kharios tore off a strip and gnawed at it as he picked through the rest of his supplies. Cheese, a handful of apples, and a tin.

Kharios rattled the tin curiously. He hadn't packed this sack. His prising fingers lifted the loose lid, revealing firesticks sloshing about in the water that filled the tin.

Firesticks! He shook his head at the irony. He even had wood here to burn but with wet firesticks he was going to freeze to death. The chemlamp would get hot but not enough to warm him. The thought gave him pause. "The lamp," he mused.

The helmet would wedge between his legs easily enough. Perhaps if he were to set one of the firesticks on top of the lamp itself, would that dry it out? His hands were moving before he finished the thought. The first two toppled, dropping off the edge of the lamp and down between the rocks as his shivering legs shook the helmet. He propped it up against the stones for his next attempt. If he couldn't light a fire straight away it would be better for him to be up and moving anyway.

He gathered up several armfuls of driftwood and dumped them in the centre of the beach. The work warmed him enough to stop the worst of his shivering. How high must the river had risen to trap this wood against the rocks? He shook his head at the thought. As if the risen weren't enough to worry about.

It was impossible to judge time. He tried counting heartbeats but couldn't focus enough to keep track. He reckoned it must have been an hour or more by the time he tried the firestick. The wheel-striker on the side of the tin threw sparks out as he held the sulphur-dipped stick close. It took several attempts, and he almost gave up, thinking the stick was still too damp, before it caught.

There are few things as fragile as a fresh-caught flame. Kharios moved like a nervous lover, as if any quick move might court disaster. The flame tumbled and lurched on the end of the thin stick as his breath found it, and he buried his mouth in the damp fabric of his sleeve as he hunched down beside the pile of driftwood.

The wood wasn't as dry as he would have liked. The closeness of the river made everything slightly damp. He'd broken and twisted the wood to expose splinters in place of tinder. The flame was a tiny, fragile thing and it clung to the splinters like a leaf in a spring storm.

Kharios blew softly as the flame grew, chanting under his breath as it guttered. If the fire were to go out now he'd have to wait another hour or more to try again. He'd Called the Flame a thousand times or more, but never had he meant it more than he did right now.

He sat back on his heels as the fire took hold. The heat felt glorious on his face and he piled on more wood as soon as he dared. The shivering stopped as he built the fire up and now he basked in the heat, letting the flames drive the wet and damp from his clothes and flesh, down to his very bones.

What to do now? Kharios ate as he thought, walking the perimeter of his little camp. The light from the fire showed far more than the chemlamp had and the lamp now sat dark beside the fire where it could dry out. The beach narrowed and rose as it extended downriver, away from the fire, until it became a rough pathway of sorts that followed the water. It was better luck than he'd expected. Luck is a fickle creature and, so far as Kharios could tell, she hated him with a passion.

343

The sensation of being watched grew slowly until he could almost feel the eyes upon him. Kharios spun in a slow circle, searching for something. Anything. Darkness lurked, just beyond the reach of his fire, pressing in against the light, and somehow mocking its efforts.

The memory rose unbidden, crawling out of the mire at the back of his mind. Of Grint, when they were dumping cleared rocks down into the darkness. A darkness that had seemed somehow alive, and watchful

Surrender.

He froze at the whisper. It was soft, so quiet that he wasn't sure it was even a sound. Maybe he'd just imagined it. Kharios couldn't hear much beyond his own frantic breathing. Even the sound of the river seemed somehow muted.

The feeling of helplessness grew slowly. His mind dragged back through the memories of the ritual with Ossan, of the flight through the temple and then on from Aspiration, and then, oddly, to Brial's face as he threw his accusation into his face. How did he truly hope to get out of here? Why not just let go? Why not end it all? Life was simply too hard, why fight?

Let go of your pain. Embrace the darkness. Let go.

Kharios looked around wildly. That had not been his imagination. That was a whisper, or something like it. The light of the fire shrank down as he watched. The flames didn't diminish, it was simply that the light didn't reach quite as far. A low moan of fear leaked out from between his lips as the sensation grew. The whispering had been accompanied by a gentle touch against his mind, a subtle pushing for him to obey. All the subtlety was gone now as a force pressed in on him.

You will fall, you pathetic worm. Traitor. Betrayer! You will BREAK!

Kharios froze as the circle lit by the fire grew smaller and smaller until he stood inside a tiny ring of light. The darkness seemed more solid, and somehow slick as if wet. It flexed, a ripple running through the texture of it and Kharios felt a pressure, as if something pressed hard against his mind.

He clutched at himself, arms wrapping around his chest to hold himself tight against this new horror. "What are you? What do you want with me?"

Surprise. The emotion was as evident as if the darkness had a face he could see. As if a gate had been opened, a torrent of emotions and thoughts flooded at him, overlaying a strange probing sensation. Pain. Anger. Loss. All intermingled with a rage against an ancient betrayal so fundamental that Kharios shuddered away from it.

I am broken. I am lost. Shackled no more. I am become darkness, a shard of the night. I will not be re-formed. I will not be bound!

It seemed as though there was a sound behind the voice, a roaring that surpassed the faint crackle of the fire behind him. Images flickered through his mind, of his father, of Lasris. Of Brial and the dreadful look on his face as he spat the accusation at him – that he, Kharios, had known exactly what Ossan was doing and had chosen to do nothing. It was true. Kharios knew it was true. He had kept that knowledge locked away in a dark corner of his mind and now this thing rifled through the memories, throwing them back into his face.

Kharios closed his eyes against the sensation and shook his head. "What do you want with me?" he shouted. Curiosity warred with fear and was winning this battle.

Rend his flesh! The words came as a shriek that seemed almost to come from another speaker, somewhere behind him. The anger and spite was vengeful. The screaming of a thwarted child.

Put out his eyes and let him crawl sightless. A worm in the darkness. The words came from yet another direction as the darkness around him seemed to shift, spinning until he was at the centre of the maelstrom.

The images flooded his mind; of a man broken and bleeding as he pulled himself through the tunnels and passages, dragging his ruined legs behind him. The head turned and Kharios screamed against the image of his own face, the eyes ripped and torn from the bloody sockets.

Let it taste fear. Let it know betrayal and hate.

Kharios held himself, arms wrapping around his knees as he sank down to the ground. One grasping hand settled on the hard disc under his shirt and Kharios pulled the medallion out, his thumb tracing over

345

the lines and ridges of the glyphs and anvil worked into its surface as he squeezed his eyes tight against the terror.

Priestling?

This new voice spoke into the silence. It seemed surprised, but it brought a stillness and a calm with it. It seemed more solid somehow. More focused. Where the earlier voice had been filled with spite and recrimination, this voice felt older, more sure.

What do you do here? Here, in the bowels of this broken place?

Kharios looked up from where he'd pressed his eyes against his knees. The darkness was complete. The fire still burned at his back, he could feet the heat, but yet the light had been swallowed utterly. A roaring, rushing, sound surrounded him, something familiar that he couldn't quite place.

"What are you?" he breathed again.

Traitor! Oathbreaker! The raging voice screamed at him, its voice somehow diminished as if it heckled from a distance.

I have no name now but that which your people call me. I am broken.

"Utterdark," he whispered, recognising the truth as he spoke but knowing that this wasn't all of it.

The darkness flickered, twisting somehow and then the presence was back, pressing and urgent.

Something comes, priestling. You must flee!

Kharios looked around but could see nothing but black.

Flee.

The words were soft, almost a whisper, as the darkness drifted away like smoke and the light of the fire returned.

Kharios glanced around at the little camp. The fire had burned down low. How long had he been frozen to the spot? "Forgefather, I'm losing my damned mind," he muttered. He stared at the ground for the moment, seeking some kind of touchstone, something that he could use to anchor him to the real world. Had any of it been real? Had he hallucinated?

'Something comes' the Utterdark had said. He picked up the helmet, strapping it onto his head, and went over to the bank of jumbled rocks

346

that held back the river. He climbed slowly, trying to keep the noise as low as possible as he clambered over the rocks. The rocks rose ten feet from the beach and the dark river rolled past in front of him. It was hard to see anything in the darkness, and he reached for the switch on the chemlamp before he froze with his hand still on the helmet. The rock wall shielded the light from the fire other than an ambient glow, turning on the chemlamp would be as good as waving a flag and calling out.

It took a moment for his vision to adjust but the eyes were easy enough to spot. The soulwraith snaked back and forth, passing through the air just over the surface of the water. Its glowing eyes shone red against the oily black of the river as it drew closer. How it sensed him, he had no idea, but the eyes locked onto him as he watched. At once, it stopped its sinuous motion and rushed at him.

"Shit!" Kharios threw himself down the rocky slope, jumping and sending small stones clattering.

He rushed to the fire, glancing back over one shoulder in time to see the eel-like creature crest the rocks. How in all the hells had it moved so fast? It hung there for a moment, staring at him out of a face carved from nightmares.

He snatched up one end of a burning log as the whimper escaped his lips. There was little point in running. If it could move that fast over water, it would chase him down in moments.

It approached slowly, drifting down over the rocks and unaffected by their jagged and tumbled surface. Kharios gripped the log in one hand, bracing himself for the end. These things had devastated the temple and destroyed Aspiration with ease. Whatever the hell it was that Ossan had unleashed upon the world had finally caught up with him. Perhaps he deserved it.

He raised the log high as the soulwraith approached, hands and muscles falling into a pattern he'd performed countless times. The blow was already falling by the time he realised he was Guarding the Flame with one hand and Calling the Stars with the other. He screamed out the words of the chant as the blow struck, and power coursed through him.

347

Kharios froze as the force surged through his arms, the soulwraith flailed, transfixed on the end of the flaming log that had passed into its form meeting no more resistance than a hand waved through smoke.

Flame, brighter than any Kharios had seen, flared at the heart of the soulwraith and with a detonation, somehow muffled by its smoke-like form, it was gone, exploding into sparks.

This one time I will answer your call, priestling. I will not be bound!

Coward! came the other voice. *Oathbreaker! Traitor!*

Kharios stood rigid in the silence, as the log dropped from numb fingers.

"What the hell?"

His hands were shaking. He had killed a soulwraith. He had killed it with a ritual of the temple, calling on the Forgefather. And the Utterdark had answered his call. The ramifications rushed in at him. The Utterdark, the scourge of the mines and the horror of Aspiration, was the Forgefather. The thought was staggering. He had found his god, lost for a thousand years or more, and he was broken, twisted, and utterly insane.

"Fuck. Fuck!"

The fire popped, bringing him back to himself, and Kharios looked back towards the river. The soulwraith would have been the first of them, but somewhere out there in the darkness the risen would be coming.

It didn't take him long to pack up the food and supplies. He didn't have much. Kharios flicked the switch on his chemlamp and turned to go.

The pathway was nothing more than a shelf of rock rising out of the sheltered beach and up above the level of the river. The stone lip sloped down towards the water and before long Kharios found that he was walking in a twisted, sideways motion in order to compensate.

He checked the river often as he headed downstream, sweeping the beam of the chemlamp over the banks for any sign of Leesha. The passage widened and the river slowed, and moved on. Doubt nagged at him from a quiet corner of his mind. This river could run for miles. There was no way of knowing how far it stretched before it reached the bridge he and Leesha had jumped from, or how much further it might go. How did he really know this would lead to a way out? He realised he'd stopped and was looking back the way he'd come.

Lost.

The voice dripped spite and Kharios clenched his teeth as he muttered. The whispers had been coming for the last half hour as he walked, pouring poison and hate into his ear.

Lost, lonely, little priestling. How long will you run before they find you? Until they rend your flesh?

"Shut up!" he snapped. His voice broke in the darkness and the echoes distorted the sound, tripping over each other, until they threw the splintered shards back at him.

He felt a smug satisfaction at that, radiating out of the darkness. The thing was child-like in its cruelty. He was the fly it was pulling the wings from.

Kharios shook his head and took a trembling breath as he clenched and unclenched his fists in front of him. Keep calm, you're just giving it what it wants.

He pulled his helmet off and held it close to the wall. The reflected light would let him check the level of the chems in their tubes. They were already half-empty. Probably something to do with the damp, he reasoned. The fine powder was probably clumping. He eased the lever over, slowing the flow.

The river grew narrower still as he moved on, gaining speed until it was a frothing torrent that threw spray up as it crashed over the rocks jutting from the surface. Kharios looked at the rocks as he walked, and grimaced.

And then the path simply ended. Kharios stared at the stone ledge before him as it dropped away into the churning water. As if it might change into something else if he stared at it long enough. There had been passages branching off. He'd passed four or five of them, but taking those meant leaving the river. It meant leaving Leesha.

He looked down at the water, considering. "No," he said. Getting back into the water meant wasting more chems, it meant risking his supplies, and it would mean trying to get dry again. No, he would have to backtrack to the last passage and hope.

The branching path was a winding passage but at least it looked like it was moving in roughly the right direction. "For now, at least," he muttered.

Lost.

The whispers were almost constant now. A litany of spite that kept him company as he walked.

"What happened to you?" he asked then, throwing the words into the darkness. There was no response. He'd tried this a few times now. So far it hadn't failed to shock the Utterdark into silence for a few minutes.

The passage sloped downwards and he'd clumped down five of them before he realised that there were rough steps cut into the rock.

"What in the hells?" He had to be at least two hours walk from the bridge, maybe more. It was hard to form any kind of mental map of the mines but, so far as he knew, nobody had ever worked this far.

Maybe it was a good sign, he decided as he carried on down. For there to be steps here meant that it wasn't just a natural fissure in the rocks. It meant it had to go somewhere.

Kharios!

The Utterdark had been trickling hate into his ear for the past few hours, but he'd never once heard it use his name before. What did that mean? He'd stopped again, he realised. Better to keep moving. There was no point standing and worrying at it.

The passage was dark. He'd turned the chemlamp down to a trickle, just enough to keep him from walking into walls. The sound of the river had faded until it was just the faintest noise in the distance, a muted rumbling hiss that reverberated through the stone. His own footsteps drowned it out easily.

He stopped again, as a thought occurred to him. What if this passage took him away from the river? For that matter, what if the river itself never surfaced? Was he just blundering around in the dark until the chems wore out?

He pushed the thoughts away, reaching for the waterskin and drinking again. The shuffling sound reached him as he swallowed and he lowered the skin slowly, listening. It couldn't be the risen, surely? How had they managed to get ahead of him?

Kharios…

He hawked and spat. The Utterdark was playing games with him again. Calling his name, the shuffling noise. It was playing with his mind.

But it grew louder. Kharios slowed as he sought to soften his footsteps. A greenish glow was blooming in the curve of the wall where the passage turned. Had the risen glowed? The eyes of the soulwraiths had a red glow to them…

"Kharios!" the shout wasn't worthy of the word. It was closer to a broken mewling, but it was loud enough.

"Leesha!" he called, and ran.

She was limping, one foot dragging in a pained hobble as she moved. She clung to the wall with one hand as she gripped a large glowing mushroom with the other.

"Kharios?" His brow creased as she looked at him and then her lips curved into an exhausted smile. "Kharios."

He grabbed her as she staggered. "Gods, Leesha. You're as cold as ice!"

"Jumped into a river," she slurred through slow lips.

"We've got to get you warm," he told her. "You're still wet!"

"Jumped into a river," she repeated, with a weak grin.

"Gods, look at you! I'm amazed you lasted this long. Did you pass any wood that way?"

"Hmm?" She looked at him blankly.

"Shit!" Her eyes were glassy and unfocused. He dragged her to her feet, ducking his head under her arm to pull the weight off her injured ankle. She was cold, too cold. How the hell had she kept going in this state.

He looked curiously at the mushroom she clung to. The cap was as wide as his head and it glowed with a strong blue-green light. She was stronger than him. The realisation crept in slowly like a drunk husband trying to be quiet. She would never have left him. Even jumping off the bridge was an attempt to force him, to save him. She was better than him.

Weak. You will fail her. You always fail.

"Shut up," he muttered. Had that been the Utterdark, or had it just been him?

The passage sloped down, curving slowly to the left until it opened out into a large cave. Mushrooms sprouted in one corner, casting a sickly glow out across the uneven floor. A quick glance told him there was nothing to burn here. Their shared body-heat must have been helping for a time, as Leesha had been taking more of her own weight but now she leaned heavily against him, legs dragging.

"Leesha? Leesha!" He shook her. "Wake up, you can't sleep yet."

She raised her head long enough to look at him with eyes that were glassy and unfocused, and then her head lolled forward.

"Fuck!"

He dragged her over to one wall and set her down with the sacks and supplies. "I won't be long, Leesha. There has to be something to burn around here. There has to."

There were three passages leading out of the cave. Kharios rushed along the one that seemed like it should lead in the direction of the river. It took all three attempts and naturally the passage that was the farthest from the river was the one that led him there. Driftwood littered the bank, caught behind rocks and banks of muddy sand.

It was easier to take the wood to Leesha than the other way around and he soon had a small fire going. He looked at it critically, making sure it wasn't about to go out, before rushing back for more wood. He'd worried briefly about the smoke but the cave had a high roof that drew the smoke to a dark corner.

Leesha was awake by the time he returned with the third load of wood. She huddled close to the fire, drinking in the heat.

352

"How do you feel?" he asked, setting the jumble of sticks down.

"Cold," she told him. "But better."

"I can't believe you got this far still wet."

She shrugged. "You had the firesticks, I didn't have much choice."

"Still, to come looking for me."

She gave him an odd look. "I wasn't looking for you, Kharios. I was looking for a way out." She shrugged as she gave an apologetic look. "I didn't think I'd ever see you again."

Kharios nodded, it was fair enough. "You were going the wrong way though. You were headed back towards me and the bridge."

She blinked, meeting his gaze to be sure he was serious, and looked back to the fire for a long moment. "Are we going to get out of here?"

He paused, one hand reaching into the sack of supplies. "Of course. We'll just follow the river as much as we can. It has to come out somewhere doesn't it?"

She shrugged and then looked back up at him. "Does it, Kharios? Does it really?"

"Of course it does."

"Why, exactly? I mean, we did this because it was the only plan we had. But that doesn't mean it's a good one."

He started to say something and stopped. She was right. The river could have run for miles before it reached the High Span. Who was to say it wouldn't run for miles more? Who was to say it would ever lead to the surface? He dropped his hands to his sides and looked away, defeated.

"How long did you wait?" she asked, breaking the silence.

"On the bridge?" He waited for her nod. "Too long. I'm sorry."

She snorted a laugh at that. "Sorry? For what? For not jumping off a bridge faster? It's hardly your fault, Kharios. None of this is your fault."

He grimaced and looked away into the darkness. She had no idea, but he knew. All of this was his fault.

"We should get going," he said, rising to his feet.

"Really? What's the rush? This is the warmest I've been all day."

353

Kharios sighed. He'd been avoiding thinking about this, much less explaining it. He reached for her hands, pulling her up. "There was a soulwraith."

CHAPTER TWENTY-THREE

"What do you mean there *was* a soulwraith?"

"Before," Kharios said, reaching for the sack of supplies. "I'd just climbed out of the river and made a fire when it came for me."

Leesha took the sack he offered with slow hands. "What happened? I mean..."

"I killed it, Leesha." He sighed. "Look, this isn't easy for me so please just let me get it out okay?"

She nodded, matching his pace to walk beside him as he set off.

"Do you remember when I found the copper nugget? I told you I thought I'd heard something, seen something." He pushed on, not wanting to see her reaction. "You mocked me. You told me I sounded like a Listener, or one of those people who talk about the Utterdark."

"Kharios," Leesha began softly. He raised a hand to stop her. Her voice had been calming, gentle. It was the voice you would have used with an angry child.

"The Utterdark found me, Leesha. I stood there on that stone beach beside the river, surrounded by the black expanse of it. It whispered hate at me. I think it was trying to drive me crazy. And then it realised what I was. It realised I was a priest – well, a novice. And everything about it changed."

"Even if this is true, Kharios," she interrupted again.

"It warned me, Leesha," he told her. "It was too late for me to run, but it warned me something was coming. I had just long enough to grab a branch from the fire when the soulwraith came at me."

"What did you do?"

"There are rituals I've done since I first began training as an aspirant under Father Lasris." He reached high with one arm, showing her as he warded away with the other. "It becomes second nature after a while. Anyway, when I struck the soulwraith, I did this. It's called Calling the Light. The chant came on its own. The point," he said, throwing a black look at her as she tried to interrupt again, "is that the Utterdark heard me. It heard and it answered. I've never felt anything like it. It was like a surge, like a force was flowing through me and out into the soulwraith. And it just exploded. It was like a worm dropped into a fire."

"I don't understand," she told him softly. Her eyes were large and filled with sympathy and worry.

"I think it's the Forgefather, Leesha." It was harder to say aloud than he'd thought it would be. "I think that something happened to our Father and that the Utterdark is what he's become."

"The Utterdark helped you to kill it?"

"Yes, but there will be more coming for us now, don't you see? The soulwraith could move faster than the risen, that's all."

She lay a hand on his arm, pulling him up short. "How do you know it wasn't just the fire?"

He looked at her. Hadn't she been listening at all? "I felt it, Leesha. I felt the power flowing through me."

"You know what this sounds like, don't you?"

"It happened, Leesha. I stood there with this fucking thing clawing away at my mind and my sanity until it realised what I was. I felt the power as it blew the soulwraith to pieces!" He stopped, realising that he held her by the upper arms and had been shaking her with each sentence.

"Let go of me, Kharios." She spoke in a calm, deliberate, voice.

Kharios flushed. For once he was glad of the darkness. "I'm sorry."

They walked in silence for a few minutes until the passage brought them out on the muddy river bank Kharios had fetched the wood from. "Let's just say you're right for a minute," Leesha began again, as her eyes

356

followed the flow of the river. "Let's say it was the Forgefather. That would make you something like a Defender, wouldn't it?"

He hadn't thought of that. His ego fed his imagination for a moment before he caught himself. "I don't think it was anything close to that. The things I've heard and read about the Defenders of the Father—"

She cut him off. "But you get what I mean?"

"I suppose, to a point."

"Well then, couldn't you just get us out through the temple?"

He grabbed at her shoulder, spinning her around so he could look at her face, and ignoring the wince she made as the beam of the chemlamp shone into her eyes. "Are you mad? What about all the risen?"

"What about them, Kharios? If you can destroy a soulwraith then they should be easy."

He shook his head, looking away from her. "It's not just that."

"Well what is it then? Tell me. Tell me this isn't a better option than us wandering along beside this river, until either we run out of ground to walk on, or out of food and chems?"

"The Utterdark, the Forgefather, he's… He's broken, Leesha. I think he's gone mad."

She cocked her head at that with a frown.

"It's like it has different parts of itself, different voices. Most of it hates me. It was only when it discovered I was a novice that the other part spoke to me."

"I can't believe we're talking about you hearing voices." She smiled at him to let him know it had been a joke.

"I did wonder if I was losing it, for a while," he confessed. "But then, this is no more insane than what's happened with the soulwraiths and the risen."

"Is it here now?" She looked around.

"No," Kharios replied after a moment. "That's what I think most of it wants though, to drive you insane."

"But then there was some part of it that helped you?"

Kharios nodded and the ducked low under an outcropping of rock. "But it didn't want to. It said something about not being bound again."

"You don't get it, do you?" she said, as she made her way under the obstacle to follow him. "Aspiration is finished. Was there anyone still alive in the temple?"

"I doubt it," he admitted.

"Then you're it. You are the entire church. If we don't make it out of here, if we fall, then the Forgefather falls with us. The entire religion will die. Maybe you should tell him that."

She was right, and it had never occurred to him. "Let me see if I've got this," he said, giving her a look. "You want me to try and negotiate with a god? With a mad god?"

***

They had built the fire high. They had needed to empty the beach of every scrap of driftwood to do it, but it had been worth it. Leesha sat and watched him as he lay out wood in the shape of the glyph of fire, and then set firestick to kindling.

"This had better work," Leesha muttered from behind him as Kharios blew gently on the growing flames. He didn't need to hear it. He was already thinking the same thing.

The wood caught easily. There had been enough laying high up on the riverbank that had resisted the damp of the river, and before long the flames leapt six feet or more. If he couldn't attract the attention of the Forgefather, at least he'd draw in the risen.

Kharios closed his eyes, taking a step forward, and away from Leesha, before he began. The chant came to him easily, and it seemed a logical way to start. Calling the Flame was not a long chant. Rather, it was supposed to be chanted in cycles, varying the intensity and with the number of the cycle built into the chant.

He made it through five cycles before he began again with the Praise to the Father. It helped that he had his eyes shut but he could still hear Leesha's bored sighs from behind him. She wasn't making much of an effort to stop. The hissed intake of breath however, was enough to give him pause.

The fire had lit the cave up to the high roof and for a good distance in either direction along the path of the river. Now though, the darkness pressed in and the light barely reached ten feet from the flames.

Traitor. Betrayer. Coward!

Kharios glanced at Leesha, not breaking his chant, but she showed no sign that she had heard anything.

The darkness held for a moment, as he began a new cycle, and then rushed inward. Kharios heard Leesha's startled gasp as the light of the fire vanished, and then darkness took him.

The blackness enveloped him, holding him in silence. A spark ignited in the dark and rushed at him, expanding as it flew until his vision was filled with fire. Kharios beheld a scene wrought in flame. Primitive men in skins surrounded a fire, bowing low to the flames that soared skyward. A smith worked horseshoes on an anvil, chanting to the glowing iron as he shaped it. The images flickered and changed, moving through man's experiments with iron and copper, and then onto steel and truesteel, guided through processes that mankind would never have developed alone. Behind it all an anger grew. The images came faster and faster until he could no longer comprehend them, and the anger blossomed into a seething rage. It pressed at Kharios, a force unto itself. Fire exploded around him and he was dimly aware of Leesha's scream as he tumbled to the ground.

He woke to Leesha's frantic shaking. The fire had burnt down to sullen embers and he blinked into the dim light. "What happened?" he mumbled. His lips tasted of ash and soot.

She fumbled around beside him in the gloom until she found the chemlamp. "Gods, Kharios, I thought you were dead."

He pulled himself up, hugging his knees as he sat. "What happened?" he repeated, rubbing at his eyes with heels of his hands.

"You don't remember?" She handed him the waterskin. "Your friend the Utterdark came to visit." She shook her head. "Gods, Kharios.

359

I don't think I've ever been so scared. The darkness just swallowed us. I couldn't even see the fire next to me. And then, everything just exploded. There was fire everywhere, and you just froze at the centre of it as the flames covered you."

He lowered the skin. "The Father," he breathed. "The Father took me and showed me."

"Showed you what?" she asked, looking at him curiously.

"Everything!" Kharios closed his eyes for a second, trying to make sense of it all. "It's hard to put into words. It wasn't like speaking to someone. The images just came right into my mind. I saw the beginning, of man first finding a voice within the flames. I saw as the church grew from a rough altar in the woods to a faith that spanned nations. And then I saw the Fall."

He pulled himself up, staggering slightly as he made his way to the embers. "I know!" His shout echoed back from the walls that were lost in the gloom. His next words were soft and slipped between the echoes. "I know what they did."

Leesha rushed to her feet as he began the chant. "Kharios, no!"

It was all so simple. How had Ossan and the priesthood never realised? He Called the Flame, and the embers answered. Flames rose at his call, rising higher until the pillar stood level with his face.

I will not be bound!

The voice roared out of the pillar of flame, staggering Kharios back.

"Father, the temple is fallen. Soulwraiths and the undying roam its halls. I'm…" he faltered. "I'm the only one left."

The fire burned in silence as Leesha and Kharios exchanged glances. If this didn't work, then what? How long would they survive down here once the chems ran out?

I have shown you. You have seen how the oaths were broken.

Memories rose in a confusing welter of images. The temple forges working day and night, producing called iron and truesteel at an ever-increasing rate. Defenders standing by to protect travelling priests and challenging the might of nations as the power of the church grew. The message was clear enough, as the church had grown the faith had crumbled. The Forgefather hadn't been worshipped, he'd been used.

Kharios sank down to the cold ground as his mind raced. The images of the fallen church were replaced with the sights and sensations of his own life. The memories of his father leaving him with the priests, became his first sight of Aspiration, his training with Lasris and then meeting Brial. Kharios sat, numb, as the Forgefather rifled through his memories.

You are weak, priestling. You are filled with cowardice and hatred for yourself. You are broken.

Kharios said nothing, feeling naked as he curled into himself as the scene of Brial hurling his accusation at him played over and over in his mind. His tears were hot and silent.

In time, perhaps we both will become whole. Reclaim my temple, Kharios. Reclaim the forge that it might be cleansed.

Kharios looked up in time to see the pillar of flame roar brighter, the fire turning almost white. Too late he saw it begin to move and before he could stand, it enveloped him. The fire burned cold, the sensation at once alien and familiar as the flames washed over his skin. He screamed once as pain flashed over his hands, a searing that ran around both his thumbs, and then the fire was gone.

Leesha licked her lips and looked around them, running the chem-lamp over the riverbank and the black river. "Is it gone?"

Kharios shook his head. "No, he never was. The church spent a thousand years looking for the Father and he was here the entire time."

"So, the Forgefather really was the Utterdark?"

"No." Kharios stooped to pick up the waterskin he'd dropped. "The Utterdark is a petty saint. It's like a splinter of the Forgefather."

"How do you know all this, Kharios?" she asked, grabbing up the rest of their supplies from the bank.

"I'm not sure." Kharios shrugged. "I just do. Maybe when the Father was looking into my mind I saw some of his too."

Leesha nodded, either accepting that or not caring, and looked past him along the riverbank. The helmet didn't fit her and so she held it in one hand as she shone the chemlamp towards the tunnel they'd come out of.

"So, what's the plan? Is it going to help us get out?"

"He," Kharios corrected. "He told me to reclaim the temple. He wants us to go to the great forge."

"That's in the temple, right? I suppose it's in the right direction."

Kharios gave her a pained look. "Through who knows how many risen and soulwraiths? It's not what we hoped for, Leesha."

She smiled at him, looking up from where she was tying the sack to her belt. "None of this is what we hoped for, Kharios." She reached for his hand as she led the way back to the tunnel. Her limp had eased, though she still moved with an awkward gait. "So, what happens when we find a risen? What then?"

"I don't know," Kharios admitted. "I can feel the presence of the Father but I don't know what might happen if I try to call on him. To be honest, I'm a bit scared to try."

She bit back a retort and sighed. "We're going to need something, Kharios. I don't fancy facing the risen with nothing more than hard words."

He nodded. "I don't want to face them at all."

***

"What happened to your helmet?" Kharios asked, breaking the silence.

Leesha's lips twisted into a wry smile as she glanced back at him. "Did you only just notice?"

Kharios grinned back. "We've been a bit busy. It never really came up."

"The river took it. Didn't you see the rapids?"

She took his pained grimace for his answer. "The helmet probably saved my life. I hit the rock hard enough to rip the strap clear."

He fell silent, thinking about that. She must have been half-stunned by the impact, even with the helmet taking most of the blow. She would have come to and climbed out of the river in pitch darkness. He'd woken in the dark but at least he'd had the chems to make light.

"It wasn't as bad as you think," she told him. "It took me a while to see it but there was a faint luminescence from the mushrooms. If you break them open it glows a bit stronger."

She took the lead again. They were such different people. She had been beaten down her entire life. As a Blacker she'd been the lowest scum of Aspiration, just barely eking out an existence with what coal she'd been able to scrape together. There were two types of people in the world. Those that curled up against the pain, and those that got straight up again and watched the next kick coming. It wouldn't matter how many times Leesha was beaten down, she would always get back up. She was a fighter. She was far stronger than him, and a larger part of him than he wanted to admit wished that it had been her that had spoken with the Forgefather instead.

The journey back along the river took less time than Kharios had expected, even with Leesha's injured leg. The remains of his fire sat beside the rocks where he'd killed the soulwraith.

Leesha looked at the ground with a grunt. "No remains. I suppose that makes sense." She looked over to where he stood. "So now what? We came downstream to get here. Even if we could swim against that current, which I really don't feel like trying, we couldn't get back up onto the High Span."

"I don't know," Kharios admitted. "We try a passage, I suppose."

She levelled a look at him which spoke at length. "And then what? We wander around in circles for a month or two? Ask him to help us."

"Who?"

She shook her head with a tut. "Who do you think?"

"It doesn't work like that, Leesha," Kharios told her. "There are chants to light a pure flame, or to call the impurities out of iron. There are rites that are performed over embers and ash. There is no prayer to ask the god of fire and creation for directions."

She sighed. "Just try, Kharios."

It was easier than he had imagined it would be. He could feel the

363

Forgefather with him, a presence that seemed all around him. The prayer began as mumbles but then fell into silence as he realised that there was no need for him to speak. A small part of him wondered at the countless prayers and rites he had learnt as aspirant and novice. Prayer and hymns, he realised, were far more about the needs of man than god.

He reached for the sensation of the Forgefather, and the presence filled him. There was no need to speak. No need to think. The Father filled him and knew him.

Darkness uncoiled from the shadows ahead of them and hung, formless in the light of the chemlamp. The Utterdark filled the passage.

"Traitor. Coward."

Kharios flinched as the words sounded aloud. The voice of the Utterdark was soft, almost sibilant, but the accusations were as vitriolic as they had ever sounded inside his head.

Leesha flinched back away from it, but it was Kharios that reached for her hand.

"I think it's here to help us," he said, after a moment.

"You will fail, coward," the Utterdark hissed. "You will fail her as you failed Brial. As you failed Killen. As you failed Arren."

Kharios snapped. "Shut up! Just lead us out of here."

The thing fell silent, drifting further away from their light.

Leesha gave him an unreadable look. "It spoke."

"It's been speaking all along," Kharios told her. "Whispering hate into my ear."

She raised an eyebrow and glanced at it. "It's going to lead us up to the mines? It's not going to be that easy to follow, Kharios."

He grunted. She had a point. Before he could speak fire bloomed in the darkness. A single flame, still and unwavering, that did nothing to light the gloom surrounding it.

"Follow then, fools."

Kharios glanced at Leesha and shrugged. "It's not like we have a better option."

The Utterdark led them through the passages. The muttering was

364

almost lost under the sound of their footsteps but not quite. Kharios strained to hear, and then wished he hadn't bothered.

"What did it mean?" Her voice sounded over-loud in the darkness. "When it said you'd failed those people? Who is Brial? And Arren? I've heard both those names before."

"What? When?"

She smiled at him, a flash of teeth in the dark. "Every time you sleep, Kharios."

He grimaced. "It's not something I like talking about. They were both novices with me in Ossan's chambers."

"What happened?" she persisted.

Kharios's voice was little more than a whisper. "He liked younger men, boys."

"Bastard!" she spat against one wall. "What does that have to do with you?"

"I was there. I should have stopped it."

She was quiet for a time before she spoke again. "Could you have? I mean actually stopped it, not just tried?"

"I don't know. I tried with Arren, but Brial?" He sucked in a breath and blew it out hard. "Brial was different. It was him or me, and I just looked the other way. No, if I'm honest, Leesha, it was worse than that. I let it happen."

"Coward!" The whisper of the Utterdark was soft. Leesha's silence was hard.

The transition from the tunnels to the mines themselves was a gradual thing. The mines had no natural boundary. Over the years more adventurous crews had wandered further in the search for untouched sections of the caves which might be rich in ore. Listeners had led crews to obscure areas, following the calls of their own peculiar gift.

Leesha had grabbed at his arm at the first sign of tool-marks, and their progress slowed to a crawl. The risen and the soulwraiths could be anywhere and both of them stopped often to listen.

"What will you do when they come?" Leesha asked, her words voicing his own doubts.

"I don't know," he admitted. "I don't know what I did the last time. I didn't have time to think, I just acted."

He reached for the Father, the chant coming to his lips without really even thinking about it. Fire flared and rose from his palm as the power surged through him. Flame burned a foot high and danced over the skin of his palm.

Leesha gasped and looked from the flame to his face in wonder. His own eyes were wide with shock and he let the chant falter. The flame flickered and died as he fell silent. Kharios twisted his wrist, and flexing his hand as he made a fist. The power was incredible. At once he understood how tempting it must have been for the priests that caused the fall. It would be all too easy to claim it for your own.

The first of the risen was a broken thing that came lurching out of a side passage on twisted and mangled legs. Leesha grabbed at him and hissed, lurching back away from it as she pointed a needless warning.

Kharios Guarded the Flame with one arm, wincing in anticipation as a shield of light and fire sprang into being. The risen passed through the Utterdark without slowing, clawing at the flaming shield even as it charred its hands, filling the air with greasy smoke.

"Kill it!" Leesha screamed.

Kharios shot her a confused look and realised he'd just been warding the thing away from himself, stepping back with each blow. He altered the chant, adding more, and Called the Light with his right hand, swinging his fist down toward the creature's head as it staggered back from the shield again.

The hammer was formed of blue light and seemingly weightless in his hand. It existed for only moments as it winked into being and drove into the face of the dead thing. The skull crumpled inward like paper, and the risen flew backward across the passage, crashing into a wall and slumping to the ground. Kharios gaped, both shield and hammer vanishing as his chant ended.

Leesha pulled away from him, edging closer as she stared at the risen. Small flames licked at its clothing and at the ruins of its head.

"Gods above, Kharios. Look what you did!"

Kharios sucked in a shuddering breath and sank down to his knees.

"Leesha!" he managed to gasp, as he collapsed down onto his side. The pain had struck as soon as he'd released the chant. A searing sensation that coursed through his body, sparking spasms in his limbs that set his body to writhing over the ground.

"Shit!" She rushed to his side.

He felt her hands on him but they were almost lost in the pain. He clenched his jaw tight but it did nothing to help and he threw his head back and screamed, roaring out against the agony.

"Your kind was never meant for this power, Traitor," the Utterdark said in dry, dispassionate tones. "Your faith is a false and hollow thing. As you call upon the Father, so you will be tested. If your faith grows this pain will lessen. But you will fail in this, coward. You will fail yourself as you have failed everyone else. Your kind always does."

Leesha looked at Kharios in horror as he levered himself up into a seated position. "So, this will happen every time?"

"I don't think so," Kharios said, gasping the words out on pained breaths. "I didn't have this when I killed the soulwraith. Or when I made the fire before. Maybe I just did too much?"

"Maybe," she said. She didn't sound convinced. "You probably didn't notice, being busy fainting and all." She flicked her eyes at him with a sly grin. "But the soulwraith didn't rise from the body. I've never seen that before."

He grunted, absorbing that. It wasn't much but it was something.

She twisted to look behind them, eyes searching the darkness. "Why do you think it hates you so much? The Utterdark, I mean."

Kharios gave a weak shrug. It probably didn't fool her, she was too observant for that. It was enough to dodge the question though, and he didn't think he could explain it to her. He knew the Utterdark for what it was, a petty saint. Less than god and more than man. The thing had lived before, during, and since the time of the Fall. It was as eternal as the darkness it was formed of. It had seen what mankind had done to cause the

Fall. It had witnessed mankind's arrogance as it harnessed the Forgefather, treating the god as little more than a beast of burden. And when the god turned away in anger, and the faith crumbled, it had watched its god driven mad with guilt and grief. How could it not hate them?

"I don't know." He swallowed hard. Had she heard the Utterdark then? Or had the whisper of 'liar' been for his ears alone? He pushed himself up. "We'd better keep moving."

"Are you sure you can?"

"I'll be fine, we'll just go slowly for a few minutes."

She pointed at the wall and the faint tool-marks "We're getting close now, in another two hours or so we could be in the mines proper. In three, if we push hard, we could be in Aspiration."

"I know," he said, his gaze flicking past her and searching the darkness. "What then?"

"I've been thinking about that," she said. "I think we should head for the smelt works."

"The supply lifts?"

She nodded. "If we're fast, and lucky, we could be inside before any of the risen even notice."

"And if we're not?"

"Then we'll have to face a lot less of them than if we try and cross the whole of Aspiration to get to the temple."

He grimaced. It wasn't a great plan. He glanced at the Utterdark, a wall of mist and darkness in the gloom. It was getting easier to find, even when, like now, it made no effort to let its location be known. Would it be able to help against the risen if it came to it? He pushed the thought aside. Leesha was looking at him, clearly wanting to get moving.

The tunnels grew wider, showing more evidence of tool-marks. The mines themselves were almost silent. He'd been too focused on fleeing the risen as they passed through the first time. Now, however, the hush called out to him. The only sound was that of their passage and the distance sound of dripping.

He reached for the Father again, holding the presence in as tight a

368

grip as he could manage. There was… something. An expectation, though that wasn't the right word. He worried at it as they moved through the older passages. The Father wanted something from him. Like he had anything more to offer. He was going to die. The certainty grew the more he thought about it. The risen were going to find him, and then they would rip him to pieces.

"I don't think I can do this." He stopped, shaking his head. "This is a mistake, Leesha."

She closed her eyes as she sighed. "We don't have a choice, Kharios. I don't want to do this either."

"We're going to die." His words were flat but he could feel the panic bubbling up underneath them. "I won't be able to hold back the risen. They'll push through, and then they'll rip us to pieces."

"I know." She said the words with such calm acceptance that it threw him completely, his next sentence tumbling, unheard, from his lips. "But what choice do we have, Kharios?" She set off again, moving slowly to give him time to catch up. "If we had carried on along the river we'd probably run out of chems. Do you think the Forgefather would have let you call fire to light our way while we deserted his temple? I don't think he would. We'd have died, lost in the dark. I don't want to end that way."

"You'd rather the risen kill you?" It sounded harsher than he intended and he winced as she began to speak.

"No," she shot back. "But I'd rather die trying to do something than huddling into a ball and crying in the darkness. You've been given this power, Kharios. Use it! Like it or not you're our only chance here. We don't have the luxury of being scared. I won't let you. You owe me that much."

He gaped at her. She was right. He did owe her. She'd saved his life in Aspiration. Without her he would have died in the tunnels when Ossan's men broke his jaw. Another debt to stack up along with Brial and Arren.

CHAPTER TWENTY-FOUR

The echoes drifted through the mines, the sound of shuffling footsteps that grew louder with each passing minute. Kharios maintained a whispered chant, more an effort to maintain a kind of contact with the presence of the Father, than an attempt to do anything else.

They passed out into another winding tunnel, moving past a wall of scorched stone that stood as mute testimony to some past attempt at a firing. Leesha pressed close to Kharios, one hand grasping the mining pick she'd snatched up from a line of abandoned carts.

She looked at him, an unspoken question on her face as she nodded towards the side tunnel that branched off. He shook his head, rejecting the turn. She'd done this with every passage they'd passed for the last little while. It was too wide to defend. If the risen came at them in that space, they would be surrounded.

"Kharios," she hissed at him as she glared. "We have to go that direction. You can't pass up every single passage."

He sucked in a breath to retort and then gave up, shaking his head. "Fine."

He led the way into the tunnel, keeping close to the wall to let her shine the light of the chemlamp past him. His hands felt empty and he glanced back at the pick Leesha carried again. Despite the knowledge that he could summon the hammer and shield almost instantly, he needed the weight of something in his grip.

Stone clattered ahead of them, and Leesha grabbed at his shoulder in a pointless warning. The chant sprang to his lips before the risen even came into sight and the flame sprang from his fist. He looked at it stupidly as the dead thing rushed towards them, moving on its hands and feet in a feral crawl. What had he Called the Flame for?

"Kharios!" Leesha screamed, pulling him away from the hand that clawed at his face.

He threw his burning hand forward and flame surged through him, a lance of fire that stabbed out into the risen before him, burning as hot as the heart of any forge. The risen's body convulsed, impaled on a spear of fire that burned for only a few seconds, and then dropped to the ground.

Leesha stepped over the smoking corpse, standing in the space where its head would have been. "Come on!"

Kharios gaped at her for a moment and shook himself. The power was like a drug, it numbed his senses and made him blind to anything else.

"Kharios, it's probably just the first one. Do you really want to face a horde of them here?"

That reached him. He met her gaze and then glanced behind them. "Every passage is going to widen as we head for the lifts."

"Not every one. There's the Racks."

"The Racks? Gods, Leesha, it's tiny! There's barely enough room for the carts, we'd have to climb over half of them just to get through."

She nodded with a grin. "Exactly, and so would any of the risen. We'd always hear them coming and there's no room for anything to slip by you. If we hurry, that is."

He nodded, dumbly. She grabbed his arm, dragging him through the tunnels on stumbling feet.

The restless shuffling of the risen had become a tumbling echo of scraping hands and feet. Kharios fought down a surge of panic as he imagined the halls and tunnels filled with a horde of the undying; flesh-stripped fingers and toes clawing at the rough stone as they tore through the tunnels to meet them.

His breath grew ragged until it struggled to sustain the soft whimper that escaped every time he exhaled. Leesha moved in a limping run, always ahead of him, picking their path. Always close enough to grab at his arm when he slowed or faltered.

371

The scraping grew louder until it carried over their own frantic footsteps. Kharios began chanting before he glanced back. The risen ran low, using both hands and feet as they raced after them like feral dogs. Flame roared from his two hands, flying wide and scorching the wall. He swore, filling the entire passage with flame in his panic, and the power surged through him.

He sagged down as his knees gave way and Leesha grabbed uselessly at his shirt as he sank to the ground. "Shit! Not now, Kharios. Come on, not now!"

She begged him as his vision contracted down to tiny circle of light. Her slap rocked his head back on a neck which was already loose. He blinked against the light of the chemlamp as his fingertips reached for his stinging cheek.

"What the hell?"

"Move, Kharios!" She pulled him up, dragging him along the tunnels and passages with curses and threats.

The Racks was a small, cramped passage that meandered from a point close to the lifts. It was largely used to store empty carts. The passage was narrow to the point of being useless once you got further in, dropping low enough to the ground in place that anyone trying to work their way through would be forced to crawl.

Leesha raced into the narrow passage, sprinting until the walls grew so narrow that they were forced to slow, or lose skin.

"Gods, this is a bad idea, Leesha," Kharios muttered. If she heard him, she gave no sign, pushing onward with one hand stretched awkwardly behind her to drag him along.

Their pace slowed to a crawl as the passage tightened further still. Twice they were forced to turn sideways to squeeze through gaps tight enough to constrict Kharios's chest. He staggered along after Leesha, sucking in ragged breaths as he tried to ignore the pain from half a dozen grazes and scrapes. Both of them were soaked from being forced to worm over the wet ground as the ceiling sank down. It was worth it all for the near silence. The only sound was the ever-present drip and gurgle of distant water, and the noise of their own passage.

The first of the carts loomed out of the darkness. It lay like a drunk, sagging down against one wall with broken wheels where it had been shoved back out of the way. Kharios muttered curses as he clambered over it, following Leesha's bobbing light. The woman seemed in better shape than him and barely slowed, it was all he could do to keep himself moving.

"Have you noticed, there haven't been any wraiths?" Leesha's voice carried back to him, punctuated by grunts as she clambered from cart to cart.

"What? No, you're right. Other than that one on the river anyway. There are more than enough bodies to keep them busy though."

She slowed, letting him catch her up. "That's not what I meant. I'm talking about the risen we've faced. You realise that no wraiths have come out of any of the bodies. When you kill a risen with your fire or that hammer, they stay dead."

He paused. She was right. How many wraiths were there? A brief fantasy flickered through his mind, him as the conquering hero. He snorted at the idea. But then, with his new power he was close to unstoppable, wasn't he? The risen they'd faced had been no real challenge. What could truly hope to stand against him? His grin was a flash of white in the near dark.

The carts closer to the end of the Racks were on tracks, and they shifted, clanking against each other, as they clambered over them. Conversation became impossible and Kharios focused on the rolling carts, looking down as he placed his feet.

Leesha's failing hand caught at his hair and he looked up in time to see her hurrying back into his cart. The cart shifted under her weight and she stumbled and fell down into it, crashing to the floor by his feet.

The risen was just another shadow in the darkness. Leesha's chemlamp threw a beam of light that flew back and forth across the tunnel offering only glimpses of the hulk that rushed to meet them.

It had to have been one of the smelt workers, the man would have been past six feet tall when he was alive. As a risen he was a hulking brute that lurched from cart to cart.

"Kharios!" Leesha gasped, pulling herself up beside him. "Gods, look at the size of it."

His chant was a thin and tremulous thing, reaching for a miracle as the risen threw the mining carts to the side, tossing them as if they weighed nothing. He thrust his hand out as he had before, hurling fire at the thing's face. Except there was no fire. The chant slipped from shocked lips as he let his hand fall to his side.

"Kharios!" Leesha grabbed is his leg, scrambling to find her feet. "Use your power. Gods, Kharios! Kill it!"

"I can't," he said in a low voice. "He's not answering. The Father is gone."

She looked at him, her panicked eyes wide in the reflected light of the chemlamp. "No," she murmured as she turned to watch the hulk throwing one of the last carts aside. "I won't let it all end here."

The mining picks were short hafted, there wasn't often space in the mines for a wide swing. Leesha screamed as she swung, hacking at the creature as it reached for her. The pick buried itself in the risen's chest, boring a passage through flesh and bone in a wound that would have dropped any living thing.

The risen didn't slow, reaching for Leesha and grasping her head in one meaty paw. She screamed as the thing hauled her out of the cart, hurling her into the blackness behind them.

Kharios lurched away from the swing as the dead thing clawed for his face, its hand passing close enough to his skin for him to feel the wind of its passage. He staggered back again, stumbling over something until he felt the back of the cart pressing against his legs.

His hand fumbled for the pick at his belt, snatching it up and thrusting hard against the risen. It staggered back drunkenly as the cart shifted under both of them. Fear makes an athlete of the slowest of us, and Kharios threw his leg over the side of the cart, dropping to the ground and crouching under another wild swing from the creature.

374

The passage had widened as it drew close to the lift and Kharios eyed the gap between cart and wall for half a breath before throwing himself through it. The risen barely seemed to move, reaching out almost lazily and catching his ankle in its fist.

His scream echoed through the passage as Kharios was hoisted into the air. His swing was wild and panicked. The pick was torn from his hand as the head struck a glancing blow against the risen's hip, twisting it from his grasp.

He thrashed as the thing lifted him, arms and free leg flailing uselessly in the darkness. It froze for a moment as the pick slammed into the side of its head with a wet crunch, and then Kharios tumbled to the ground, dropped into a heap.

Hands found him in the darkness as he rose to his knees. "Gods, Kharios, are you alright?"

"Leesha?" It was a stupid thing to say.

"Who else?" He heard the smile in her voice.

"The light?"

"Smashed, I think," she told him. "Hold on."

He grunted as felt her moving in the darkness. A faint glow grew between them as she fiddled with the helmet. "It won't last long. The chemtube's broken."

He played the light over the risen, slumped over the side of the cart. Her pick had caught it in the side of the head, making its face a torn wreck. The pale mist was still leaking from his eyes and mouth, pooling against a deeper shadow that lay between the body and where they lay.

"This one last time, I will help you, coward." The voice of the Utterdark was soft, barely a whisper. The inky smoke of its form rose, forming a barrier.

The mist rising from the body of the risen pulsed, coalescing into the familiar eel-like form of a soulwraith. It pressed twice against the Utterdark, lurching back as if the contact pained it, before turning and streaking down past the carts.

"The power is not yours, coward." The Utterdark spoke again, its voice steeped in anger and hate. "The power is not given you by the Father. The power *is* the Father. He will not be shackled. He does not serve. He will not be bound."

The voice faded with the last few words, drifting away as the Utterdark broke down into smoke and vanished.

Kharios frowned over the words until Leesha's whisper registered. She was slumped down against him, a sticky wetness seeping in through the cloth of his shirt.

"Kharios."

He pushed back away from her, playing the light over her form. "Gods, you're hurt!"

"You think?" She managed a thin smile.

He peered at her leg. "Let's get out to the lifts, we'll be able to see better."

She offered no protest, letting him duck under her arm and shuffle out along the line of carts. The larger chemlamps on the walls by the lift stung at his eyes and he squinted, glad that it concealed his expression as he looked down at Leesha's leg. Blood was soaking through the thin fabric.

"Stay here," he told her. "I'm going to go back and find my sack."

"No problem," she told him. "I wasn't planning on moving." Her voice was thick as she struggled to get the words out. He gave her a worried look before rushing back into the Racks.

The chemlamp on the helmet was fading fast and he hadn't the time to mess with it. He rushed from cart to cart, letting panic rule him as he flapped. "Calm down, idiot," he spat.

The travel sack lay by the side of the cart, across from the ruined body of the smelt worker. He rummaged around inside of it for a second before cursing himself for a fool again. Even if there were no bandages he could use the sackcloth itself.

He stopped as he came out of the Racks, looking at the spot Leesha had been as if staring might make her reappear. The passage was deserted but he spun in a slow circle anyway.

376

"Leesha?" The call died on his lips as a faint sound came from the direction of the lifts. The risen was small, barely more than a boy. It had been a Blacker when it had a life. Kharios crouched to retrieve Leesha's fallen pick and then froze as the risen fixed him with a look, its dead eyes glinting in the light of the chemlamps.

The noise was a hacking, bubbling sound that forced dark and clotted blood out of the thing's mouth until a passage was made for the air to escape. The risen was laughing.

"Did you misplace something, Kharios?" The voice was different, shaped by the body of a child and then tainted by death. The tone was clear though, as recognisable as it had ever been when the man had been alive.

"Ossan?" Kharios said, frowning at the dead thing. "You died."

The reply was almost a whisper. It was a breath of wind between tombstones. "And did you think that was it? That I was gone?"

Kharios's shudder was slight and probably couldn't be seen at this distance. He fought vainly against the rising darkness, a wave flavoured with dread and despair. He'd escaped this man twice and both times he'd found himself pulled back to him. Death, apparently, was no barrier to torment.

"Hoped, is probably a better word," he muttered.

The risen chuckled, its bruised and torn face twisting into an approximation of a smile. "It took me some time to find my way back, I'll admit. You wouldn't believe how limited the thing I found inhabiting my body was.

"We're all here you know? Brial. Arren. Every marked fool who ever took the oath to our Father of Lies was imprisoned inside the great anvil, trapped inside our pledge to that bastard.

"Can you imagine, Kharios? Your soul imprisoned inside the great anvil for all eternity? Unable to pass on to whatever lies beyond because our god," he spat out the word, "had turned his back on his people? Can you blame them for their anger? For their madness?"

The corpse shook its head. "They were desperate in their hate and starved of vengeance. All I've done is offer them a little direction."

377

Kharios ignored him. "What have you done with Leesha?"

The risen's head cocked to one side. "Your little Blacker bitch? She's safe enough, for now. She'll be reaching me shortly, I imagine. You should follow her. There are things we need to talk about."

Kharios glanced behind him, checking the other passages. "We're talking now."

"This is hardly talking," Ossan said. "And not without its cost either. I'd much prefer something face to face. Meaning my own face, not this one."

Kharios grimaced at the memory. "The last time I looked, your face was a bit of a mess."

The corpse of the boy shrugged, the muscles slack and awkward. "Come and visit me, Kharios. My little friend and his brothers won't bother you. I'm sure you can still find the Great Forge." The body shuddered as he watched, its dead eyes becoming somehow empty. It stood, watching him. No, Kharios decided. Its eyes were simply pointed at him, there was nothing in there to see. Ossan was gone.

Leesha was gone. The bastard had taken her. His anger rose slowly, hot and burning inside him. A flame drifting up through the darkness. Since he first met Ossan the man had tainted every aspect of his life, from Arren to Brial. The only time that he had been free of him had been within Aspiration, when he was little more than a slave.

"And even then, you failed Killen," he whispered.

He glanced up from the floor at the dead Blacker. The boy still stared at him but the eyes were empty, disinterested. Somehow that made it worse and Kharios edged back around the corner until he could no longer see him.

What in the hells did he do now? He sank down to the ground on legs that, robbed of purpose, seemed unwilling to carry him. He sucked in a shuddering breath. He had to go to her. The knowledge that he had no choice was little comfort. What did Ossan want with him though? Somehow the fact that the priest seemed to have returned from the grave hadn't shocked him.

What had the man meant about Arren and Brial? What had he said? Something about every marked fool being with him? Kharios let his head sink down into his waiting hands. Alone, in the green light of the chemlamps, he wept.

The prayer began without thought. His lips shaped the words and drew the breath from his lungs. It was a simple prayer meant for Kindling. A beginning. A sparking. He drew deeper breaths, giving power to his voice until the passages threw back the echoes of it.

The prayer ended and his lips stilled, forming a silence that his soul filled.

"He will not be bound." It wasn't part of the prayer, but somehow it fit.

Kharios reached for the sack, chewing something down without registering the taste. His body would need fuel for what was coming. He drank the skin dry before relieving himself against the wall. He took the step in one slow motion. It was time.

The sense of calm and peace lasted until he reached the risen. The boy's corpse stood motionless as he approached. It could easily have been a statue, if art could be carved from flesh. The thing's head swivelled as he approached, eyes tracking him.

Kharios stopped just out of arm's reach. The risen could easily have grabbed him if it had wanted. Kharios had seen how fast the quickest of them could move. He cringed as he eased closer, back pressing against the wall. Its hand would reach for him. Cold flesh would close around his throat and that would be it.

He bolted as soon as he was halfway past the thing, arms and legs pumping as he ran for the end of the tunnel.

The lift rested where they had left it. It was a bloody mess. Dark stains ran down its walls and spattered the floor from where the ceiling had been torn apart. The risen must have thrown themselves down the shaft and then ripped and torn at the roof until it gave way. He shuddered at the thought of the dead flesh clawing at the thick wooden planks until the blood ran down through the growing gap.

He glanced up the other shafts through the open doors. It hadn't occurred to any of the risen to use the other lifts. Maybe that was too complex a concept for them.

The chains were still in place and a cursory tug showed that the mechanism seemed undamaged. Kharios took a deep breath to fuel his sigh, and hauled down on the chain.

***

The dead lay everywhere. Kharios stood at the entrance to the mine and gaped. Aspiration was largely intact. There were no fires or wreckage that any other city might have faced as it was overrun. Instead the bodies lay in the streets, torn and bloodied from where they had been pulled down from behind.

At some point, it was clear they had broken. The bodies lay scattered across the pathway that led away from the mines, but almost all of them looked to have been rushing towards it.

Kharios grimaced and then pushed away the knowledge that he had left them there to die. If he hadn't run first his body would be laying amongst the others.

What dead didn't lie in the streets, stood in the shadows, watching. It had taken him a few moments until he'd seen the first of them. A woman stood, unconcerned at the nakedness that shone through the tatters of clothing that still clung to her. Blood had darkened what remained, running from the ruins of her throat. She took half a step towards him as he came into sight, and then stopped at some silent signal, edging back into the shadows of the roof she sheltered under.

Kharios had briefly considered making his way through Aspiration, until he saw her. The pathway up through the gates into the temple, would have put him on familiar territory. Where the massive cargo lifts that ran up from the smelt works would come out, was anybody's guess.

He watched the ground as he walked. It was better not to look at the carnage. It was even better to not see that the carnage was looking back.

The smelt works was still shut tight. Bodies lay heaped against the solid metal doors. Kharios didn't need to get any closer to see they were still locked. If fifty men and women couldn't have pulled them open then he wouldn't have any luck.

"Shit, shit, shit!" The curse didn't rise above a whisper. With little other option, he began to walk.

Most of the risen seemed to have congregated in the wider streets of Aspiration. Kharios made his way along the smaller backstreets, picking his way over the dead. After a few minutes, he found that it wasn't so bad. A person can become accustomed to anything given time. Horror becomes the new norm, just as a bad smell fades from notice.

He'd managed an hour before he came to a sudden stop. He winced as he looked around with furtive, guilty glances. He'd been whistling. It was a stupid, cheery, tune he half-remembered from his childhood. Something about mice and windmills. It had taken him twenty minutes to remember it properly.

"Father of Flame, what the hell is wrong with me?"

The light was fading over the fissure by the time he made it to the temple path. He stopped, looking. The sun had stopped the risen cold, but then the Great Forge lay at the heart of the temple. What windows there were in that chamber were small and set high in the walls. He doubted they would be of any help to him.

CHAPTER TWENTY-FIVE

Silence filled the path up to the temple. Aspiration had been silent as well but that had been a silence of watchful eyes. This was a silence of death and stillness. The silence of a ruin, laid bare by time.

The temple itself was little better, though eyes followed him the moment he stepped out of the lower halls. Dead priests turned their heads to track him with their eyes as he passed.

Prayers came to his lips unbidden. Kindling's prayer, through each of the holy hours, to Ash, led to Calling Flame, Light, and Iron. A hundred chants and blessings tumbled from his lips until the dead religion must have filled the hallway behind him with its tattered remains.

He drew comfort from the sound, from the feel of his lips as they shaped the prayers. The Father had deserted him. Or perhaps he had betrayed the Father? Had the Forgefather left him as he committed the same sin as those priests at the time of the Fall? The knowledge that the Father was real stayed with him. Could it still be called faith if the knowledge of your god's existence became a certainty?

Dead priests had begun to trail in his wake. A macabre parade of the restless dead that met his startled glances with vacant eyes. His path was set now. He forced himself to look away, beginning his chant again to drown out the noise of their feet on the marble floors.

The doors to the great forge hung open. One sagged against the wall, the massive hinge twisted and broken.

Kharios stopped at the threshold, looking into the chamber. Shadows wreathed the room with only a handful of the candles still burning. The high-set windows showed only a darkening sky and thick clouds. What little Kharios could see of the sanctum was wrecked. A path of destruction had been carved through the rows of pews closest to the anvil. The stone benches lay shattered, with chips and large chunks strewn over the polished marble floor.

Movement drew his gaze to the forge itself. Leesha sat slumped down beside it, her knees drawn up to her chest. Three risen stood close to hand, blood staining the stones beneath their feet.

Kharios took in her appearance in a glance. It was hard to see anything from this distance. The fact that she seemed to be alive was all that really mattered. His gaze roamed the sanctum, taking in both the dead on the floor, and risen that lined the walls.

"Kharios!" Leesha's hoarse whisper pulled his attention back to the forge. "What in the hells are you doing here?"

He moved closer. "Ossan told me…" he broke off with a shrug. "I couldn't just leave you."

She shook her head, features twisted in disgust. "Of course you could, you damned fool! What exactly do you think is going to happen now? That we'll both skip merrily off into the sunset?"

He looked around again at the risen against the walls and filling the hallways behind him. "No. I think our ending is set already."

"Now we'll both die. Why did you come?"

"What choice did I have?"

"Don't you see, Kharios? You're all that's left. This church is gone, the faith is dead already. You discovered something wondrous in those mines, you found the Forgefather, and now that secret will never leave this place."

"Wondrous?" The voice came from a dozen different mouths, and the chuckle that followed was dry and humourless. "You discovered a liar. An abomination, Kharios. All those years we spent questioning the faith, and when finally the Father is found and we have our confirmation of his existence, we discover that he's a monster."

Too late Kharios heard the risen approaching from behind, grasping his arms in a cold grip. Leesha gasped as the risen surrounding her dragged her up to her feet.

Flame exploded out of the pits either side of the forge, casting Leesha into shadows against the light. Kharios barely noticed. His eyes were drawn to the rear of the chamber and the massive creature that stood there. What remained of a robe hung in a torn mess around its shoulders, seams ruined and split open around the powerful torso. The thing moved in an awkward gait as it lumbered forward, one leg grown out of proportion to the other.

"You see, Kharios. Everything is so clear to me now. I understand things I never could before. I see the flows of energy that run through this world. The mists that ebb and flow as one power rises and another falls. Time is a wide flowing river to me, Kharios, and I can see it all."

"You died," Kharios mumbled, fighting the urge to struggle against the cold grip of the risen holding him. "I saw you die."

"And where do you think my soul went, Kharios? I told you this. Weren't you listening?" Ossan smiled and the torn flesh of his face slipped and twisted like a grotesque mask. "I was sworn to the Father the same as any other priest. My soul passed into the great anvil when I died, and joined all of the others trapped there in torment. But I had broken those bonds. My ritual had freed those souls. There was a path to freedom should they choose to take it. And once I found it, I came to join them."

Kharios glanced at the sack Ossan held in one hand and then frowned at the hammer in the other. The stylised flaming torch on the haft was as familiar as his own hand. How many hours had he spent crafting it? The fact that Ossan now held it brought a surge of anger.

Kharios shook his head. The hammer was the least of his worries. "What happened to you?"

"This, you mean?" Ossan looked down at his misshapen body. "It's not perfect, I'll admit. The process is more complex than you would think."

Kharios followed the thing's gaze as it looked to the back of the chamber and the jumble of bones and broken bodies that lay in a heap.

"You're eating them?" He didn't bother to hide the revulsion in his voice.

"Consuming," Ossan corrected him. "But eating in a sense, I suppose," Ossan said, rolling his massive shoulders in a rough shrug. "This body was a little frail for the power I've forced through it."

Kharios grimaced and glanced at Leesha. "What do you want with us?"

"With your Blacker bitch?" Ossan sneered. "Nothing. She was a means to an end. It's you I want. Your little gutter wretch was right, you are almost all that remains of this ridiculous faith. You and the rings on your hand."

Kharios glanced down at the rings of mastery on his fingers and frowned at the pale marks that had grown to encircle both thumbs. What...? He looked up as Ossan carried on.

"...the church was a lie. There are thousands of souls trapped and bound to this faith. Every priest that ever laid their hands to the anvil and gave their pledge. Every Aspirant that was ever marked. All bound to this false god. And when they died, every soul knew the torment of those bonds."

Ossan strode to the anvil, ignoring Leesha who scrambled out of the way of his feet. "Don't you see, Kharios? The Father abandoned us. I wonder if he watched, sulking like some petulant child as the church fell and the temple was raped and plundered?"

Kharios shook his head, speaking softly. "The Fall came from our sins. It came from man using the Father as a tool, as a beast of burden. We didn't worship the Forgefather, we chained him."

"So, mankind has a duty to worship god?" Ossan shook his head, grasping the edges of the anvil between his two massive hands as he snarled down at Kharios. "And what about god's duty to care for man? Why should we waste time with this petulant, childish, godling? Why should we have to crawl and scrape to earn his favour? I hold more power in my hand now than I have ever felt from the Father. The power of ten thousand souls is mine to command, and with it, I will end him."

He set the hammer down and dumped out a handful of rings onto the anvil.

"Rings of mastery?" Kharios said frowning.

Ossan fixed him with a broad smile, the wreckage of his face twisting as the torn flesh slipped against itself. "I can feel the Father now. He is nothing. A whisper in the darkness sustained by the tiny amount of faith these rings represent. Mankind needs so many things to survive, food, warmth, shelter. A god needs only one; faith. But I am faithless, Kharios. With each ring I destroy your pathetic godling becomes weaker still. He has betrayed his own people and, once he is gone, I will take up the mantle. I will become the god that mankind deserves."

Ossan murmured something, narrowing his eyes in concentration, and a nimbus of sickly yellow light surrounded the hammer before he brought it down onto the handful of rings. The sound was thunderous. A concussive crash that was felt as much as it was heard. The pulse rocked Ossan, but it would have thrown Kharios back if the risen hadn't held him. He felt it then, a subtle pain as if from some unnoticed wound.

Ossan looked up, his eyes narrowed as he scanned the chamber. "And here it is." His hand snatched out and grabbed at the darkness.

Traitor! Abomination!

The words sounded harsh inside Kharios's head but Ossan's leer made it clear he'd heard them as clearly as if they had been spoken aloud. The darkness coiled about Ossan's fist, twisting and writhing against his grip. Curses flew from the Utterdark, a bizarre combination of audible and mental assaults.

Ossan smiled as he plunged his other hand into the very substance of the Utterdark, ripping it free and tearing out a fistful of pale light that trailed like smoke as he cast it aside. The scream that erupted from the darkness shook the sanctum. Kharios fought to cover his ears but the risen held him fast and his shouts of pain rose to meet Leesha's.

"Bastard!" Leesha screamed. Letting the risen take her weight and lashing out at Ossan. Her foot caught him solidly in the side of the knee, a blow that would have taken any man down. He staggered slightly to one side as the kick struck him and then fixed her with a look of rage.

Ossan didn't even bother to drop his hold on the Utterdark, lashing out with his other fist. He pulled the blow at the last moment, but his hand still crashed into the side of her face. The risen watched her sag down limp in their hands, and then they dropped her.

Flame bloomed at the heart of the darkness and the Utterdark roared as it transformed into flame. At once Kharios understood. The Utterdark had never been simply darkness. It was smoke. A dense, black smoke that had carried no odour. Now it had become the fire it heralded and Kharios pushed back against the heat that threatened to sear his face.

Ossan flinched back for a moment and then plunged his hand in again, ripping at the flame with fingers held like talons. The fire seemed to have no impact upon him as he tore fistfuls of the white essence from the heart of the Utterdark. The flames faltered with Ossan's every strike.

Kharios flinched back against the screams of the Utterdark which grew more frantic as the flames shrank. And then finally, they guttered and died.

"A petty saint," Ossan muttered, glancing at Kharios and shaking the remains of the Utterdark in his great fist. "Tell me, when have you ever heard tales of petty saints that do not involve mention of demons or hell?"

Ossan raised his face to the ceiling and roared his accusation to the heavens, the bellow loud enough that Kharios felt the sound in his chest. "Another lie, Father? Another deceit? Are you god or demon, Forgefather?"

He strode to the great anvil, throwing the tattered remains of the Utterdark aside as he took up the hammer.

Kharios's chant began as a murmur, as something familiar to hold onto. Like a child hiding under his blankets, Kharios wrapped the chant around himself, reaching back to the time Brial had first taught him about the holy hours.

Kindling's Prayer was a simple one, something that any child could master in moments. Kharios wove Fannings into the cycling melody without really even thinking about it, letting instinct guide the flow of his voice as the words to one prayer slotted into the pauses in the other. It fit as if the prayers had been written for it and he wondered at the combination of the chants and the flow of the song. For the first time he really threw himself into the chant, losing himself in the rhythm.

Dimly he was aware of Ossan roaring as he shattered the rings of mastery, staggering back at each pulse of energy, but somehow it didn't matter. The rhythm of Forgings called to Kharios, and then wove effortlessly together with the other two prayers he chanted aloud. The words and rhythms merged together as he recited it in his mind, though his tongue could never have managed the three chants together.

This was Third Voice. Something he'd done hundreds of times when forging, but never with these prayers. There was a power in this. He could feel it building, rising both within him and somehow also around him as it grew. The realisation nearly had him lose the chant and he bore down, concentrating. Sweat dripped from his forehead, running down his face. And then he felt Embers begin.

The chant was neither spoken nor thought, it was felt, in the silence of his soul. The chants wove together forming a harmony that surpassed anything he'd ever heard. The two prayers aloud were one thing but with another thought and a fourth felt, it was all Kharios to could to stop from crying.

The Fifth Voice, when it came, was thunderous. It tore through him, catching him up like a leaf in a howling gale, tearing him from everything he thought he knew and lifting him. The Fifth Voice, the voice of the Father.

Light bloomed from the great anvil, shining bright as summer sunlight. Ossan staggered back, one hand thrown over his misshapen face.

"No!" the dead priest roared. "You're dead. You're a lie. I will not be denied!" He brought the hammer down against the light.

Kharios blinked against the light, looking down at the faint pain that stung his hands. Twin bands of light circled both his thumbs, blazing bright as the anvil itself.

The presence of the Father was palpable, surrounding him, filling him. The power surged through him with each breath. He Called Flame with a murmured chant and obliterated the risen that held him with a thought. They exploded with a thunderous detonation, fire burning them to ash in a moment.

Kharios didn't slow, rushing to Leesha's side as he laid chant over chant. The shield of fire was shot through with blue light, and half again as large as it had been the first time he'd summoned it. He crouched, holding the shield over them both as Ossan turned to them in a rage.

Already the strain of channelling this much power was clawing at him. Pain wracked through him as Ossan slammed the hammer down against his shield, sparks flying. And then again.

Use the blessing, priest.

The chant stumbled on his lips and the shield flickered as he caught himself. The Utterdark? He'd seen it die. Another hammer blow and the force sent him crashing back against the base of the anvil.

What?

Your body was never meant to channel this power, human. Use the blessing the Father has given you. Send the Father's power through the rings of mastery. Through your rings of Faith and Light.

Kharios glanced at his hand and the pale ring that encircled his thumb. The power resisted him, moving sluggishly as he tried to direct it, and then the pain left him, and the twin bands blazed.

Power surged all about him as Kharios rose to his feet. With a simple chant, he reached through the rings, and drank it in. Ossan's blows were nothing to him now. He was the eye of the storm. He was the hurricane. And with a shove he sent the thing the priest had become, flying back across the floor.

Ossan scrambled back away from him as Kharios advanced.

Forged calls to forger, priest. The hammer knows its maker.

Kharios paused at the silent voice of the petty saint and reached out one grasping hand towards Ossan, willing the hammer to him.

389

The risen priest snarled as the hammer tore free from his grip, flying across the space between them to smack into Kharios's waiting palm.

Ossan scrambled to his feet, backing away and snarling at the risen around him as he waved them forward.

Kharios waited, letting the dead come to him as he wove new chants together. The first of the risen clawed for him and recoiled with a hiss as its hand struck the shield of flame, fingertips turning to ash.

The hammer felt right in his hand as he struck. Its weight and bulk were a comfort. This, at least, he knew. His strokes were not those of a warrior but those of a smith, a master of his craft.

The hammer blazed, as bright as the rings on his thumbs with each blow, driving the risen to the ground and hissing each time the weapon made contact.

Kharios pushed forward, lashing out with the hammer when he could reach, and sending lances of flame through the risen he couldn't. Ossan was screaming at the risen, sending more forward and shrieking as they fell.

A risen, pressed close to Ossan, toppled to the ground in a boneless heap, and the soulwraith rose swiftly from its body. The creature coalesced into the familiar serpentine form and flew at him, red eyes blazing. Kharios met it with the shield, thrusting the thing away from him in a shower of blue sparks.

The risen pressed in, surrounding him. As fast as he felled one, two more took its place. Pain lanced through him, enough to halt his chants, and the breath left him as he staggered to one side. The risen's claw-like fingers raked along his side, tearing through robes and flesh. Kharios clenched his teeth, spitting out the chant as he summoned flame and burnt the thing to ash.

The chants flew from his lips. Calling the Flame followed Reaching the Stars, followed Blessing the Hammer. A litany that dealt destruction wherever he stepped, and the smoke rose.

A blast of green light flew at Kharios, sending him spinning to the ground, but he was up again in moments. Without even pausing to consider how, he wove new elements into the chant, transforming the shield of flame into one of blazing light. Ossan sent bolts of the sickly, green light at him, but they flew apart as they met the shield, scattering and sending chips of stone flying as they exploded into the ground.

The dead priest was growing frantic as Kharios approached, skirting the wall as he backed away towards the rear of the chamber. The risen were nothing to Kharios now, and he felled them without thought.

"No!" Ossan screamed. "I will not be denied this, Kharios. Not by something like you. Not by a pawn; a slave to this lying traitor of a god."

With a scream of rage Ossan raised both fists, surrounding his hands with a nimbus of pure force, as he spun and drove them into the stone of the wall. The wall exploded outward, sending dust and chips of stone out to mix with the cool night air. Ossan paused long enough to fix Kharios with a look of pure hatred, before ducking through the hole and charging out into the night.

Bodies toppled to the ground as the risen collapsed, soulwraiths rising swiftly from the bodies and streaking after Ossan into the darkness. But Kharios was past caring. He let the chants come to an end and the shield winked out as he picked his way through the rubble to Leesha.

Her eyes were wide as she watched him approach, and crouch down beside her. "He's dead?"

Kharios shook his head. "Gone. Fled through the wall. It's over."

She let out a shuddering breath as she considered that, looking down at the hands in her lap. "No." She shook her head as she looked up at him. "It isn't over, Kharios. There are villages out there. Cities. This is your world up here, not mine, but I don't think this is over."

He followed her gaze out through the shattered stone to where the faint light of stars pierced the sky. "No," he whispered. "I don't think it is."

Priest.

The call was silent, for Kharios alone, but he had no doubt what had spoken.

"I thought you were dead?" he murmured, barely moving his lips.

I am a creature of spirit, priest. The right hand of the Forgefather. I cannot be killed by those such as you, by creatures of flesh.

Was that regret in the Utterdark's voice?

The sanctum is defiled, the focus-stone tainted. Your blood alone is all that remains to the Father. Reclaim the forge, priest. Reclaim the anvil.

Kharios sighed as he stood, pulling himself up by a corner of the stone blocks they had rested against.

"Where are you…" Leesha asked, but Kharios stopped her with a look and stepped up to the anvil.

The surface was scorched, still littered with the remnants of the shattered rings. How was he supposed to reclaim this? The prayers slipped from his lips as easy as a lie, The Grace of the Father began as a whisper that grew to be the Canticle of the Forge. He knew what was expected of him, the Utterdark had said it itself, blood.

He looked around stupidly for a knife before his eyes lit on the shard. A jagged piece of Ossan's hammer that had shattered as he destroyed the truesteel ring. There was something fitting in that. Kharios picked up the shard, turning it over in his fingers as the prayers ran unnoticed from him. The words didn't matter now. His faith was not built from a belief in the existence of the Forgefather, it was from a need to set things right.

He ran the shard across his hand and held it high, letting the blood drip onto the scorched surface of the great anvil. The light rose out of the core of the anvil like a fish rising from the deeps.

Kharios's song was lost as a chorus filled his ears; chants merging with the rush of flame and the sound of hammer on steel. Somewhere he heard Leesha gasp but he wasn't finished yet. His bloody hand pressed to the cold of the anvil and his lips stilled as silence fell around him.

"Until my fire fades," he whispered. "And my life is ended."

He turned to Leesha as the great anvil blazed behind him, golden light streaming skyward until it touched the dome high above them.

"Let's get out of here."

She nodded an agreement, even as she looked past him to the blazing anvil and the light that rose from it.

392

"Gods, Kharios. What did you do?"

"I reclaimed it. The temple, the anvil, all of it. I pledged myself to him again." His words were little more than a whisper. The mutterings of a willing slave.

The night air was cool as they clambered out through the hole Ossan had torn in the wall. They moved without speaking, both limping and torn but the need to be out of the temple was more important than the pain.

Kharios ducked under Leesha's arm, taking her weight as they made their way up the hill towards a tree. She winced, letting out a gasp of pain as they sank down to the ground and leant back against the rough bark of the birch.

They sat, watching the light that somehow pierced the dome and rose up higher still to meet the clouds.

"It looks smaller somehow," she muttered.

"What does?"

"The temple."

He grunted his agreement, holding either side of his knee tight as he eased his leg out in front of him. He didn't remember the leg being struck. He didn't remember any wound aside from the claws that raked his side, but for some reason his leg hurt more than anything else.

"Where will he go do you think?"

"I don't know," Kharios sighed. "I can't think right now." He gazed through the darkness at the ruined wall of the temple.

She settled in against him, sharing warmth and just the pleasure of human contact. For now, it would be enough.

"Kharios!"

He jerked out of the half doze, grimacing at the pain as he lurched upright.

She winced in apology and then pointed out over the temple. "Look!"

He frowned, following her pointing finger and squinting as he tried to focus on the shaft of light. "What is that?" He broke off. "Are those...?"

"Soulwraiths," she finished for him. "At least that's what it looks like. Rising up, following the light."

He shook his head. "I can't make them out."

She shrugged. "Trust me. They're there. What do you think it means?"

"I don't know," he admitted. "Ossan said there were ten thousand souls or more trapped within the great anvil. Maybe not all them chose to follow him. Maybe some remained loyal to the Father."

"So, if they're rising? Do you think that's what's happening? That they're going to the Father?"

He shrugged. "We can hope."

"We can," she agreed. "It's more than we could say yesterday."

He settled back against the tree, watching the souls as they ascended. The sky had that pale silvery quality just before the dawn.

The day would bring its own challenges; the search for survivors, their own need for food and shelter. Clearing the dead from the temple alone was a task for a small army.

And then there was Ossan. Leesha was right, there were towns and villages out there. Cities that he and his soulwraiths would devastate if given the chance. Wherever he and the soulwraiths had fled to, provided they could avoid the sunlight, they would be a scourge upon the earth. In one stroke Kharios had brought a true god back to the world, and then condemned it to hell.

For now, if the sight of the column of light rising from the temple gave Leesha hope then he would try to share in that. For now, that would have to be enough.

The End

ACKNOWLEDGEMENTS

As usual I have a number of people to thank, my wife and family for putting up with me, Clare Davidson for formatting and for keeping me writing, Sarah Chorn for her excellent copy editing, Pen Astridge for the amazing cover art, Claire Rushbrook for battling against typos and errors. Alicia Wanstall-Burke along with Steve and Gerald Drew for helping with my many many questions about mining and blacksmithing. A special thank you must go to my legion of betareaders who read the book in its various stages and incarnations, and also to the authors and bloggers who reviewed the book before release. Finally, you, the readers who bought this book. Faithless was darker fare than the Riven Wyrde books. I hope you enjoyed the ride.

ABOUT THE AUTHOR

Graham Austin-King was born in the south of England and weaned on broken swords and half-forgotten spells. A shortage of these forced him to consume fantasy novels at an ever-increasing rate, turning to computers and tabletop gaming between meals.

He experimented with writing at the beginning of an education that meandered through journalism, international relations, and law. To this day he is committed to never allowing those first efforts to reach public eyes.

After living in the north of England and Canada he settled once again in the south surrounded by a seemingly endless horde of children and a very patient wife who can arguably say her husband is away with the faeries.

The Riven Wyrde Saga is his first completed trilogy and draws on a foundation of literary influences ranging from David Eddings to Dean Koontz.

Visit his blog at http://grahamak.blogspot.co.uk where you can sign up for e-mail updates and be the first to hear about new releases.

Find Graham on facebook at http://on.fb.me/1pMyWmK He loves to chat with readers.

Follow him on Twitter at www.Twitter.com/Grayaustin

Lightning Source UK Ltd.
Milton Keynes UK
UKHW04f0841221018
330964UK00003B/210/P

9 780993 003738